THE CELDAN HERESIES

THE REACHING MAN SERIES, BOOK ONE

Megan Carnes

FAMILY OF LIGHT BOOKS
An Imprint Of Milspeak Foundation, Inc.

© 2024 MEGAN CARNES

All rights reserved, including the right of reproduction in whole or in part in any form except in the case of brief quotations embodied in critical articles or reviews. For permission, contact publisher at the following email address: info@ milspeakfoundation.org.

This is a work of fiction. Names, characters, places, and incidents either are the product of the author's imagination or are used fictitiously, and any resemblance to actual persons, living or dead, businesses, companies, events, or locales is entirely coincidental.

Manufactured in the United States of America

Carnes, Megan, Library of Congress Control Number: 2023941530
ISBN 979-8-9881203-0-8 (paperback)
ISBN 979-8-9881203-1-5 (epub)

Design: Michelle Bradford Art
Editing By: Margaret MacInnis

MilSpeak Foundation, Inc.
5097 York Martin Road
Liberty, NC 27298
www.MilSpeakFoundation.org

For my parents and my sisters
And for James

Acknowledgments

First, I want to thank my husband, James Robinson, who listened to me talk about the beginning of this book while we stayed in a cabin on our honeymoon, and who has been listening ever since. Without his encouragement, feedback, and patience, my novel would never exist. Gratitude goes to my parents, John and Jackie Carnes, and my grandparents, Jim and Nancy Hawks, who never stopped believing in my work, and who kept me believing. I thank my sisters, Ali Carnes and Izzie Fleury, who helped me grow up with adventures and jokes, and who still tell me when I'm being too strange. I'm indebted to my grandmother, Miriam Carnes, who inspired a character in this book, and finally to my father-in-law, Fred Robinson, who sat on a California pier and told me this novel was worth the work.

Great help came from my readers: James Robinson, Fred Robinson, Bruce Fischer, Nathan Williams, Mike Williams, Mary Simmons, LeeAnn McCoy, Paul Harding, Julian Bernick, Amy C. Waninger, Nan Griffin, and Jan Adkins. Jan is the English teacher who started me writing, way back in high school, so I'm indebted to her twice. Thanks go to Annie Dillard and Bob Richardson, whose friendship and support showed me the kind of author I want to be. I'm grateful to Marilynne Robinson, for offering me a remarkable education in literature, history, and theology—and for introducing me to Paul Harding. Credit goes to Brad Gardner for telling me how to use a personal wiki, and to Giles Anderson for answering my contractual questions. I acknowledge Inkarnate.com for the wonderful software that allowed a non-artist like me to design the map in this book. My Facebook community gets a big thanks for listening to me kvetch, laughing at my jokes, and giving their two cents on any question I asked. In addition to their help, Pentwater, Michigan, offered me quiet winters where I could write by a lake, and West Branch, Iowa, rented me an essential study space above the best pizza shop in eastern Iowa. My gratitude goes to Davenport University for hiring me to teach along a schedule that actually promotes creativity. And with deepest respect, I acknowledge Maximo Presbyterian Church of St. Petersburg, Florida, and the Congregational Church United Church of Christ of Iowa City, Iowa, for showing what good religion looks like.

I thank the Milspeak Foundation for their noble and important work. Its president, Tracy Crow, changed my life by taking a chance on this story and encouraging more light. I'm also indebted to my copyeditor, Margaret MacInnis, for her many insights, including her decision to put my manuscript in Tracy's hands. And I'm grateful to Michelle Bradford Art for giving the book such a wonderful cover.

Finally, I recognize all the strong women who have been waging their own resistance, whether in silence, in public, or in print.

Celdan Nursery Rhyme

Es-aosh established Celd,

Visjaes found us where we dwelled,

Visjaes scattered loss and strife,

Es-aosh fought for our life.

Es-aosh drove Visjaes hence

Es-aosh called every Prince

They, together, chase Visjaes

Over time and over place.

Es-aosh, of light and thought,

Visjaes, hot and chaos-wrought,

Es-aosh will surely win,

And come to be our Lord again.

(The hyphen rarely exists in Esaosh's name, except in verse.)

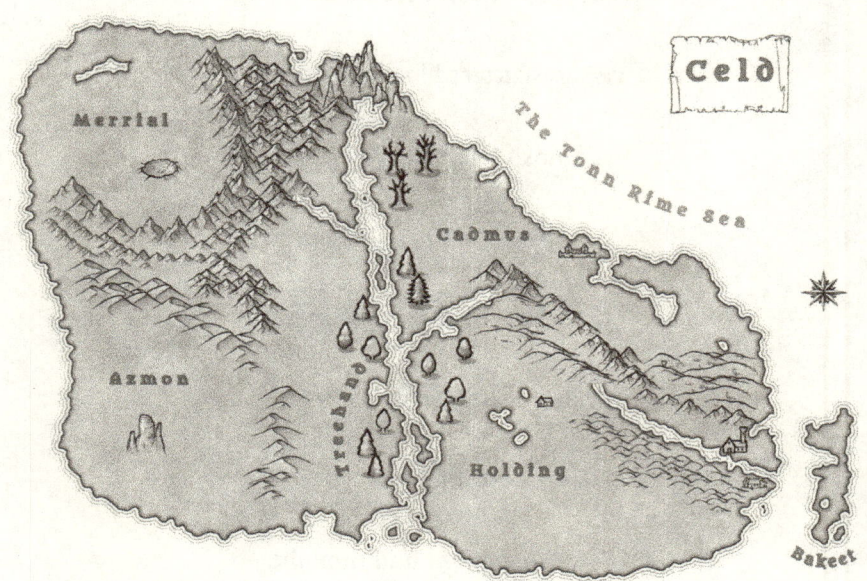

Map created by the author with Inkarnate.com.

Key Tenets

of the

Imperial Church of Esaosh

Esaosh is the lord of clarity, reason, and strength. All decisions, transactions, subjugations, and primacies must emerge from those same virtues.

Every subject under Esaosh must reckon his own worth, and behave accordingly.

Esaosh eschews over-emotion, unfairness, and magic, as they derive from the demon-god, Visjaes, who is the lord of chaos.

Esaosh wills that celdans adhere to the teachings of the Church, as the Church will keep them safe until Esaosh returns.

It should be unnecessary to codify any other law, as Esaosh has already inscribed his will on every mind, including even that of a slave.

A Brief Celdan Timeline

Year Shadowed:
Esaosh, wanting freedom from Jaes and Visjaes, flees the heavens.

Year 0:
Esaosh discovers a new world, and calls it Celd.

Year c. 300:
Esaosh orders Celd into provinces.

Year c. 600:
Esaosh establishes both the Church and the provinces' ruling Princes.

Year c. 1150:
Visjaes invades, and commits a worldwide ruin called the Bale.

Year c. 1154:
The Bale drives some princes into dormancy.

Year c. 1200:
Esaosh and the remaining princes leave Celd, to pursue Visjaes.

Year 1202:
The Imperial Church of Esaosh becomes Celd's steward.

Year 1203:
The provinces of Treehand and Merrial become pagan.

Year 2306-2422:
The Church and Treehand wage the Clearing Wars.

Year 2763:
The present

Months of the Celdan Year

1. Zeffar
2. Af
3. Bardion
4. Core
5. Rochon
6. Alpion
7. Lehashon
8. Sislau
9. Zaffion
10. Potch
11. Altarib
12. Wax

chapter 1

INCREASE

I was born because I was afraid. I still remember the fear and the falling, and for a long time, I considered that drop the first transgression of my life. These days, I recognize how at least the fear came from reverence, but it would take a near-burial for me to realize such a thing. Now, at the end of my life, I enjoy the irony of waiting in a Church prison cell that hangs high in the air. The ones who hold me are the Imperial Church of Esaosh; in fact, they hold control over most of the world. My people, the Riven, have warred with them for most of a century. I don't think I ever told the Church about what I felt when I was born, but these days, it still seems they're trying to send me back.

They've dangled me high above Cathedral Ordinal, which is the Empire's chief fortress. What they haven't realized is how they've given me a view of the Gomadong Plain that is so reaching and splendid that it could drive me to defy the Church's religion, simply because the land's own beauty hints at something better. And in the meantime, what neither of us has realized is how high-hanging solitary doesn't keep every visitor out.

As it happens, I'm telling this story to a bird. That's ridiculous—I thought so too. But as a prisoner, I don't get much company. As I'm both a heretic nun and a former advisor to the Riven's army, my jailers consider me too dangerous to keep around anyone but a handful of guards. Nor does it help that I'm one hundred thirty-two years old. Even if I didn't talk to a bird, the people around here would consider mine a witch's lifespan. And to be honest, it scares me too. I don't know why I'm still alive. Lumis Caspar, the head of the Church, is at least fifty years older than I am, but I believe he purchased his longevity from the same demon who made Caspar's power nearly unspeakable.

The bird appeared nearly a month ago, with the late summer's first snow. I'd stuffed my hair out the window of my prison cell, as the freshest water I can get these days is what I can wring from my hair. I had lain over the brick, watching the snow mute the glare from the cathedral's mirrored spires, and the bird half-collided with the sill, giving a sort of guttural moo.

I watched him from across the room. He was about twice the size of my head. He had pulled himself the rest of the way onto the sill with a beak nearly long as he was. The thing was almost thick as my arm, and it had the color of dark wood that's begun to wear. The bird himself was featherless, except for three blue, disheveled primaries. Now he ground his bill. He was naked enough to make me wonder if he was some wayward chick—maybe an owlet with an unusual neb. But he had a withered foot and some film over one eye, and his chest skin sagged so much I worried he'd spear it. Not that I should talk. As he sat on my sill, I wondered if the weather had blown him here. He couldn't possibly have flown.

At first I didn't want to move. If I startled him, he might pitch off the window, and land near the sentries below. One of his three primaries stood nearly vertical in the wind. I shoved my three-legged chair toward the window. The exertion of it all made me huff some, and the bird spread his stance. I piled straw from my pallet into the seat of the chair, as this seemed the best way to show welcome to a bird. The wind pitched, and landed me in the chair. Then the bird, with his feathers a-breeze, stood on one foot, and used the other to comb his head.

Except for my potbelly, I'm mostly skin and bone. Sometimes I hold my hand to the sun, and half expect to see through it. But my prison is made of sandstone brick, and the weather off the Gomadong can tilt my cell to the point where in the mornings, I occasionally wake in a different spot from where I went to sleep. In the wind, now, this bird clutched his pink head with his gray toes, and he did not move.

The only other time I'd seen something like this was in the wastes of Merrial. Its chasms run deep enough to create their own gales, while Nabush—the chitinous stalk that leads up from this world—stands firm. The bird on my sill had an eye film reminiscent of the stalk, but the rest of him did not. Nabush was a creation of Esaosh—the Church's own vile god—and he used it to climb from this world, the way a snake slips its cage. Among his other domains, Esaosh is allegedly the god of strength. But even on this first visit with my bird, I decided that despite his immovability, he was too woebegone to serve a monster like Esaosh.

Now I stood from the chair. The creature's beaded gaze suggested expectation, something like the stare a dog uses when he wants his dinner. With such a beak, the bird probably speared meat. "You can't be one of our messengers," I said. Our army does use birds as couriers, but we usually stick to blue jays, as they're nearly as smart as ravens but not as obvious. This bird would be far too noticeable, if not also too magical. Not that magic is the right word; these days, most magic is an evil purchased through the bargains of the Church's plutomancy. I knew this, but I wasn't yet ready to call the bird a miracle.

Now the wind gusted the scent of the cathedral bakery, the flesh-golem pens, and the smeltery that prepared the courtyard's new summoning altar. The bird flapped his naked wings, and gave a shake to his stub of a tail. The snow must have been uncomfortable. I touched the chair and invited the creature to sit. He stared from the sill. I offered some bread crumbs that, along with a spider, had somehow traveled to the folds of my lowered hood. The bird wanted none of it, so I offered pig jerky; he stood on it. I offered him more straw from my pallet, and he picked at a strand. He left a pile on the flagstones, and returned to his previous demands.

I peered at the guards on the cavern floor. They'd probably shoot the bird, if they thought I had any rapport with him. The young watchmen aren't usually so vicious; in fact, whenever I'm able speak to them, I do what I can to keep them from turning cruel. But their superiors have taught them such fear of me that, last week, when I dropped my hair dongle onto the portico where they stand outside my cell door, a boy crept upon the dongle with a shoe.

Now the bird sat, too large for the window. "Come in," I said, and I took a step toward him. His eyes widened, and he lowered his head, with a hiss like a turtle. I found the wall behind me, and eased myself down to sit.

A bird hunted me, once. I still remember it pushing the tundra's boulders out of the way, as it rummaged while I ran. Now the bird on the sill seemed to rummage me with a look. "What do you want?" I said. If I needed to chase him off, he likely wouldn't make it easy.

He picked at his chest fuzz while he leveled me his gaze. His one clear eye was so black that when he shut it, I could still see the color through the pink in his lid. For a long time, he didn't move, and as the early evening deepened, his shadow on the flagstones grew immense. In my chair, I sat far away from the silhouette, as if my touching it would somehow register as impertinence. And my worry here was ludicrous. I've stood before whole armies, some of them not even mine. "You're a bird," I said. He leaned on his feet, from side to side. Those talons could probably hold both of my hands in one. The creature settled on his haunches, and that made his claws tighter grip the sill. He slit his good eye, but kept open his filmy one, as some little answer to the rising moon. The cataract likely muted distraction so he could doze, but I figured he still watched. I certainly did. Nearly every bird can be disarmingly keen; a ship captain once told me how the crew's ravens would decide which of a sailor's hands to perch on, depending on the one they discerned was dominant.

At some point, I slept. At my age, sleep descends like a pillager. The dawn came with a high rumble and a pop, and I awoke in a sweat that might have come from a fearful sleep. Amid the orange of morning, the bird stood in the window, on taller legs than I'd reckoned he had. He leaned somewhat in from the sill, because he likely needed the space, and he watched me with both eyes. Something in his neck quivered, and the sound that came from him was like somebody tattooing a hand drum in a glass jar. All birds sing at daybreak; even, in a way both terrible and holy, the raptor on the tundra sang.

My window bird's ritual went on for a while—long enough for me to manage to stand. Then the song ended with that percussive noise people can make when they snap the side of their open mouth. This was apparently the pop I'd heard when I awakened. The bird bowed a little, and shat. But I figured his song wasn't the workup to that finale. He tattooed for the duration of the sunrise, pressing me his same black, white, and imperious stare. The day rose higher, and he finally made a third mouth-snap sound.

"Good Mother," I said.

The bird had jumped into the room. I stood behind the chair. Then I offered him the chair. Then I sat in the chair. My heart fluttered a little, as it does these days when I feel the creep of panic. The bird walked the edge of my cell, with legs so bent, he had to raise his beak from the floor. He stepped over a swatch of burlap I'd been trying to sew into mittens. His chest fuzz spread to some kind of eczemated scales that stretched up his nape until they gave him a brownish pate. And just then, despite his intrusion, he reminded me of an old man in his underclothes.

He sat, and the brick cell pitched. It pitched. Its roof chains creaked, and I folded my hands in my lap. My knees shook.

"Please show me," I said, "what you'd like me to do."

The creature remained in his crouch, and rattled something in his beak. I couldn't think of any bird his size who could pitch a sandstone cell.

When people are lonely, they talk to whatever's available; I understand that. I've seen a hermit hold parliament with a hive of bees; a senile blacksmith who daily considered the urge to hug his fire; and a man from a dungeon who scrawled miles of walls with his own discourse, so he could encounter parts of them again to start new conversations. At my age, from either the years of mortar or the decades of gritting my teeth, I've developed a tinnitus that sounds like cicadas—and in the summers, when the real insects come, I can never tell if other people can hear them or not. I'd forgive you if you thought this bird was a phantom of my own loneliness. But in my life, I've encountered magic and demons, and a divinity who throws us against both magic and demons. And if I dismissed my bird as something blown here by chance, I'd deny much of what had killed so many, and much of why the rest of us keep trying to live.

In the morning after he sang, the bird watched me while I thought. Those people who spoke with bees and fire and the warren of themselves: some of them were lonely—shunned, even—but I promise they were never forsaken. In fact, they'd been visited, sometimes repeatedly, sometimes to the extent where they had sought solitude so they could enter a space large enough to accommodate the very exchange. And I know this, because, in a room beneath the earth, in a place that could be this hanging cell's opposite and companion pole, something visited me as well. Like those hermits, I have been seized, touched, *twisted*, as every heretic supposedly is. After a while, most of us learn how miracle carries with it an obligation. And this duty is one reason why, at first, I didn't want to recognize miracle at all.

After some reflection, I've come to suspect this bird has arrived, because I've been tasked to impart a dispatch to you. Such a demand would coincide with everything I've seen, including what lives at the top of Nabush. But I won't press the point. I don't have to. If you're aware of what I'm saying, the miracle has also addressed you.

It took me some time to realize the bird wanted a dispatch. You'll agree most of them don't. But throughout our second day together, I noticed how if I began to speak at length, the bird shut both his eyes. Throughout that next week, I discovered how if I began to tell him what I knew of this world, and of my people's opposition to the Church controlling this world, he tucked one of his feet up into himself. So I started to recite, and he started to doze. And then if I diverged from my account—say, if I noticed a boy in the courtyard sneaking a morsel to a dog—the bird rousted with a gaze so black that I kept an eye on his bill.

These days, when I speak, my bird lets me have the window. He leaves at dusk, using those talons to climb his way to my roof, or to a beam someplace, or I don't know where else. But after dawn, he takes up my mittens as a kind of mat. I lean against the sill and let my voice carry. It helps something if the old guards below me think I'm crazed, and it heals something else, if the other guards are young enough to wonder if I'm not. I'm careful not to tell them everything I share with you; sometimes I whisper to the bird. But as an old lady who has already mostly left this earth, I'm probably more forthcoming than you'd guess. From my stone jar, midair, I start my story at the beginning:

My name is Gaelle. It's pronounced most often as the strong wind, although a friend of the family once suggested I should pronounce it *Guile*. In addition to being a nun, and a heretic, and a military advisor, I'm the niece of Jillian (the outlaw who raised me) and Miriamne (a mage whom the Church burned). I'm other things too, and I haven't divulged some of the most important ones; those things take time to tell. As for the bird, I don't know his name, at least not yet. In the weeks since he landed on my sill, he's grown two feathers, so I've begun to call him Increase.

The world we live in is called Celd; that's with a soft C. To me, the name suggests a variant of *sold*. Or more recently it's reminded me of a place imprisoned: *cell-ed*. It turns out that in certain ways, both interpretations are correct. But such an idea is part of my own heresy.

Well, we heretics may be twisted, but along the way, the mere fact of such attention shows we've also been selected. Today, a spindly redhead stands guard at the portico outside my cell door. It's a wide enough space that a person could probably get used to sleeping there. But we are in midair, and he stands flat against the wall while he glances along the suspension bridge connecting my cell to Ordinal's main fortress. I would love to free him; in a critical sense, he's a prisoner too. Throughout its history, the Church has conscripted boys, right from their parents. Because they've been snatched from both their families and any semblance of choice, there's a time when these young are vulnerable to people like me. So many of these captives proliferate the Church's empire, that if they revolted, they could turn it all inside-out. My people hope for an uprising, anyway. It's what I hope, provided I can find a boy who would be receptive. For all I know, such turning is also what Increase hopes; maybe my dispatch can reach these orphans as well as you. In any event, what this prison's architects have also forgotten is how a roost in midair is a brilliant place from which to preach. So if I am in fact crazed, and if Increase isn't receiving my testament, you've come upon it through a recording issued by someone else. And truly, that would be a miracle too.

chapter 2

Cart and Horse

part ONE

I was born, afraid and two months early, in an oxcart. We'd been on the way to a midwife. My mother did not survive. My father kept the oxcart by the cottage for years afterwards. He planted bluebeard shrubs in its bed, where every summer they blossomed, and every winter, they turned to bone. When I was young, I made myself thrust my head, wide-eyed, into the shrubs, at least once a winter. During all this, I imagined my mother watched me face the dread and the pain. I imagined her accepting my apology for being born early, and lethally, from fear. And from the beginning of those days, my shame bid I spend a great deal of time trying to resist all personal fright as if it were the worst form of idolatry. Actually, it isn't the worst. But it was the worst I could recognize for a very long time.

My father's name is Lloyd. My mother's name is Barbara. After she died, my aunt on my mother's side, our Jillian, came to live with my father and me. For a long time, I thought she was the only aunt I had. My family worked an orchard of apple and eddlefruit near the thorp of Ludington, which is in Holding province. Holding is under the dominion of the church currently keeping me at Cathedral Ordinal—that is, the Imperial Church of Esaosh.

Their god is whom my side of the war has come to oppose. And in retrospect, I think I first started looking for a different faith, way back when I decided to reject him.

Esaosh is the god who led us, his people, to Celd. He brought us to this world after his rulers, Jaes and her son Visjaes, turned against him. Contrary to what we Riven know, the Church declares Esaosh is a wise and devoted savior. They teach that after he established our redoubt, Esaosh set a Prince in power over each of Celd's five provinces. These Princes settled the lands of Holding, Cadmus, Treehand, Azmon, and Merrial. But then Visjaes, the supposed demon-god, attacked, and committed a violence known collectively as the Bale. During the Bale, Visjaes cast some of the Princes into a torpor. Esaosh and the rest of the Princes drove Visjaes away, and they then gave chase. Evidently they hunt him still. For over 1600 years, Celd has awaited the return of Esaosh and the Princes. The Church says it keeps watch the best it can, especially for invading agents of Visjaes. It sets worldwide laws, both religious and secular, as it seeks, allegedly, to regulate peace and security. It claims to instill Esaosh's virtues of reason, strength, and fairness, while also stamping out all passion, magic, and trickery that might attract Visjaes, the Demon Son.

In my old age, I am a nun of Visjaes. She's our god, not a fiend. And her very divinity suggests how most things anyone proclaims about her don't even come close to what she is. This *Demon Son*, for instance, most often reveals herself as female to me. But assigning any gender to divinity is like assigning color to water, when on some days, it will change its hue as soon as your reflection appears inside it. I will assert how Visjaes is a god of creation, which means she's a god of possibility. Creativity also means she's a god of love, and such love suggests she's also a god of correction. I will further admit Visjaes is indeed a trickster. She seizes her mystics. Through her enemies' own protest, she makes them announce her existence. And regardless of how the people of Esaosh claim to defeat her influence, the gloom of this world is one place she goes to get back up again.

Still, I didn't become a nun of Visjaes for a very long time. During my childhood, my immediate family had dealt little with cosmology, for reasons ranging from irrelevance, to irritation, to outright resentment. We were an irreligious group. The Imperial Church—who equated weakness with sin—had begun to institute a steel-shod reform that, in the name of security, debased the poor and made villains of unbelievers. We were both. And my aunt Jillian, who was also flagrant, fought to save as many of the poor and the faithless as she could. In her twenties, she became an outlaw, who then became savvy in the ways of theft and infiltration, who then became captured. And since then, the Church had sentenced her to a kind of open servitude, where they snatched her into any ruin they discovered, for the purposes of clearing out its dangers, as well as its coffers. In short, Jillian was what the Church calls an intrepid. That's an apt name for her, considering how while she remained indentured to them, she sent some of the best treasures to cabals opposing the Church. She also spent a great deal of time on the run. In fact, since the day she arrived at our farm when I was nine, I spent a lot of my youth wondering why she had run to us.

This story is about my encountering that reason, and it's also about my encountering the remains of my family, as we struggled to fight a church of demons. My part in the fight began when I refused to harm a cosmic and accursed horse, which everyone under the sway of those demons was trying to find. When we came upon the horse, I didn't know she was either sought after or cursed. I was all of fifteen, and I simply refused to kill her. I refused. No true injury ever came to the horse. But in sparing her, and in sparing her master, I committed a rebellion that would shape the rest of our lives.

The horse arrived on a day in late summer, when Jillian talked me into an elder tree. It was the eldest tree on the farm—the greatest sire tree—and when my aunt looked up at me, she seemed as small as I was. "Your father is dead, Child." She said he'd been killed by Wilm Albertson's mare. She called this to me while I was at the top, next to nothing but some feaster's down and talon marks. I looked around for something, as if in response to all this I could find a switch or a tool. My hands had gone numb; in a way, they made the tree feel absent. Those who came to the farm said Jillian and I resembled each other, and now she stood, looking like me calling up to myself.

She dropped her gaze and lay a hand on the sire's trunk. The tree smelled of the resin my father would get on his face and hands when he trimmed the orchard. Even though other woodsmen appreciated it for improving their grip, my father believed it perverse to use a tree's own sap in the process of cutting it. He loved the trees. With something bordering on indignation, he loved the whole land. Jillian had told me love obviates economy, and she was exactly right. Perhaps she was also correct in deciding that by clutching this tree, I would smell my father.

Now pale, short, and shorter-tempered, she peered at me as if she were something inevitable. In a few ways, she was. The tree jostled, where Jillian had already climbed into the lower branches. She could climb as fast as other people swim, but now she took her time.

Jillian settled among the middle limbs, as invitation. She confessed she'd decided to tree me before she told me of my father, because she hadn't wanted me to run. Enough predators lived in the surrounding forest that running made a person resemble prey. So now I held, whole bodied, to the branches, and wondered how long Jillian had spent the anguish of the day, anticipating this trap.

Earlier in the afternoon, she'd told me how, from the roof of this tree I could see the fall festival in Ludington. And I could. In many ways, she hardly ever lied. Jillian's attachment to the truth is part of what made her inevitable.

So when she sat there, looking away from me as if she tried to tame a wild animal, the animal inside of me jumped. I don't know if it jumped because it was afraid or enraged—whether it fought to live or die—but I hit the ground rolling. Jillian had taught me that instinct. I tumbled, by reflex, into a stance, and she watched me where she stayed.

She climbed down head first. This was a trick she'd been trying to teach me, that she was probably teaching right then. In addition to unsettling any onlookers, the position lessens your chances of getting surprised. Now I thought of punching Jillian, in hopes she'd kill me by reflex. But even at fifteen, I knew she had deeper instincts. She pushed into a sort of roll, and landed on her feet.

"You're a thief," I said. Poor Jillian; it was the worst I could think of calling her.

She sheathed her hand-held climbing tines, and wiped an eye. "Yes."

part TWO

Earlier in the day, my father had purchased the mare responsible for killing him, from Wilm Albertson. Wilm was apparently inconsolable about the death. Imperial Law decreed that Wilm should be beaten senseless for selling a murderous animal, and for the animal to be killed. Jillian told me how Wilm was overcome more for the sake of himself and the horse than for my own father (whom he disliked). And this was consistent with what we knew of Wilm.

It so happened that before I'd learned of my father's death, Wilm had found Jillian, and told her of the accident. He had admitted he'd told the horse how he suspected my father loved plants more than animals. But Wilm told my aunt he'd never suggested anything more violent. This was Wilm's defense, as if a horse could be spoken with, about murder.

The story Wilm told is that after agreeing to the purchase, my father mounted the horse for only the first time, and that as soon as he sent her into a trot, the mare threw my father forward, so he broke his neck on landing. Wilm had run to my father when he'd heard the horse's scream. And in the meantime, the scene had also attracted a merchant from Azmon—an Azman—who had seen the entire incident, including the final parts of Wilm's and my father's transaction.

The witness, being a foreigner, couldn't give legal testimony in a court of Holden law, but Wilm worried the Azman would pay someone to be a witness in his stead. This could happen sometimes. Furthermore, Wilm feared the Azman could use the accident to turn both Wilm and his horse into flesh golems. These creatures, called mindless, are catatonic, necromantic creations that, although a staple of the Azmonian economy, were forbidden in the rest of the Church's empire.

Now, on the day of my father's killing, Jillian told me Wilm knew more about talking horses than he knew about either Azmen or mindless. Still, she said such ignorance was helpful in how, without the witness, Wilm may have tried to hide my father's corpse.

I'd been selling dried fruit at market when Wilm had first gone to Jillian with the news of my father's death. Afterward, she had gone to Wilm Pasture to see for herself. Now, after we'd both agreed she was a thief, she told me what had happened, while we traveled back to Wilm's hut. She spoke in her regular voice. She clicked at Godiva, our other horse, in the regular way, and her words sailed above me as if I sat at the bottom of a well. I rode with the outrage that, at the moment, Jillian could speak anything but outrage. And I rode with the outrage that she, at the first, hadn't gone to Wilm's in my father's place.

My stance was harsh, perhaps; I spent a great deal of my childhood throwing my rage at Jillian. But we both knew how animals baffled my father. They would do little for him. He had no business buying an unfamiliar horse, a horse he hadn't ridden until after her own purchase. I often wondered if my father even had business being a farmer—but then, he could grow anything. Vines flowered for him when they were out of season. He could look at a bare acreage and tell how much grain it would yield. I, myself, was short, like my aunt and my mother, but like him, I was stout and easily muscled. Wilm once suggested my father could raise me to win a prize in Ludington. I remembered that.

Now the cart creaked with Godiva's uneven pull. She walked faster for us than she did for my father. She always had. A year earlier he'd sat, enraged, two miles from home because Godiva had stopped to graze, as if my father begrudged her the grass.

We had always expected a living thing would kill him. Sometimes it seemed he couldn't harm anything, even to fend it away. For him, we feared the bears and the cougars, the adders, and the rocs. Infections lingered in him. In the fields, at the peril of running, he would rush at the feasters, to chase them from the crops, and they wouldn't fly away. He could run them off only when they actively harmed the fields, and then only over time and just barely. Eventually, or so it seemed, he just out-produced the predators more than he ever defended against them.

I'm amazed how my father had only one child. But then, my mother did die in childbirth, leaving a hole in my life somehow in the shape of my own self. And I'd long wondered if during that night, while she screamed in the oxcart, my father had pulled, pushed, and finally whipped the obdurate ox to make it go. In any event, he likely blamed himself for my mother's death, as much as I blamed my own fear. Maybe he'd blame himself for his own death, too.

Because blame was at issue here. I knew this the way a person knows another's character. The Church invested a great deal in assigning blame for anything, after even the most senseless tragedy. That was its idea of keeping security. Both Jillian and my father had said as much, in these six years since she'd arrived. And in the oxcart now, I tried to hear my father's voice while shutting out my aunt's, even though they were both telling me the same thing.

"It isn't what you want to focus on," said Jillian, "I know it isn't." I wished she'd stop talking. "But around here, you know, if it's not dealt with soon, punishment becomes contagious."

The road rumbled the cart's bench, as if the whole world sped by. "Somebody should get punished."

"Fine." She slowed the cart. "If you know what that means."

"Speed it up."

She stopped the cart, and Godiva stomped. "Gaelle, do you know what this punishment means?"

"Wilm gets punished."

"And the horse."

The wind kicked across the fields, and it jingled the reins. Maybe it blew my father's hair. "That's fine."

"Gaelle."

"It's fine."

I could smell her sweat, darker than usual, as if something welled from deep within. "You and I," she said, "We need to think about what we're going to do, when we get to Wilm Pasture."

"You can start the cart."

"You are the next of kin." She put her face in mine. "Do you know what that means?"

"He was my dad."

"Yes." This was everything it meant. "But the law."

"I know about the beating."

"You don't know everything about the beating." She released a little gasp, as if from pain. "You know, I reckon no one's ever told you."

"I think I've been told plenty today."

"Fine. But what you don't know is that the rule of law says the beating—the punishment, all of it—has to come from you."

The wind ruffed my hair, like my father's. "No." I watched the set of her jaw. I wanted her to disappear. "No, that's not right. That doesn't make a lick of sense."

"It's provincial law, applicable to the countryside."

"Wilm gets the garrison—"

"And the countryside is where the garrison doesn't have the resources to serve."

"Resources?"

"Or motivation. Either way."

Along her fist, the skin on her knuckles pulled thin. Her hand still had dirt from her chores; just this morning, we were all doing chores. "We can send him to Northcraft," I said, "or Hal's Bride."

"Gaelle." She put her palm on the side of her stomach, as if this was where her pain lived. "The law says you need to beat Wilm. Senseless. And right now. And then you need to kill the horse."

"No." I scrambled from the cart. Godiva, two heads taller than I, looked on. "That isn't even possible."

"I can help you with the horse."

"Help?"

"I can."

I couldn't imagine how she'd do such a thing. I didn't want to imagine. "My father is dead."

"Come back to the cart."

I turned a little circle.

"Gaelle." Jillian looked behind us. "We can't have this argument in the middle of the road."

"Then you go to Wilm yourself."

"Honey," She never called me Honey, "the longer we wait, the more the news will spread—"

"What, that my father is dead?"

"And that you have yet to carry out the Law of Retribution."

I wanted to sit down, right there, or lie down. I imagined both the horse, and the man who sold her, shuddering on the grass.

Now Jillian had her hand around my arm, and she was leading me to the cart.

"Jillian," I stopped, but she tugged. She was stronger than I, and faster. "I haven't even thrown a punch."

"We can talk about it more."

"I can't do this."

"We'll get you through it."

"You're going to make me do this?"

"No." She looked sadder than I'd ever seen her. "I can't make you do anything. But I," she looked as if she needed a witness, or a partner, "I need to take you to them."

The mile marker to Wilm's pasture stood just up ahead. She had waited almost to the end of the trip before we had our talk. "You trapped me," I said.

She beat the reins.

"You trapped me," I said, "the way you did in the tree."

She looked at me sideways. "Would you have come of your own?"

"No."

"Then it's better that I trap you than they do."

In those days, Wilm was brown-haired, blue-eyed, block-headed, and wiry. He had a paunch that, next to his frame, made him look like he was trying to abscond with something. When we reached him, he said my father carried the taint of the Treehanded. Jillian jumped from the wagon so fast that Wilm took a step back. Treehand is the province to our west. They worship the trees, and their forests swallow anyone who wanders their rim.

Now Wilm looked at Jillian as if he'd never liked her, and that she was confirming every reason why.

She came up to his shoulder. She said, "You're disgracing the dead."

"I forget," he said. "You prefer to disgrace the living."

"Speak to Gaelle then." I didn't want him to speak to me. "That's why we've come."

Wilm wiped his face, and looked around. A tawny man who could have been an Azman stood under a nearby oak. I looked at the ground, and kept looking. I didn't want to look at anything else, because I might end up looking at my father.

"Gaelleda," Wilm approached where I sat in the driver's seat, "you've gotten big."

I thought of striking him. "I don't want to talk to you."

"Gaelle," said Jillian, "he has the right."

"I do. I have the right," said Wilm, "and the sadness. I am truly sad to say your father could not handle horses."

"That's twice," said Jillian. "You've put the blame on a dead man."

"The law says I can cast blame on a dead man, if the grievance affects the living." Wilm grasped the front of the cart, and it leaned. "I'm the living."

"You're quoting a court law," said Jillian.

"Well, all I can do is quote," said Wilm. "I don't get to go to court."

"And that's because you confessed," said Jillian.

He heaved a look at the Azman. "You know why I confessed."

"What I know," said Jillian, "is how your bigotry helped condemn you."

"Bigotry." Wilm turned to me and back again. "I keep a good life. I raise good horses."

"Clearly," said Jillian.

"They are good horses!" said Wilm. "We make an honest living. We chart the stars."

"So the horses help you chart the stars?" she said.

"My father made an honest living," I said.

Jillian wiped her mouth. Wilm shoved his hands in his hair, and stood there, as if he'd glued himself. "Gaelleda. I know. It was a terrible mistake. He must have scared the horse he owned."

"The horse he bought," said Jillian. "And he bought her just now."

Under the circumstances, this lawyering might feel unseemly, even obscene. But the law stood as the apparatus set to grind us. And even at fifteen, I knew the Church enforced over half its statutes with some kind of death.

"Gaelleda," said Wilm. "You're a big girl. You're strong like your father. Maybe he was too strong for the horse."

"Wilm," said Jillian.

"My father didn't break the horse's neck," I said.

"All right," said Wilm. "Gaelleda, you know he was bad with horses. We all know."

"You could have stopped him," I said.

"How could I do this?" he said. "Gaelleda, your father was here. I was there. You shouldn't have to tell a farmer not to scare a horse."

"I have to kill your horse!" Maybe, somehow, my father could hear me. "I have to beat you till you drop."

Wilm squeezed his hands. Jillian looked to the sky, and gave three quick blinks.

"That's what I have to do," I said. "You have killed my father, and you've made me decide whether to do these things." My aunt had said she needed to deliver me, as if she'd been making a confession. "Either I do this, or I break the law."

"Law? You people don't follow the law," said Wilm. "You have no reason to start following it now."

"She's fifteen," said Jillian. I looked for my father, and stopped. "For a fifteen-year-old, I think you can take a beating."

"No beating!" said Wilm. "Let's reason instead, all right?" He kept an eye on Jillian. "No one has to go unconscious. No one has to kill anymore—"

"You forget the witness of the Azman," said Jillian.

"No," said Wilm. "I have so very not forgotten—"

"And this isn't to mention," said Jillian, "any person who was, or is, nearby."

"Who else is nearby?" said Wilm. "Robbers in the woods?" He had a point. And I couldn't tell if this made things better or worse. "There are accidents!" He glanced somewhere toward the porch. "Gaelleda. Gaelle. Will you beat and kill for an accident?"

"My father died of an accident."

"Your father," said Wilm. "Would your father want you to kill my own horse?"

"He's using your father," said Jillian.

"And you're using your niece," said Wilm. "Listen. Gaelleda. She is using you."

"Stop," I said.

"She wants to make you like her," he said. "Rifling old church piles, making your mother weep."

"You will leave her family out of this," said Jillian.

"You like to think, Gaelle?" he said. "You like your skepticism?" He took a heavy breath, and something rattled in his throat. "Then show your independence. Yes? Don't let her tell you what to do. Because from now on, she will be the only one who tries to raise you."

Over the years, Wilm would become a better man than this. But now, as with the rest of us, he had a long way to go. In the pasture, his lips had gone white.

"Gaelle," said Jillian. "If you break the law, the Church will try to find you for the rest of your life."

I felt weightless. Sometimes the heaviest decisions have such an effect on me, as if they can lift with their own enormity. I was only fifteen and had just lost my father. He was somewhere on this land, and I didn't want to see him. And I had just discovered that with this wagon ride, my aunt had trapped me all day long, to keep me from getting caught.

"Gaelleda." Wilm was squeezing out a ghastly smile. "Gaelle." His eyes flitted to my chest.

"I'll do it," I said to Jillian. "I'll get it done. And you will help with the horse."

"Now wait," said Wilm.

He clutched at his belt. Jillian stepped behind him, and put a foot in his back. Wilm fell to the ground, and Jillian started to tie his hands. Wilm was weeping.

I backed up a small rise, away from all of them. The Azman, since forgotten, had sat. Jillian had Wilm kneeling. He tried to stand, and she held him down. I looked around, half hoping for someone to intervene, and I found the wagon bed holding dappled sun. Under the seat lay a case Jillian had filled with her kukris, as well as a club and a spade.

I gagged, but nothing came up. Beyond the rise, about fifty paces away, a white horse stood in its corral, rigid and still. Facing Wilm's commotion, it pinned its ears. Maybe the horse had a sense of its own peril, or maybe it just responded to its keeper's cries. A blue accordion slouched on the stump by the horse's stall.

Jillian stalked toward me, with Wilm, as if she had brought me a gift. I stepped back, to the edge of the rise. Wilm leaned, and Jillian tugged.

When she first appeared in my life, Jillian had essentially arrived with my puberty. And now, while deep in the throes of both it and other catastrophes, I figured Jillian never brought anything good. She never did. She'd just appeared at our cottage one night, the way my mother had just died on another.

At the rise, Wilm shuffled with his ankles tied together. Jillian gave the horse a once-over. It paced. Wilm called to it, calling it Lucinda, telling Lucinda she was blameless. The horse snorted while it trotted in tight circles. It was clearly afraid. My father could never intentionally frighten anything, so I half climbed the fence, and screamed at the horse. It jigged, and I screamed again.

"Gaelle!" Jillian pulled me off the fence. "Stop it. Gaelle!" Wilm doubled over, and wheezed. Jillian held my wrist. "You want to kill a horse when it's calm."

I stood loose and out of breath. What she suggested made sense, but it also felt like a betrayal.

Jillian placed Wilm, facing me, between the pasture and me.

Wilm arched his back, and squinted. "Please."

"We haven't even hit you yet," said Jillian.

"Then turn me so the sun's not in my eyes." He looked as far as he could over his shoulder. "Please." He tried to meet my eye. "At least let me look at Lucinda."

"I want Gaelle to see your face."

Wilm rubbed his nose on his shoulder.

"And I don't want her to turn her back on the horse," she said. "How dare you sell it to Lloyd?"

"She's a good girl," he said.

Jillian said, "There are hoof marks on the barn door."

That straightened him a little. He said, "She has a spirit."

"Damn it, Wilm," said Jillian. One reason Jillian was such a good guardian was that no matter what she actually knew, she intuited the stakes better than anyone.

Now she left for the wagon. Over her shoulder, she said for me to keep Wilm between the horse and myself. Wilm hobbled on his knees. He spat. I looked away, and felt myself blanche at the thought of knocking him senseless. If I hit Wilm with, say, the wagon's club, he would likely fall over. That would make it easier to hit him a second time. The trouble was that I had no idea where I would hit him. I would break his nose, if I hit him in the face. I might make him bleed from the ears, if I hit him on the side of the head. He had tiny earlobes. He had a necklace tucked into his shirt.

He was smiling at me again, while a droplet of sweat moved along his jawline. My aunt was unloading the wagon. The Azman watched. On his knees, Wilm rocked from side to side.

"Stop it," I said.

Wilm stopped. He'd likely been trying to work the ropes.

"She'll catch you," I said, "if you try to run."

"I won't run, Gaelleda." He gave a strangled kind of laugh, and sniffed. "I won't leave my horse."

"You were going to sell your horse."

"It was all I could do to sell her." By the way he sat, the opening in his shirt showed the deep hollow in his collar bone. "I won't leave Lucy like this, not ever. By the stars, I will not."

He grunted, and grunted again. Jillian, when she'd made him kneel, had used a hook to fasten the rope on his hands to the rope on his feet. I hadn't even seen her do it. I didn't know we had a hook like that. Wilm couldn't stop arching his shoulders.

"My aunt will be back."

"She always comes back." He sucked the sweat from his lip. "Lucinda had the longest eyelashes when she was a girl." He shrugged off a fly. "Looked as if she were all dressed for a party."

"You should stop talking."

"I didn't like to sell her."

"Then you shouldn't have."

"No? Well I am poor, Gaelleda."

"And I am an orphan."

He made a hissing sort of laugh. "I think you're all grown up."

My father once told me of the Cadmul—the people of Cadmus—in the north, of how they crossed into adulthood when they killed the first animal larger than they were. In the Cadmul culture, my father would have never grown up. He would have been a *girash*, a grown child, for the rest of his life.

Wilm and I startled. Jillian had dropped the spade, and stood behind me, with the club and the kukris. The Azman stood behind her.

"No." Wilm squirmed. "No, you get him away."

Jillian steadied Wilm, who had started to tilt. Wilm hollered at her touch. Lucinda whinnied and pranced. Jillian was saying that the Azman brought cords only, that he was here to secure the horse.

Wilm shouted a curse.

The Azman told him to listen. "Wilm Albertson," he said.

"Don't you say my name."

"You must please understand," said the Azman, "I keep no mindless."

"Oh, yes," said Wilm. "I know how all of you visit whole brothels of mindless." I didn't know it at the time, but the Azmen have trouble producing female offspring. And as such, this insult was doubly, even triply, grave.

In the pasture, the Azman looked at Wilm with a softness. "I'm afraid I can't calm you."

Wilm bent a little forward, as this was the best way he could protect himself with his shoulders pinned open. The Azman unwound long straps of leather he apparently carried by wearing them around his legs. He spoke in a low voice to Lucinda, who had raised a front hoof. She was far taller than Godiva.

Wilm hollered for Lucinda to fight. He told the Azman she would never go mindless, that he could take my dead father if he so wanted a slave. Jillian hit Wilm, and he hunched over himself. She glanced at me. She righted him. I wanted her to carry him away.

"We'll beat you first," she said. "We'll knock you senseless."

"And when I wake up," he said, "you'll have killed her."

"You won't have to see it," she said. "We'll act as fast as we can."

"I want to see her now," he said.

"I told you why you can't," she said.

"Let him do it," I said.

She turned to me. I tasted acid, and fought not to cough.

She worked quickly, almost automatically, as if I'd spoken an order. While she helped Wilm toddle to see the horse, she looked to me, the way she'd do if she positioned furniture. And it dawned on me that if I told her to turn him back, she'd probably comply.

My mother. I wondered what she would have done, if she had wanted this person to be my only guardian.

The Azman's lips had a tattooed blue. He made a low whisper as he mounted Lucinda. And now with his mouth set, he stroked the sides of her neck. Wilm watched him, unblinking, as if he willed the horse to throw her mount.

The horse kicked her right leg, and the Azman squeezed to hold on. The fence slats around the corral had splits.

My father. I kept expecting either his retribution or his help. And then I realized his retribution was me.

I moved between Wilm and his horse. "You sold it," I said to him. "Why?" Jillian tried to move me, but I held. "You sold a crazy horse."

"She has a spirit," Wilm said.

Geese pushed through the sky. Wilm's nose whistled when he breathed, and I thought of it bleeding. Lucinda stood by the fence, wide-eyed and tossing her head. The Azman was down now, securing her front legs. He worked like some kind of mechanism.

"Lucinda's dying," I said, "because you sold her."

Wilm said, "We were hungry."

"Don't talk," I said.

"Gaelle, you should hear him," said Jillian.

"Why?" I said. "This is more of the law?"

"No." She held the club, blunt and wooden as fact. "What it gives is a full picture that frames the law." She faced me, but now she spoke to Wilm. "Tell her why you needed the money."

"I said why." He stretched against the leather. "We needed the food."

"We could have given you food," I said.

"I don't beg!"

The Church kept a law against begging; Wilm would get beaten for that, too.

"I wouldn't beat you for begging," I said.

"Well, you should know it's thievery," said Wilm. "And every thief deserves beatings and worse."

Jillian dropped the club. She opened the box of kukris, and they gleamed like fish. "You'll have to use the longest blade to kill the horse." She held up a kukri. "And, Gaelle, you must be prepared for a lot of blood."

"Lucinda shouldn't be punished," said Wilm.

The Azman put a smear of mud on the horse's neck.

"Drive in," said Jillian. "Jump back."

"You're supposed to help," I said.

"I will help you by holding the horse."

Wilm was toddling.

"I thought we were going to do him first," I said.

"We will," she said. "But what you learn about the horse will help you with him."

"I don't want to learn any of this," I said.

"Beating Wilm will be harder," she said.

"Harder than killing a horse?" I said.

She made a chewing motion. For all I knew, she was trying to destroy what she most wanted to say. "It will change your life to beat a man."

"My life has already changed," I said.

She took a breath, and offered me the club. "Do you want to cause pain, or just knock him out?"

"What?" I said.

"Do you want to break his bones?" she said. "Do you want to scar him? Do you want to ruin his hearing or his sight? Do you just want to make him hurt without permanent injury?" She wiggled the club for me to take.

"I don't know," I said.

"Take the club." She pressed it into my palm. "If you want simply to knock him out, you can hit him in the temple. But be careful not to kill him."

"I won't kill him," I said.

"If you do, you're a murderer." Her face sat in all straight lines. Wilm was sort of muttering. The Azman had pursed his lips until they'd disappeared. He kept the horse still as a monument.

"This law is stupid," I said.

"Which part?" she said.

"I don't know," I said. "Which part isn't?"

"You listen." She dropped her gaze to mine, almost shoving it there, "You can't speak lightly."

"Gaelle," said Wilm. "Think of what your father would want."

I refused to look at him. "You be very quiet."

"Gaelle," Jillian grasped the club above where I held it, "think of what your father would want."

The repetition felt like a betrayal. Even Wilm looked up.

"Jillian, you're the reason I have to do this at all." I shoved the club at her.

She pushed it back, and stepped close enough that I could smell the smoke on her from our kitchen fire. "If the victim doesn't immediately carry out the law, the victim becomes a criminal."

"You're a criminal," I said.

"And you want to be like me?" she said.

For the first time, she didn't look inevitable. Instead, I felt somehow inevitable, except I had no idea what to be inevitable toward.

Something felt heavy, and I remembered Jillian still pressed the club. My father couldn't hurt anything. In one society, he'd be a child. In another society, he'd be an outlaw.

"Did my parents break the law?" I said.

Jillian stepped away from the club and me.

"Jillian," I said.

"They tried not to," she said.

Wilm sneezed. We looked at him, and he said he sneezes when he's nervous.

I thought of my father running off the feasters, of him whipping the ox.

"I'll just knock him out," I said.

Wilm started to mutter, but I couldn't tell if it was a thank-you, or a curse, or a prayer for a curse.

"Wilm," said Jillian, "do you have an eddlefruit?"

"Are you going to bake a pie?" he said.

Eddlefruits are purple things, about the size and shape of a baby pumpkin, and with an inside like an artichoke. Only one tree of them has ever grown in your world. Jillian told Wilm an eddlefruit was the general thickness of a celdan skull, and that she wanted me to practice hitting it first, without breaking the shell.

Wilm's cheeks had gaunted. "No, I do not have an eddlefruit."

Jillian looked to the Azman.

"I have one skull," he said. "A worg. For the apothecary."

"Worg mindless," said Wilm. A worg is a wolf the size of a boar.

"We'll use the skulls," I said.

"No. Too dry," said Jillian. "They're far too brittle."

The temple was a small part on anyone, and Wilm had a very small head. I could hit his eye, or his ear, or both.

The Azman said, "You could kill the horse first."

"No," said Wilm.

"Afterwards," said the Azman, "you could practice hitting the horse head." He touched the horse's face, and she shied. "There is, of course, some difference, but—"

"No. You won't!" Wilm worked the ropes. A joint popped, he cried, and he started again.

"Stop!" I'd grabbed Wilm's shoulder and shaken him. "I'll hit him." I looked to Jillian.

The Azman, standing in front of her, drew his hand down his mouth.

"I mean it," I said. "No practice on the horse."

"That's good, Gaelleda." Wilm gasped a look at the sky. He felt surprisingly soft.

Jillian mouthed something I couldn't hear and stepped in front of the Azman. She said to me, "You will at least practice your aim."

"Otherwise," said the Azman, "you might close your eyes."

Jillian took me by the shoulders, and led me a ways off from the others, to a fence post. She told me to practice hitting the post about a club's width from the top. Her hands were rough and cool. She squared my stance.

She looked me in the face, as if she assessed a wound. "When you hit the post, the club will sting your hands. Though to a lesser extent, the same will happen when you hit Wilm."

I pushed that image from my mind. Then I drew back the club, and struck. The fence shuddered, and my arm felt both electric and numb.

"Aim higher." Jillian had me spread my stance. "That would have hit him in the neck."

"Esaosh."

"Esaosh might, in fact, help you here, if you want him. I don't know."

For some reason, calling on Esaosh felt even riskier than calling on the garrison. And as the afternoon progressed, the garrison had begun to feel deadly.

I lowered the club. "I can't do it."

"You can."

"No."

"Gaelle, it's the law."

"No. Please. You do it instead."

"I can't.

"You can. You like to break the law."

She touched my face, and held it. "I never do violence for anyone else." She rubbed my cheek, and let it go. "And if I did it for you, and if anyone saw, you'd be charged with enticing the services of a criminal."

My eyes stung. Whoever my mother was, this woman felt like the exact opposite. I wished she hadn't touched me at all.

I swung at the post, and hit it squarely.

"Good," said Jillian. My arm felt it might split at the elbow.

She told me that when I was hitting Wilm, I'd have to pause between blows to re-aim. She described how when it's hit, a head makes a different sound than a fencepost. Wilm would be making sounds as well, she said. And I'd have to reset my whole stance after each blow, because he was likely to move.

"Tell him not to move," I said.

"It's involuntary."

She took off her belt, punched a new hole with the kukri, and buckled the strap just below the elbow of my swinging arm. This brace, of sorts, would help with the arm sting. Wilm watched, perhaps thinking it perverse that I was protecting myself from the pain of hitting him.

My arm throbbed around the band.

"This isn't fair," I said.

"It doesn't matter."

"Well it should."

What we planned to do simply tripled what was already terrible.

Jillian sat with her hands on her knees. At my age, in my grief, she seemed to do nothing but watch. But from what I know now, she likely tried to keep herself from collapsing into the grass.

Behind us, Wilm strained, bowing his head one way and arching his back the other. Beside him, the Azman sat astride a horse the stranger had tethered for the kill by straps that looked much like the one on my forearm.

"Jillian," I said.

She didn't even give me a blink.

My mouth had gone dry. "I can't do this."

She looked like an idol.

"You said it was my choice." My lip started to tremble, and I lifted it into a sort of sneer.

She reached out her hand, and took it back.

"I can't," I said. "I'm sorry. I can't do this." From my hands and my gut, I'd started to grow cold. "Please don't make me do this."

She turned to me with her face unmoving. I couldn't even see her breathe. "You must realize," she looked above me, "you must truly understand that if you do not do this, you are an outlaw. That you are fifteen." She put her hands under her knees, and she stiffened herself. "And that for as long as you live—for the next ninety-so years—you will always be an outlaw. That the Church actively pursues outlaws, especially of our kind—"

"I don't care."

"Think about who might care."

I thought of my father, who couldn't kill. I thought of my mother, who died giving birth. I confess, at the time, I did not think of Jillian.

"Jillian."

"When the Church finds out, they can punish you." She closed her eyes, and of all things, she seemed to count. "They can beat you." She opened her eyes. "They can watch you for the rest of your life."

"But right now, who's to see?"

"I've hired the Azman for lookout. I'll tell you this much. But I don't know him. And he can't see it all—who's in the fields, on the road, in the woods. Gaelle." On her knees, the veins on her fingers protruded with the strength of her grip. "Your outlaw fate would not be fair either."

"Well." In a shudder, I inhaled a stretch of cool air. "Life isn't fair, is it?"

She drooped her elbows. It's what my father used to say, and I always thought it sounded as if it were something you said to a child. And the pain of this day was in small part about my no longer living as anyone's child.

She sat some more. She wiped her hands in the grass, and I felt both planted and blown.

"You need to ask yourself," she said, "down to a certainty, whether this refusal is worth the rest of your life."

But I didn't want to ask myself anything. Other people, yes. I had a crate full of questions for them. And one was how life could be so unfair if our world was supposedly established by the very god of fairness. It was a philosophical question for a decidedly visceral day, but God knows it outlasted that day.

I once caught a bass in Lake Kelmer, which is where our orchard draws water. The fish was four inches long, but it was my first fish, and I wanted to eat it. My father kept it in a bucket while he told me the meal would last only for two bites, and how afterwards, the fish would be gone. The bass was silver, like a piece of the water. Its mouth moved open and shut, as if somehow, the creature looked for the rest of itself. In the end, I returned the fish to the lake, and watched it hover in the shallows, like a proclamation.

Now I sat in front of Jillian, and spread my legs before me.

"I think," I said, "that my father would decide nobody wanted to kill him."

"Intent isn't the issue."

"No!" I looked her in the eye, and I made myself keep looking. "Intent should be the issue. And I will not hurt them."

The corner of Jillian's eye moved, as if in some kind of spasm. I waited for her to yell, or to grasp my face.

"Jillian."

She dug in her pocket for her handkerchief. She offered it to me, and it smelled of resin. I used it, and handed it back.

Jillian wiped her brow, and she held the kerchief to her mouth.

I was still holding the club, so I let it rest on the ground. "I won't beat them."

She stood in a single motion, as if for a while, she had gathered herself to do so. "I'm sure," she focused on folding the handkerchief, "I'm quite sure he will be happy to hear it."

I walked on sturdy legs. The air was cool on the sweat in my palm. I'd left the club behind, and Wilm watched it while he tried to straighten his shoulders.

Jillian led me to his hands, and said, "You're free." I tugged at the hook. Wilm started to laugh or cry, and Jillian told him to sit still so I could work. He stopped squirming. He trembled. I unfastened the hook on the second try. Wilm stood, and Jillian helped him, and then he knelt and thanked me.

"Get up," I said.

"Gaelleda," he said, "you are magnificent."

"Shut up," I said.

Wilm straightened while Jillian handed me a knife. Wilm was so exposed, with his feet together and his arms tied behind him. I had a flash of evil. Then I sawed at the ropes on his feet, and as each one gave, it was like the loosening of something inside me. I suddenly wanted to sleep.

Lucinda stamped her hoof. The Azman sat on her, as something that had just caught up to us.

"You can get down from Lucy," said Wilm.

The Azman sat.

"Get off my horse," said Wilm.

"This is still an issue," said Jillian.

"No," said Wilm.

"Let it go," I said "It's a stupid horse."

The Azman, with hazel eyes, gave me a look that was open for a stranger's. Wilm appeared caught between cheering and correcting me.

"Wilm can't keep the horse," said Jillian.

"You aren't the decider," said Wilm.

"If he keeps the horse," said Jillian, "the law can see he hasn't been punished."

"Who's to see?" said Wilm.

"Her father is dead," said Jillian. "Don't suggest that none will wonder why."

From the corner of my eye, I thought I saw my father's boots, toe-up, in the field. But when I looked again, two pigeons lifted.

"Jillian," said Wilm, "we can lie about why."

"We will lie about how the horse killed him, but we will not lie any further." She drew her kukri. "Gaelle has forgiven you. But she won't have the burden of that horse."

This was wrong. It went against everything we'd talked about. "Jillian," I said. "I get to decide."

"Wilm is one thing. But the horse killed your father—my sister's husband." She stood in front of Lucinda. "It killed a decent man. A young man." She drew back the knife.

"Gaelle," said the Azman. "Look away."

Wilm hollered.

I was standing in front of the horse. I don't remember the move. Jillian stood six inches in front of me, with the kukri level with my head. For a moment, her face went slack. "I love your heart." She'd never said this before. "But the horse has to die."

"No," I said. "She doesn't."

She lowered and raised her kukri.

"My father's dead," I said.

"You don't have to be here," she said.

"He couldn't kill," I said. "He wouldn't kill the horse."

"Gaelle makes an excellent point," said Wilm.

"Your father would kill to keep you safe," said the Azman.

"You don't know my father," I said.

"I just am a father," he said.

"Think of the law," I said, "of how it says you can't do this for me."

"My doing it will be bad enough," Jillian said. "But it's easier to hide one moment of my doing something for you than it is to conceal a horse for her whole lifetime."

Jillian nodded at the Azman, and something flew from him. She grabbed Wilm, and somehow lashed his torso, to the fencepost, with a leather strap. Wilm was screaming. Jillian turned to me.

I stood my ground.

"Gaelle." She turned me around. "Look. Look at the horse. Look at the yard." She pointed to the splinters in the fence slats and stall door. She showed me the roll of the creature's eye, the scar on its front leg. "If we stripped Wilm, I imagined we'd find scars on him too."

"I'll scar you," he said.

"Never mind the law," she said. "We've put you outside the law. But think of Wilm keeping the horse. Think of him selling it to somebody else."

"I won't," said Wilm.

"If you're hungry enough," she said.

"We can feed him," I said. The words had come out like a spell. "We grow food. We have plenty." She shook her head. "Jillian."

"Hush." She pulled the base of her braid. That's what she did whenever her mind raced. Now she turned to the Azman. "Can you take the horse?"

"It's not conditioned to the screel," he said. The screel is the wind that scours Azmon. "I'm afraid it would die horribly."

"Just let her go," I said.

"Such would be a miserable life," said the Azman. "She'd have to find her own shelter. Her own food."

"She'd want to go home," said Jillian, "and that would be miserable for Wilm."

"You don't care about my misery," said Wilm.

"Somebody does," she said, "which is why you're still upright."

The horse tried to shake her head, and the tethers creaked. My father would have had to fight to get her home. He would have shown up bruised and half-senseless, as if he had just tried to ride a tornado.

"We could take it home," I said.

Jillian laughed.

"We wouldn't have to ride it," I said. "We could just feed it."

"That's called a loss," she said.

"I could feed her," said Wilm.

"You can't even feed yourself," she said.

The Azman peered at me with his head back. A scar, an old slit, ran horizontally beneath his chin. "You'd give shelter," he said, "to the horse that killed your father."

I had no answer to where this generosity was coming from, or why it wouldn't stop. I said, "She just threw my father."

"And you'd add this crime of mercy," he said, "to all your others?"

I looked to Jillian. The skin beneath her eyes was dark, as if the day had drawn away any rest she'd had.

"You're all thieves," said Wilm. "You're experts at avoiding the law."

"After all this," said Jillian, "each of us will be an outlaw."

I sat, and the horse sniffed in my direction. "You said it was my choice."

The horse whinnied, and the Azman bounced. "And what if," he said, "you take home this horse, and you wake up one morning and change your mind?"

Even then, I recognized this possibility as a consideration. I had no real reason to save the horse. And I remembered what Jillian had said so recently, while she held my face. "If I changed my mind," I said, "then I would have to kill it."

"You won't kill Lucinda," said Wilm.

"Lands, you people!" Jillian stepped so close to me, that it took all I had not to move. "You have no idea how hard it is to kill a horse like this. How hard it is to train a horse like this. It's a liability just to have this horse."

The Azman said, "It would make a good warhorse."

"That's what I always thought," said Wilm.

Jillian had thrown her kukri into the ground. Now she stared at the Azman.

"I could stay on," he said. "Train her, if you like."

"Esaosh on a chamber pot." Jillian climbed the pasture fence, so she was almost eye level with the Azman. "What part of anything grants you the right?"

"I have helped you here. I know what you have, and haven't, done."

"Oh no." She crouched on the fence. "You do not want to blackmail—"

"I misspoke, perhaps." He had a split dagger in his belt. "In my province, death isn't nearly the worst punishment. And yet, your young woman refrains from bestowing it."

Jillian pulled her braid with such force that I thought she'd yank it right out. "I hired you for an afternoon's security."

"Ah-ha!" said Wilm.

"You hush," said Jillian.

"Truth be told," said the Azman, "I'd have stayed here out of interest." He stroked the horse's neck, and the horse nipped. "This horse's color isn't common in your province, but it is common in mine." From the horse, he leaned sideways, toward me. "What would you say if somebody decided this horse looks a lot like the one your departed father tried to buy?"

"Who?" I said.

"Someone," said the Azman. "What you could say is that Teph, your Azmonian friend, has given you an Azmonian warhorse—that this was given in sympathy for the loss of your father."

"Why would you do this?" said Jillian.

"He wants a mindless warhorse," said Wilm.

"Horseman." Tears stood in Teph's eyes, and as if to keep me from rising, Jillian pressed my shoulder. "It can't be done with animals," said Teph. "They become dire. Uncontrollable. They kill everything in sight."

Wilm sagged in his strap.

"And yet with Gaelle's leave," said Teph, "your horse's life will be in my hands."

"Is that all you want?" said Jillian. "A sense of irony?"

"No." He dismounted. He was tall. "I wanted something other than expedience." The horse walked its back legs, side to side. "I want to honor this rare complication." He peered at me from his bleached brows. "I believe what I've spotted is compassion."

"So that's what you've spotted." Jillian muttered.

"Just so," said Teph.

Wilm sat, and his waist strap slid to his armpits.

"What about your family?" I said.

"My children have family of their own. I see them seldom."

"And we're supposed to feed you," said Jillian, "and give you shelter."

"For a month," said the Azman. "Afterward, I'll have finished."

"Well, how about that," she said.

"It suits me fine," he said.

The Azman had bushy eyebrows and a beak of a nose. His skin was so leathered that you couldn't tell if the desert had done it, or if he was simply old, or if the desert had actually made him old. He wore silver studs in each of his ears, where his left had another, smaller one of dainty green. It wasn't a color a man would choose, usually, but it was maybe a color a child would give her father.

"It sounds good to me," I said. Wilm exhaled as if all of him deflated. Jillian unfastened him.

The fence creaked as the horse pulled against it with her back legs. I'd had no idea how much effort Teph had spent to keep her still. "You're good with horses," I said to him.

"I'm friends with Cadmul riders," he said.

"Jillian," I said.

She leaned against the fence, with her top half hanging over her thighs. "If you wish to take home the horse that killed your father, I really can't stop you."

"With the Azman," I said.

She laced her fingers behind her back. "And if he touches you, I will kill him."

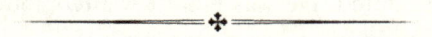

This is how we resolved my father's death. Wilm wept, and stroked the horse's nose. The Azman rode to our farmstead, zigzagging, presumably to tire her.

From the back acreage, Jillian and Wilm carried my father, wrapped in a stable blanket. They placed him in the wagon bed. A shock of his hair hung, black, from the top of the roll, and when I saw it, I vomited until I could barely stand. When that happened, Jillian held my head in the crook of her arm, and Wilm returned to stand against the fence, as if he were still strapped there.

During the trip home, I was barely strong enough to sit in the wagon seat, but I couldn't bring myself to lie in the back with my father. I leaned against Jillian as she drove us. She pressed somewhat against me, and I waited for tears.

Jillian spoke during the ride, sensing, perhaps, how silence was something I couldn't yet bear. She told me she had hired Teph when Wilm had first brought her to my father, that she'd liked how, before she'd arrived, Teph had stayed to ensure the death received an answer. She told me Azmen cry not from sorrow, but from fury, and that there are stories of whole Azmonian armies hacking their foes while tears streaked the Azmen's own faces.

She said my life would never be the same. The point was so obvious that I asked to walk home. "Your father," she said, "is another issue. We will mourn your father." She held up her hand, as if to shush me. "But what you've done can never be found."

"You rarely get found," I said.

She handed me the reins, and undid her blouse. On her right breast, just above the aureole, was a brand in the shape of an **I**. I wanted to ask what it was for, but I couldn't speak.

"Once they find you," she said, "they don't ever let go."

I was too young and too overcome to grasp everything Jillian was telling me. But even then, the sight of the burn made something in my own chest flop a little. "How would the Church know any of today?" I said.

Right then, she could have told me of the Shield Potent, which is the Church's secular constabulary. She could have mentioned the Sword Potent, which is the religious equivalent that, even then, schemed to cut off the Shield entirely. Jillian had informants; she must have heard the rumors. Instead, she closed her shirt. "Many times the Church doesn't know what we do. Even when they're watching, they don't. And this very reality," she pulled tight her eyes, "is why I even let you take these risks."

"Plus you agree with me." More than once, I'd seen her bite into a particularly sweet carrot, and save the butt of it for Godiva. "You do agree. You know? It's where we come from."

"I agree, Gaelle, that under the right protection, you are the one to make your own choice." She took the reins, slowing the horse, until I looked at her. "But all they have to do is find out once."

"There will be only once."

"Gaelle," she glanced into the wagon bed, and was slow to turn back around, "will you never feed a beggar? Will you report a man who can't pay his debt?"

"You said my parents tried to keep the law."

"They did. And they spent a lot of time alone on this orchard."

"Well, it's a big job, Jillian."

"Here's another thing you have to consider. What your parents would want for your life." She looked at me, the way she'd peered at the wagon bed, but I didn't look back. "It is, in fact, what I've been trying to consider all day."

I watched Godiva's rump, brown and stiff. She was old enough to have known both my parents. Her age, in fact, was probably why my father was so intent on buying Lucinda in the first place. I wondered how Godiva would survive the other horse.

My parents had spent almost all their married life in their orchard, until it had become a kind of cloister. After what I learned on my father's deathday, I occasionally wondered if this cloistering was the reason Jillian had come, if when I was nine, my father had actually sent for her. She could do the work in town, maybe, while he remained with his child and tried, apparently, to abide by the law. He must have missed the town and its opportunity to do good beyond his own flesh.

Raising me, of course, was a bigger job than I could see at the time—a job far bigger than growing the orchard. This wasn't just because, to put it succinctly, I was a willful and spiteful cark, but because, on the way home, I was utterly correct about where we came from. I was more correct than I knew. My father, an anathema of gentleness, raised the only child of four related women. At the moment, I'd learned of only two. In their own way, all of these women opposed the Church—sometimes in the hedgerows, and sometimes at the gallows. Wilm, who was older, knew all of my family, at least in passing. He certainly spoke as if he did. And I like to hope their acquaintance with him helped him grow into what he eventually became. In any event, each of those people had an influence on how my father, the quiet farmer, had cultivated me. And when my aunt glanced into the cart on our way home from his death, I suspect she had also acknowledged him about what he begat.

The whole project of my childhood was to teach me not to run. With the horse, even Wilm had rooted for me to remain *intrepid*, as one might say. And both before and after my father's death, when my family doled out the truth of this world, they taught me how at least half of resistance amounts simply to standing fast.

When we got home with my father, Jillian stoked the fire for the night. I sat so close to it that it stung my eyes. Teph put Lucinda away without addressing us, and per some previous arrangement, he spent the night in the shed.

On this first evening, I was the last to bed. I fed the fire, staring as long as I could at its blue eye. On one side of the house stood my mother's cart. On the other side stood my father's horse. In a way, I slept between them. Upstairs held the sound of Jillian weeping.

chapter 3

GARFIELD

This morning, the sun rises over the Gomadong, as if we're crossing into a new country. The guards have posted a bowlegged boy as sentry on a rampart that's even with the Bell. The dawn gives a rose color to his helmet, softening it into something better than itself, and I wish he could see that. One way Church possession works is by making you believe you are nothing in this world, except where the Church itself touches you.

Despite the rampart's relative proximity, Ordinal's jailers have disconnected me from just about everything. My prison hangs in a canyon whose west mountainside both lifts and partially encloses Ordinal's main fortress. The eastern cliff juts with catapult and cannon. When everyone started this war, nobody had much artillery, but Celd apparently enjoys an accelerated evolution of weaponry.

Between the cliffside church and mortar, passes a cobblestone road. My cell is too high to see the faces of any travelers, but I can discern them by flag, or uniform, or gait. A Riven scout once told me it's easy to recognize even an acquaintance by their gait.

From my prison, I watch the wagonloads of marble, iron, and gold. I pray over the prison carriages as they crawl like monstrous beetles. I try to count the troops as they move in and out. They're loudest when they march on the part of the road directly beneath my cell, but of course, this is also when I can't see them. So I close my eyes, and let the sound overcome me, the way I imagine it ringing along the cell's suspension chains. That Riven scout I knew: he could interpret the thunder of an army the same way a sailor might read the thunder of the sea. I cannot. But I try, if only as a way to think of the man who could. Now when Increase is here, the bird hunkers in the marchers' sound, sitting black-eyed, white-eyed, naked with contempt, motionless as if someone's had him stuffed.

Despite the noise, I admit a part of me is happy for even an army's approach. If I could get a message to the Riven, I could tell them precisely who moves along the canyon road. But I'm also just glad for the company. As much as people in my life have tried to prepare me for confinement, prison is still monstrous in its reality. My cell is about the size of a small barn, hexagonal in shape, and slanted toward a drain in the middle. The whole thing resembles a diamond, or one of those prison carriages. The chains suspending the cell are at least as thick as what sustains a drawbridge. And I think about their size, because this cell must carry tons of stone. I don't know how the engineers made it hang. Maybe they used ossumancers—bone mages—to infuse the rock with a kind of living, interior scaffolding. If so, I'm not as alone as I thought. But then, as a hostage to dark magic, I'm also worse off.

None of these things is worth considering. My cell holds a rush floor, a straw pallet, a wooden stool and chair, and a woolen blanket. The jailers have since given me a double-lined, burlap cassock which someone has blotched with yellow paint. Yellow is the Church's warning color; it implies sickness, pus. I tell Increase the yellow shows how I'm turning into light.

I have two windows, facing north and south. These have no shutters, but I can use the stool to plug the north window most of the way. Then I can sit in the chair, with a torch, in front of a wall, and keep warm enough.

When the weather's nice, I like to sit by the portico that's outside my cell door. Most of the time, a guard stations there, clutching a rope handle someone has bolted into the wall. Even if this guard doesn't speak, I like to hear him fidget in his mail, or maybe hum before he catches himself. Most of the people who guard me are teenage boys. I don't know why. Perhaps the boys are the only ones young and expendable enough to brave the portico. A suspension bridge stretches from the porch, to an alcove in the castle cliffside, where another guard keeps post. The bridge prevents my cell form swinging more than it would otherwise, but the wind pitches my prison to the extent that the guards call it the Bell. They call the wall's rope handle *Mama*. Among the sentries, you show your manhood by not holding onto Mama.

The portico has a wrought-iron railing. And even without it, the platform is wide enough to keep most people from falling. But when the guards get so they don't hold to Mama, they do sometimes clutch the bars on my prison door. I watch their leather-gloved fingers, and sometimes after their shifts, I hold the places where their hands had been.

Increase does not show himself to any of the sentries. He stands in the windowsill, sometimes on the draft-blocking stool. Or he sits out of sight, on his burlap. Or he goes climbing somewhere outside, with talons that could encircle a flag pole. When he returns, I tell him about the guards. Even if he stayed nearby, I tell him. My account seems important, somehow, as if my interpretation of events is as meaningful as their recital. When I talk of the boys, I don't preach those things out the window. And lately, I've begun to tell about them just after sunrise, when Garfield, my new night sentry, leaves me with too many things to say.

―――――― ✠ ――――――

Garfield puffed at me during the first night he came to the portico. Somebody must have told him the posture would make him feel brave. And really, it wasn't the worst strategy. During our initial evening, he kept stepping onto the bridge, and though he probably did so out of fear, part of me wonders if he just needed a place to let himself fully exhale. Sweat stuck his hair, black, to the nape of his neck. His eyes, wide and a little bit bugged, had the same ruddy brown as the birthmark that ran along his jawline. On the portico, his fingers slid along his halberd's haft. He kept correcting himself from holding it like a broom.

In the middle of his first shift with me, I asked him where he was from. He shrank a bit into his cuirass, and his nose ran. The old fighter in me thrilled at how I'd just scared the actual snot from the enemy. But the fact remained that Garfield was a boy. He shouldn't have been guarding old ladies any more than I should have faced the decision over Wilm and Lucinda.

I asked Garfield again where he was from, and he said his home was the Church.

"My home is a church," I said. "I'm a nun of my church."

"You are the Reaching Man's whore," said the boy. His voice cracked, and perhaps to cover it, he scuffed the butt of the halberd.

"I've been called worse," I said.

For a moment, the child in him looked fascinated. Then he touched the Esaosh holy symbol he wore around his neck. "You should know there's nothing worse than the Reaching Man."

The Reaching Man is a Cadmul iteration of Visjaes. The Church describes him as a demon the color of sand that can change its length and its thickness to the extent where it can watch from within a bush, or hide flat along the steppe's rare wreck of a tree. The Church maintains the Reaching Man makes a habit of stealing children, so it must be a particularly terrible creature for Garfield. In all honesty, I know how it feels to dread the Cadmul expression of Visjaes. And in any case, Garfield was onto something when he faced me in my cell; before my life ends, I do mean to draw at least some of these boys away.

Garfield and I didn't talk for the rest of his initial shift. Perhaps because Esaosh is the supposed Lord of Light, Garfield lit the three torches that hung around the portico, and he brought two more from the castle. Judging by the smell from his brigandine, the boy started to suffer from the heat. I didn't mind the temperature; warmth is good for my shoulders and knees. And I could always lean on the cool of the sandstone. The Bell angles its walls so a guard in the portico can see just about any part of the cell's interior, except for what's right next to the door. Poor Garfield seemed hesitant to turn his back to me when I was still visible, while evidently he also didn't like how I looked in his direction. So he stood, at the intersection of all that, until I took pity, and tried to sleep.

This prison in Cathedral Ordinal is not the most vicious or even the oldest, but as it resides at the Imperial capital, it is the most officious. One could call it prestigious, if one were in the habit of deriving prestige from the Church. As I tried to sleep while Garfield shed his anxiety, I wondered if any of my family had languished here. Most of us met our end at Abbey Holding, in the farmlands far to the south. But if I extended my kin to include all the resistance—if I counted the Riven who fight the war, and the Cleft who run the charities, and the Syndicate who serve as our spies—then many of my people have slept at Ordinal, if not this very Bell. The gallows in the courtyard recall the many who have also died here. And I suspect a reason the churchmen have hung me above the Gomadong is so I might see our final defeat along the plain.

As I lay in the Bell, that night, I drew a pebble I'd lately found in the floor. The surface of the stone had worn nearly smooth from what must have been centuries of prisoners rubbing it. Now I shifted my hips, as they had gotten boney of late. I put the stone to my lips. Then I imagined Garfield agog, and I put it down. But I needed the company of the thing, so I placed it back at my mouth, where it felt cool as an egg.

After about a week at the Bell, I could tell how despite his fear of me, the heat from all the torches made Garfield want to drowse. Such a lapse would nearly kill him. He wouldn't likely fall, but the Church has mirrors they position on the plain, where they use light to punish any guard they've caught asleep.

"Garfield," I said. As he stood in place, he shuffled his feet. "Garfield, where are you from?"

"I'm from the Church, Old Woman."

"Of course." I grasped the bars. "But I mean before then. Where was your home?"

He touched his birthmark.

"It'll keep you awake," I said, "if you show me."

With my finger, I drew a streak through the grime on a flagstone near the cell door. This, I told him, was the Ariadne River. It bisects the Empire, and Garfield had almost certainly never been west of it. I placed a dead cricket in the northeast to designate Cadmus, and a breadcrumb in the south to show my province of Holding. Where I squatted, I kept hold of the bars, because these days, it's hard to sit so low. "Garfield," I said, "point to something before I can't get up again."

Maybe on account of the torch's heat, he removed his gloves. He rubbed a pimple, and approached close enough to waft me his breath redolent of dried fish. With one hand, he grasped my cell bars, and with the other he hovered a finger over the stone. He'd chewed off all his nails. Then he lightly touched the Cadmul border, just to the north of Holding and to the south of the Gomadong. He kept his finger there before speaking.

He told me *Garfield* means *plain of the spear*, and that his father had named him. "My name is for the battle there. You cotton?"

"At Ketch?"

He tucked his pointing finger into his fist. "That's where we routed you all."

"I see."

He stood, with a jangle. I worked to stand too, and for a moment, I thought he would offer his hand. Instead he just watched.

"So." I straightened. "How old were you?"

"I'm fourteen."

"I mean when you were conscripted."

"I was the oldest boy."

He hadn't given an answer. Instead he maybe offered a reason he'd given himself for why the Church took him so young. The way things go, he'd probably been a little over six. A member of the Sword Potent likely suggested that, held in the arms of Cathedral Ordinal, Garfield would remain safe from the war against us infidels, while he also showed his family's loyalty to the cause. Maybe the Sword also gave Garfield's mother a sack of barley. If so, she probably never brought herself to cook it.

Garfield had turned his back to the conversation. These days, he'd grown comfortable enough to do at least this much. I watched him relax until his free arm started to dangle.

"Garfield," I said, "you must love your parents."

"Love is your business, Whore."

He had stepped from me, and now he half spilled a wall-mounted chalice of salt. They throw handfuls of the stuff at any prisoner who shows signs of demonism.

"One more thing," I said.

"What now?"

"I reckon you never get mindless on this bridge?"

"Mindless?" He tossed the salt into its dish. "No." He adjusted his girdle. "No, they'd have to get into the castle."

"Then I'll let you get back to your stewing."

The mindless—the flesh golems—if they ingest salt of any kind, they enter a rage. The Church had lost whole mining operations this way. I suppose I shouldn't have needled the boy about his salt piles, considering all that, but he did just twice call me a whore.

With his back half-turned, he watched me with a kind of resentful need. Garfield probably wanted me to agree with him about the castle, but as I was a heretic, we weren't supposed to agree at all. I'd let him work on that for a bit.

"You know," I said, and he startled. "I'm sure you're right. About the mindless. And they'd make so much noise that you'd hear them jumble on the castle stairs."

"They'd have to get out of the pens."

"And dismember so many people along the way."

"Stop it."

"I'm sorry." I offered him some salt I'd gathered, and he watched to see, maybe, if I'd start to crisp up or something. I left it all on the cell door's crossbeam. He positioned himself on the other side of the portico, and sucked in his top lip.

I'd forgotten how much the Church has to make people fear the world, so the people can decide to let the Church rule the world. Our resistance has whole regiments who ridicule such fear. My dear Patrick, who heads our church, used to be like Garfield. Nowadays he could make the boy fear the Reaching Man so much that Garfield would flee the haft of his own halberd. And then Patrick would make him laugh about why he did. I miss Patrick with my whole heart. He is one reason why I try to connect with these boys in the first place. And if I can connect with them, I can save them from their masters.

From where he stood, I couldn't see Garfield's eyes beneath his helmet. The Church had put him in an impossible position. At his post, he was required to watch me, and yet he wasn't allowed to learn anything from me. And what he was likely trying not to absorb was the fact that we were both alone.

Besides a sort of regimented appreciation for teamwork, attachment is at best an indulgence, in the eyes of the Church. It can spell disaster, such as what happened with my decision to spare Lucinda. And at the very least, it leads to altruism, which deprives the people of Esaosh from becoming their strongest selves. Love, then, is an outright catastrophe, which it is. It can lead you to hide your face in the shadows, say, because you can't stop glancing at a spot, next to a dead cricket, that reminds you of a woman weeping beside a sack of grain.

A little later, I said, "Garfield."

"You should stop talking."

"You should stop chewing your nails."

"You should stop telling me what to do."

"Fine. But I'm not the only one who'd say so." I let him think who else. "Chewing your nails will make your fingers pucker."

"Well, your face has puckered. Who's chewed on that?"

"Watch your sass, Boy." He blinked. Good. "I'll do you one better." I swung my elbow. "My fingers have seized up, completely. I can't let go of the bars."

He swallowed, perhaps to keep his voice from cracking. "I'm not stupid."

"I swear on my life." I yanked. "It's what happens when you're one hundred thirty-two."

"You are not one hundred thirty-two."

"We can count on all our fingers, if can you help me get mine loose."

My shoulders had begun to ache. I've told lies in my time, but this was not one of them. The other day, I bit a heel of bread, and thought my jaw had just come off its hinge. Now I lengthened my arms, and stuck my rear out as far as I could. "There. I've gone as far from you as I possibly can." I wondered if he could see down my cassock. "Please undo my grip."

He bent to peer at my hands, from across the portico, and the pair of us looked as if we'd entered some kind of joust.

"Look," I said. "You don't even have to put down the halberd." I managed to straighten one finger, and it clamped back down. "Just put your hand here, over the bar, so you can push my fingers away when they try to latch on again."

He looked along the bridge.

"If I'm so dangerous," I said, "why am I my own set of manacles?"

"Why are you so old?"

I chuckled, and bounced, and the motion made some part of me twinge along my ribs. "Because your people didn't get to me till now."

Garfield and his halberd stood in front of me. He reached, briefly, for Mama, then put his dainty fingers beneath mine. He pressed with the back of his hand, until my left grip came loose. He pushed my hand away with his knuckles, and rolled it over like something gone belly up. "Keep it there," he said. For emphasis, maybe, he pressed my palm with his own. I tried to keep my face slack. He slid his fingers between my other hand and the bar, grasping my fingers while he did. He pulled them away. "There."

He stood by the salt chalice, and wiped his hands on his greaves.

It would have been pleasant to thank him, but I didn't want to draw attention to how he'd touched me more than he needed to. Boys do that though; they ratchet in their trust, sometimes at the pace of forgetfulness or need.

"I'm going to sleep now, Garfield." I settled on the floor. "If you start to doze, you just give me a holler."

"The sun's almost up."

"Oh. Then it was a night well spent."

chapter 4

Milkweed

part ONE

On the first morning after my father's death, I saw Lucinda lie down for the only time that we lived in Ludington. Just after first light, I stood in the doorway of our still house, watching Lucinda's still sleep—her resting on her side, the slow rise of her belly in the dawn. She was clean; Teph must have groomed her after their ride. He likely brushed her down, smoothed her coat, and followed the shape of her as if he outlined what I had decided to save. Now, in the rising sun, she heaved whatever unknowable things she dreamed. She really did have long eyelashes. And in that moment, before we hadn't yet buried my father, I was glad I had saved this horse. After everything since, I'm still glad.

Now Teph emerged from the shed, and shut softly the door. Lucinda raised her head, stood, and snorted. Hers was the first full sound of the morning. He reached to her, and she stomped. She nuzzled his arm, and she shied. He reached again, she reared him her head, and he stroked both sides of her face. She swished her tail. She gazed from the pen, looking east, and for a moment, she rested her chin on Teph's head. This morning remains one of the most serene moments I remember from Ludington. It was a break from the expected, the way compassion usually is.

My father once told me how if you save an animal, it will know what you did. No matter if it's your pet or your livestock, or some wild thing you found in the woods, it will sense what you've done, the way it senses both fear and this thing that is somehow its opposite. The animal might still kill you someday. It, like you, is a creature of this world. But then again, it might also leave you alone. It might even attach itself to you, as if it remembered what you had done, or even, as if through an impulse deeper than instinct, it recalled something older than you both.

part TWO

Despite Lucinda's first calm, and its rebuttal of everything to come, I soon surprised myself by how much I wanted Teph to take this horse and leave. Contrary to his earlier promise of four weeks, Teph stayed for two and a half months. And regardless of that first morning, he said Lucinda was more difficult than he ever thought. His bruises, and the split in his lip, were proof enough of his sincerity. Early on, Jillian once told me she'd wondered if she should have found a better horseman. But she stopped doubting, she said, when she approached the horse alone one evening, and felt her palms sweat just from the curl of Lucinda's lip.

"What horses snarl?" I said.

She stood with me at one of our windows. "Maybe it honors your father to know she's so difficult."

The time was certainly difficult. And in many respects, I was more difficult than even Lucinda. Call it grief: an orphaning at adolescence. Call it an outlawing at adolescence. Or simply call it adolescence in general. After a full day of taking Lucinda's screams, Teph would lurch into our cottage, and take some of mine.

For the entire time he was with us, he spent most of his evenings in the shed. Jillian still slept in her partitioned part of the upstairs. Next to it, my father's room effectively produced an extra bed, but Teph had the manners not to ask for it. I had the authority to offer, but I never did. Each night, before he retired, he checked all the fence latches, and he chopped the wood. In the wee hours, before light, he milked the cow. I'd hear the cough he had just after he'd awaken. Then I'd listen to my aunt's voice when she opened him the cottage door. They laughed, sometimes. They banged familiar pots. I would get out of bed, both loving my parents and hating everyone else. At times, I wanted to make Teph outright kill Lucinda, just so he'd leave.

And yet, even among all my grief and rage, I doubted if any of us could kill the horse. There was something about her, so implacable, that you feared how even after death, she would rise again, screaming. Teph worked to break her, perhaps as much from compassion as from a promise. Or maybe, when he struggled to sit on her, he'd begun to feel the turn of the world.

Of the world, in a broad sense, I should say more. Its coastal southland is Holding province. This province has the most farmland, including my childhood orchard. Holding is also our most temperate land, where it has ice only six months out of the year. On the southern coast, presides Abbey Holding, where the abbot is the ecclesiastical authority of the whole Church empire. Much of my family has died at Abbey Holding, or on their way to or from.

To the north are the plains of Cadmus. In their east, by the coast, sits Ordinal, which is the seat of the Church's bureaucracy and military. Historically, the Church's chancellor directs all of these matters, as a counterpart to the abbot. In command of both the chancellor and the abbot is traditionally the principe, who lives in a palace on Ordinal's shore. As part of his reform, Abbot-Principe Caspar has since combined some of these offices. But they still remained distinct in my youth. Of more present concern is the fact that Ordinal also houses Cathedral Ordinal, which is where Increase and I currently roost in our cell.

To the east of all this is Bakeet, a chain of islands many would call the empire's tail. It runs halfway up Cadmus and halfway down Holding, where the extreme portion of each end sits in perpetual ice. Bakeet used to belong to Holding, before its remarkably peaceful bid for independence. And now the province hosts merchants, pilgrims, or smugglers, depending on which is most suitable for any of the Bakeet to become.

To the west of everyone, running the full length of Celd, lies Treehand. Its taint, as Wilm called it, can be many things: its sacrifices to the trees; its hate for the Church empire; its pallid settlements that few outsiders see. The province is technically under Church rule, as the Church proclaims everything in Celd is part of its empire. But Treehand rejects so much of the empire that Treehand was the first sign to us revolutionaries that the empire was not invincible. Treehand used to spread over a large portion of the east, until the Church launched the Clearing Wars three hundred years ago. But even this incursion, and its loss of thousands, served only to push the Treehanded back. To this day, we burn Treehand's artifacts whenever we find them. Even we rebels do, and with the blessing of the Treehanded who have joined our ranks. Those immigrants came to us from a century-old schism between the priests, who demanded child servitors, and the parents who refused the tithe. Both the Imperial Church and the Treehanded Priestly Grove practice conscription. And you can see why some of the Treehanded parents eventually found sympathy with the likes of us.

On the other side of Treehand, to the southwest, shift the frigid deserts of Azmon. Here is the seat of gem mining; the ruinous wind called the screel; and the criminals who live out their endless deaths as the flesh-golem mindless. Despite present exceptions that didn't become clear for years, the Church traditionally condemns mindless as unabashed artifacts of necromancy. For centuries, the relations between the Church and Azmon have been correspondingly strained. In fact, if not for Treehand, war would certainly have come between them long before our current revolution led them to it.

Finally, to the north of Azmon, sits Merrial. Nobody lives there, as far as we gather. Even the present-day Azmen stay out. The land is poisoned, where the mineral content is high enough to disorient navigating birds. The Church says Merrial is the land where Visjaes arrived, already wounded, while also wounding the world. A few of us also now know that Merrial houses

Nabush, the stalk of Esaosh's impertinence. Fewer still have also seen how Merrial holds a monster's tomb. And I don't mention either of these facts from my prison window.

During nearly every day of Teph's stay at our orchard, he tried to build on what I knew of this world, in the way of a man who truly missed his family. None of it felt interesting to me. I was obdurate, sarcastic, and at least as caustic as Garfield. The world's wounds meant nothing to me; from where I sat, the world had them coming.

During all this time, Lucinda screamed. Teph outright called it keening. He never harmed her, never so much as hit her, even when she dislocated his shoulder. After the occasional day or two of rest, he'd return to crouch in her pen as if he danced with her. She would peal in such a way as if to leave me tearing, as if she alone could make a sound appropriate to my father's death. Other times, I wanted to smother her myself. To my mind, she had no right to keening. She had no right to risk the fact that Wilm might hear, so he might come to kill us for bringing misery to his horse. But Jillian suggested if I thought such a thing, I didn't know Wilm. (And largely, I didn't.) She suggested that for all we knew, Lucinda had gone on like this her entire life. "We don't know," she said. "We can't hear Wilm's farmstead." She put her hand on me. "There's nothing to make us suspect he can hear ours."

Two months passed this way. Then at breakfast, while eating preserves of eddlefruit, I asked if maybe Lucinda missed Wilm.

Teph coughed, and I hated his cough. "Of this," he said, "I heartily doubt."

"He was her family," I said. "A horse might miss her family."

Teph bristled his beard, which was coming in white. Even more than that cough, I hated the sound of his bristle.

"Why?" I said.

Teph banged his pipe against a bucket we'd set by the chair.

"Tell me," I said.

"Gaelle," said Jillian. "Don't start."

"No," I said. "I want to hear it. Why do you doubt?"

"Because," Teph said, "the horse is restless."

"But she's keening," I said. "You called it that."

"You know this isn't my first language." He stood, and knocked one of the herb baskets hanging from the ceiling. "She's keening like a child shut in her room."

"Bellowing?" said Jillian. "Screeching? Howling."

"Howling. Yes." He cleaned the dishes, and left for the corral.

I squinted at Jillian, the way she squinted whenever she had a doubt.

The knocked basket swung its scent of lavender. I made sure the door was shut. "He's lying," I said.

She watched me while she slid a sprig of the herb into her mouth. It's supposed to soothe a person, and it's a wonder there weren't days when she reeked of it.

"Jillian," I said. "He's lying."

"So you say."

From the window sill, she produced a bag of dominoes.

I said, "You know he's lying."

"I teach you to play rimstack, and now you catch liars all of a quick?"

"He's a bad liar. Worse than Wilm."

She bounced the bag against her thigh, and the rattle was a little fast to match her calm. "Would you like to name me his tell?"

I'd waited for this. "He meant *keening*. He's fluent in Holden. He writes Holden poetry."

"Well, it's terrible poetry."

Jillian arranged the dominoes around the rim of the flattened stack. She had taught me this game to teach me observation—to read bluffs and expressions. It's where I'd learned her squint. Now she told me to ante.

"So once again," I said, "you're refusing to answer."

"If you think he's lying, then tell him he's lying."

"Because that's what you would do."

"No. It isn't at all what I would do. But say what you want. I'm not you."

This was something she said a great deal these days. It was, perhaps, her counterpoint to the fact that like her, I'd become an outlaw.

"At market," I said, "I won five rimstack matches in a row."

"Then you should stop playing there for a while."

"Why?" I figured she'd at least be a little proud. "I think it would be nice, don't you? If I could win all the time?"

She'd been walking a domino along her knuckles, and now she snatched it. "That doesn't lead to a good place."

I flipped a domino, letting it clack. "I think it would show I'm good at sussing bluffs."

"Gaelle, do you know what they call people who always win?"

I almost said *winners*, but I thought better of it.

She gave me a look as if I hadn't held my tongue. "They call them *sorcerers*."

I barked a laugh and dropped the domino. "Sorry? Sorcerers?" I thought she'd say *cheaters, scoundrels, crooks*. Her eyes had gone hard as peach pits. I'd never heard her use *sorcerer* before. "Well." I rapped the domino. "I guess they'd say I've ensorscelled my ante." As I noticed the pun, I gave an elongated gasp. "Wait. Jillian."

"Stop it, now."

But the joke was too good. And I didn't yet know of my mage-aunt, Mirimane. "Jillian. You're my ensorscelled auntie!"

She was on me, grabbing my collar. She pushed my back against the wall. "You cast magic?" My neck scraped. "Is that what you do?"

"Magic—"

"You can't prove that you don't."

"I don't—"

"You cast it," she said. "We saw you."

"I don't cast magic!"

"Woman, we have witnesses."

"Jillian—"

"Jillian? Jillian Who? Who's Jillian?" She fumed lavender. "You're calling to your friends now? Other mages, perhaps?"

"I'm sor—"

"Sorry? Well, now we're getting somewhere." She gestured to an invisible audience. "*Sorry* shows guilt. And now you've admitted you cast magic."

"I don't cast magic!" I scrabbled beneath her. "What the hell, magic? There's no magic in Holding!"

"No?" She removed a hand, but she pushed me harder. "And what do you make of the rack, then? And of the stake, and the grinning engineer who sits in his cell all day, thinking of things to put in you, or cut out of you?"

"What?"

"And what will you say while he makes you confess you spoiled the river, or killed the dean, or turned the dairy cow into the temple idiot who moans all day?"

She let me go and with her other hand, she held her fist.

I clung to the wall while my heart thudded in my neck. "I wouldn't—"

"God help you." She leaned a little over her hands. "God damn your lip." She knocked a chair. "You are fifteen years old."

"Jillian."

"I have drunk bottles of wine older than you." She didn't even like wine. "Your father died. You are an outlaw. You think your biggest problem is a tinker who isn't entirely forthcoming about a fool's spook of a horse." She threw open the cottage door, and sunlight came in with the cold. "So you call your dominoes, Gaelleda. And you try, maybe, to keep a day ahead, or a week, or a year." From her forehead to her gut, she shuddered. "And who knows? You reckon? You might even have figured out how to read by then."

She left the cottage and its swinging door. I still leaned against the wall, where she'd just been at my throat, and I pressed the cool of my palm against the throbbing side of my neck. That shudder had washed over Jillian as something trying to get out. I'd never seen it before. I had sprung her like a trap.

Jillian had never before laid a hand on me. I'd provoke her; she'd yell. It wasn't a dance, but it wasn't a duel either. As I stood by our table now, I figured she would never have done such a thing with my father alive—pushing me into a wall, shouting insults loud enough for Teph to hear.

I opened the door, and the sun was so bright that it practically pounced. I stalked to the corral before my eyes had adjusted enough for me fully to see it. Teph sat on the railing, rubbing his side.

"You write poetry," I said. "You know what *keening* means."

"You fighting everyone today?"

"You're lying about Lucinda." I climbed onto the railing.

"A creature can be sad and restless at the same time." He made room for me to sit by him. "Don't you agree?"

"I don't agree." I stayed where I was. "And you haven't denied you're lying."

He had a spot of freckles between his eyes, and when he squinted, they disappeared. "What I'm doing, Gaelle, is guessing."

"Either that or you're dodging."

"Guessing is an honest stance. I can honestly not know."

Just lately, when my aunt had me pinned, I'd pleaded for her to believe my ignorance.

"Fine," I said.

"There."

"Then what do you guess?"

"I guess," he said, "that Lucinda has always been restless about something other than Wilm."

"Something what?"

From where he sat, Teph used his hand to hoist a stiff knee. "Wilm is a horseman. That's his trade. I also ride horses, in my traveler's trade." He straightened his knee, and it popped. "But it takes all I have to mount Lucinda."

He hadn't answered the thrust of my questions, but he'd said enough to show some kind of pain in himself. And maybe I should have considered how honest I wanted Teph to be.

"To be frank," he said, "I'd have an easier time riding a bear."

"Then you'll have to kill her?"

"No. That would seem a bit like killing her for my own shortcoming. And I refuse to become a bully." He wasn't one of those. He never was.

"Then what makes her restless?" I said.

"I can't confidently say."

"Then what can you guess?"

"Perhaps something that isn't clear enough to say wisely."

"Well try me."

The horse screamed. Teph put his hand on the fence, and I noticed Lucinda's bite marks farther along its planks.

He dusted his palms and climbed back into the corral. "Would you like to help with some of the clarity?" While facing Lucinda, he held out to me one of his leather straps. It was the kind he'd used to bind the horse, when he didn't wear it around his legs. He waggled it. When I took it, he tied the other end around his waist.

Teph told me to stand on the far side of the fence. He was going to try to lead Lucinda by the halter, and as he pulled against her, I could help pull too.

"She could snap your fingers," I said.

"Most adult fingers are as thick as the average carrot."

I sagged my grip on the strap. "Most adult horses like carrots."

"I'm aware." He nodded at my hands, and I tightened my hold. He tugged at the horse, and she wouldn't yield. I tugged at Teph, to give him my strength. I may have also helped to hold him upright. And I considered whether, if I needed to, I'd be able to pull his body from the pen.

We pulled for maybe ten minutes, for a time that seemed longer than it was. Afterwards, my ribs were sore from the horse yanking me against the fence, and it's likely Teph's had nearly cracked. Lucinda had moved two steps.

I rubbed my nose, and smelled the leather from the straps. Teph took deep breaths, as if when he'd been bound, he hadn't been able to.

"Tell me something else," I said.

He shook his head. He spat. "She's just too big."

Lucinda moved in the pen, like water poured into a bucket. What none of us knew is that she would have outright killed almost anybody else.

Teph stretched tall, until his back popped. His bewilderment, and his struggle, felt nearly as unsettling as Jillian's rage. All of it made me want to retreat to the comfort of an old fight of my own, and I wandered to my mother's oxcart.

When I got there, I was shaking. Maybe it was the fatigue from all the pulling. Then again, I might have shaken from the very thing we'd pulled against. Whatever it was felt like something both within and beyond Lucinda, as if it, and not Teph, had ridden her here. This thing had made me shake during the weeks before; sometimes I even awoke, shaking. It apparently made Teph try to break it. And somehow it also made my aunt shudder as she pressed me into a wall.

Certainly, I'd also had something to do with her pressing me. While I sat by the oxcart, I had to admit I had been obnoxious this morning, maybe even belligerent. Such meanness was as frequent as my shaking. But lately, if I wasn't unkind to people around me, I was simply unkind to myself. And it was easier to be unkind to Teph and Jillian, because I felt safer around them than I felt even around myself. Maybe it was on account of the anxiety of it all: the upendedness, the father who ceased. Or maybe it was also because of the fact that while he literally pulled at a mystery, Teph was a riddle himself. I paused over this, while I worked at the tightness the morning had left in my chest. Teph was the safest to pick at. Then came my aunt. Then came this other that had put pain in their eyes.

While I sat at the cart, I plucked a dandelion. Lately, I seemed to be the only one who remembered Teph was temporary. He had nearly the transience of a stranger. Despite his self-granted extension, this was all he had. In the evenings, if we saw him at all, he smoked and wrote. Over the last week or two, he had lingered some after dinner, and he and Jillian had started a contest where he tried to tie a knot she couldn't undo. He tied, and she unfastened, and he let his beard grow in. As a guest, he made the meals we ate, and he cleaned up after them. Jillian protested every time, but Teph said the guest rendered service to the host. Such was the custom; he invoked custom in our house. Jillian cleaned while he wasn't looking.

Now as I sat by the oxcart, she was nowhere in sight. Whenever Jillian used to yell at my father, she would finish by striding into the orchard. Today, this was probably where she'd shuddered off. She told me once she liked the cool of the trees. Maybe she also liked the concealment. There were times, when, after a fight, if my father needed her to complete a chore, he would go out and bellow orders at the fruit. She was so temperamental that it was a wonder she could ever be discreet enough to serve either as an intrepid or a revolutionary. In the years while she lived with my father and me, she screamed. Her eyes darkened and flashed. But I didn't know how she could look at me, ever again, after pushing me into a wall. I missed my father, and how he must have contained Jillian. And in fact, I'd eventually learn he did contain her, in part because my mother had asked him to.

By the cart, a breeze blew, and the weather started to sprinkle. I missed my mother, even if she was a person I never knew. I wondered what she would do about Teph and Lucinda, if she'd bid me think more about the horse, the way I imagined her urging me to stick my head in the oxcart bramble. Maybe my mother's hand was like mine. I cupped my own chin, and pressed my mouth shut. Jillian had cupped my face too, on the day my father died. On that day, she'd fought both me and herself, for the sake of me and herself, but mostly of me.

Something small buzzed, and a hummingbird, with its yellow head, flew straight up into the rain. I blinked at its suddenness and its interruption. It was a little, rising sun, or a star falling the other way. I watched it until I lost it. Then the rain increased, and although it was cold, I let it wash me until my hands unclenched.

part THREE

I would dry in the sun, which returned almost immediately. The weather did this in Holding, especially during the warmer months. Maybe the inconsistency somehow helped the plants. *Helpful inconsistency*: like Teph and his buttoned-up guesswork. But we'd already picked at him; the dandelion seeds had blown away. The oxcart dripped. It reminded me of Godiva's cart, where after a visit to Wilm, we'd carried everything home.

Lucinda was the next thing to look at, even if it unhinged me to do so. Despite being half the age of Jillian's wine, I would not sit and wait to think about the horse. So in early afternoon, while Lucinda and Teph did battle, and my aunt cooled off in the trees, I decided to find answers with Wilm.

The road wound through the Holden foothills, some three miles between Lloyd Farm and Albertson Pasture. We lived probably half that distance apart, on the straightaway, but a forested ravine lay between us. Much of it was ember pine and birch, mostly too packed together for anything larger than a bear to live inside. But despite how we had only just entered early fall, the ground could change to mud, and then freeze. Even most of the hunters stayed out.

The road running along the ravine was rooted and unpaved. In recent memory, no noble had come near Ludington, or even Northcraft, our largest sister village. To the Empire, this meant there was no reason to repair the path beyond anything barely passable. My father had told of the occasional wagoner who brought sand to fill the biggest holes. And yet, because sand was heavy, and thereby precious to carry, the wagoner dug up the sand before he went on his way.

The road to Wilm's was a decent walk in the daytime. The third of the trip that cut near the woods was in the middle of the route, so as long as you planned, you could afford to be on either side of the forest at dusk. The fields on both ends were safer, in how you could see something coming whole minutes before it arrived.

Still, you never ran. You packed a torch and a means to make fire. You carried a wool cloak in your bag, year-round. And if there was a chance you'd face the actual night, you brought a coin or a tradable good. Cottages usually scattered close enough to reach, and if you offered payment, or even work, the owners often gave you shelter. Payment for hospitality followed the Church Law of Hospitality; it's why Teph insisted on doing the dishes. When I was small, and Jillian had yet arrived, a slender man with an unknown accent came to our door at supper. He offered us rabbit skins, and said, "Cat. Follow." We let him in.

The road today still crunched from the night's frost. From a habit Jillian had taught, I walked on the grass beside the path, to muffle my footsteps whenever the grass was soft. Now I slowed. The road itself had no fresh tracks, but patches marked the grass, about a stride apart. The practice of walking on the side of the road wasn't a secret, but it wasn't common either. I squatted, as if to adjust my boot, and as I bent, I peered beside me.

I crouched against the wind, so scent-wise, I had the advantage, unless something came from behind. The breeze blew and the branches creaked. The smell of Lake Kelmer lifted from the other side of Wilm's property. Lucinda's sound didn't reach me here, and this meant Jillian had been right about how Wilm was protected from her screaming. In fact, it's possible Jillian knew such a thing, because she'd checked.

I walked the rest of the way alone, although the side trail continued. At the start of Wilm's fields, the path wound toward his shack. Smoke rose from his chimney. At first I thought I had just followed his footprints, and from our property no less. I was that suspicious of the man. Then I heard him speaking. He sneezed, which could have meant anything. And yet the fact he was outside and speaking might have meant he didn't want to let his company in. A move any closer would risk exposure. Wilm had harvested the fields, so I had little place to hide. And after a while, the only way to stay unnoticed was to keep pace and walk in the middle of the road, as if I were most anyone in the world.

I should have gone home. It would have been reasonable not to intrude on a man I knew only from a distance, aside from our sharing such an oddly intimate exchange. I could have at least waited until Wilm was alone. But this would have involved standing still, which had its own dangers, if you were out in the open. And besides, the inertia of the morning kept me walking through any amount of indecision, until I heard the voice of my aunt.

I dropped to the ground, and gouged my chin on a frozen clod of earth. The smell of my own blood made me mutter. You didn't bleed in the open here, any more than you would bleed around predators in open water. Bleeding was worse than running. The smart thing, now, would have been to reveal myself, and then make up some lie about needing Jillian at home. But I crept, holding a wad of shirt to my chin, hoping that somehow both Jillian and Wilm faced away from me, so they wouldn't have a chance of seeing movement in the fields.

A haystack close to Wilm's cottage would offer the best place to hide, and when I crouched there, I found enough sun-softened mud to daub my chin.

Jillian handed Wilm a milk canister and a sack. "So we brought you more," she said. "On account of the cold."

"And you make sure you have enough for Lucinda."

"You aren't eating her food, Wilm."

"She downs a lot of oats."

"You don't have to tell me that."

"Well, I have no one else who can listen to these things."

"Right. So what do you know?"

"Nothing. People go by, but they're usual."

"Nothing from the west?"

"No," he said. "I said nothing. You pay me to look west, so I look west."

Jillian looked around, and I froze. "It might not come from the road."

"So you do think it's mindless."

"I didn't say mindless."

"You said *it*."

"Them. They."

"Esaosh."

"Listen. Wilm."

"No. You listen. You get that man outside this village."

"We don't know if Teph is attracting anything."

"But you suspect!"

"Right now, *that man* is the one who is saving your horse."

By the haystack, my knee crunched a snake skin. Teph really had been lying. Or at least he never told me he was potentially trailed.

Wilm slung the bag over his shoulder. "You aren't going through all this just to save Lucinda."

"You would," said Jillian.

"You wouldn't."

Jillian scraped her boot sole on the porch. "I have a fifteen year-old who made a deal."

"And you would kill a horse three times for the safety of your girl."

This was true. I couldn't see it at the time, but Jillian's shudder, this morning, showed how this was exactly true. "Check your food," she said.

Wilm rummaged the sack. "You think the mindless will stop and play rimstack?"

I clamped my mouth.

"They're a gift," said Jillian. "They make a signal."

He tried to hand them back.

"They aren't marked, Wilm."

"No. I am tired of your signals." He dropped the bag. "You want me to watch the west, so I watch the west. You want me to keep the smoke going until I see something, so I keep the smoke going."

"You'd keep it going most of the time anyway."

"But it's an obligation!"

"Well toughen up, Neighbor. And listen to me. The dominoes will give you two things."

"You mean two that aren't my horse."

"The first is that they can show a signal that tells us precisely that the mindless are coming."

"See? You said it!"

"Wait a minute. The second thing is the assurance that from the very beginning, we have not suspected mindless. Otherwise we'd have given you the dominoes from the very start."

I put my hand in the mud. The muck felt primal, real, far more real than what Wilm and Jillian discussed. *Mindless*, uttered even in terms of their contradiction, was a word on par with *sorcerer*.

"I'm wondering," said Wilm, "if you got these dominoes just now, from a tricksy friend perhaps."

"Wilm, they're faded. See? Gaelle used to suck on them as a girl."

Wilm grunted. I'd been betrayed by my dominoes, to say nothing of my aunt.

"And so what do I do," said Wilm, "if the mindless come in my sleep, and you can't see the stopped smoke?"

"In the night? You know better. Men don't move at night. And because men made the mindless, the mindless don't either." Jillian likely believed this, the way she believed the mindless were not coming at all, but from what I've lately seen in the war, it is absolutely untrue.

Wilm had been studying Jillian, and now he turned away. "This doesn't help me."

"It does help you, because if we see the signal—"

"The mindless-only signal—"

"If we see the domino signal, we'll rush to help you."

"But I'm alone if it's only men." He sort of sung a sigh. "And I could use the signal anyway, just to get you here to help with whatever. But lately, *Outlaw*, you've become violent when you're mad."

I couldn't see her face, but Jillian was probably giving Wilm a look that said he was making her angry right then. "If it's men who are coming, they will not bother you, *Outlaw*. They don't want extra trouble."

He examined the dominoes as if they were a sack of poison. "So these dominoes make a distress signal you'd respond to."

"In the event of mindless."

"And yet you say there should be no mindless. So the dominoes are mostly useless."

"In the way of, say, a snake-bite kit."

He pocketed the dominoes. "It would be better if I were able to send this signal, and you would come riding on Lucinda, your warhorse, to save me from any possible danger crossing my path. No matter what it is."

My aunt lit her pipe. "You raise an interesting notion. But it does add a bit of value to the gift." Jillian would light her pipe whenever she wanted to negotiate. It was a tell, perhaps, that hid how she gritted her teeth. "If this is what we're going to arrange, with the help and the warhorse, I think I should ask for something more before I tell you how to activate the signal."

"You already said you'd show me!"

"But the use has just enlarged."

Wilm spat.

"The spitting is a nasty habit, Wilm."

"And so is cheating."

Cheating carries the penalty of amputation. "We will tell you how to activate the signal," she said, "and we will come to the signal, on our warhorse, with utmost speed, in exchange for one thing."

I squeezed the mud. Jillian was wily; this offer she'd maneuvered was likely what she'd been arranging all along.

"What do you want?" said Wilm.

"You need to tell us the truth about where Lucinda came from."

I nearly jumped from the haystack.

"No," Wilm said. "There's nothing to tell. I got her when she was a baby."

"You know more than you say."

"She was fluffy and white, like a milkweed seed."

"From where?"

"From Northcraft."

"From Northcraft."

"Yes."

Jillian rummaged her pocket, and tossed Wilm a handkerchief. "This is for you."

"I don't want your rag—"

"And it's because you're going to start sneezing, because you're starting to get nervous, because really, Wilm, you're lying your face off."

"I am not!"

"And you better hope you don't get nervous when the mindless come, because they have very delicate hearing."

"And now you're trying to scare me, Sticky."

"I am."

Wilm set his shoulders, and turned toward his hut.

"But the fact is, Wilm, I'm scared myself." She drew the pipe from her mouth. "And actually I wish it was just mindless. Because what I'm starting to believe is that the horse—your horse—is starting to call something."

I felt as if Teph's horse straps pulled around me.

Wilm had grasped the doorpost. "The only thing Lucinda is calling is me."

"She's been keening. Screaming."

"She wants to go home."

"She's been doing it before she left home. Or at least before leaving your home."

"You don't know anything about our before."

"But it's what I think."

Wilm opened his door. And even from where I sat, I saw how chunks of wattle had fallen off its rim. "Go home," he said.

"You played the accordion," said Jillian. "You played it to soothe her."

"All animals enjoy the accordion."

"But she's your only horse, these days. She was too wild to race, so you just kept her. And you started to lose money."

"You know nothing."

"I know you loved her."

He slammed the door, and stepped forward. "You get off my land."

"Wilm." Jillian backed half down the porch. "I need to know what she's calling."

"You don't need to know anything."

"I have a family. We live near a village."

"She is my horse!" He leaned forward so hard that he pushed his arms farther from his sleeves. "She's my horse. We'd have meals together. She ate off my plate."

"Meals."

"I happen to have a rapport with the creatures—"

"What kind of meals?"

"What?"

"Vegetables? Meat?"

He wiped the back of his neck. "Whatever I had, which wasn't so much."

"Meat?"

He turned a little, side-to-side. "Only sometimes, with the meat. I admit such a thing is special, eccentric—"

"If you could tell me anything—"

"You'd tell me how to use your special dominoes. And you'd say, 'Stop the smoke for western unusuals, and use the dominos for the mindless. And for whatever else, you just keep on sleeping.'" He'd moved back to his door. "And if you're so worried about your family and your village, you should get yourself rid of the Azman."

He had a point, and a good one, if Teph had people tracking him.

Jillian said, "They have indigo and auramite."

"What? What they?"

"I just altered the dominoes this morning." She must have returned to the cottage. "You burn them. They've enough indigo and auramite to turn the smoke green."

Wilm let go of himself, and clutched his hand as if he wanted to seize something else. "This is your signal? Your defense against the mindless? You think they won't notice if the smoke turns green?"

"They're colorblind. And they're mind-less."

"Colorblind?" He started to laugh. He kicked a nearby shovel, and Jillian moved the rest of the way down the steps. "Get off my land." He stopped laughing. "Get off it. Now."

"I've told you the truth."

"Other people aren't colorblind."

"We've talked about other people. Other people won't bother you."

"No, just your other people, as if they were the only other people in the world."

"I just said—"

"Oh, you say and you say. But you don't talk about bandits, or soldiers, or rocs, or cats, or pity knows what else." He hollered. "I have reason to fear other things. I have as much reason as you. And now that you've taken Lucinda, I'll have to wait for however long it takes for you to get here, while in the meantime, I do not have a way to run."

Jillian had let her pipe bowl tip, and now it dropped an ember to the porch. Wilm watched it burn out.

My aunt was honest, and intrepid, and she did suss the stakes of a circumstance better than anyone. But she was most attentive to these things, in terms of the people she loved. One might even say it was a way she loved.

"Of course," she said. "All right." I don't think she ever got to the point where she loved Wilm. "Don't use the cards for those things. Stop the smoke. We'll come to that signal—"

"No." He leaned on his arms, from inside the doorframe. "What you think is that if someone doesn't fit in your world, they just don't count."

"No. Wilm."

"Oh, yes, Wilm. Exactly, Wilm."

"We reframed the deal."

"Because you wanted to get fancy."

"I hadn't thought it through."

"I think of everything." He looked small. She looked smaller. "Get off my land."

My knees trembled, maybe from how I'd been squatting, or maybe from something else. Jillian had, herself, sprung a trap.

"Wilm, I need you to tell me what Lucinda is call—"

"Woman, she is just a horse."

He picked up a shillelagh from inside the doorway, and she backed toward the road.

Wilm sat on the porch steps, still holding the club, with his legs apart. The sack lay behind him.

"Wilm." Jillian had reached the road. "The love you gave to Lucinda may well have been the only thing that kept her from killing you."

"Get out!"

She walked as if she'd been caught in heavy rain, and she threw a stone, hard, into the fields. Jillian was passing beyond me now, where she could turn back at any point, and find me astonished and exposed, on the other side of the haystack. Because Wilm still sat, I couldn't get to the other side. And truth be told, I didn't want to move. I half hoped Jillian would call after me, perhaps without looking, to show me she knew I was hiding, that she'd meant for me to hear the conversation, that the dialogue, in all its turns, actually went as planned. Now she stalked down the side of the road, the side opposite the one we'd previously traveled. Her exchange with Wilm was the first time I'd seen her commit such a serious mistake.

The sky stretched bare. I could hear Lucinda without hearing her. I didn't know what to think. What I'd just learned was part of what I'd sought, and way more besides. But the answer was that nobody knew what to think. If Lucinda was actually calling something—if she ate meat—if love was the only thing keeping her from killing the idiot who offered such love—then she did have to die. It didn't matter if I'd once seen her, as something redeemed and dreaming. She had murdered my father. For all I know, she'd wanted to eat him too.

Lucinda also had to die so Teph could move on. Such resolution would be brutal, but tidy. With him gone, nothing would come from the west: not any soldiers, or bandits, and certainly not what Wilm feared about mindless. And if something did approach, it would keep going, because whatever it searched for would decidedly not be here. I now know that if we had tried such a thing, our whole farmstead would have scattered to ruin. But whether such destruction would have come from the mindless, the Treehanded, or the horse herself, I still can't fathom.

Along the roadside, my aunt kept walking. At his hut, Wilm still sat, staring at the road.

I could call to Jillian, to tell her what to do. But if I did that, Wilm would hear, and I did not want him following us home.

Jillian was angry, and she took strides that meant business. A moment ago, I could have gotten her attention by throwing a stone. But now she was too far off. And then, she started to run. She did such a thing, when she was furious. She'd do laps in the orchard, almost daring something to chase.

On his porch, Wilm had clutched the sack in his lap. Well. By not moving, he was prolonging Lucinda's life one last time. At least he'd like that. We would wait to tell him we killed the horse. Afterward, we could maybe find him money for a replacement, or at least for a cow.

Something flapped behind me. A feaster—a large, carrion bird—had landed a stone's throw from where I sat. I swung my arms, and it lifted away. I palmed my chin, and felt the blood before I saw it. The mud was failing.

I leaned against the hay, and muttered. Wilm rested his hand on the sack. It didn't matter. The feaster was likely a scout. They're larger cousins of vultures, and they eat in packs. Feasters hunt by smell, or taste. They fly with their mouths open, and as a side effect, they chug enough air to give them astonishing endurance. I couldn't stay by the haystack, but there was too much danger in walking home without first stopping the bleeding. Wilm would have to help.

Three feasters landed, and hissed at one another, for position. They devour flesh by pinching it with their beaks, and twisting. I ambled toward the road.

Wilm faced the other way, as if he'd finally decided to cooperate. My plan was to make it to the road without his noticing. Then I'd walk backward, until Wilm looked my way, or until I crossed his property line. Then I'd walk forward, to appear as if I were just approaching.

When I was halfway out, Wilm turned and I stopped. I walked forward and waved. He half hunkered a glower, snatched his sack, went into the house, and shut the door.

I needed to appear innocent and inevitable, something of an obligation, even if the Law of Hospitality gave Wilm the right to turn me away. By the time I reached his porch, he'd propped the shillelagh against the nearest post.

He swung open the door. "Leave me alone."

"Please." I took my hand off my chin.

"Gah!" He fisted his hands. "Go back to your auntie."

"My aunt? Where? I'm not with my aunt."

"You were."

I turned behind me. "She's here?"

"You people even lie when you're bleeding." I dripped on his porch. "Take it." He handed me Jillian's handkerchief. "Go."

"Wilm, I can't—"

"Yes, you go. And you tell her not to be so cheeky with her gifts next time."

"I am not with Jillian."

Poor Wilm expected treachery from everyone. Of course, I was deceiving him now.

"If that's true," he said, "your auntie walked down the road. You can catch her soon enough."

"I was just on the road. I came to find her."

"Then you must have seen her."

"Wilm."

"Oh, how you remind me of her!"

I shrugged. It was funny how when he said such a thing, it somehow made me proud. "You know," I said, "she does go into the woods sometimes."

"The woods."

"Lately, yes. She's been going in there. I think—it's as if she's checking for something." I met his gaze; it was deeper than I thought it would be. "That's how I missed her. I bet that's how."

"Take your kerchief and go."

"I want to go."

"Splendid."

"But there are feasters."

He closed his eyes, and his eyelids trembled. "No, there aren't."

"Yes, there are."

"Did you see one?"

"It landed right by me."

He peered over my head, toward the fields, and puckered his mouth. He didn't have to help me, especially if I didn't pay. But I knew he would, because he was never cruel. This is something that united all of us on our two farms. Amid the grinding laws of the Church, we were a squabblish and self-vexing community of anti-cruelty.

Wilm had left his door open, and he'd entered the house.

I followed. The cottage was one room, small and warm. Everything smelled of smoke. The accordion listed on a central table. The bed had a stable blanket, as a possible remnant from Lucinda. I shut the door. The walls and ceiling, whitewashed, had markings all over them.

Wilm handed me a bowl of water and a rag. I kept trying to read the house's marks. They were familiar, somehow: points with dotted lines connecting them.

Wilm stood me by his window, and told me to look at him. He asked about the blood, and I said I fell on a rock.

"Unlucky you." He leaned on his knees, and studied the wound. The last time I saw him, he'd glanced at my chest. "You've nothing inside it," he said, "but the cut is deep." He pressed on the wound with fingers that smelled of apples. He drew some garlic from a bucket, and began to chop.

I stepped closer to the nearest wall, and knocked a hand-scythe. The wall points seemed like spots on a map.

Wilm put the garlic into the bowl, and placed all of it above his cookfire. "They're stars, Gaelleda. In the summer. You should be able to tell that."

For some reason, I thought of the hummingbird, of it rising in some magnificent storm. "You painted these?"

"Of course."

I'd forgotten he did such a thing. Looking back, we were all mostly unaware of what he did it. At this point, anyway, I don't think even he knew he was building a cathedral.

Now he handed me a candle and told me I could look at the wall more closely. "Don't drip wax, Gaelleda."

I held the candle near the stars. He must have painted hundreds of them, with a dark ink. The distances between the points seemed proportional and exact, and the stars themselves varied in size, to the point where they gave the feel of depth.

"How long did it take you?" I said.

"A summer. Last summer." He took back the kerchief. "The sky isn't the same now."

"So they're like clouds that way."

"They are nothing like clouds, Gaelleda."

"They're both in the sky. They both change."

He snatched the bowl of garlic, sprinkled in some water, and threw in a handful of fireplace ashes. Then he started on the bowl with the grinder.

"So, it's like going back in time?" I said. "Your ceiling?"

He set down the bowl a little louder than he needed to. "It's a summer night in my house, even if I can't go out."

"Is that why you did it?"

He wiped his hands on his thighs, and the soot left a streak. Then he steered me by the shoulders so I stood in the middle of the room, with the candle. "This is where we are, and these are the stars around us."

"But they've changed."

"A little. I've told you that." He turned me in a slow circle. "Do you think the stars are getting closer, or farther away?"

"I don't know."

"Good. You've stopped being smart." He positioned me so I faced the fire. "They are, in reality, coming closer." I jerked. He put his face in mine, and that made me jerk again. "You should think on this." Without looking, he grabbed the bowl. "All of them are coming, Gaelleda. All at once. A little each year." He stirred the garlic mash. "I have measurements."

They say a person will react with fear to the sound of a rattlesnake, even if they'd never learned what a rattlesnake is. I reacted with similar fear to what Wilm just said.

He held my chin, and began to apply the paste.

"What happens when they get to us?" I said.

"Nobody knows."

"Are they made of light?"

"Don't talk." He stiffened his own mouth, and he dabbed my cut. "Nobody knows anything of the nature of the stars, except that they move."

"How fast?"

"You mean you want to know how old you'll be when they get here."

"How old will anyone be?"

"I don't know the answer. Nobody does. You'd have to know how far they'd come, or if they moved at a constant speed."

The charts around me felt like a net. "Who else thinks this?"

He leaned back. "It's a fact, Gaelleda. It's like saying there's a desert beyond Treehand."

Nobody had told me any of this: not about the stars, or their arrival, or their slamming all of us into what likely was some kind of final mash. The idea must have terrified everyone I knew. My aunt must have been afraid of it. My father must have feared it, long before he fell off the horse.

Wilm's paste made my eyes water, and I hated that, because it probably looked like I'd begun to cry.

"Gaelle. It likely won't happen for a very long time." Wilm gave me a flat look. "You'll be completely dead, along with the rest of us."

The relief was small and blank. "That's fine."

He turned away, with the pot. "You don't even know what death is."

"I have an idea."

After setting the pot down quietly, he gave a hesitant reach to my shoulder, and patted it. "You do. That's good. Don't worry about the stars."

I wiped my eyes from the garlic's stink, and put the stars out of my thoughts. They were Wilm Albertson's stars, and to my mind, at the time, Wilm was a git. I put the stars out. But the stars came back. They kept coming back, and I wiped my eyes again. The stars came back to the farm, falling on the Azman.

"Gaelleda."

My lip quivered.

"Now now," he said.

My poultice fell off.

"I didn't mean what I said about death." He muttered something as he retrieved the dressing. "You know plenty about death."

"I'm fine."

"Oh, but stop now," he offered me the poultice, "Oh, let's hush so."

I squared my jaw and my stance.

He set the poultice on the table, and sighed. "Everybody's afraid these days. All the time."

"Why?" I turned, and he stepped back.

"Gaelle."

"Why?"

"Because we have eyes, Dearie."

"Why did your horse kill my father?" Something felt to break in my chest. "Why was Jillian here? Why were you talking? What's trailing Teph?" He shrank a little, the way some men do when they realize they've upset a woman. I breathed, and to my fury, it came out as a sob. "Why did she push me?"

"Who pushed you?"

"She shudders."

"Your auntie?"

"Yes, *my auntie*. She cries in the night."

He stood with his feet together, as if I'd cornered him. "Gaelleda." He glanced at his accordion, and for a moment, I wondered if he had a notion to play. "I think you are all in crisis."

We were. We bordered on catastrophe.

"I think she is frightened for you," he said. "All right?"

The garlic had started to sting. "She's frightened for more than just me."

"But especially for you. Yes." He waved at his ceiling. "And not because of the sky. Parents don't worry about stars smashing their children from the sky."

At my father's death, he'd tried to curse me with the fact that Jillian was now my parent. "She isn't my mother, Wilm."

He waggled a nod side to side. "You're a smart girl, Gaelle. She has good reason to fear."

"What? Because I'm smart?"

He tsked. In fairness, he'd likely seen smart members of my family get carted away. Now he glanced at his horse blanket. "Gaelle, what I think is that when the time comes for your aunt to tell you what to do, then really you must do it." He spread open his palms. "This is what I think." It was as if he showed me his hands were empty.

I looked for any kind of tell. His siding with Jillian was somehow terrible, nearly as bad as seeing him on his knees. It made me believe everything he said.

"And what do you think about the Azman?" I said.

"You must do it. You must listen to your aunt."

"You both think he's attracting something."

"Foreigners attract things."

"But Jillian doesn't care if he lies."

He looked sharp. "About what does he lie?"

Of course. This was a major reason I'd come in the first place. In all the excitement, I'd nearly forgotten.

I said, "He says Lucinda isn't keening for anything." He can barely ride her, and he's still guessing enough to hide what he thinks. Something kept me from speaking all that. "He thinks she's just restless and sad."

Wilm flared his nostrils. I had given us an irony I didn't intend, where in this matter, Wilm and Teph were also on the same side. And by the same token, come to think of it, I'd just suggested Wilm was lying too.

He grasped my elbow, the way men sometimes do, and guided me to the door. "Jillian loves you, Gaelle. You listen to her." He clutched me harder than he probably meant. "And you must ask her these things—but as an adult." He beaded a stare at me, nodding until I nodded too. "And if she doesn't keep you safe," he peered at the table, which held the sack of dominos, "if she doesn't do that, then you just run."

Under no circumstance would I flee. Even then, I knew I'd be dead if I was alone.

I said, "You should get another horse, you know." He let go of my elbow. "Maybe we could help you to buy one." His stars flickered in the candlelight, and I wondered if he found solace in them. "I don't want any of us to be this afraid." I thought of us killing Lucinda. "Not even the horse."

His eyes widened, and hardened, and softened. He leaned against his doorjamb, and for a moment, he seemed to hug his house. He had a pail of horse oats by the door, as if he wanted to keep ready for even an improbable return. "What you tell your aunt," he said, "is that the milkweed came from a peddler from Treehand."

I crossed my arms, and tried to keep hold of myself. "Treehand."

"Don't ask me anything."

I wanted to kick that bucket of oats until it spilled.

He said, "It's still usable milkweed. You see? It's beautiful and soft." So was fire, in a way. "You tell her so."

"I'll tell her." Then I'd tell her to kill the horse.

"Good girl," he said, and I squashed a blossom of guilt. "Go home now. If you stay, I'll have to make you work."

chapter 5

Perch

Every few days, even this late in the fall, the sun shines long enough for me to gain a little warmth at my hanging cell's window. Increase and I share the spot, elbow to claw. This co-sunning is the closest the bird has allowed me to get to him, so far. What I consider sharing might actually amount to his version of a territory war, but he doesn't hiss or posture. When the warmth makes him redolent, he smells a little of dust.

As we've sat here, I've decided I should use my vantage as a little lighthouse for you. I should show you the landscape, both personal and otherwise—the swells of history and the wrack—so you can get a better sense of what converged on us when we let Lucinda live. This clarity might make my story less mysterious, but I think it will let you know what the stakes were, and are, even better than Jillian had reckoned. Such understanding will help you come to terms with what we did, so you might do better in any similar context. My stance means I'm preaching history, which, when coupled with my prayers, probably heads toward prophecy.

As it happened, our Lucinda, cursed and bewildered, was the steed that heralded a world war. It's the war we fight now, what's come to be called the Reordering War, and it will decide who dominates Celd when Esaosh (the Church's god) starts his final battle with the true god, Visjaes. Before the Reordering War, when Jillian and I still puzzled over the horse, every province that knew about Lucinda tried to take control of her. Lots of times, they couldn't find her. In fact, her misplacement is how she ended up with Wilm at the start. Years later, we learned the Treehanded peddler who sold Lucinda was a smuggler who worked at cross-purposes with all the provinces, and who also wanted the horse to kill as many Holden as possible. But that is a story for another time. As a foal, Lucinda must have been malleable enough to sell. Or at least she wasn't strong as Wilm, who was drawn to her as much as he was drawn to the stars. He never mounted Lucinda while she stayed with him, but then you don't sit on a foal.

For a long time, this errant selling was more than what most people knew about how Lucinda came to Wilm's pasture. But every province has resources, and as the years passed, those regions learned enough of Lucinda's trail to send agents to our orchard. Those visits provide the context for the first episode of my story.

Decades afterward, as the Reordering War commenced, each Celdan province fought for primacy, while my revolutionaries and I forsook those provinces, to fight for Visjaes. We call ourselves the Riven, because we believe that, in utterly opposite ways, both Visjaes and Esaosh have maimed us. Every episode of my story will try to divulge why we think these things, and how they've influenced our side of the war.

When I came of age in Ludington, the Church's new abbot had begun the reform I mentioned. Although he never made his true reasons public, the campaign was his brutal attempt to purify and strengthen my province, Holding Province, in anticipation of the Reordering War. These preparations are why he sought Lucinda; why he'd eventually make moves against every other province; and why he later started pogroms against his own subjects when they didn't sufficiently support him. This abbot is the same Lumis Caspar I've mentioned in terms of his age and power. He's now the abbot-principe, which is a position he invented for himself when he took over the entire Church. He's been a constant enemy of both the Riven and my family. He's become a warlock in every sense of the word. And he keeps me in my hanging cell, because as we'll discover, he likes to store anyone who means something to him, inside a jar.

Still, from the Bell, I can see the gallows and the mindless pen. There's the summoning altar, with its cages and its chests, where the Church practices its plutomancy. Farther out, the priests and engineers have begun to construct an altar of white marble and cinnabar, which is the white and red of the Church's colors. Lately, the monks have positioned some kind of yellow brick in the center. I don't know what that is, but apparently no one without dispensation can go near it. And even then, most of the people with permission approach only once.

From my window, I watch the young guards, and try not to glimpse the mindless. The Church didn't always keep the creatures in the open. In fact, I was in my early twenties before I discovered that, despite their pronouncements against necromancy, the clerics had begun to raise the golems in secret. But these days, the Church is as flagrant about displaying its mindless as it is about displaying most of its victims. So I try to look above the creatures.

I peer along the length of the Gomadong, toward the horizon, watching the ground open itself almost in a kind of trust. If Caspar has his way, the plain is indeed where the Riven will fight our final battle. We will almost certainly lose. From my vantage, mirages lie as lakes on the aching earth, and I figure we'll fight like this: a temporary promise that ends up going elsewhere. There was a time when the Riven might have beaten Caspar—when, in the wastes of Merrial, we could have unearthed a weapon capable of reducing everything to atoms. But it was poor Teph who helped us to see how winning at all costs does not help Visjaes with the battle he'll fight. And though I believe Visjaes will win regardless, it's imperative both for us and for you that the Riven help him the best we can.

You notice Teph has a part to play throughout most of my life. At this point, I've known Teph longer than almost anyone. Meanwhile, my aunts, though long dead, have kept me company in their own way. Jillian's life is so similar to mine that our resemblance gives me a kind of anticipation. And beyond her, I'll also tell you of Wilm again, and of Patrick, and of many more who made both this world and myself what we are.

Mine is a long telling. Maybe it needs a plain to work with and a bird to carry it away. But through it all, I ask you keep hold of one thing: my account is how truth came to a world that gouged itself with madness, and how the Riven grew in the truth's farthest reaches, as the truth itself tried to make us whole again.

I hang here in my midair oubliette. On the battlements, Garfield shakes sand from his helmet. If I could speak openly about such things, I would tell him to re-cover his head. One day, the desert will become holy.

chapter 6

Wilderness

part ONE

One evening, when my father and I still lived alone, he looked up from the fireplace, and told me of an encounter he'd had in the marches near Treehand. He'd gone there before he'd met my mother, as if in visiting the plants, he would stand before the aspect of the world's vastness that opened him the most. He told me he'd heard the largest tree before he saw it, severe and creaking and bare. Bundles crowded the branches, dangling like fruit. They were the largest fruit he'd ever seen, sagging the canopy, in silhouette. He got closer, and he saw they were people—not hanged, but bound, wrists to their own ankles, in the shape of water drops. They bent the branches and smelled sweet. One had fallen, and smeared itself along the exposed roots.

I was probably eight years old when my father had said these things. In the few moments after, the fire popped. He sat with his hands on his knees, and looked somewhere beside me. I'd been playing with a doll, and I dropped it headfirst off my lap. My father left the room.

He never said anything else about what he'd told me. I never asked. It's hard to guess what brought him to share this haunting with his eight-year-old daughter. Someone had accused him of loving Treehand, maybe, or he wanted to warn me, or he just needed someone to witness what he had seen. Perhaps he thought I'd forget.

Since my father's confession, I'd willed myself to think of the body-fruit tree, so nothing like it could ever surprise me. I suppose it was like my mother's oxcart, this way. Even now, on the barren Gomadong, I think of Treehand when I too dearly miss the green. That province grew its own evil, as many gardens do.

———— ✤ ————

On the way back from Wilm's, I found my aunt standing in the middle of the road. Her braid hung, half-mangled, as if she'd been yanking it like a bell pull. Now she clasped her hands over the slight of her paunch. "You must want your father to climb from his grave."

I clung to her, and she tripped a step back. I stared up the blue length of her cloak, and into her face that had gone wide.

She held my cheeks. "What hurt you?"

"The horse is from Treehand." She leaned back, and I said, "Wilm says the milkweed seed is from Treehand."

She looked me in the face. "Tell me what happened to your chin."

"I hit the ground. Wilm fixed it after the feaster." She glanced over my shoulder. "He says you're all scared. And he told me of Treehand."

Jillian's braid strands wafted in the breeze. "Do you believe him?"

"I do. Kill Lucinda."

"Should I believe you?"

"Jillian!"

"It's a legitimate question. And on our way home, you can tell me everything that happened. Including why you wandered off."

"Jillian." I stepped in front of her. "Lucinda could be calling to something in Treehand."

"That's a good guess." She put her hand on the back of my neck. "But it will hardly exclude you from punishment."

I didn't care about punishment. "So in addition to the horse calling Treehand," I slowed, "you also believe that Teph is calling something of his own?"

"This is something you will have to ask Teph."

I stopped, and she bumped into me. "I will."

As we walked, the sun stretched the afternoon light. Jillian told me she had seen signs of my passing on her way back from Wilm's. She pointed to my tracks, evenly, but on my neck, her other hand had gone cold.

In many ways, my father had taught how we can ruin ourselves if we underestimate the trees. Whether wittingly or not, he became one of the first wise men who spoke to me on behalf of the land. He said that trees can sense light, that they sleep, and that the Treehanded believe their elders grow into trees after they die. Such transformation is why, despite pressure from the Church, we Holden call the largest tree in a spread the sire tree. But the Treehanded actually worship the elder trees. The elders are their temples, where priests bury corpses at their bases. The Imperial Church considers it a capital crime to eat the fruit from these trees. And this was another reason that, if Lucinda were actually calling something related to Treehand, we would want nothing to do with her.

Many in the Church would want a second Clearing War with Treehand. Even without one, the Church scratched at the forest's perimeter. Occasionally, a band of scouts ventured the edgewood, where later, a borderman would come across an array of weapons, clothing, and utensils neatly arranged outside the forest's rim. Rumors suggested some of the materials didn't belong to the people who entered, how some were of Cadmul or Azmonian make. The Church burned it all.

According to my father, the Church used to set fire to the forest. But they discovered the trees become aggressive amid at least certain kinds of fires, where some of their seedpods burst only when they incinerate. On the border, Holden farmers still talk of smoke rising deep from within the forest, as if the Treehanded set fires of their own. When that air wafts into Holding, farmers won't go outside, for fear of what might be inside it. Whole crops suffer this way. And once the smoke has passed, both the locals and the Church will pull up any new saplings they find growing within a year after the event. As a result, the Holden side of the border suffers whole patches of desolation. And in these marches, the soil is turning to sand. This is true even now, as I hang in my prison. And one of the great projects my people share with our defected Treehanded is that we try to give what now remains of Treehand back to the land.

At the time when Teph stayed with us, the Azmen were the only ones who lived on manageable terms with the Treehanded. Certain traders, such as Teph, could pass through the forest during specific seasons. Apparently, the trees knew them by scent. And because Teph and the trees were so copacetic, I'd spent evenings with the fear that Teph, tying his knots, would speak an image like my father's.

———— ✣ ————

Teph was sharpening his knives when we reached the cottage. Jillian said to him, "It's what we thought."

He clicked his tongue and Jillian went into the house. Teph's beard was gone.

"You'll need to kill the horse," I said.

He set down his knife. "It's a struggle, but I can in fact ride her."

"She's Treehanded."

"Well, that's an assumption."

"No, it isn't. I decide."

"But not anymore." He handed me one of the daggers. "You'll help to sharpen these."

"What do you mean, 'not anymore?'"

"Lucinda has gotten too big for that custom. And we can't kill her."

"Like hell we can't."

He offered me another knife, one for each hand. "Your punishment is to help me sharpen."

"Punishment?"

"Of course. You scared us by wandering off."

I didn't like the heaviness of what I held. Despite my talk of killing the horse, the knives scared me. And for all I know, that's what Teph wanted them to do.

I said, "Why are you sharpening?"

"Because I'm leaving tomorrow." He thrust the dagger into the ground. "Do it like this. Over and over." He waited for me to start. "And after the knives, you'll learn the whole alphabet."

I thrust the knife. "Wait. You're leaving?"

"I figured this news, at least, would make you happy."

It should have; it should have made me feel safer. But it didn't. "So you're saying somebody's found you?"

"No, I'm saying that right now, we'll have no talking."

He worked the dirt until he dug out an old bone. It made no sense how he could punish me for leaving, when he, himself, planned to go for good.

"You're leaving us with a horse from Treehand?" I said.

"I wouldn't do that if even your aunt had asked." He peered at the bone; it looked like part of a fox. "Treehand, in fact, is where the horse and I will go."

"Lands, why?" I said. He gestured at my dagger. "Teph, why?"

"My dear. You have to work first."

We stabbed the earth until nightfall.

part TWO

After all eleven of Teph's knives, Jillian fed us pottage lacking turnips. She said we'd exhausted our supply for the week, and I imagined Wilm eating one in the silence of his starry hut.

I sat across from my aunt, who had given Teph the largest portion of the stew. She and I hadn't spoken since the road. The last time we had been at this table, she had shoved me against the wall.

I said to Jillian, "You lied about what you thought."

She gripped the table edge.

"You lied about pursuers from the west," I said. "And about what you knew of a Treehanded horse. You lied about the possibility of mindless." Technically, she hadn't lied, but by my lights it was all the same.

With her free hand, Jillian spooned her dish.

I said, "You talked to Wilm about mindless."

"There will be no mindless," she said. "I told him so. And the fear he gave you is the price you pay by eavesdropping on a faulty source."

I said, "He's the only source I have."

Jillian glanced at Teph. "And what do you know of your source?"

"That you're feeding him," I said, "to keep watch."

She nodded.

"That the horse," I said, "came from a Treehanded merchant."

"And?" she said.

"And that you gave Wilm my dominoes."

She said, "We'll get you more dominoes."

"I don't care about dominoes." I checked to see if the door was bolted. I did not want Teph to leave, and I did not want to know why he had eleven knives. Just this afternoon, Wilm had hugged his house. "My father died from this horse." They both turned to me. "I decided to save it. You approved." They stopped eating. "I was mature enough to judge Lucinda, to make a decision involving life and death. Jillian. You made me decide."

She said, "The law made—"

"No," I said. "You did." It wasn't an accusation, but it was a fact. "And then today I learn how something I spared is calling another thing that might be coming from Treehand. And that the man who came home with us could also be attracting something else." Mindless or men, it didn't much matter. "You know how all of these things practically panic Wilm."

"Well," she puffed a little, as if to disturb a fly. "It isn't hard to panic Wilm."

"And how they also panic you," I said. "And how they also make your hands go cold."

She touched her braid. She'd mended it since the road.

"This," I said. "All of this, has something to do with me. I saved the horse. I brought Teph here."

She folded her hands.

"You could die." My throat tightened. "I could die." I swallowed. "I'm grown up, because you made me grow up." I squeezed a blister from the knife work. "And I'm grown up enough to know."

Jillian, exhaling, almost showed relief. Teph smiled into his lap.

Jillian said, "That is the most reasonable thing you've said in a while."

"No." I stood, and the chair scraped. "This isn't an enrichment opportunity. This isn't a chance to teach me a grown-up lesson."

"Gaelle," said Teph.

"And I'm through being punished," I said.

He raised his eyebrows.

"Out of decency to me," I said, "and to Wilm—and to my parents—you have a responsibility to tell me what you know."

I still stood, risen from the table as if to make a toast.

Teph said, "You have a talent for speech."

"That's enough," said Jillian, and it was hard to tell if she was speaking to Teph or to me. "Gaelle, sit."

I spread my stance. Then I sat.

She chewed her bite of pottage longer than she probably needed. "You are not yet an adult, no matter what the world has demanded."

"I'm old enough," I said.

"You are old for your age," she spoke louder, "but you are not an adult."

"Nor should you be," said Teph. "And when I leave, you will have to be even more of an adult."

"You were always going to leave," I said.

Leaning back, he favored a rib. "I was hoping there would be somewhat more time." Maybe he'd wanted to stay as long as he could, then, even if it meant getting mauled by a horse.

He told me he and Jillian had essentially settled the truth about Lucinda, as soon as Wilm admitted she could eat meat. They'd discussed such a thing after Jillian returned from Wilm that morning. When I met her on the road coming home, she had retraced her steps, in search for me.

Now at table, she and Teph told me how horses aren't indigenous to Treehand. The province offers too little to graze, and what vegetation a horse can eat is hooked, carnivorous, or narcotic. Most species in Treehand are carnivorous, or soon become so. Still, those Azmen able to travel to Treehand have come across the occasional wild horse—one whose line has somehow survived long enough to grow feral, the way domestic pigs can change into boars. The Treehanded horses grow bigger than domestic ones; the males develop tusks; and they eat meat. I asked why it wouldn't be easier to adapt to just eating fruits and leaves, and Teph said not even the Treehanded will eat most of those. The communities cultivate specific groves which they petition for food. They decorate the trees with animal skins, and with bone and wood they've carved to resemble fruit. Some of the trees wear a collection of bells, and Azmonian lore holds that when you hear those bells, you get away.

The Treehanded are also scarce. Teph had seen only one of them, dead and covered with moss. The animals are equally rare, and extremely quiet. Only the insects are ubiquitous. And by far, they make the most noise. Still, many of the plants also speak, if you have a practiced ear. Some of the Azmonian guides can differentiate the trees without seeing them, by the sound the wind makes in their leaves.

"Lucinda is Treehanded," said Teph. "But she is not a quiet creature."

"Neither is Wilm," I said.

But Jillian and Teph thought Lucinda keened long before she came to Wilm's pasture. For one thing, Wilm couldn't soothe her. And if Wilm had been able to purchase her, he had likely gotten her at a very low price. Somebody probably wanted to get rid of her as soon as possible.

"Nobody willingly comes from Treehand." As if to emphasize his point, Teph wiped a spot off the table.

"But," I said, "you do."

"That's through Treehand," said Jillian.

"Merchant routes," said Teph. "They're an old tradition."

Teph the merchant. He had a dark fleck in his left eye. Aside from his knives and the bag he'd used to keep his worg skull, he kept only a pack. And it was just slightly larger than what I would take to market.

"Teph." For some reason, I flushed. "What do you sell?"

He rubbed his green earring. "I sell knives, of course."

Jillian sat still.

I said, "All of your knives are used."

He held the earring. "You make a very good point."

He and Jillian might have waited weeks for me to ask such a thing, for me to notice.

"Esaosh," I said.

Jillian rested her mouth on her hand. I began to feel cold.

My gut tightened, as if to withstand a blow. "Teph. Do you sell horses?"

"Gracious no!" he said.

"Are you even a merchant?" I said.

He let go of the earring, and pressed a finger to my wrist. He watched Jillian. She gave him a nod.

"I procure," he said, "certain things that go missing."

"You're a bounty hunter," I said.

"More hunting," he said. "Less bounty."

"He's what Azmen call a Retriever," said Jillian. "It's a noble's post."

He told me Retrievers are knights, of a sort. They are trained in combat, but they struggle against the elements, mostly. Azmon is primarily dunes and scrub. The screel—the ravenous wind—is so strong that it twists vegetation and blows sand until it polishes stone. Much of Azmon lives in caves. And Azmonian fortresses have bladed, above-ground walls which the sand blows to razors, until the walls have to be replaced.

The Retrievers venture into the howls of the screel, and elsewhere, to find those who have become lost. Sometimes their targets are travelers, or animals, or fugitives. Sometimes they are goods, or caravans of goods, which as a pre-emptive measure, Retrievers occasionally escort. This is how Teph learned the trade routes through Treehand. Azmon doesn't trade with Treehand's inhabitants, but Azmon does trade with Holding. And the trade-routes go both ways. One would expect Treehand to want a share of the profits, or at least some kind of toll, but they don't. They don't want anything. And they'll kill anything, if it wanders off course. They will especially kill the mindless, who flout, they say, the cycle of life and death. That, and allegedly according to the ground itself, the mindless are inedible.

"The Treehanded talk with you?" I said.

"Occasionally. To our great man," said Teph. "In any event, the Treehanded declare the Retrievers must return any mindless that actually reach Treehand. The Treehanded refuse to approach the mindless themselves."

"That's a weakness," I said.

Jillian glanced me up and down.

"Oh, it's a weakness for everyone." Teph rubbed his chin scar. "If too many mindless are left unretrieved, they constitute an act of war."

He said the largest danger involves mindless getting far enough to wander off a domestic part of an Azmonian trade route. This, however, is blessedly difficult, because beyond the paths, the vegetation is almost willfully dense. Because the mindless have no inhibition to regulate their efforts, they are horrid in their strength. They can topple a group of men. But they are still celdan bodies, and they are degradable. The screel can tear the flesh from their bones, so that by the time they get to the forest, they rarely have the strength to push through Treehanded vegetation. Still, in rare cases, the wind can also hone their bones. And these sharpened mindless can cut the ground by walking. Such a creature can hack through plants, if it has enough time. But typically, even the keenest mindless take weeks to cut a path. And as a result, the Retrievers can find them, grass-stained and thrashing, while their bladed hands and elbows have broken off around them.

"This," said Jillian, "is why we believe that Wilm will never see mindless."

I put my head in my hands. The gesture felt very adult. "So there actually is a chance?"

"Again, you sound like Wilm." Jillian scraped the turnip pot with a bit of ardor. "I just told you no."

"But Teph is attracting something," I said. "You said so."

"It will likely be Azmen," said Jillian, "and it has nothing to do with Lucinda."

"You're attracting Azmen?" I said. "Countrymen?"

"Well naturally," he coughed, "we don't all get along." He said his leaving with Lucinda would solve two separate problems: it would remove a Tree-handed horse who was calling for something, and it would divert whoever separately followed him.

"We picked up two unrelated fugitives," I said, "in one afternoon?"

"Gaelle, you can't forget," said Jillian. "At the same time, you became a fugitive, too."

I walked to the fire and back. The depth of what they told me made me want to move. Teph and Jillian watched me from where they sat at table, looking like my parents, or a mockery of my parents.

I laughed. It was the only thing I could do to keep calm. "I have no idea what you're talking about."

"I've come to Holding because I've fled my brethren." Under the table, Teph kicked his bag of knives. "The Retrievers are now likely retrieving me."

If Wilm heard this, he would puff triumphant. Jillian made a calming motion with her hand.

"You're a criminal," I said.

"An Azmonian criminal." He reached for a mustache that wasn't there. "Your laws won't punish you for harboring the likes of me."

"But the Retrievers," I said.

"I'm a very good criminal," he said.

All of these people wanted me to resist becoming an outlaw, when they sat in my own house, evidently thick as literal thieves. "Jillian," I said.

"Listen to him," she said.

"You knew!" I said.

"I told her after the first day," said Teph. "I needed a place to hide. I could help you with your horse. And if anyone appealed to the authorities, I could help to keep them from you."

I glanced at his knife bag. "By force?"

"By whatever it took," he said.

"And besides," said Jillian. "I also support his cause."

I wanted to bang the table. "What cause?"

"We'll get to that," said Teph. He surveyed the table I wanted to smack, as if he wondered if it would hold everything he had to lay out. "First, in their hunt for me, the Retrievers would have a lot to contend with before they ever got as far as this farm."

"We're talking about nearly half the width of the empire," said Jillian.

"First they have Treehand." Teph cut a piece off a parsnip. "Then," he cut another piece, "they have the fact that I took their weapons." He nudged the pieces in his bowl. "The weapons you sharpened."

This afternoon, I had held the weapons of a company of man hunters.

"Not even a skinner carries eleven knives," said Jillian.

"Are there ten Retrievers?" I said.

"Five," said Teph. "Sensible people carry two knives."

I said, "Then one of you is half-sensible."

"I lost one," he said. "That's why I carry two."

I sat on the hearth.

Teph said, "The Retrievers also have to contend with the mindless."

"Wait," I said. "Now there *are* mindless?"

"Just the ones," said Jillian, "who won't make it through Treehand."

I'd begun to sweat. With Lucinda calling something, and the Azman Retrievers separately after Teph, two shoes had already dropped. Now, with mention of the mindless, it felt like somebody had landed, dead, on the floor.

"Still," I said. "Mindless."

"Escaped mindless," said Teph.

Of course. These days, everybody ran from something. "How many?" I said.

Teph drummed his fingers on his bare cheek. "There are three."

Teph and his fellow brethren had been trailing four mindless that had escaped to Treehand from an irrigation farm. Most mindless have been geassed by the golemancers who made them; they have been bound to follow orders from their master. Ingesting salt of any type will eventually produce some kind of metabolic change that dissolves such control. This is what frightened Garfield, when he knocked the chalice on our portico. While it's free, the mindless ranges without purpose. Depending on the disposition of who it once was, it may set about destroying everything it finds. "This is a problem when you use mindlessness as a sentence for violent criminals," said Teph. "Many are vindictive by nature." Once this salinization takes hold, the mindless's maker has two days, on average, to reassert his command before the salt wears off. Otherwise, the creature is forever free to wander, semi-conscious and purely reactive.

Now there happens to be a particular kind of salt—called sanchal—which has the potency to affect mindless on contact. The mindless on the irrigation farm had come across a thin vein of sanchal after it had opened with a lightning strike. The salt had entered the creatures' degraded skin, and the mindless had fled. The Retrievers' task was to return them to their owners.

As was his custom, Teph had visited the farm during his investigation. But what he found was a reek of decay that even open air couldn't flush. Six mindless wandered, all tattered nudes. Some had walked their feet to bone. Others had lost their arms, so the owners ordered them to dig with their mouths. Teph found mindless teeth in the ground. Then other mindless would come, and take the teeth-ridden heaps into their own mouths. The sight made Teph vomit. And afterwards, he stood by the retch so nothing could carry it off.

The memory stayed with Teph like a scent. The day after the irrigation farm, he and his Retrievers followed a trail leading to Treehand. And as the screel gave way to clots of life, Teph decided even the most stunted version of the living should be inviolable.

In our cottage, he rapped the table softly, as if he were still bringing order to some kind of dispute. "Nothing deserves a blasphemed existence."

He's right: nothing in this world, nothing in your world, nothing in history or imagination deserves a blasphemed existence. And among all the things Teph became, among all the blasphemy he nearly embodied, I pray that Visjaes recognize how it was all in service to this truth.

At our table, Teph said how after three days along the trade routes, the Retrievers heard the wet hacks of a mindless clawing through the brush. They readied their leather strips as a means of lashing the creature. The Retrievers surrounded the mindless. The mindless attacked. Teph let it knock three men senseless, and he did the same to the remaining two. "Then," he said, "I killed the creature."

Jillian rubbed the split of her thumbnail.

"How," I said, "do you kill a mindless?"

"It was in bad shape by then." He still knocked his knuckles. "The killing takes a fair amount of severing."

Perhaps it also took a fair amount of time.

"So," said Teph. "I stole from the men. I doubled back to another trade route. And I moved east."

I stood from the table with no idea what to give him, no notion of how to respond. "Did your comrades see you attack them?"

He stilled his hands. "One."

"But then you knocked him out," I said.

"Yes."

"So they don't know where you went?" I said.

"Possibly not." He touched his earring. "But they are very good at retrieving."

A thought welled in me, almost as if it were an emotion. "Were some of them your relatives?"

Jillian inhaled. Teph seemed to search my face. "That is rather trenchant."

"No." I'd just read how often he'd touched his earring. "I'm sorry," I said.

"There was a son-in-law, who didn't see me. I attacked him first." He looked at the pieces in his stew, and he pushed away the bowl. "I left them supplies, and wrote a note with directions for the shortest way home." He held his own wrist. "Their knives I took. I left them three clubs." I imagined him leaving them in a stack, like a little campfire. "I figured the reduction might make them turn back."

My mouth felt loose. "What about the escaped mindless you didn't find?"

"That's one of the reasons they'd have to turn back," he said.

"And what about the Treehanded rule of no mindless?" I said.

"Or few mindless," he said. "The remaining two would be tolerable. And I hoped the land would eventually kill them. For their sakes, in addition to others'."

I tried to imagine Jillian knocking me out, and leaving me in the wilderness, of her approaching a family that had just faced tragedy, and asking to be hidden.

"Gaelle," said Jillian. "Teph is an abolitionist."

He said, "It's nothing so grand."

"Mindlessness," she said, "is a form of slavery. He risks himself to end that."

We had slavery in the cities, but it was rare and usually reserved for captives.

"You end slavery by killing mindless?" I said.

"A type of slavery," said Teph.

"It's another reason why the appearance of the other mindless would be astonishing," said Jillian. "Other obstacles aside, they'd have to be ordered to hunt Teph by the Retrievers Teph attacked. And this would probably mean the Retrievers would have to catch them, and have them re-commanded by their maker."

"Wilm's fear is moot," said Teph.

"Wilm's fear is prejudice," said Jillian.

"And in any event," said Teph, "I had taken great care, before I ever involved you." He always would.

"But you're feeding Wilm," I said. "You're keeping him as lookout."

"We're mostly just feeding Wilm," said Jillian. "He stays alive and out of debt. He gets to feel some control."

With the poker, I whacked the fire, and it flashed. All of his was just like Teph and Jillian: so very shady and so very kind. One was the first thing, and the other was the second, and you never knew who was which.

"You were afraid," I said, "when I talked about Lucinda."

"Yes," she said. "Lucinda is a monster." A monster calling other monsters.

"Then we'll kill her," I said.

"We found a weed in her pen," said Teph.

I said, "It's too cold for weeds."

"For normal weeds, yes," said Teph. "That made it easier to notice. It's still out there, if you want to see. It has hooks."

Maybe my father, in front of the fire, foretold his own death.

"You should know," said Jillian, "that we suspect we'd find more of them in Wilm's pasture."

"Treehand killed my dad?" I said.

"Gaelle," said Jillian. "We should have taught you more history."

She started to tell me of the Clearing Wars, how so much of the land used to be Treehanded.

"You'll learn more when you can read," said Teph. "And this is a reason you must read."

The table's wood had come from a tree that had been in the center of the orchard. It was a larger elder, probably centuries old.

"So, kill Lucinda," I said, "and the weed."

"Gaelle," said Jillian. "You are so eager to kill."

"I'm eager to right a mistake," I said. "I should have killed her the first time." The herbs cast crazy shadows from our hanging baskets. "I should have let you."

"Well, I'm glad you didn't," she said.

"The horse is from Treehand," I said. "The weed is from Treehand."

"Do you see the connection?" said Teph.

"Who cares about the connection?" I said. "The horse poops the seeds.

The seeds grow into a plant."

"Holding doesn't have the right seeds for the horse to eat," said Teph. "Not many. Not enough. And Lucinda's been with Wilm for over a year."

"Fine," I said. All of this felt both trivial and dark, as if I was supposed to find the monster in the room, so it could get on with eating me. "What is your point?"

"Eddlefruit," said Teph. "It doesn't grow unless a feaster scores the tree-bark by perching in the branches. This is why it's a mixed thing to kill a feaster."

"It's a mixed thing," said Jillian, "to kill in general."

"Certain seeds," said Teph, "won't germinate unless a certain animal inhabits the land. Maybe it's the weight of the animal. Maybe it's a substance in the animal's dung or a mineral in its hooves. But unless the animal is present, the seeds lie dormant."

I still held the fireplace poker, and now I tightened my grip.

"Lucinda," said Teph, "is awakening Treehand in Holding."

We needed my father to be here. He didn't know about horses, but he knew about plants.

"You see now," said Jillian, "that we cannot kill her."

"Absolutely we can kill her," I said.

"But when you kill something," said Jillian, "you shut off a spring of information."

"We'll shut off a spring from Treehand." I glanced at the fireplace. "My father told me about Treehand."

"Who sent Lucinda?" said Jillian. "Did she just wander here?"

"Where did Lucinda come from?" said Teph. "Why is she here?"

"How many Lucindas have been planted in Holding?" said Jillian. "Or to the north, up in Cadmus?"

"How many horses truly live in Treehand?" said Teph. "Is there some kind of Lucinda ranch?"

I watched them more than I listened. Either they'd rehearsed this argument beforehand, or they'd just talked about it again and again. An entire dialogue had germinated during these weeks after my fathers' death, and now that I had finally found it, I'd uncovered an infestation.

"If Treehand is using a horse to take back its land," I said, "you need to call the garrison. You have to tell the Church."

"Gaelle," said Jillian. "We are all criminals."

"I don't care," I said. But maybe I did.

"In fact," Teph hung his head, "it might come to that. But rumor is that the Church is already becoming more militant."

"So let them go after Treehand," I said. "They hate Treehand."

"They hate heretics," said Jillian.

"Well, some of them deserve it," I said.

"Dear Gaelle," said Teph. My aunt stood, and stood still.

I hadn't meant to lump all heretics with the Treehanded. I certainly hadn't meant to lump all outlaws.

"That's not what I meant," I said.

"I have many friends who are heretics," she said. "Many innocents. Many people of warmth and courage."

"I know," I said.

"You would have been lucky to know them," she said.

She was right; I would have known my family.

Teph had drained a cup of water. In some act of partnership or maintenance, Jillian filled it again. "If we alerted the Church," said Teph, "more horses would die. Just out of precaution. Whole farms would fail."

"The Cadmul are horsemen. Then there's the Tonn Men," said Jillian. They live in the far north of Cadmus. "They're nearly nomads. What then?"

"And then there's the people," said Teph. "Innocents killed as Treehanded agents." And the thing was, he said, that if the Treehanded really meant ruin, all they had to do was raise this exact sort of alarm.

"But aren't you talking," I said, "about a worst-case scenario?"

"We don't know the scenario," said Jillian. "Not nearly. Not yet."

In the meantime, they said, they would send the news of Treehand among their friends—the heretics, presumably, or at least the people whom

Jillian's intrepid work sometimes supplied. And there were also the Retrievers, if we could assume Teph could find friends among them. Or at the very least, he thought he might get the news to another group of abolitionist Azmen.

In the setting sun, Lucinda was screaming. We barely noticed the sound anymore.

"And you say you're taking her to Treehand?" I said. "Even though you can barely ride her?"

"That's what I'm guessing," said Teph. I imagined him riding full tilt, into the men who chased him. "Still," with a finger, he parted the beads on his cup's condensation. "Well. Wherever we go, I will let her take me. And that allowance should make the ride at least a little easier."

We cleaned up from supper, in silence. Jillian told Teph to sit, that he'd have enough work to do in the morning. I cupped my hands around the warmth of the stew pot. Then the dish reminded me of Wilm's garlic pot, and I set it down.

In retrospect, what's astonishing is how correct we were: The horse was indeed from Treehand; she was sent to bring up the grass; the mindless were on the move, both for reasons that didn't connect with our predicament and others that attached to use like hooks. We were wrong about one thing, however: Lucinda wasn't calling Treehand. She was calling the Church.

part THREE

After supper, Teph sat by our fire with a book in his lap. He hung his arms loose at his sides, as if he gave the pages a kind of freedom. I'd never seen a book before. It was smaller than I thought it would be, and moldy enough to smell like wet dog.

When he'd opened the book, Teph told me we were going to meet the alphabet. He settled deeper into his chair, and I had little doubt that all of his children, no matter how many, had learned to read.

I stood in front of him.

"You play rimstack," he said.

He explained that I already knew how to read dominoes, that the dots were symbols holding an idea, a quantity. He said letters hold sounds, or a choice of sounds. He went on this way for a time, not yet showing me the book, but writing out letters on a separate page.

I kept standing, and after a while, Teph stopped. "Despite your opinion of the opposite," he said, "I actually don't believe in protecting most knowledge." He lay the book, face up, in his lap. "Please sit."

I found a chair from the table. Teph said how in the Imperial academies, students were in fact required to stand during instruction. He told me the tradition had taken on reasons ranging from respect, to sadism, to sleep prevention, but that in the beginning, it was a means of making a citadel of students. Education was for the select. Teachers could burn, if they instructed the wrong person. A professor's voice carried less when he sat within a standing circle. And the students could better see intruders, if they stood while they learned.

I asked Teph if he'd ever had to stand, and he'd told me he didn't learn in an academy. Still, he suggested I think of the name of our province: Holding. He said it receives its title from the monastery it houses, the chief monastery of the Imperial Church. It is the greatest academy in all of Celd, and it keeps its knowledge—it holds it—for those who are worthy to attain such things.

While I sat, Teph arrayed each letter of the alphabet in a line. He hummed into his pipe. Then he moved us to the table, where he had me practice the letters over and again. At first, he held his hand over mine; I was surprised at how warm it was. Then he watched me work alone, with his chin on his forearms, as if I were the one teaching him.

When darkness came, I stopped. "Is this illegal?" I said.

"In your case, not." He pushed the paper toward me. "You own land. Your aunt serves the Church." I snorted. "So. Let it serve her."

He etched with me for half the evening. He smoked more than usual, as many as three pipes. All of this must have been hard work, teaching me the alphabet in a night.

At first the urgency was hard to parse. My aunt certainly knew the alphabet; in fact, she knew several. But I suspect Teph had always planned to teach me to read, and that with Lucinda's sudden turn, he had both to shorten and to sharpen the goal. Perhaps, considering the danger he'd just learned he'd face, he simply wished to impart something to someone for whom he'd developed affection. In all the years I knew him—among all the studies and plans and altercations we shared—this night is one of my most salvific memories. Teph wasn't ever quite my father, but he did give me my words.

Well into the night now, he opened his book to show me a map. He read me climate descriptions, and history, and poetry. In a small way, the study of it all was an alchemy of understanding. I've tried to recreate something of it, while bidding Garfield show me his home on a flagstone. During the last night Teph spent with us, he taught me till dawn. And when the sun came up, it was as if the world had opened its eye.

part FOUR

At sunrise Teph looked at me from across the table, bleary and stubbled. He smoothed the page of his book and gave a sticky cough. "I've kept you all night."

"It's OK."

He scraped the chair as he stood. He put his hands on the back of his hips, and looked around as if he were somehow embarrassed. Then he made a stiff walk out to where he slept in the shed, and I saw again how he was not a young man.

Jillian returned to the cottage, with cold on her clothes. I hadn't even noticed her exit. She boiled eggs, warming her hands in the steam. The morning, she said, brought freezing fog. She touched the book Teph had left on the table. And while he was outside, she told me she thought he would leave it for me.

In the gray of dawn, it appeared so very inert. "I suppose if he took it,"

I said, "it would only weigh him down."

"Gaelle, that's cynical." It was. It was a protective stance. "You must avoid cynicism. Deliberately."

Teph entered the house with a backpack and wet-slicked hair. His eyes had a sort of forced brightness.

Jillian gave him bread and old oats, and some honey I didn't even know we had. She offered him two sausages.

He put his hand on the book. "Read all of this," he said to me. I told him I would. "Your aunt will help." I didn't want her help. Such a thing would feel like an intrusion.

When we got outside, Lucinda stood bolt-straight in her pen. Except on that first day, I'd never seen her as silent or watchful. Teph bent to wrap the leather straps around his legs.

"Kill her if you have to," said Jillian.

Teph grimaced, as if the horse had heard. He said he had no intention of freezing the trail. He looked to us. Our breath came out in clouds, as if it were itself a conversation.

He rummaged his pack, and pulled out a box that was longer than what I'd seen him use for his knives. It held an arrow that had a crust of black salt.

"Sanchal," said Teph. "As a last resort. You should have no occasion to use it."

"You might," said Jillian.

"I kept one," he said.

He handed her the box. Salting the mindless would be a saving measure, if the mindless's purpose was us. Otherwise, the shot could yield anything.

I asked what would happen if the mindless was already sanchaled. And Teph said that in such a case, the arrow was mundane. "Use it in any event," he said. "Just aim for the eyes."

He stood in front of me, took my hand, and kissed it. "Bear well your unborn children."

He took Jillian's hand, and kissed her palm. Something fluttered in her face, and while he still bent, she patted his head.

He entered the horse pen, and Lucinda stomped. Jillian noticed a dangling buckle, and he thanked her as he fixed it. He mounted the horse, in a smoother way than I'd seen before. He sat still while she pranced, and asked me to open the gate. I swung it slowly—and the horse went out. They already approached a gallop, halfway to the barn. Teph held on with both hands, peering back at us from around his crouch. He sort of half waved, and shouted something we couldn't understand. He and Lucinda headed southeast, away from Wilm's.

I could still feel Teph's kiss on the back of my hand. No one had done that to me before. It was surprising, in its bristle. Without looking, I sensed Jillian stood as straight as before. Even at my age, I knew it was a different thing to kiss a person's palm, and that maybe a pat on the head was not the desired response.

In the barnyard, near the gate, I listened to the fading hoofbeats. I said, "Was his poetry really that bad?"

"Lands yes!" She leaned into my shoulder, and laughed.

chapter 7

MEDICINE

As you age, you want to keep in touch with your feet. We Riven learned this when we recruited older peasants to help in the war. Look at an aged person's toenails. If they're clawed, the person might not be limber enough to cut them. Bad flexibility accompanies bad circulation, and such a thing will threaten a lifespan. The Church might claim my longevity comes from witchery, but in fact, nuns like me can grow very old. Some say it's from the contemplation, but I think it's the prostration. I used to be able to rise from the floor on one leg, while holding a child. Now I have to use my hands to stand. But every day, I make them touch my toes.

In my sandstone prison, about ten days after the boy, Garfield, helped me with my fingers, I used the heat of the afternoon to do my stretches. Ordinal's steppe is dry, but the Bell traps enough moisture to dampen any dust. The result is a heap of sludge in the corner, with the most recent layer powdering the top. Sometimes I wonder if I'm turning into the same thing. Lately it's taken me so long to bend to my feet that my head starts to pound.

I was in the middle of my stretches, in the yellow of the afternoon, when some boys started to howl below the Bell. I could tell it was them, because of the reediness of their voices. A husky, day guard stood on the portico next to Mama, and he laughed a curse. The guard sergeant kept post directly across the bridge, in an alcove within the castle wall. Otto, they call him, is tall and in his forties, with a habit of beating my prison bars with his torch. From what

I could tell, he hadn't reacted to the howling.

The howls rose to shrieks. Shrieking is different from screaming; any parent will tell you so. One boy shouted while another one laughed, and I pressed my forehead to the bars. It was good the children were safe. I once saw a church massacre. And no matter its circumstances, the fact of it followed its perpetrators, afterwards, into every room, like a stink.

That night, Garfield stood by a salt chalice, and tugged at Mama. I wished him good evening, but all he did was lean his head against the haft of his pole arm, and push his gaze along its length, to the floor. At first I thought he'd gotten embarrassed by how he'd touched my hands the other night—but that had been days ago, and he'd since even brought me a cup of mead. The floor-map's cricket, now half-smashed, lay on the flagstone. With his head bowed, Garfield touched his mouth. He looked at his fingers, and with the back of his hand, he touched his mouth again. I waited for him to spit, and he did. But he spat into a handkerchief he kept in his belt, and the fastidiousness of it caught me so off guard that I nearly lay my head on the bars again. These signs of life can seize you with affection.

"Somebody hit you," I said. He hunkered his shoulders. "Either that or you fell on your face."

"Mind your business."

He bowed his head, but he wouldn't be able to do so for long. Those guard helmets are heavy: solid iron, and made for full-grown men. I'd seen boys, not much older than Garfield, with bald patches from where the helmets chaffed.

Garfield leaned against his halberd. It must have helped support his head.

From where I stood next to the bars, I stretched to touch my toes. My plan was to bend far enough so I could get a look into the boy's face.

"I'm not going to help you if you get stuck again," he said.

"Oh no. They wouldn't let you in my cell."

"And you're a woman besides."

"At least you've noticed." At least he could speak clearly. "Sometimes, lands, when you're my age," my hamstrings started to shake. "Sometimes, I swear, I stretch like this, and it feels like part of my spine will snap right off, and fly across the room."

"I won't pick that up either."

I chuckled. At least he'd started to joke. I bent my legs some, and got lower. Garfield had a smashed lip. The sight of it made my knees a little weak.

A blow like his could have come from a shield at sparring, but he'd probably be proud of that instead of embarrassed. More likely, someone hit him with a gauntlet, once, or with a bare fist, repeatedly.

I leaned back on my palms, and my breastbone popped. "Salt will help with the swelling."

"Salt is for you all."

"Get a little water, mix it up."

"So you want me to set free the mindless?"

"What, you're going to kiss the mindless?"

He spat into his handkerchief. What he needed was ice, but the latest snow had melted, and it was arid enough at Ordinal, that any ice the Church had was not for the boys.

I said, "Honey works, if you have it."

"Then I guess I'll just mash my face into the abbot-principe's toast."

"Somebody already mashed your face." I could get down on his level, if he needed me to. Patrick, the father of my church: he and I have a childhood home on that level.

Garfield was muttering about my being a witch.

"Ask your own herbalist," I said. "I couldn't care less what you do with your lip."

Field medicine is what I know. And before then, I guess I learned farm medicine. But although I love an herbalist, I never was one. Unless they work for the Church, most of them are dead these days, especially if they're female. The Church has decided women are less rational than men. And seeing how Esaosh is the lord of reason, this means we're less holy than men. So if the Church finds we've mastered a skill we aren't rational enough to learn, we must have acquired it in the least holy way possible—such as through witchcraft.

From within the castle's guard alcove, somebody howled. Garfield shrank, and puffed.

"What's that?" I said.

"Be quiet."

"Lord, preserve us!" shrieked a boy. "It howls at night, like a mindless in heat."

"Hey!" Otto, the watch sergeant, hollered from the alcove. "You pipe off!"

"What howls?" I said.

"Please," said Garfield. "Be quiet."

"Otto!" shouted a boy from inside the castle. "Otto, ask Garfield what he did."

"I don't give a rip what he did," said Otto.

"Ask him why the rector smashed his mouth."

"He what?" said Otto.

"Ask him," hollered the boy. "Otto! You'll bust your gut."

"Garfield!" shouted Otto. "You going to make me bust my gut?"

Otto's torchlight bobbed along the bridge. Garfield shuddered a breath. "Garfield," I said. "Look him in the eye."

"Boy?" Otto is the most hirsute man I've ever seen. His arm hair pokes from his cuirass sleeves, like a little fringe. Now, on the portico, he stood in front of Garfield while his torch hissed. "So tell me why the rector popped you." Garfield started to speak, but Otto grabbed his jaw, and held his face to the torchlight. "You're lucky you still have your teeth." Otto let him go. Garfield teetered, and he clutched the prison railing. "So?" Something clattered from around the corner. "Bust my gut."

Garfield let go a little breath.

"You huffing at me now?" said Otto.

"No, Sir."

"Oh. Well." Otto braced his torch, business-end first, against the crossbeam of my bars. "Maybe with a busted seal, you can't keep all your air in!" He'd shouted this across the bridge, and from the alcove now, the boys cheered. Otto beamed like a performer. "Now," Otto said to Garfield, "make me laugh."

Garfield half raised his handkerchief, saw that Otto noticed it, and pushed it into his belt. My hands had gone cold. I could do nothing for the boy. Any help I gave would be worse than his climbing into my cell.

"Tell him, Garfield!" cried one of the boys.

Garfield planted the butt of his halberd, and stood behind it. "We'd talked all week about the buffet. Right?" Even I'd heard of the buffet. It's a new kind of banquet, where nobody sits. "We talked about it all week." So Garfield said he had to read the lectionary during the afternoon's service, and that he was assigned a scripture about the buffeting winds of change, and that he read, "Lord Esaosh, preserve us," he looked Otto in the eye, "from the howling boofay."

The boys, now halfway across the bridge, split into fits. Otto tucked in his lips far enough for his upper chin hair to stick out. Garfield grasped my prison bars, and he held his ground.

"You chump," said Otto. "You complete thickhead." He laughed like something you'd imagine from a folktale swordsman. "*Howling buffet?* Does it also run around the room?"

The boys guffawed. Garfield had his mouth open, but maybe this was because he couldn't all the way close it.

Otto snatched the torch. "What do you think, Whore?"

From where I sat, I piled all my attention on an old singe mark in my lap. "What?" I lied. "Is it a joke?"

"Worth and Freedom, *is it a joke?*" Otto nudged Garfield. He dug two fingers into a salt chalice, and dumped a gob of it into Garfield's hand. He told him to go make a saltwater poultice. "They were right to pop you." He nursed a limp I hadn't noticed. "But a laugh is worth the balm."

Garfield made his way through the crowd of boys who had pushed nearly onto the portico. One of them patted Garfield on the back of the head.

Otto followed everyone out, flapping his hands as if he herded geese. For a moment, I was alone, and I laughed till I cried.

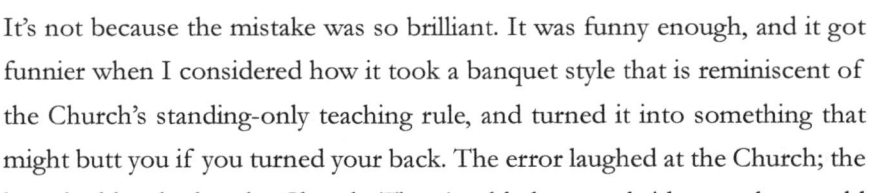

It's not because the mistake was so brilliant. It was funny enough, and it got funnier when I considered how it took a banquet style that is reminiscent of the Church's standing-only teaching rule, and turned it into something that might butt you if you turned your back. The error laughed at the Church; the boys had laughed at the Church. They jumbled onto a bridge, so they could make other people laugh. And Otto, who is forty and a fire hazard, he laughed too. If my god, Visjaes, is a trickster, Visjaes lives in the joke—especially if it's at the expense of Esaosh. Maybe this is why, for all its mirrors, choirs, and architecture, the Church of Esaosh is so very dour. Esaosh isn't a creator. He didn't make this world; when he landed here, he took it. And just like their god, his Church of Light doesn't make any radiance, either. The priests just redirect it from those who do.

I didn't laugh much when I was young. From all the danger, loss, and dread, we lived with such gritted teeth. Perhaps because she was so good at sussing our immediate stakes, Jillian did not joke. And these days, it touches me to think of the times when she made herself uncomfortable enough to try. I didn't start to laugh until I started to hope; that is, until my view of the world became large enough to show me I had room to play. And this is why I wept after Garfield filed off the bridge, with Otto and the boys. Whether they knew it or not, humor is frequently an act of faith.

Of course, it doesn't always come from such a place. The news mongers, in the rebellion's Syndicate, are mostly atheists, and they can write satire so funny that I've watched an executioner laugh as he recited the writer's crimes. The atheist's humor topples fear with an acceptance of defeat in the first place. But humor from faith topples fear by urging us not to accept the end at all.

Garfield returned to his post with a dripping, burlap sachet. His voice box bulged while he leaned back his head.

"Does it sting?" I said.

"It feels good."

That made me feel good, and I almost said so. With the salt-water poultice, Otto had confirmed my treatment. For somebody truly bent on hating me, the endorsement wouldn't destroy all suspicion. In fact, the Church teaches that so-called healing witches are more dangerous than the hexing kind, because they show how magic can be helpful. But despite how he occasionally postured, Garfield wasn't bent on hating me. If he was, he wouldn't have admitted the poultice helped. Nor would he have taken my advice to look Otto in the eye. And when Otto commanded Garfield to make him laugh, Garfield certainly wouldn't have grasped my prison bar. As much as anything else, his little reach was why I'd wept.

It was late now, but I still sat. I'd taken to sleeping during the days, so I could talk with the boy. From behind his poultice, he made little slurps, and I tried not to find them annoying.

"Garfield," I said, "your brothers loved your mistake."

"They thought it was all right."

"They brought you to Otto."

"They wanted Otto to laugh."

"That's right. And he did."

Garfield lowered his voice. "Otto's not bad."

These days, I wonder if he isn't, at least not to his brethren. Regardless of whether the Church looks askance at affection, Otto enjoys the boys' adoration too much to harm them. And for all I reckon, the boys brought lip-busted Garfield to him, because they knew Otto would treat him. "You faced him, though. Garfield. Today you showed your spine."

"Don't butter me up, Whore."

"I haven't buttered anything. Salted, maybe."

"Ha."

"But I mean it."

"About my buttered spine?"

"Yes. Just remember the funny things. Or at least the hopeful things." I tried to remember Jillian's laugh. "Both of them can help you."

He grasped the halberd. "And help me do what?"

I couldn't say they might help him stay good. I couldn't suggest how hope can grant a laughing faith. I couldn't even hint at how it may help him face fear. "If you can list them—the hopeful and the humorous—they can help you influence your brethren." There. This was a perfect goal for someone in the Church of Radiant Might.

Garfield told me to go to sleep. Influence, in fact, was where the Church and I agreed. When the time comes, I'll want Garfield to persuade as many people as he can.

chapter 8

VISITATION

part ONE

Jillian once told me how, in terms of her intrepid work for the Church, a building's secrets are relatively simple in themselves. It's the people, she said, who have an architecture far more devious. All of us are occult. At first I thought Jillian meant to warn me, of treachery, say. And it's true how a friend can show us to some part of themselves, all while they're bricking us in from behind. But it turns out the surprise can also go the other direction—as it would do with Wilm, and as I hope it goes with Garfield. And in terms of the self, it can go every which way, and occasionally at the same time.

In the barnyard, while Jillian had her arm around my shoulders, I put my arm around her waist. We didn't do this sort of thing very often, and I checked to see if she shuddered. She didn't; she just breathed with an evenness that seemed deliberate amid the tossing wind. I matched her without even trying.

In these parts, woodsmen teach people to walk the forest two or three tightly abreast, so at a distance, predators will perceive them as a single, large creature. And in the yard, that's how my aunt and I stood: one shorter than the other, but both wary and quick. We watched a man ride away on a darkness that likely attracted more darkness. And with both Teph and the darkness disappearing, my father's death began to stretch unmitigated, as the edge of a wilderness. Now a flock of rooks rose from the valley Teph had entered, and then there was nothing left to watch.

"You should get sleep," said Jillian. I didn't want to sleep. "You go. I'll do the chores."

I entered the orchard instead, and she didn't seem to mind. For all I knew, it's where she slept from time to time. I'd imitated her exactly. The thought made me move only deeper, so as to walk through her, toward something more like me, or my father. I came to a tree, and climbed without purpose. This was simply a way to keep going. And only when I sat in a branch, did I realize I was repeating the very day that Teph's departure had returned to us.

The notion made me want to jump from the tree, but somehow I couldn't. I held to the branches, as if overridden by instinct, hugging the tree as if holding my father. In my mind, I spoke to him.

This was a practice out of Treehand. I opened my eyes. The apples, withered, hung like bundles. I jumped, landed in a roll, and sprinted through the rows. Only fools ran like this, but I needed the recklessness, the way Jillian sometimes did.

I thought somebody had their arm around my neck—Jillian, maybe, because the grip was long and thin. But the grasp felt too rough, and I had no one beside me, and the thing was a black-and-white pattern in my hands, before I realized I held a snake. It lay red-ended and inert on the path, before I realized I had torn it in two.

Trembling, I felt myself for bites. I'd killed a snake. Over and over, I whispered what I'd done. From my merest effort, and without even knowing, I'd ripped the creature in half.

I'd never done any killing before, outside of eating. But this killing felt so very non-deliberate; Jillian would call it a non-deliberate descent.

"I'm sorry," I said. The snake lay with its mouth open, as separated as its own interruption. The creature's stubble of fur made it a felt climber, a venomous constrictor that drops on its prey. Most farmers shoot felt climbers from trees.

The moment made me nauseated. With my hands on my knees, I leaned my head toward the ground. But this only made my heart thud. I took account of my hands and feet, and found a part of myself keeping me company. Some part of me observed. I looked around without moving, and I listened to my breath. My heart already had returned to normal, loping along, mostly undisturbed. After killing something, I had an undisturbed heart.

It's not unheard of for a man to pull apart a snake; this is what the Observer part of myself said now. A snake's skeleton will show how fragile it is, even for a girl so much smaller than a man.

I placed a twig in the snakes's mouth, and the snake bit, from reflex. The stick maneuver is what you're supposed to do, so as not to leave the corpse as a kind of loaded spring. And because somebody had taught me this, they'd implied that snakes are sometimes killable. Farmers kill snakes. But what I'd done felt like prowess. The Observer said so.

The thought was repulsive. My aunt had claimed I was far too eager to kill, and here I gave her proof in two pieces. I pressed my ears, as if to block out any further thoughts, but the silence just amplified my undisturbed heart.

My palms were so sweaty that they smelled of metal. And for a moment, I hated the trees, how throughout my entire life, they'd reached around me like fingers. I hated how I stood among them now, as if they'd pulled me here. The reason you aren't supposed to run in the forest, is because the rashness might tempt death for something. And along the way, it might introduce you to the watchful part of yourself that is just as opportunist, just as ruthless, as any predator wanting to stay strong. I didn't see it, at the time, but from the height of old age, I can tell you that Instinct—the Observer—keeps at least one door open to Esaosh.

part TWO

Predators aside, the most prosaic reason for not running in the fields is that the rows of plantings can make it difficult to tell where you are. Two years before I was born, my father and mother purchased our orchard during winter, after its farmer and his family had died of the stuttering plague. My parents bought over twenty-four furlongs, at a fraction of the cost, and for the first few months, if my mother saw the approach of a visitor she didn't want, she would meet him while stammering.

Because the original family had died, and because the land was so vast, my parents had only an inkling of what could grow from the trees. The acreage had so very many, dormant in winter. Come spring, my parents learned they had eddlefruit, plum, and apple. My folks made good use of what they had. But when my mother died, and when my father was alone with an infant, he let some of the trees go. And never being a man to sacrifice comfort for wealth, he returned the rest of the trees to the wilderness. When I was a child, he kept me from them. They became more feral with each year; in fact, we began to call the whole of them the ferals. Over time, they called to me, testing my courage. And in a sense, I came to view them as an extension of my mother's oxcart.

I stood in their outskirts now. The trees stretched, low-slung and brambled. From the ground, rose the ferment smell of fruit that had landed in a mash. A few years ago, my father and I watched a black bear stumble into the barnyard, and sit, holding her back feet, swaying a look behind her, while our dog, Kettle, barked and snarled. The bear eventually wandered her drunken self away. Out here, the hunting scenes were probably spectacular. In fact, it's possible my snake had simply fallen after eating some marinated rodent. But this wasn't worth the thought.

Now I peered down the rows. There's a star, Pol, in the south this time of year. It's small and faint, but my father taught me to find it, even through daylight. Wilm could probably do the same. I found the star now, and oriented myself toward home.

part THREE

When I reached Jillian, she was cleaning out Teph's shed. The few times I'd been there, he had kept it immaculate, but my aunt was sweeping the floor, and she'd set up a table. "We'd never given him a table," she said. Sweat stuck strands of her hair to her temples. She was out of breath. And even while part of me still rattled from the ferals, I realized how Jillian acted as if she hoped Teph home. She wore isolation like a net.

I held to the doorjamb.

"You didn't sleep," she said. I had a thought of the snake, and I tight shut my eyes.

"That still isn't sleeping." She tweaked my elbow as she passed.

She had me dust the table, and help her move a crate. She swept under the bed, and something scraped. I took a step back, and she pulled out a wooden box that was shorter and fatter than the one for Teph's arrow. She set it on the floor, and opened the lid toward her. On the other side, lay a scatter of white string which Teph had tied into ridiculous knots, some so ornate that they looked like flowers. Jillian laughed into the back of her hand.

"At least it isn't poetry," I said. Jillian, the intrepid, giggled.

I realized, then, that she still needed me to stand with her while we fought to keep our breath even; I couldn't tell her about the snake today.

"You could practice on these," she said. "Undo those five, and they'd arrest you for larceny just to save time."

"I think he meant them for you."

"Well," she stood, and her knee creaked, "he thought you the scholar and me the thief."

"They say the two have things in common." But I liked how she'd made a distinction.

"Gaelle." She shut the box, and pressed her finger on its lid. "We have to start teaching you things."

Here we'd reached Wilm's very prediction, of Jillian alone and raising me.

"You've been asking to learn things," she said.

"I know."

"And with Teph, and your father, and Lucinda—"

"I'm an outlaw."

"Honestly, given the way of life, I don't know if you could have remained a non-outlaw." She set down the broom, and a beetle fled the bristles.

"You said my father followed the law, most of the time."

"No, I said your father tried." She carried the beetle to the door. "By associating with the family, your father was absolutely an outlaw."

"You mean by associating with you?"

"No."

"I meant no offense."

"No. Not that." The wind brushed the barn, and I realized the air here still smelled of pipe smoke. "All right," she said. "Maybe this is where we start."

"Start where?"

She placed the beetle on the ground, and stepped outside. "Actually, I'm going to take you there."

After these months, I expected Jillian to bring me to a Treehanded idol, or a pile of narcotic petal ash, or a churchman tied up by his britches. From the barnyard, she glanced back at our cottage, as if she'd leave it all behind. Then, horribly, she led me back to the orchards from where I came.

As we walked, I feared we would go in the direction of the snake, that we'd find it in its two pieces, or worse, find half of it gone. Then Jillian hooked us left and away, winding us deeper and more easterly into the ferals, until she pointed to a gleam in the trees. It sat low to the ground. The shine stayed constant; whatever caused it kept either stationary or heading right for us. Jillian moved us along, and I discovered the gleam came from a box, barn-shaped, made of glass. The thing held something green inside.

I had seen little glass in my life. We had some on the house's two windows, but it was bleary and uneven. From where I stood, this box's glass appeared as clear as thin ice.

Jillian nudged me toward a glassed-in bush.

"Esaosh," I said.

She chuckled. "Absolutely not."

The box came up to my shoulders, and the shrub came up to my waist. The plant had rough bark, and even this deep in autumn, it had long, oval leaves. The branches held clusters of green pods, each the size and shape of a horse's eye. One had split, and revealed a line of brown.

Finally, I considered Lucinda, Treehand, and the plants. I scrabbled to a tree.

"Gaelle!"

"You have a Treehanded plant."

"What?" She followed my gaze. "No. Not hardly." Maybe little snakes would hatch from its pods. "Gaelle." The plant looked back. "Listen." She gave me a little shake. She squared my shoulders, the way she'd taught me to hit Wilm's fence post. "Your mother and I." She capped my shoulders with her palms. Then she let go, as if she couldn't keep them there. "Your mother and I have another sister."

I felt a stab of adrenaline, not unlike what I'd felt with the snake. My heart pounded. It kept time.

"You mean," I said, "my father had a sister."

"No. Your mother." She took a step back. "She had two."

Jillian never lied, but she parceled the truth in such a way as to frame it. Throughout my adulthood, I'd do the same. But in those later years, I tried to remember how such delivery amounted to a trick. Now in front of the plant box, I felt nearly fed to the truth.

"My mother," I said, "did not have another sister."

"Yes. We did."

Jillian grasped her elbows, the way she'd palmed my shoulders. Then she raised her arms to her sides, part ways, as if they filled with air.

She dropped her hands.

I sat on the ground, as if Jillian had directed me there. But I couldn't get up. I felt splayed, if not torn in half.

"This. Here," she was saying. "This is a hot box. A greenhouse." Her hand shook while she touched the top. "It grows the almond plant."

Had, she'd said of them having this sister. *Did*. The box was a memorial.

I punched the ground, and Jillian jumped.

"She's dead," I said.

"All right," said Jillian. All the people in my family were dead.

"So she is, in fact, dead?" I said.

Jillian's mouth looked soft. She nodded.

I shot to standing. "You kept another aunt from me?"

"And I'm telling you now."

I'd later learn that Jillian kept two.

But now I couldn't speak. It was as if, in response to some partial drowning, my throat had narrowed.

Jillian said, "She was—"

"Don't talk to me."

"All right."

Jillian walked a little circle around the greenhouse. I squatted, and put my fists to my eyes. The ferals could hold any number of things Jillian had deposited, according to her own architecture.

"Gaelle. Please. I need you to listen."

I shouted at the trees. "Why should I listen?"

"We were going to tell you."

"We?" I snatched two handfuls of grass. "So my father knew?"

"The box is old, but it was never a secret."

"That's Esaosh's fat pock."

"It was never a secret, but it was something to work up to," she sort of flapped, "to prepare you so—"

"Prepare with what? My father's death?"

"Sit." She pointed to the ground.

She hunched the way she'd done when, in Wilm's pasture, she thought Teph had blackmailed her. I sat.

Jillian leaned on the box. For all I know, she consulted her reflection. I wondered what this dead sister would think: how she'd take in all this secrecy while a horse killed her brother-in-law and her niece tore apart reptiles in the woods.

Jillian told me my father helped to build the greenhouse. She unfastened a latch I hadn't noticed on the box's side. The lid opened without a sound. It released dampness and warmth, and the aroma of green, and wood, and something like cherries.

"Gaelle, I am telling you as much as I can right now." In hindsight, she probably was. "When you live this life, and especially the life of an outlaw, and especially the life of an outlaw in this family," she spoke to the trees, as if she litigated. "You have to understand that information is a weapon. And you don't give a weapon to a child."

"I am not a child—"

"You are all of fifteen, when much of the world lives a century, at least."

She once compared my age to a bottle of wine. "So which alcohol's maturity did this aunt reach?"

I regretted saying it as soon as I did. I'd been trying to show my maturity by showing how deeply I could cut.

Jillian had spread her hand over the open top of the box, as if she warmed herself at a fire. "You know, I come here to calm down. And I ask help being patient when you say your things. But this time," she pinched a dead almond leaf, "I think the person you insulted is her." I'd forgotten how few people could cut as deeply as Jillian. "Maybe this isn't my affair," she said.

"All of this is your affair." But I didn't know half of what I meant.

Jillian tossed the dead leaf, and for a moment, she looked to leave me too. "Information is a weapon, Gaelle. Information can kill you, if you don't know how to wield it, how to keep it."

"Nobody has died for anything I know."

"And how fortunate for you."

I remembered her tattoo just above the aureole. Even when my father was alive, she'd stand on our hill sometimes, watching for messengers from the Church.

"You mean the Church kills people," I said.

"I mean the Church killed your other aunt. Yes." She closed the box.

Here may have been the very reason my family hadn't yet shown me the grave. This box held a stack of information. "The Church killed this aunt because of what she knew?"

"And because they didn't like what she said."

"So, what did she say?"

Jillian looked to the plant, as if to read it. "What I can tell you is that she claimed how different events have impacts that go farther than their immediate circumstances."

"What do you mean 'farther'?"

"I mean the consequences can be unknowable."

The notion gave heft to Jillian's excoriations to avoid violence. "Well, that's just history."

"So there you are."

I didn't feel I was anywhere.

"Furthermore," said Jillian, "she claimed the Church doesn't have divine authority."

"Well, it doesn't have divine authority."

Jillian shrugged.

At the time, I figured that if my family didn't know what divinity was, at least we all reckoned how the Church didn't either. "So," I said, "does this mean she'd been part of the Church?"

"No."

"So she just baited the Church, from the outside?"

"Gaelle, you don't have to bait the Church, either from inside or out. This is a critical point you have to remember. They're adept at making their own reality."

"What, so they just hunted her? For what she said?"

"Yes. They do that." Especially if the speaker is a woman. "But I admit, in this case, Miriamne was conspicuous."

"Miriamne."

"You haven't asked her name."

This was true. "Miriamne of Ludington?"

Jillian sighed. "Miriamne of the Book."

"Which book?"

"Every book. And she wasn't supposed to have them."

Teph's book still sat on my bed. "Teph said they weren't illegal."

"They aren't illegal. But if you learn badly in the eyes of the Church, they can keep you from reading."

I started to imagine how the Church would prevent such a thing.

"Of course," said Jillian, "after Miriamne's arrest, all she did was keep reading. And then she started writing books. And when she couldn't write them anymore, she began to dictate the books."

"To whom?"

"To friends, family." She pulled at her braid.

"Then how did they stop her?"

"I just told you they caught her."

"But if she kept going, then they must have let her out."

"Well, they didn't really kill her all at once."

They didn't. Mutilation, such as the amputation of the upper lip, was a warning to both the heretic and anyone who might listen to them.

In the clearing, the wind picked up. We'd get snow any day now. This box had an eloquent reversal, with its green in the winter and white in the spring. So much of my family had found memorial in plants.

"Was she like you," I said, "or was she more like my mom?"

"Miriamne? Me." That somehow brought relief. "You have more of your aunts in you than you have of your mother." That somehow stung.

"That's more than what I asked."

"Like me, you have the temper of a peat badger. And like Miriamne, you have a propensity for obtuse defiance."

I stood up.

"Gaelle, you can be angry."

"That's good."

"But don't ever make me honor you with a box."

They say mothers become aware of how they both birth their children and set them on the road to death. Through my century and a third, I have never become a mother, except in how I've started to woo Garfield. And although it's a pale version of what she gave me, such motherhood is the same sort Jillian embodied at our farm. It's a kind that birthed a person toward the good fight, while also sending them to face death at the very hands of the world they tried to save. This power to set somebody on that path—it will strip you of your sleep. It'll leave you reaching for a bird in your hanging cell, while you wonder if he's some sending from all the fighters you reared and lost. Or this power might leave you missing your sisters, as you try to raise your niece, while you steal a moment to hold your face over the warmth of an almond box.

I didn't speak for a while, after Jillian forbade me from making her mourn me. She'd stepped away, as if she'd left a little marker with what she'd said. I shuddered. Then I remembered when she shuddered, and then something made sense. "They thought," I said, "they charged Miriamne with using magic."

Jillian gave the almond bush a glance. Mage Miriamne.

She said, "What you did receive from your mother was her intellect."

"You mean I'm right."

"Yes, Gaelle. That's what I mean."

"Then who killed her?"

"I said the Church—"

"But which people?"

"Too many to name."

"Then maybe you tell me the worst ones."

"Why? So you can kill them?" I willed myself from thinking of the snake. "Gaelle, they kill people every single day."

"Not our people."

"Yes." She wheeled on me. "Our people. Our friends. Our allies. Good people. They kill one another, for God's sake."

"They don't kill our family every day."

"But only because there's so little left of it."

She made to hug herself, and stopped. In this clearing, she'd begun to show me how much she had lost.

"Miriamne and I," she said. "We gathered things. Objects. Knowledge."

"Did she cast magic?"

"What? No. It takes very little to convince the Church that somebody casts magic. I thought I'd shown you this." Such as she did with my dominos. "Now your mother was someone who could recognize, among all our collections, the things that were most good."

"But—"

"Your mother was for peace. She didn't directly speak against the Church, and she didn't kill. She was like your father this way."

Maybe she would not have wished to end Lucinda.

"And your mother wasn't perfect," said Jillian. "But Miriamne." She let herself smile. "Miriamne would come to the cottage, and Barbara was pregnant with you, and Miriamne would dictate what she thought, and your mother would write only the things she'd agree with." She let herself smile some more, as if it came with her letting herself say these names.

"She dictated to my mother?"

"She did." She rubbed a scar on her forearm. "Miriamne had gotten so she'd lost a hand and both eyes."

I thought of an eyeless, one-handed woman gesturing in our house.

I said, "So my mother was a heretic?"

"Oh absolutely." She tossed an old eddlefruit. "Barbara the baby. Sweet and unassuming."

"It was an act?"

"The sweetness? No. It was kindness, thoroughly." She gave me a look of affection that might not have been for me. "No. With what Barbara sensed, I think she was the most natural heretic of us all."

I'd often imagined my mother pregnant with me, of how she and my father spoke to me while they sat on their bed. Now I considered a tall woman with a loud voice, telling my mother every manner of thing, while my mother refined it, and I grew. It began to settle, this comparison Jillian had made.

Now she told me I'd never met Miriamne, how she died a few months before I was born. Jillian knew the exact dates, both her death day and my birthday, which, of course, was another sister's death day too.

In the clearing, I rubbed my forehead. My hand smelled of apple mash. Jillian had lost one sister, and then the next, with only a season between. The trees stood around us as students.

Jillian was talking about how almond was Miriamne's favorite plant, and that Miriamne had a friend who was an herbalist. Almonds grow only in Bakeet, said Jillian, along their liquid coast. But you could force bloom an almond plant, almost anywhere, even in winter.

"Gaelle," she was saying. I had drifted from the conversation. "The bloom. It's true. I'll show you." She'd cut off a twig that had five, tight buds. Then she told me to shut the box, and she led us home.

At the cottage, she warmed water in the cook pot, poured the liquid into a shallow pan, and laid the twig inside. She told me to wait.

She left me with the pan, while she finished in the shed. The cold rolled in from beneath the cottage's door. I looked around, stood beside the plant, and waited for it to lengthen, or to become something other than a twig. Maybe this was magic. Or maybe I'd been set up for a joke.

After a while, I sat by the fire. It was only early afternoon, but I wanted to sleep. The day had given me too much to absorb, mashed in a ball. I closed my eyes, and the ball turned to snakes.

I opened my eyes, and I wiped them. It hadn't been decent to tear the snake. Nor would it have been decent to kill Lucinda. One day, killing the horse might be necessary, but in a sense, that would just add to the pity. This is what my gut told me, from a place somewhat deeper than instinct. And if I was canny, like my mother, this truth is what I knew.

If I was canny, like my mother, and if my mother both recognized goodness and worked to spread at least some heresy—if, in fact, she was the biggest heretic—it must follow that some heresy was good. I'd always held this opinion, probably, but thinking these things would be the second time in three months when I'd knowingly committed a crime.

My father's death was the first occasion of that crime. My mother must have recognized him as good. And having allowed Jillian to help raise me, my father must have believed Jillian was good. And all of this suggested how when he died, and when Jillian let me decide whether to follow Church decree or become an outlaw, she was letting me choose at least a partial stance about what I thought was good. When, in Wilm Pasture, I was deciding what to do about Wilm and Lucinda, I had used the name of Esaosh. I'd meant it as a curse, but Jillian had said Esaosh might help me there. When she kept secret the heresies of my aunt and my father and my mother, she was actually offering something. Even at fifteen, if I was calm enough, I could accept that she was. Such secrecy was a way she tried to give me freedom about who I'd be in relation to everyone. And if I had chosen the Church's side, I don't know what we would have done.

In our cottage, the almond soaked in its pan, smooth as if the sprig still waited under glass. I sat at the head of the table, in our small room, and I imagined it crowded with family. "We are all heretics," I said. We were. And whether Jillian foresaw it or not, I would further learn how Miriamne was indeed also a mage.

My aunt, in the late afternoon, pushed through the door with a load of firewood. She chattered and stomped in front of the fireplace. She stuffed it tight with pine, which burns hotter and sappier than what we usually chose. You really shouldn't burn pine in a chimney; the creosote builds too fast. Jillian must have walked a ways to get the wood.

I took off my top shirt, and asked to open the door. Jillian said no. She removed the twig from the water, and set it in a cup by our places at table. Then she told me to sit while she fixed us supper.

The twig began to bloom.

My aunt was rummaging our oddments chest. I touched her shoulder, and she stepped beside me.

"That's why she loved them." She straightened the twig. "Nothing force blooms as fast as almonds."

I touched the petals and I loved their newness. They did look like magic. "Miriamne must have gotten along with my dad."

Jillian laughed. "They didn't talk much, really. But they knew they loved the same folk."

Jillian fetched us the supper, and we sat at the table with Miriamne's blossoms before us. With this plant, Jillian had managed to keep friends around for another night.

My father's chair sat empty, as it had for months. It had a layer of dust and three fingerprints from someone who may, or may not, have been paying attention. We had buried him next to my mother, on top of our nearest hill.

As she ate, Jillian described how in the springtime, for about a week, the almond bush blooms white. And when you're around it, you can believe there is snow inside its glass.

"When is Miriamne's birthday?" I said.

"In Altarib."

"There can be snow in Altarib." To this day, in an early blizzard, I think of Miriamne.

Slowly, almost as if she snuck, Jillian grasped my hand.

"Did she want it," I said, "her almond memorial?"

"Actually," she sucked some soup off her finger, "that idea came from your mom."

Something of Jillian's noise chaffed.

"And what of my mother's memorial?" I said.

Jillian tightened her hold on my hand.

"Or my father?" I said. "What about his?"

She finished chewing. "That memorial is you."

This was true. But part of me hated how Jillian knew my family better than I.

We ate. Then Jillian said, "So we'll start tomorrow."

"Start what?"

"The teaching." She crossed to the stairs. "We'll plot all the things you need to learn, if you're going to live as an outlaw."

Or a heretic. That's the word she should have used.

She started up the stairs. "Thank you for holding your temper today."

"I didn't hold it much."

"I know it isn't easy. Good sleep."

"It isn't even dark."

"Well," she pulled at a knot on her tunic, and I thought of Teph, "I didn't sleep much last night either." She finished climbing, and shut her door.

I turned to where the almond branch leaned in its cup, solitary as light.

Now that I was alone, something in me trembled, as if I would laugh, or maybe cry. Jillian moved up above, with heavy steps. Unless she was sneaking, her steps were always heavy. If you only heard Jillian, you'd think she was a hulk of a man. And even after all this time, to hear those thuds, and then to see her descend as small as she was: it was as if she was bigger when we weren't watching.

Everything was bigger. Everything opened with a death, the alphabet, and the drop of a snake.

That evening, I stayed with the almond branch. Jillian said it would open only for a few hours, and tired as I was, I felt I should sit vigil. The sprig was like a window appearing where I hadn't even noticed a wall. Somebody moved inside of it—an image smeared, barely a form—perhaps becoming as big as my aunt could sound. We all seemed so perilously large. When darkness fell, I stuck my head out the cottage's door. I sneezed in the cold, and I thought of Wilm. The night was clear, and it showed the stars coming to meet us.

part FOUR

The first part of what Jillian taught was cosmology. This was both a surprise and a disappointment. Equally so was the fact that Jillian didn't see reason to postpone our chores. We stood with our ladder and our baskets, in the eddle orchard, while she echoed Church teachings and I checked the fruit for worms.

Jillian told me how Esaosh had supposedly lived in the courts of the chief deity, Jaes, until Jaes' son, Visjaes, provoked Jaes to join him in a plot against Esaosh. To avoid war, Esaosh took us, his people, to this world, and established Celd.

"I know all this," I said.

And I knew how Visjaes had found Celd, and waged the destruction called the Bale, and how Esaosh and at least some of the Princes drove Visjaes away.

"And they kept chasing him," said Jillian.

"And they kept chasing him," I said. A worm curled around my knife, and I uncoiled it into the worm sac. We would sell them at market as boar bait.

"The important thing," said Jillian, "is that the Church still waits for the end of the chase."

"But we don't," I said, "because it's all buzzard grease."

"Maybe." In fact, it wasn't all so greasy. "But if it's important to your enemy, then it's important to you."

It was strange to think how a people I hated got to choose what I cared about.

"So," I said, "the Church really is an enemy."

From her ladder, Jillian gave a big, slow nod. "And it waits, as I said, for either the return of its savior, or the return of Visjaes, who is the savior's enemy."

These names meant nothing to me. What mattered was the mindless, or the garrison, or Lucinda

"Wait," I said. "They think Visjaes could get past Esaosh, or even defeat Esaosh?"

Jillian spoke from inside the eddle branches. "If they were honest about it, they'd admit the fear itself walks the line between faith and heresy." She shook the branches, and four eddlefruit fell. "Esaosh is supposed to be the god of radiant clarity and strength, and yet he can apparently become hoodwinked and rendered fairly weak."

The eddlefruit bobbed around us as some bruised and wormy galaxy. "You'd think that if they invented a god, they'd make him a little smarter."

"All through history," said Jillian, "the Church has both wielded, and been wielded by, fear." But, she said, this anxiety has made the Church pay almost a fetishist's attention to those who might cause this fear. "Suspected sorcerers, necromancers—"

"But those don't exist. Not really."

"Well, go ask Teph if necromancers don't exist."

The wind blew cold enough to made me want to hide my hands. "You said that magic is a myth."

"No, I don't think I ever did." She hadn't. She'd parceled. Now she wiped a piece of worm from her knife. "Gaelle, I don't know everything alive in the world. I hope I never do. Then again, I have decided belief is real—and how in many ways, this is all that matters."

"But still there are facts," I said.

"And they matter all the more, in terms of absolute truth. But we live under a Church that seeks to regulate truth."

"And they're also the ones who say that magic is real."

"And in doing so, they try to claim what magic is."

"Right." I stood at the bottom of her ladder. "So what is it? What's magic?" Jillian didn't know about the Church's summoning circles and the bargains of plutomancy, at least not consciously. Back then, maybe two people knew.

She sat at the top of the ladder, as if I'd treed her. She put her hands on her knees. "From what I've seen in manuscripts and murals, magic centers on getting the world to behave in ways it normally does not."

"What, like prayer?"

"Maybe. But prayer mostly asks an indulgence, while magic tries to impel an exception. And this sort of forcing of the rules can never end well."

This stance might have been as religious as Jillian ever got. She figured that if nothing else, reality deserved respect.

"So," I said, "magic is bad?"

"It's ethically arrogant and practically foolish." She tossed a flattened bird nest. "And if you're risking the way the world works just so you can get what you want—"

"You've put yourself at the center of the world." I've since learned how most mages do such a thing. The Church certainly does.

"Anyway." Jillian climbed down the ladder. "I should admit I haven't seen any actual magic."

"Oh. Then—"

"I've seen signs of rituals, old attempts to compel. But it's mostly quite ancient."

If magic remained so moot, I couldn't see why she was wasting our time. I helped her pick dead catkins from her shoulders. The pods made me think of my father telling his story about Treehand. And Treehand made me think of the mindless.

"The mindless," I said.

"Yes. Good. Necromancy is rudimentary—less art than craft." It uses tools instead of secrets, she said, recipes instead of leaps. "It doesn't really raise the dead. It just moves them around." Apparently she found this comforting. "In general, necromancy is part agriculture, part slavery—"

"Plantationism." Golem farming. "Teph used that word."

"Yes." She stood akimbo. "It's technique anyway. Magic, but baby stuff." She wiped eddle mash from her boot. "It's blasphemy against what death should be, but I think it's less individualistic." I couldn't imagine a world where mindless making was baby stuff. "It's malignant, certainly."

"I'd say *very*."

"But it doesn't invite self-deification."

The wind pushed through the orchard that my father had reared. I could barely accept that we harvested the fruit he'd grown, while we talked about different stripes of sorcery. "So my father knew about magic?"

"He'd heard me talk about it."

"And Wilm?" All of a quick, Wilm seemed wiser.

"Wilm knows about the mindless, of course, but I don't know what else." Even now it's hard to say what the stars were telling Wilm.

"And the Church hates necromancy," I said, "even if it is a baby magic."

"The Church hates anything that gives the peasantry power." She examined a hail-pitted fruit. "The mindless are powerful. And so are the people who can argue against the Church itself." She stood with her bruised fruit. "Thus went Miriamne."

"Mage Miriamne."

Jillian cut the fruit, and the juice ran pink in her hands. "You can see how calling someone a mage would invite terror and infamy."

At some point when they were together, Miriamne must have put her hand on my pregnant mother. Maybe she had told me something, and maybe it was so true that my mother let her.

Jillian smelled the fruit.

"So," I said, "we define magic the same way as the Church?"

"In theory." We all agree magic manipulates. "In theory, we each agree how real magic tempts the unforeseen."

"Those are Miriamne's consequences. What she talked about."

Jillian wrapped her hands around what remained of the fruit, and it disappeared completely.

"Miriamne critiqued the Church," I said. "Was she aiming her consequence bit at them?"

"She aimed most of her anger at them."

"Jillian. Does the Church cast magic?"

"Now, remember that, as I'm their intrepid, the Church sends me into their own ruins."

"And those are where you saw the magic traces?" When Jillian parted her fingers, the glimpse of the eddlefruit looked like a wound. "Jillian."

"I think the Church excuses itself of its own exceptionalism."

"So the Church does cast magic?"

"Or at least they try. More likely, they try."

"And they make you help them? They have you do their research?"

"I figure they don't know what they'll find in old ruins. So they send in the convict." She dropped the eddlefruit's rind, and I expected my orchard snake to crawl out.

"So what did you find?"

"No grimoires, if that's what you're asking." She gave me a look as if to dare me to guess what a grimoire is. "Mostly, I give them trinkets. Maybe if I can pad the Church's coffers, they won't tax the hides off the peasantry."

"Fine." Her evasiveness sounded like her exact kind of parceling. "But you said you have seen signs of magic."

"Depravity. Destruction." She handed me a worm for the sac. "A whole underground courtyard covered in grease that was once people's fat." She tossed an eddlefruit. "Is this what you want me to tell you?"

"God, no."

She softened her face, and straightened the collar of my tunic. "It's actually what I tell them. And it is the truth." With one finger, she patted my collarbone. "I want to see that expression—the fear, the disgust you showed—when it alights on them." It must have relieved her when she did, and she probably saw it often. But then, there must have been times when she didn't. "Gaelle, you should know I tell them I've seen signs of demons."

Demon was a term the Church used for Visjaes and his followers. "That's all right," I said. "You used the Church's word against them." Such a tactic sounded something like what she would do. It sounded more like her than any other possibility attached to the word.

She moved her eyes, but she stood still. And again, it seemed she was counting. "It's true," she said, "the Church uses demons, or the threat of demons, to exert its control." She described how the one thing a dictatorship needs first is to convince its people how the people have a problem. The second thing it needs is to convince its people how only the dictatorship can solve the problem. And then it needs to locate other people who personify the problem. Heretics, and sorcerers, and those with either peculiar or ardent passions: they become that personification. And so do demons who can, conveniently, possess anyone—and who also, conveniently, possess mostly women. "Demons, you cotton, help the Church keep its power."

"Well, the Church is all about power," I said.

She dropped her knife. "And one could argue how power itself is a demon."

Maybe Miriamne had argued as much.

"But," I said, "there are no actual demons."

"Gaelle, I don't know." She knelt before me, to pick up her knife. I didn't like her peering up at me, with her open face, with all that honesty. She could tell me about dead sisters and undead crafts, but I could not accept her talk of demons. While she stood, I turned my back to her. The side of the worm sac moved with what it held.

I said, "What did Miriamne think?"

"Miriamne believed in demons." That made my neck feel tight. "But I think she decided most of them were off somewhere else. Or maybe they were otherwise occupied, or at least not worth looking for."

"Off fighting Esaosh's Princes?"

"Hard to say." Jillian had moved to the weeds along the backside of the eddletree she'd climbed. "Our Miriamne believed in some very far reaches." She returned with a snake skin, and I took a step back. "I thought I saw this from up there." She held it out, and it lifted in the breeze. "Gaelle." She dropped the skin. "You can't be afraid of demons."

"I'm not."

"If they exist, they are likely much different from what we expect—because this is probably how everything will turn out to be."

"Except we figure they like people's fat."

"All right. Maybe. But that, whatever it was, happened long ago." Maybe demons, like snakes, shed their skin. "And the fat's discovery shocked even the Church."

There is, in fact, great hope in what Jillian said. Lots of men who grow up in the Church devote themselves to fighting evil. My dear Patrick, our church father, certainly had. Such courage isn't so hard to find. The difference is that when Patrick saw where the demons actually were, he had the humility to keep fighting them. Such humbleness is scarcer than courage, especially among his old brethren. Still, it can be taught.

Jillian and I moved to another tree, working in silence for a while, as if it took a moment for all we'd said to follow us. The wind rustled the snakeskin in the grass, and I kept track of its rising as if it were a ghost.

"So," I said, "are there supposed to be any hereabouts? These demons?"

"Other than the ones who apparently infest the designated heretics? No." The snakeskin tumbled. "The Church is very fortunate in how, for some reason, demons don't afflict its most well-behaved provinces."

"So they're in Azmon and Treehand, with the mindless and the weeds."

"And actually, there's one in southern Cadmus." This one was closer to home. "You've heard of the Reaching Man."

In that instant, I felt as if something watched my back. This was not the first time I'd heard his name—this iteration of Visjaes, this aspect of who would become my god. When I was little, way before Jillian, a girl came with her peddler father from town. She taught me the rhyme about the Reaching Man, as we stood in the fields, taunting both the sunset and each other.

> *The Reaching Man searches, the Reaching Man sees*
> *The children of Cadmus, on their mothers' knees.*
> *He comes to their cradles, and plucks out their breath*
> *And leaves them unblemished by all save their death.*

Jillian now said how although it primarily wanders Cadmus, people tell stories of the Reaching Man all over the world. Enough infants die suddenly in their sleep, that the demon keeps considerable power. All these years later, the boy, Garfield, might even know the peddler-girl's chant. The Reaching Man connects with death, I suppose. And though he is a facet of my god, and though I am old enough to prepare to meet my god, I do not want to meet him.

Jillian grunted, as we hauled the fruit into the cart. "You have to admit he's a good metaphor."

"What?" I said. "The Reaching Man?"

"Here's a demon that snatches a life at the beginning of its potential. I mean, it's a parent's worst nightmare, the very worst." Worse, even, than honoring me with a box. "Then on top of everything, you have the myth of Visjaes retold—his committing the Bale against the world once it had just established its infant empire, his taking Esaosh and the Princes away."

"So the Reaching Man is an aspect of Visjaes," I said.

"Well, all demons are," she said, "but the Reaching Man is a chief aspect, yes."

She told me about Limdul the Marchman, who gathers lost pilgrims, and turns them into a field of howling grass. She talked about Babath, who poses as salted meat in roadside way-stations, and flies back together as it attacks a visitor. And she said how villages daring to host necromancers also tempt the bone wagons, which are the settlement's own houses whose beams ossify from the inside out. The buildings barrel off, with their inhabitants locked inside. Jillian looked down from the wagon seat to where I'd gathered our worm knives. "And I'm sure the Treehanded have demons, and any blasted people in the heart of blasted Merrial have demons." She spat an eddle seed. "Wherever there's death, or something to protect, there's going to be a demon."

"Shit," I said.

She laughed. "Is that disbelief or dismay?"

I didn't know which. I clutched the knives, just like Teph. In hindsight, I should have asked Jillian if there were angels too. Then again, I'm not sure if she'd ever heard the term.

"The demons are mostly myth, Gaelle. But as myth, they do motivate." I grasped the cart's seat. "They make people suspicious. They let people focus on some distraction to hate, instead of spending their energy on what really is at issue."

"Such as the tyranny of the Church," I said.

"Yes."

"Or the spread of the Treehanded plant."

"Now we don't know enough about the plants yet." She started the cart. "But you see it now? How raising the alarm could be a bad idea?" An eddle-fruit rolled in the wagon-bed. "And it's especially bad if it plays to people's prejudice."

The cart bounced, and I let it loll my head. I imagined the snakeskin rolling around in the wagon-bed, too.

The sun still held high, and it streaked its rays through the eddle branches and the wind's dust. We passed our old, ruined storage barn, and the holes in the roof looked as if light had knocked them clean. I should have thought on this—of the heft of light on a day I learned of magic and demons.

"So what about Star Fall?" I said.

Jillian gave me a sidelong look, as if I'd just used bad language. "Wilm tell you about that?"

"Well, I'm glad somebody did."

"It's Church teaching."

Maybe that was why she'd never mentioned it. "So it's a lie?"

"No. It's the end of the world, and I'm sure one will come." She let the reins vibrate against the seat.

"So the stars are coming? Like the Church says?"

"I don't think anything will happen like the Church says."

I huffed. "The stars are collapsing?"

"It's what the sages say." She pointed to a pheasant. "And not just the Church sages." Back then, it was hard to imagine Wilm as a sage. "But, Gaelle, it's so far off that you might as well worry when the mainland will break into islands."

"Wait. It'll do that?"

She laughed, and I wanted to stand with indignation. "Gaelle. It does so over thousands of years. You don't know this?" It wasn't my fault I was ignorant. "A little piece of us breaks off." I thought of Wilm's pasture floating away. "If you ask me, it isn't such a tragedy."

"Then the world will end?"

"Well, yes, Gaelle. I mean, everything does."

I thought of my parents floating away, and then exploding into light, of myself doing the same, of the snake.

"And do you think," maybe I asked on behalf of everyone. "Do you think that'll just be it?"

She turned to me. A branch had scratched her face. "You're asking if I think there is life after death."

"Sure."

She gave a long inhale. "The Church would say this is up to Esaosh."

"Esaosh, who can't find his way home?"

"That's the one." It was insulting to think how anyone's continuance would depend on such a thing. "Now Miriamne would say it's a definite yes." Miriamne, who might have coped with this world by looking away from it. "Miriamne spent a lot of her life trying to learn something, anything, about what comes next."

"So was she that unhappy?"

Jillian watched a red squirrel with his nut. "She was both the happiest and saddest of us all."

"Was that because she knew things?"

"Well, we all know things."

"Jillian, don't be cryptic."

"Fine." She closed her eyes, and looked toward the sun. "She just rarely seemed at home."

I now realize Miriamne was a mystic, and that she searched for what was beyond Celd, because some intuition made her feel confined to Celd. And it follows, really, how someone who wrote opposite the Church didn't want to live in the kingdom of the Church's god.

In the cart, Miriamne felt almost as mythical as magic itself. "So what do you think?" I said. "About where we go."

Jillian hunched a bit, in the same cart that had carried my father. "I just know it isn't up to me." She spoke toward her knees, and I could barely hear. "And I figure I'll take what I can get." She turned to me with a forced kind of brightness.

"You don't believe in an afterlife."

"Not Esaosh's afterlife, no."

"And what about Miriamne's afterlife?"

"You know I'm a fan of protective pessimism."

"But not cynicism."

She chuckled, and poked my thigh, as if to give me a point. "I think,

Gaelle, that if there ever were a paradise, then the first part of it would be for us to have the power to make amends, for every single regret."

She gave a pat where she'd poked me, and she looked away, as if she'd somehow pushed off from the conversation. She was right, though. At all of fifteen, I knew she was right. And after what has aged me, and after what I learned of what aged her, I figure you can't have any kind of rest until the gift of amends.

I looked at her on our way home: the notch in the rim of her left ear; the bump at her hairline, the sweat streaks along her neck that touched a pock mark she may have received in a hideout, or a ship's hull, or a prison. Sometimes, when I watched my aunt, I felt I'd come upon a kind of forced march. Now a white spider ambled the toe of her boot. She told me I should work on reading Teph's book, how it would give me the rudiments of this world. It puzzled me, at first, why nobody had taught me these things before. But academics tend to slide away when you try to survive, when you need to find someone to help you raise your child, when there's food to grow, and when the Church can pounce on what you know the way a snake can drop from a tree. I remembered the fright I'd felt from the ferals' viper, and the power, and the creature's inertness, and the Observer telling me not to be altogether displeased. The Observer would not make room for amends.

When we got to the farm, we released Godiva into her old pen. She nuzzled me, and I pressed my forehead to hers. Jillian put the worm sacs next to the bushel bags reserved for market. I imagined the creatures in their mass, dividing and sprouting hair. The idea made me feel a little sick, so I hung my head, breathing through my mouth.

"Yesterday," I said, "I tore apart a snake."

I'd said it, while Jillian stood on the cottage's step. I meant to say it just to myself, but it leapt out of me, like a ghost.

I couldn't look at Jillian. I could speak only to Godiva, and then in a kind of push, about my running and the felt climber and its drop on my shoulders. Now I looked at my hands, and at how they weren't big enough to reach around an eddlefruit.

Jillian had folded hers. I watched them from the corner of my eye, the way I'd watched the spider on her boot. She said, "You weren't supposed to run."

"I know."

"The snake has stopped existing."

"Jillian, I know."

"You could have stopped existing. That would have been a thousand times worse."

"Well, I was afraid."

"Yes, Gaelle. You'll likely spend your whole life afraid."

"That's not true."

She raised her arms and looked to the sky. "It's how we live."

Not existing did not jibe with an afterlife.

"Child," she said, "you have become so eager—"

"No. Don't." I was not eager to kill, not ever.

She was leaning on the cottage door—and she was leaning me a look that, despite all, was not so unkind.

I wanted to lie down. I figured she did too. She'd have to go inside, though, because I couldn't move until she did.

"Next time you're afraid," she said, "I want you to try to count."

I'd seen her do this. "What, like my times tables?"

"I know it sounds like something they do in the madhouse, and if you stop for a minute, maybe this will give you a clue as to why some people are there in the first place." Maybe the mad house's bones would spread from the inside, and carry them off. "Gaelle. If you count, you can slow the moment. And it's best if you count the good."

"You're teaching me something from when I was little—"

"Well, so was potty training, and we're all glad it took." She'd given a little laugh. I was glad she could joke. "Count the good. And if you can't find the good, then count the neutral. Count what you see." I counted snake pieces—one, two. "Gaelle, it sounds silly, I know. But if you count, it will keep you anchored."

I was supposed to put away the knives, but I didn't want to touch them. "And this counting will somehow keep me from killing?"

She grabbed the knives for me. "The counting will keep you from panic. You will keep yourself from killing." I vowed to myself I would. "But counting is a ritual. And rituals keep you connected to yourself."

"You make me sound like a monk."

"Well, mystics do it. There's a reason they regiment so much of their contemplation."

Maybe Wilm sat in his hut, counting his stars.

"But so do soldiers, Gaelle." The pairing felt odd. "So does anyone who needs to keep hold of themselves."

On the ground by the shed, Teph's knife-sharpening divots had turned to puddles.

"And here's another thing," she said. "And this will help you more as you learn things more." In her hands, the deworming blades looked like scissors. "You must serve something larger than you."

"I don't think I'm all that self-serve—"

"No-no. But find something you'll die for. Better yet, find something to live for." Maybe my mother had done so. "This is another thing we do."

She deposited the knives, and returned to where I stood.

"Like what then?" I said. "Like what do you live for?"

"Me?" It was a personal question, but I had just told her some personal things. "I live for truth. And I live for loved ones." From her tunic, she offered me an eddlefruit, whole and polished. "Sometimes, even, it's most helpful to count those."

"Loved ones." I took the fruit. It was warm from where she'd kept it. "And what if you don't have that many?"

She stepped into the house. "Then you just shuffle them back and forth. Like you own feet."

Jillian wasn't a bad teacher; I knew as much, back then. And now, as someone who's managed to live longer than most, I can say she was one of the best teachers I'd ever have. The technique with the counting is a mystic's trick; it's a resort for anyone who faces the awful, or the awe-full, or the sliver between the two. Such a technique is part of what I teach Garfield, as I bid him to list what's comic and hopeful. You shuffle what you name, like feet, so they might lead you home.

In the barnyard, I brought an apple to Godiva, and in a weak patch of sun, we ate our fruits together. With her nose, she butted the back of my head, and she wafted the warmth of her breath. Of loved ones, I could count her, and Jillian, and my parents, and maybe Miriamne. I felt it a duty to love Miriamne, who had never seemed at home. She was the first person I'd heard of who wanted something beyond this world, who wanted better, who believed if she plied herself hard enough, she could ascend to better. In this way, she was like Esaosh and his high-reaching Merrial stalk. And I would learn that, for reasons utterly opposite, they both sought Visjaes.

Miriamne is, in fact, mostly dead, so all I can mostly do is guess, these days. But I suspect her pursuit came largely from how she was right about the reality of demons. Centuries ago, they'd held primacy in those ruined Church vaults, nearly as much as their lord Esaosh. I don't know if even the most depraved members of the current Church realized such a thing, while they bid Jillian to perform her excavations. But soon I would end up in one of those ruins myself. And I tell you that while, in my childhood, we tried to reckon a horse and the spread of a plant, those demons excavated the Church itself. In fact, that was one of the reasons why, at the moment, Lucinda hurled Teph in the Church's very direction.

part FIVE

Before the next morning, I awoke with the certainty I was not alone in my room. I was lying on my side, facing the wall that flickered from the front room's firelight. Nothing new cast a shadow or made a sound, but something gave the heft of attention.

I wondered, at first, if I was dreaming, but my body accepted none of it, the way the body knows these things. My hands clenched, and my heart beat in my neck.

Holding to the bed, I started to deepen my breaths, to keep them as normal as they had been in my sleep. I tried to count them, but counting seemed just a way to waste time. In this position, nothing but a quilt and pillow offered protection. Even the chamber pot sat across the room. The room itself was dark enough that I could slit my eyes so I could still see under them, while no one normal would know I was looking. But to get any sort of vantage, I would have to roll over in pretend sleep.

The move took discipline, like slowly pulling a shard from a wound. And I used the fact to convince myself the watcher was Jillian, that this was one of her lessons I could pass without hassle, if I could just move myself as smoothly as thought. I turned, counting the increments in the movements as if they were waypoints. I rolled over, and saw no one. The room was small enough for the bed nearly to touch both side walls. The space between it and my clothing trunk offered no place for anything to hide, unless it was very small, and I didn't want to think about that.

I pulled a long inhale, and my eyes watered. The attention persisted.

I jumped from the bed, landing in the doorway, and the attention sharpened.

Jillian sat by the fire. I looked behind me and back again, while she sipped a cup. The window showed the orange of dawn.

Something still studied me. I'd started to tremble—and both to protect and steady myself, I put my back to the wall.

The thing was her.

"Gaelle, come by the fire."

For a horrible instant, I wondered if I should grab the bread knife on the table. Then I pressed to the wall. "You are the mage."

She coughed. "Hardly."

"You were watching."

"No."

"But you're here."

"And with tea."

I clutched my elbows. "But you know why I'm up."

"I do."

The feel of her attention had been so heavy, as if it carried the weight of how her steps sounded when she moved upstairs. She poured me some tea from the fireside pot. "You know, I can't read your mind."

"What?"

"Are you trying to think at me, or are you just thinking?" She held out the cup, and I thought of an almond pod floating at its brim.

"What the hell are you?"

"What am I?" she said. "I'm a person, if you haven't noticed. A sister. A friend."

"Tell me what you did in my room."

"I didn't do anything in your room." She moved from the hearth. "Please. Sit by the fire." She wrapped her arms around herself. "You don't have to sit by me."

The attention she'd wielded was gone, as if she'd rested it on a rack.

I shivered in the morning chill, afraid it looked like fear, afraid it might actually be fear. So although it was exactly what she asked, I crossed to the fire, and let its warmth soak into me. Jillian took a step farther off. I sat on the hearth, and something in my back started to loosen.

Jillian mentioned how my father had taught me to find the star, Pol, in daylight. She told me of the Treehanded guides who could tell the plants by their sound in the wind, and of the west-Cadmul tribesmen who can sing two notes at once. "Such abilities aren't magic," she said. "They're skills."

"Well, you were impolite with your skill."

"Dear. The problem is that I think the skill is yours." She placed my tea on the hearth. "And though I hate to tell you this, you seem particularly skilled at sensing me."

"That's absurd."

"Why?"

"Why is it absurd?"

"It's just a skill, Gaelle." She picked up the old almond sprig. "Or it's a sense, if you'd like."

This is how she introduced me to Touch. We didn't use such a term, even if by my lights, *Touch* is the best word for it. We didn't call it anything that acknowledged its intimacy. It is a deep thing, Touch. It feels exactly like what it sounds: a nudge, or a push, or a brush. The particulars depend on the emotion behind it, but in every case, it is a personal reach.

In any event, Touch is not telepathy. That first morning, Jillian told me the difference over and again, with the same vehemence she'd had when she told me the mindless wouldn't come to the farm. Touch can't send thoughts; it can send only presence. It is essentially a call and response.

"What we have," said Jillian, "is a simple connection." She pulled tighter her sleeping gown.

I hate to imagine the dismay I might have had on my face. "So you can tell, with this skill, when I'm thinking of you?"

"Well, no. You have to send it. And I have to receive it." It's a cooperative connection. "It's like a game of toss."

"Well, your Toss felt more like fetch."

"I know. It did. I'm sorry I woke you." She said that as if she'd just dropped a pot. "But I had to get your attention, and I had to do it when you weren't expecting me. And sometimes a person can toss hard enough so the other one notices, even if," she shivered, "they aren't consciously open to receiving such a thing."

"Open. I don't even know what to say."

"What I would say is how this morning's kind of toss isn't ever easy." I didn't want it to be possible. "If you aren't already open to me, it takes a great deal of effort to toss so hard. In fact, it makes the sender want to sleep."

The fire popped, and I jumped. I didn't think I would ever want to sleep.

"I'm able only to make you aware of me," she said. "But that's all I can do."

"Well, Jillian, that's a lot."

"I know. You've been handed a lot." My aunt was a private person. And when I look back, I realize it must have taken a great deal for her even to attempt to Touch with me. "Gaelle, I cannot make you answer."

"Then why did you do this?"

"All I did was try."

"All you did?"

"Yes. I tested the connection. I'll admit this much," she said. "In light of last night, I wanted to see if we had it. But please." She leaned forward with that word. "Please believe this is not an invasion."

She rarely pleaded, just as she'd never looked at me with such openness as she did when she'd knelt in the ferals. Such vulnerability made what she said about Touch as inevitable as she was—which is to say it felt so damnably true.

"We were just talking about demons," I said.

"I know. And you'd just told me of the snake."

I had. And the divulgence of Touch in relation to the snake made the snake even more sinister. "So you think you have to save me from killing?"

"Gaelle, no. No." She leaned again. "I just want you to know you aren't alone. You are never alone, unless you want to be."

In the firelight, her elbows poked sharp in her sleeves. She had lost weight since my father died.

"So who linked us?" I said.

"Nobody knows." I thought of Miriamne. "In fact, this is all very rare."

"Then why us?"

"Because," she drew her knees into her shirt, "I think we're some of the only ones left." Her loneliness. She'd confirmed it. Maybe when she'd swept the shed, she'd tried to Touch with Teph.

"Have you done this toss," I said, "with other people?"

"I have."

"Did you do it with people I know?"

"No."

"Did you—"

"In fact, this is a very good way of showing how we can have this connection, while still maintaining all privacy."

"Then can I do it with someone else?"

She looked as surprised as I felt. I couldn't imagine doing this with anybody, certainly not anyone left in the world.

"If you have it with one, you can sometimes do it with another, but such a thing gets," she flicked a dinner crumb, "exhausting. And even then," her face was blunt, "there has to be a strong, emotional connection with the receiver."

That's what it meant, then, both for us and for the people she'd previously lost. She turned to look out the window. She stayed that way, facing my opposite direction, with shadows on her cheeks.

I said, "You're wearing your nightshirt."

"And so are you."

"Yes, but you were expecting me."

She shrugged, and clutched her arms. "If I'd have dressed, you'd have felt more exposed."

She'd even left her hair loose, and no matter how early or late we were up, she'd always kept it braided. I'd seen her nude more often than I'd seen her with her hair down.

She had goosebumps.

I stepped away from the fire, and sat in the table's far chair. "I'm starting to sweat."

While she crossed to the hearth, she gave me a glance that might have been gratitude. She spread her hands to the fire, and sat.

"Gaelle, when you're afraid, you can play our game of toss. All right? It will help you to manage."

Maybe we'd both count snake parts—one, two. Or maybe we'd stand on my father's burial hill, counting horses in a churchman's team.

To convince her I had been too warm, I opened the door. The sun had risen into the clouds, and the light spread milk-silver. Near Wilm's horizon, there was a missing plume of smoke.

part SIX

Jillian and I stood outside in our nightshirts, and my knees trembled. The sky was turning the clear blue of brutal cold.

"The fool," said Jillian, "he's likely overslept." She told me to dress in my furs.

She headed for the barn, and I thought of horse herds spreading the Treehanded weeds. Then I thought of the Retrievers, and even the mindless, who followed Teph. At least the smoke was missing, instead of green. I pulled on my father's old bear-pelt breeches. Jillian had taken them in, after he'd died, and she'd had the courtesy to do it somewhere private. This morning, the breeches felt like the heaviest clothing I had ever worn, as if part of my father remained inside.

In the barnyard, Jillian handed me a dagger, whose haft was freezing. She said to use the knife as a last resort, and I noticed, gladly, that I agreed. Under a gray cloak, Jillian wore a suit of leather armor I had never seen before: a cuirass and greaves that had the boiled, auburn color of a saddle. It comprised of hand-sized pieces overlapping as scales, so Jillian resembled something between a seedpod and an insect. The armor smelled oiled. She said, "We should go."

"Where did it come from?"

She ushered me along. "I'm glad you're impressed."

When we got to the road, she took my hand—and I stopped.

She gave our arms a little yank. "It will keep us from running."

She held on and walked fast. Her gait was more like a march, where she lengthened her stride and fell into a rhythm that had us inhaling for three steps and exhaling for two. Maybe she'd learned this pace in prison. Maybe both then and now, she counted her loved ones. This morning, she walked right past Godiva and the wagon. I almost asked why we didn't take them. But Jillian pulled us off the path, and skirted the hem of the woods, along what was a prodigious shortcut.

The air was so clear and the trees were so bare that it looked as if they could scratch each other. We passed turkeys gleaning a stubbled field. They strutted and puffed. I blinked, and watched them for longer than the moment seemed to allow. The land somehow demanded it, and yet at this instant, I couldn't fathom how anything in the world could be normal, let alone restful. Jillian glanced at the birds as if she too sought the good.

I kept waiting for Wilm's smoke to start. The dagger made my belt tight, and when I rested my hand on the pommel, the belt squeezed more. We might find bandits in Wilm's pasture, or the garrison, or a scatter of mindless reaching him before he'd had time to color the smoke.

Jillian led me to a tree in Wilm's outskirts. "Stay here." She dropped my hand. "If I yell for you to run, you head for the ferals. Not home."

She started across the fields.

"Use the haystack," I said. "You can hide and still hear."

She gave me a look.

In a crouch, I held the dagger before me as if it were a candle. Jillian strode, bent over, to the side of the hut. Wilm didn't have windows, so she stood flat, and pressed her ear to the wall. Then she moved to the front of the door, and did the same. She knocked.

Wilm opened the door, and grasped her arms in what looked like relief. He pointed to the treeline, which was about a hundred paces from where I stood.

Jillian turned my way, and Wilm dropped his arm. She marched toward the line.

I started to count, stepping from the tree, as if I removed myself from a snare. Wilm met me at the haystack, and he clutched the top of my arm. Jillian stood near where Wilm had pointed. From nowhere, she'd drawn a kukri.

Wilm held me back. "She's all right," he said.

She stepped into the trees. I struggled, and Wilm held his shillelagh. "Gaelleda, I will knock you down."

We waited. Whenever I opened my mouth, the cold made my teeth ache. Wilm was warm next to me, and I fought the impulse to huddle with him. He stamped.

"What's in there?" I said.

"I think it's dead." He had scraggled cheeks, this morning, and he smelled of pipe tobacco. "I don't know."

I could try to Touch—to think toss—with Jillian. Maybe she could feel the pressure of my considering it. I strained to see her.

Wilm let go of me. Jillian had come halfway to the haystack. "We need a bonfire," she said. "And a rope."

"Why?" I said.

She said she'd tell us after, that the work would be easier this way.

Wilm and I looked at each other.

"Is it dead?" he said. She nodded.

"Is it mindless?" I said.

"It isn't mindless," said Wilm. "Dead mindless still move."

He left to fetch what he could. Jillian put her hands on my shoulders, and for a moment, she was deep in my eyes. "Mind Wilm today."

"Why?"

"If he feels some control, he'll feel less afraid."

"He's a tiny-eared cretin."

She nodded with the look she had when she'd flicked that crumb. "He actually happens to care for you." Maybe when I shuffled my loved ones, he'd hang onto my feet. "Gaelle. Everyone in these pastures cares for you." It baffled me why she said such a thing. "We need Wilm now, so we can do what we have to."

"What do we have to?"

"We have to burn his land."

This was the first act of war I would ever be party to. "Esaosh, Jillian, what did you find?"

The forest behind us stood as an army. "It's a Treehanded corpse."

part SEVEN

Wilm waited by his assembled firewood, and peered up the road. Church law allows large fires in the wet of spring—but this was autumn, and you were supposed to pay a fine as a form of insurance.

Near the treeline, Jillian had knelt where I could see, and tied the rope presumably around the Treehanded's corpse. Now Wilm peered at where it still lay hidden in the grass. "This is one of your enemies?" he called to her. "Maybe something you raised when you picked through its crypt?"

She lolled him a look. "Seems that it came for you."

"I found it dead on my land." He stood on his toes. "Pale as my own backside."

"Wilm Albertson," she said, "ever enchanting."

He said, "You reckon it infected the porcupines?"

"It didn't fight any porcupines," she said.

He gestured at the body, and looked at me as if I'd smarted off. "Whatever left the spines," he called to her. "You think it turned carrier?"

"Whatever killed it," she beckoned us over, "is likely dead."

"Then it's a fast illness." He approached where she squatted, and I followed. "You should leave the corpse. We should burn the yard."

Jillian stared at what still lay in the weeds. I stared at Wilm. He had wandered precisely where Jillian wanted him. She could burn the body and the plants, and do it all in the name of a plague—which, I figured, was what Treehand amounted to.

Jillian looked above the treeline, and tugged the body from the grass.

It was thin and curled in on itself. It wore a gray-hooded cloak that still cowled the head and stayed tight around the neck. Black quills, in singletons and bunches, poked from the opening in the hood. They reminded me of catfish.

"Wilm," said Jillian. "You've been calling the Treehanded."

Wilm sat down.

"You've heard the term *tree ghosts*?" she said. "From the pallor?"

He jumped to a crouch. "I don't know what you're saying."

"The quills here, they actually grow from the skin, as a sign of nobility." She touched one with the blade of her kukri, and the spine clicked against the edge. "It's from a trait that's rare. Hereditary. It makes people grow a sort of nail from their follicles—"

"Evil Speaker," said Wilm.

"The Treehanded priests," she said, "they're all of one family—"

"It's a Treehanded priest?" I said.

"Judging by some of the fading gray," she said, "he's still rather young. Low stationed."

Wilm wheezed, and looked to me as if I could help him again. "I know nothing of the Treehanded."

"That's evident." She lifted another spine. "So let me tell you it was Lucinda who first called them."

"No. No!" He sprang from the ground. "You stop with the horse!"

"The horse herself," she said. "The very horse you coddled and fed."

"Lucy isn't calling anyone."

"We've discovered, in fact, that she has been sent from Treehand," she said. "And not just peddled from an emigrant."

"Jillian," I said. We'd agreed to keep this from him.

"It's true," she said. "She even brought up some Treehanded plants."

"No," he said.

"She did it in our pen," she said. "She did it with her hooves."

"Jillian," he said, "you are lying again. And you unreasonably hate my horse."

"Have you noticed any strange weeds?" she said.

"Weeds?" he said. "No. And I suppose you know every plant growing in your back thickets."

"No, we don't know," said Jillian. "We don't know what we could be touching with our bare hands, or what we could be breathing in."

"Jillian," I said. Wilm had gone red.

"Gaelle's father," she said, "was probably the first death in a long-extended Treehand invasion."

"That," Wilm pointed. "Jillian, that is not true."

"I think it is true," she said. "And you were likely next."

I couldn't imagine why she had to assault him like this.

Wilm said, "You must be eating bad fruit." He cut a laugh. "Something gone fizzy, I think." He turned to me. "Gaelleda."

"Stop," I said, maybe to both of them. Jillian had told me to mind him, but she never said he might ask for my help. "I think she's afraid," I said to him.

"Think what you want," she said.

It was the only reason for her actions that made sense.

Jillian pulled the corpse's rope. "We will start by burning the body and then the house."

"My house?" Wilm rushed to her. "It wasn't anywhere near my house."

"Afterward," she said, "we'll burn the pasture."

"Stars in heaven." He snatched a piece of firewood. "You burned Lucinda."

"Stop," I said.

He stepped toward Jillian, and they both motioned for me to stay back.

"We let her go," I said. Jillian glanced at me.

"Teph's riding her now," she said, "to see where she goes."

"You're lying," he said.

"Does this look like a lie?" Jillian pulled back the corpse's hood, and even she looked away. The eyes had closed. The lids and the sockets were black, so together, they made the eyes look dark, huge, and somehow fuzzed. They resembled scorch marks on wool.

"You can't say for certain how that's a Treehanded." Wilm pointed with the wood. "You can't say for certain that it wanted my fields. Or that it came for me."

Jillian said, "You admit it died on your land."

"I told you I found it dead on my land," he said. "You also think something might have dragged it here."

"I never said so," she said.

"Yes." Again, he looked to me. "You said something killed it. That means something could have dragged it."

This was true.

He pushed the corpse with his foot. "Check for animal marks."

"You check," she said. "I'm going to be ready if it moves."

"Gaelleda." He held out his shillelagh. "Use this to search."

This was cowardice from Wilm; maybe even he would admit it. But I've since treated the moment as proof that when he later grew his courage, he did so in a very short time.

Now Wilm touched me with the club's handle. He was explaining how he'd look himself, but that he wanted a neutral party to investigate. Jillian either nodded at me, or worked to hold back bile.

I peered at the creature, as if it were Lucinda on two legs. And the comparison recalled my parents and the oxcart. I took the shillelagh, took a breath, and prodded the corpse's shoulder with the thick of the club.

"You have to get closer to move it," said Wilm.

"She told me not to touch it," I said.

"You'll be fine," she said, "as long as you don't."

"You know," I said, "you can be the one to do this."

"Will you beat it if you have to?" she said.

She'd given a low blow, and I promised myself I'd remember to tell her she did. I squatted, and smelled death. I wished the cowl still covered the Treehanded's face; beyond hiding the creature's eyes, it would make me less likely to rattle the spines. I rolled the body.

Flies lifted. Maggots filled a wound on the back of the neck. Wilm was talking fast, about how the gash was definitely the mark from a talon. He said the flies showed how the creature had been dead for a while.

"It's still Treehanded," said Jillian.

"Fine," said Wilm. "It may be. I don't know what it is, or otherwise I wouldn't have called you." With his elbow, he covered his mouth from the smell. "We border Treehand. Rocs pick up their prey, and fly low from the weight, and then drop whatever demon they've grabbed, onto my property."

"Well," said Jillian. "We're going to burn all of your property."

"Jillian," I said.

"You won't!" said Wilm.

"You admit," said Jillian, "that you have strange plants in your yard."

"No, you said I do," he said. "I never know what plants I have in my yard. I don't have a fetish for plants."

"I can guarantee," she said, "that I could show you strange plants."

"I wouldn't know if I could trust you, Sticky. I wouldn't know if they were strange or not."

Jillian put a hand on her sheathed kukri. "We will burn the Treehanded. We will burn your things."

"No!" said Wilm.

"We will make it so the garrison has nothing to take as a fine," she said, "even if they do detect the fire."

"Jillian." I stepped in front of her, the way I'd done with Lucinda. "This isn't what my mother would want."

She looked up, as if someone had entered the room. I'd never invoked my mother before.

"He prompted a Treehanded invasion," she said. "His horse killed your father. It tainted this land."

"Gaelleda, she is out of her tree."

"You will live in our ferals," she said to Wilm. "You will carry your shillelagh. You will eat enough of our food to be strong."

"Wait." Wilm looked around, as if he were under attack, but he couldn't tell where it was coming from.

"We will build you a house," said Jillian, "and we will build you a watchtower."

"As if you'd build me anything," he said.

"You will have windows," she said. "You will keep armor, and have a hearth for a signal fire."

"How?" he said.

"The tower will be high enough for you to watch both field and sky," said Jillian, "and your job will be to guard against both Treehanded weeds and the Treehanded themselves."

She leaned up at him. He put his hands to his cheeks. Heaven knew what I should have done with mine.

"How long?" he said.

"As long," she said, "as you feel the consequences of being alone in the world would be worse than the work I demand."

"Jillian," I said, "you're talking about slavery."

Wilm still clutched his cheeks, and his eyes had gone wide. They moved as if he read, and he held up a hand.

"She wants to burn your house," I said.

He nodded and made a fast, humming sound. "For this, she will have to let me keep something." Wilm showed a flash, then, of how often he and Jillian haggled. "Now. If you grant me property after rendering me completely destitute, they can fine you for easing a beggar."

"Then I guess you'll have to keep something," she said.

He puckered his mouth, looked her in the eye, and took a step toward his house as if he wanted to converse with it. Jillian gave me a small shake of her head, and she scraped mud from her boot with a stick.

Magic, it seems, is not the only one that manipulates. In retrospect, I figure Wilm probably realized he needed Jillian at least as much as he hated that he did. After all, he's the one who had stopped the smoke. So perhaps it made sense how he would give up the poverty he had, if he could feel he had no choice but to haggle for something better.

Now, Wilm muttered as he sort of petted the haystack. He threw a stone toward the treeline. "I suppose there's really no stopping you."

"Wilm!" I said.

"Bring a torch," said Jillian.

Wilm jogged toward his hovel. At the halfway mark, he slowed. Then he jogged again.

"You need to let it go," she said to me.

"I don't think I can."

"Gaelle." She stepped so close, I smelled tea. "We'll have to burn everything."

Wilm brought out his belongings in two, large turnip sacks. He wore his accordion around his neck. I asked what he'd do with his painted star charts, and he said that if he could get his hands on some colors, he could make himself new maps. "Would this be all right with you, Your Landlady Highness?"

"I'll do what I can." Jillian wrapped the Treehanded in a shroud of ripped seed bags. Then she dragged the corpse back to the weeds, where the rope, still attached, splayed like a serpent.

We fed the fire for the whole afternoon. Jillian wanted us to fatten it on everything. She wanted the flames to grow higher than Wilm's hut. We burned his table and his chairs, and we fired his rug and his trowel. We pulled down his porch. Jillian told us to wrap cloth around our noses and mouths. She talked about extermination.

Night began to fall, but the fire was more unsettling than the darkness. It shone orange in Jillian's hair. She threw a stool, and it crashed on the pyre, and it was astonishing to think how at dawn, she'd shivered while giving me space at our hearth.

Wilm approached, clutching his water bucket. It's an item with domestic significance in Holding and Azmon. A man's home is where he *sets down his pail*. "I refuse," he said. "I don't want to burn this."

Jillian paused with half a fence-post. "Wear it on your head, for all I care."

I'd removed my hat. Steam rose from the ground. It was a feudal act, Wilm reducing himself for our protection.

"I'm doing a good thing," he said to me. "You know, for the two of you."

"I hope it helps everyone," I said.

He'd stopped to look at me, but I couldn't see his expression. "Have you seen this plant, Gaelleda? What she wants me to find?"

I hadn't, not once in the two days since Teph's departure. Wilm's mortar and pestle rattled in the bucket. "We'll show you," I said.

He set the bucket beside the turnip sacks. "Your auntie's still trapped me, you know." It was what she was good at.

Jillian whistled for us to keep moving, as if she worked a mule team. With Teph, I had seen her fear of Treehand. It had matched the fury with which she'd now sought to cauterize Wilm's land. But today something else appeared in her—a loss of best reasoning, a panic stretched to cruelty, a lack she'd once vowed to help me prevent. And whatever my father did, or dreamed of doing, I knew this: he'd never want the ferals to hold a half-indentured pauper, no matter if the pauper had a part in killing him. This certainty, in fact, was the sturdiest thought of the day.

Jillian leaned on the shovel we'd used to make a firebreak. In the dimness, she appeared to rest on shadow. I strode to her, and as I got close, I slowed. I couldn't tell if she was looking my way, or where she was looking at all.

"Did you lose your hat?" she said.

Perhaps ironically, I counted. "Did you lose your mind?"

"Don't start."

"You want to burn a neighbor's field, and make him permanent company?"

She raised her shovel high, and let its point fall to the ground. "If we aren't careful, Gaelle, we'll have more company than we can ever survive."

"You put the blame of all of Treehand on a single man."

"A man who killed your father."

"A horse killed my father! A horse we let go!" Maybe my parents watched me defend Wilm. "And really, Jillian? That's what this is?" I gestured at the breeze's embers. "Revenge?"

She stepped toward me, and dropped the shovel. "I think he knows what he's getting."

"He thinks you've fabricated a trap."

"I told him the truth."

"You beat him with the truth, until he couldn't sense anything around it. You made him reject the truth."

"My God, you are self-righteous." She grabbed my elbow. "Did it ever occur to you how I want him to think such a thing? That he has to believe I've made all of this up?" She pulled me close, and she pinched. "If he thinks I just concocted a ruse, to burn his crops and to take his things, he won't suspect there really is a Treehanded invasion."

"But there is an invasion!"

"Of course there is. But we don't know enough. And if we tell him our uncertainty, he will really start to panic. And panic will kill him."

I yanked my elbow from her. "So in the meantime, you just plan to leave him in danger, out in our ferals?"

"In the meantime? No. In the meantime, we keep him near, standing watch."

"For something he doesn't believe in."

"Yes. And he'll go through the motions, because he's getting better than he got."

"He's smarter than you think."

"And he's prouder and needier than you can imagine." She brushed her hands on her greaves. "You have to entice a man into doing something he resents." She bent to her firebreak. "You beat him into doing it, the way the Church does, and all you make is an enemy."

We stood far enough from the fire that the sweat in my hair had begun to freeze. I had ash in my nose and ears. It probably grimed my face, and if I could see Jillian clearly, I'd probably find she was just as smeared. Across the pasture, Wilm placed something in a turnip sack. I said, "I don't know if lying is any better."

"You listen to me." She squatted, and I took back a step. "I've told the truth. I've spoken enough truth to make whole garrisons want me dead. And all of this, every day, has been in service of preserving the truth." She stood with a sack she'd apparently kept at her feet. "You'll wear this as a bonnet until we find your hat." She tossed it to me. I caught it, and I half hated that I did.

"We'll burn the body," she said. "Then the fields."

"And the garrison?"

"It's what I said. They'll find nothing to take away."

"Except Wilm's turnip sacks."

"They'll have to find him first. And if they do, we'll claim everything but the remainder is actually ours." She watched Wilm cram his saddle blanket into a sack that had already overflowed. "It's the truth."

"So this is what you really want? To own most of Wilm?"

From the fire, she fetched a torch of burning dowel. "You follow me now. And you follow like we're friends."

At the haystack, with a gloved hand, she split a piece of hay to reveal a fiber, white and twiny. Its hooks made it resemble an appendage from a pallid insect.

"This is the Treehanded plant," she said. "The one he's been baling. The one you cozied up against."

The sky reeled. I removed my mask to breathe—then shoved it back on.

"Clearly it's dormant," she said. "It's caused you no harm."

Wilm tossed his pillow onto the fire. "Has it harmed him?"

"Well, we'll have him close enough to watch."

I wanted to vomit.

"Gaelle."

"None of this feels right, at all."

"No, it isn't. But keeping him alive is why we're moving him. And his rejecting the truth is why he'll come with us at all." She adjusted my bonnet, so it fit over my ears. She held her hands over them, and everything went soft. I closed my eyes to the perversion of trying to get Wilm to believe how the truth about Lucinda and the weeds was a lie. Jillian wanted us to carry him to our home, on the back of that lie, while he saw the opportunity—if not the twisted generosity—in becoming our warden. Jillian released me, and I opened my eyes. "When we burn the Treehanded," she said, "I want you to face away from the fire as much as possible."

In the dimness, she brought me to the corpse as if we approached the edge of a chasm. Something buzzed from the ground, and we stopped.

"If what Teph told me is correct," she said, "the flies that grow from the maggots are not from Holding." This made sense; I'd never seen maggots so late in the fall. "The larvae are inside the Treehanded." She pulled the rope, and the corpse lurched. "Air matures them. And they're leaving through the opportunity of an open wound."

I should tell you Jillian was right about all of it. Lucinda did bring up the Treehanded weeds. And when we learned how Lucinda ran, with Teph, toward the Church, we would see that Treehand had not at all forgotten the Clearing Wars. In fact, it positioned itself for the next one.

part EIGHT

It took us a month to build enough of Wilm's new home to get him out of ours. He lodged the meantime in the shed where Teph had stayed. And yet if he knew of the previous guest, he never mentioned it.

Instead, Wilm changed nothing. During those days, I saw him draw nothing from his turnip sacks. In fact, I began to suspect he was using as many of our goods as possible, so he could preserve every crumb of his own. I said as much to Jillian, after a week of watching, and she drank it down with her tea.

Wilm rose later and retired earlier than anyone else. He slid from the shed, long after I'd started the mid-morning chores. He said little to either my aunt or me. Instead, he attached notes to our door, listing things he needed in precise, block-letter script. I didn't know how to read much of what they said. And by my lights, he counted on that.

When Wilm did work, he built the new cottage. When we heard his hammer, Jillian would set out to help him, leaving the rest of the chores to me. And truth be told, I didn't mind the task. The race was to hasten Wilm's departure. I didn't like living with a man who glanced at my chest and helped kill my father. Nor did I like how decency had demanded, twice, that I defend him. And as for Wilm, he likely couldn't abide a stay with the women he needed to protect him, in a shed where once lived the man who absconded with his horse. Nor could he feel easy on a property where my father's absence had its own chair.

Every evening, my aunt would come home, and teach me knots, or history, or writing. We'd discuss the Clearing Wars the Church fought to establish the boundary with Treehand, or how Holding and Bakeet have the warmest climates in the world. Beyond chores and study, I performed guard duty, twice a day, while Jillian and Wilm labored. I visited our old pumpkin patch, which came up each year, whether we prompted it or not. There must have been fifty of the gourds, these days, warm and sleeping in a crowd. At home, some house rodent had started storing beans and millet in an old glove that had fallen behind our front room's carrot crate—and I let it. Maybe we had burned its field.

In that first week, I'd followed the smell of smoke to the part of the ferals' rim that opened to the remains of Wilm's pasture. Elk had bedded among the warmth of the ashes, and when I startled them, they stood pale and alert as Lucinda. I don't think I noticed it at the time, but this beauty asserted itself as its own testament. It still does; it's why I watch Garfield ponder the setting sun. Beauty might be the first step mystics take toward awe.

But none of this diminished the world's ferocity. While Wilm lodged with us, I walked the ferals with a dagger and a pot I could bang if I needed help. I hated feeling safer with the dagger, but I did. And part of me acknowledged how in any event, cutting something might be less monstrous than tearing it apart with bare hands. We showed the Treehanded plant to Wilm. Jillian had one in a block of ice that kept the shape of our wheelbarrow's basin. The weed was the pale strand only; not the sheath. Wilm said it resembled a cabbage root, and we didn't disabuse him. In the meantime, while I guarded, I kept watch for unseasonal insects. I used a scythe to open random patches of brush. And though I knew this wasn't how the infestation took hold, I imagined making a slice, and setting free a cloud of flies.

Nothing came of my work. The weeks rolled into winter. If there was a Treehanded invasion, it progressed at the speed of plant. And regardless of how belligerent the growth might have been, it would have had trouble outspreading the slow menace of the freeze.

At the end of the first month, we'd completed the first floor of Wilm's cottage. Its bottom had a dugout, where someone could crouch. Pine logs made the walls, with moss filling the cracks. A stove, purchased in Northcraft, ticked in the front room's corner. Its narrow chimney would keep out any creature larger than two handspans. And because of the closed nature of the stove, its fire would incinerate anything that could otherwise roll into the room.

On the day Wilm moved in, we gathered to furnish his first floor. He treated us to a handful of hazelnuts. Then he checked the stove latch, and gave the iron pipe a little knock.

"Wilm," said Jillian. "You should come for supper."

I stopped midway through crunching a nut.

Wilm said, "Kindly, no."

"I think" she said, "it would be the neighborly thing."

"You've been quite neighborly enough," he said.

"And I think I told you," she said, "that you should eat enough to be strong."

"And I think these days," he said, "I am stronger than you."

"Good," she said. "Let's keep it this way."

"Jillian." He rarely called her directly by name. "Will you order me into that house?"

He'd said a curious thing. It gave Jillian the authority, but it also gave him a dignity.

"I'm ordering Gaelle," she said. "It's actually warm in our house."

"Well, how nice for you," he said.

She nodded for me to leave, and I stepped outside.

I shut the door, and relaxed in the forest's hush. Jillian had bossed me from the room, but she still got me out of it. Tossing the rest of my hazelnuts for the creatures, I started for home.

A few moments later, Jillian caught up. Her breaths came shallow, and she bumbled against me, while we walked in the snow.

"He's a git," I said.

"He makes his choices. But his night will be cold."

"We give him all this, and he won't even consent to coming to dinner?"

"Oh, and you'd want him to come?"

"No. Not after he insulted our house."

"And if you were him, you think you'd be eager?"

I stopped. "Well, I guess I'd be polite."

"No." She laughed. "You?" She put her arm through mine. "So you'd be willing to eat in the house of a man you helped kill?"

For Wilm, everything in our house must have loomed like a haunting. It was a way we both were the same.

"You know," said Jillian, "his refusal to come could actually show he's a good man."

"Well, I wouldn't mind if he thinks our house is hallowed."

"And I wouldn't mind if he thinks he's welcome."

It's what my father would have wanted. My father was a good man. "Wilm must have had it out with some squirrel for those hazelnuts. They tasted a bit like pee."

She yanked me a little. "I gave him those hazelnuts."

"Oh," I said. She yanked me harder. "Better him than me." I stumbled through the branches, and listened to the wolves. In the twilight, the snow stood gray as the elk bed.

part NINE

In early winter, Ludington's snow had had crept so far up the trees, that Wilm had stopped building. Every morning, he emerged from his hovel to brush drifts off the second floor's scaffolding, and during the rest of the time, he lived underground. Each day's new snow covered the entrance, as if it were the den of a polar bear.

On a clear morning, after a storm, my aunt rode Godiva to Northcraft.

That afternoon, more weather stranded her somewhere along the way back, and this left Wilm and me to hunker with only a horseless toboggan, a set of field skis, and two pairs of dry-drift snowshoes. The day's snow was wet, and walking the barnyard felt like climbing stairs.

Aside from a visiting marten's occasional bark, the barnyard held a stillness that felt like an extension of the cold. And like the cold, the stillness seemed both an invitation toward, and a reason against, sleep.

On the second dawn while my aunt was away, the sun rose crimson, while the afternoon stayed pale, as if morning had bled it. The colors meant weather, and I hurried my chores. Then in deep afternoon, when the temperature was warmest, I entered the ferals to collect the sap from the eddletrees. I wore my father's breeches, and with the effort in the silence, I felt as if I could be his ghost.

In my snowshoes, I tapped the trees for what they could afford. Sap trickled, yellow, down the spout. The stuff ferments enough that it rarely freezes, but my father always joked that the trees' best defense is how the sap is slow enough to render a person hypothermic while she waits. You can warm yourself by ingesting it, in the matter of any sort of alcohol, but afterwards, you might also wander off, toward a stupored finality the Holden called a groveman's romp.

Now the weather had begun to snow, and my face throbbed with the storm's approach. A push of wind flung the spout from its hole, and landed it a ways off.

I tried to keep sight of the spout, and my eyes watered in the wind. The trees canopied enough to obscure the clouds straight above, but beneath them hung the smell of a lake. That's what a snowstorm smells like: a lake. I tied a rope around my middle, and looped the other end around the tree. Such was the practice when conditions got bad; we had too much work and too much weather to do little else.

The line stretched as I moved to the spout. The wind shifted and keened, and I hummed to match the blowing's pitch. The howls can make people crazy if they can't get a handle on it. You have to learn to control the wind, in a tune.

Now in the ferals, the gusts had two notes that rose high, like a whine, and then fell to the pitch's bottom. I didn't like the sound; it wasn't the usual wind, and it might prove dangerous, if invited as music. So I started to recite the alphabet Teph taught me; this too was a kind of counting. In the sky, to the west, hung a gyre of feasters.

The birds spiral by the dozen when they find carrion, but today there must have been hundreds. Their number looked almost like a whirlwind: dark, circling, nearly solid. And in light of all that looming, the two-tone sound suggested the the cry of something dying. It was hard to tell where it was dying. Snow, ice, and wind can all play such tricks with acoustics that you misjudge the provenance of your own footfalls. But today, one thing was clear: with so much sound, and so many feasters, this dying thing would have to be at least the size of a man.

The orchard seemed to hunch. Snow covered the spoutless eddletree in long spots, and the look of it made me clutch the back of my neck, as if my nape needed a shield.

This would be my last tree. Jillian, so waylaid, would understand that the snow had gotten dangerous. The two tones whined. I gathered my gear. The feasters had moved. They wobbled, in their spiral, above a smoke of birch. Their approach meant they moved fast—east, against the wind, toward the farmhouse. Their pace had a speed most anything dying couldn't reach, unless it was on a wagon, or a sled, or a mare.

The thought of Jillian came like a punch. I unhooked the rope from the tree, and heaved my steps. I crossed the tread of my snowshoe trail, and forced myself to stop.

Snowflakes fell amid the cloud of my exhale, like the stars Wilm declared were coming to meet us. Many things in the fields move both fast and eastward, and whatever careened out there now offered no proof that the feasters followed Jillian. And even if I could happen upon some proof, it had taken me half an hour to enter the ferals. And this was before the snow had started, and before I'd have to fasten the rope, tree by tree, on the way home. If she could, Jillian would tell me these things, while she sat away from the fireplace, swirling her tea.

The two tones howled and the feasters moved. I moved to another tree, and to another. It was as if I pulled the trees in my direction, on some fat, creaking line, until I could reel in the thing that cried.

At an intersection, I ducked. A feaster buzzed my shoulder, with the wind in its wings. Behind me now, it lifted off a dark thing that stood in the trees.

The thing had the basic frame of a man, with pale, yellow eyes, no hair, and skin reminiscent of burnt leather. I would have known it was a mindless even without Teph's description. Some things match the worst of what you imagine.

The mindless howled the two-toned song, and it stepped toward me, through the snow, the way I stride through a room. The rope still attached me to the tree.

I pulled the line, but the loop had caught. The mindless snuffled. I climbed the tree. Another howl rose from the west. I climbed higher, remembered my knife, and cut the waist rope. It dangled from its loop, and the mindless stood near its end, looking up at me with eyes like lights in a prison.

A feaster brushed the branches. The mindless jumped onto the trunk, and we rocked. The creature slid to the ground, and I threw snow in its face. It didn't blink. It scrambled onto the trunk, fell back to the bottom, and howled. The west howled back.

More birds followed a second creature, similar to the other, but blonde. The first mindless jumped against the tree. Then the other jumped, while its skinless triceps flapped. My feet snapped a twig, and I thought of the mindless's weathered bones. I thought of my bones, and I climbed into the swaying branches, amid snowflakes that danced the way things look before I faint.

The two mindless jumbled. Thank God they couldn't think well enough to climb. The tree made a sound like an ache, and I clung to the trunk, the way I'd done when Jillian had told me of my father. She'd been training me, even then, with her handspring from the stock. Now I scrabbled a limb that reached into the canopy, located a lower branch from the next tree over, yelled for Jillian, and leapt.

I landed hard in the next tree, and bit my tongue. The mindless stood at the bottom. I kicked and I climbed, and all feeling left my hands. The creatures shuddered the branches.

The blonde mindless punched the trunk, and something cracked. I jumped, again, and landed on the next tree, square. My breath was gone. The tips of my gloves were gone. My nails were gone from their beds. I hollered for Jillian, and Wilm, and my father. A mindless batted a screeching feaster, and the bird fell to the ground.

A second bird hissed, heavy with the stink of Kelmer's marsh. Beneath me, the mindless curled the eddle tree's bark. All this worry about my inclination to kill, and now something was going to end me first.

The circumstance was unacceptable. The dry, Observer voice told me this. The orchard had more trees that were close and jumpable, but landing on each was like sustaining a fall. And after only these two, my arms had gone stiff and some of my fingers had most certainly broken. And even if I could jump from tree to tree, I'd eventually reach the end of a row.

The wind threw merciless drifts. I stuck my head into the upper branches, and thought of my mother. Then I thought of Miriamne, nearby in her box. Below, the mindless snuffled. My teeth chattered. I tried to count my loved ones, the way Jillian taught me, but the attempt just felt like goodbye.

The tree snapped. I caught the next trunk, and the impact shuddered from my hips to my brain. Two of my ribs felt so driven into each other that it hurt to breathe—and I had to breathe. The mindless scrambled.

I inhaled, and with the pain, I screamed through a burst of light. I screamed, I don't know how many times, or how loud, or even if I screamed a word. It was as if part of me had finally gone free, and taken off running, anywhere.

Jillian answered, like a hand against my breast bone, heavy and warm. The shock opened my mouth. Air went back in. My self went back in.

This was toss; it was Touch. I started to weep.

part TEN

Jillian had slowed my thoughts enough for me to wonder if I could cut some branches, and fling them. Maybe I could use my rucksack's flint to set fire to the tree.

The blonde mindless's bones protruded from its knees. The fire would harm me before it harmed these creatures.

Jillian Touched, and I breathed. From the swaying tree, the sky had begun to tilt.

West from here loomed a black locust with spines, mildly toxic, that spread a hand's width apart on the trunk. The locust was the only large tree in the orchard, and it was also the most unassailable. The tree wasn't far; it lived by the lake. I would move toward it as slowly as I could. Meanwhile, somebody would have to pray for the orchard; the mindless had already left a line of ruin.

part ELEVEN

The afternoon filled with falling trees. I'd gone so numb from jumping that even most of the sounds seemed far away. I seemed far away from myself. But the black locust stood next, dark as a reckoning. Something warm ran down my neck. The mindless with the flappy triceps whacked my tree trunk, and the creature's arm fell off at the elbow. I wrapped my scarf around my eyes, in a way for it to let me still see out the bottom. Then, tucking my chin, I leapt.

The landing brought a burst of light. The locust had knocked the top of my forehead, and now I fell onto a second branch, and a third, rolling like a child falling from bed, smacking another branch, another bed, until landing on my stomach with something sharp against my cheek. Yellow eyes peered from below.

Jillian Touched. I lifted my head, and my cheek went warm. My legs went warm.

The mindless had thorns in their fronts. Thorns stuck into me, and jostled with pain as far off as light.

To the left, in the direction the snow fell, a deer bolted. I tried to call for her to go, but no sound came out. The snow fell on her withers. It speckled the fur, as if the doe turned back into a fawn.

I loved this world, even if it ended me, and I asked it to count me as one of the good.

part TWELVE

Wilm's voice pulled, then slammed me awake. South of the tree, he hoisted a torch while he sat on Godiva. I pushed myself from my belly, and the thorns came with me. Wilm bellowed, and Godiva screamed. Behind them, the mindless shambled.

Something twanged from above, and the bald mindless buckled with an arrow in its eye. Wilm swung the torch, beating Godiva into the trees, and the blonde mindless followed. The struck mindless screeched, flung itself at its fellow, and bit its neck.

Someone's hand pressed my shoulder. Jillian, headfirst, climbed from the branches above me. She pulled me onto her back. I lay on her short bow. Something snapped, and we tumbled down, through light and snow.

We landed, splayed at the bottom of the tree. The shot mindless grappled the other, and the both screeched a sort of four-tone duet. Jillian pulled me by the arm, through the snow. My hands were probably too broken to hold.

Wilm rode to us, bug-eyed and praying, with the torch in one hand, and a reach for me with the other. He gripped Godiva with his knees, and he heaved me up. "You're a horseman," I mumbled.

Jillian landed behind us, and pushed me into Wilm's back. He was warm, and he gave me a warm torch.

"It's coming," said Jillian.

Wilm kicked Godiva to a gallop. Jillian muttered. The bald mindless followed, and it dangled blonde clumps.

Jillian shot for the creature's eyes. She wiped the sap from my palms onto a regular arrow, and I watched her as if I were a doll. She lit the arrows with the torch, and when they hit the snow, they sizzled. When they hit the mindless, they sizzled.

Lake Kelmer lay before us, flat with snow. Close behind, the creature snuffled, with arrow shafts in its eyes.

Wilm grabbed my torch, and jumped with Jillian to the bank. He stuffed the reins in my hands. "Go!"

The horse bolted up a nearby rise, and I bounced against her neck. As the mindless reached the shore, Wilm wafted his armpits in its direction. "Hey!" He hugged himself, and let go. "I bet my ma smells better than yours."

The creature shuffled toward him, and Wilm looked to Jillian. She was righting a rowboat that lay along the shore, and I angled Godiva toward her.

"Get back!" She swung at the horse, and the horse shied.

On the ice, Wilm waved the torch, and swore. The mindless approached, and Wilm did a little jog in the snow, where he swore again with each step. Jillian had the boat keel down, where she'd pulled it to the ice. From the hull, she drew a stone as big as a melon, such as the type you'd use to hold down a cover.

The mindless keened. I held Godiva's mane, and scanned the trees. The mindless had no answer.

Wilm, farther out, cattle whistled. The mindless ran toward him. It slipped on the ice, and landed on its chin.

Wilm said something about missing toes. The mindless leapt up, skittered, and crashed. Wilm laughed a tearing laugh. I closed my eyes, and the darkness felt like falling.

Wilm shouted, and the mindless lurched toward the rowboat. Jillian threw a stone at the creature's head, and bone crunched. I gagged. The creature stumbled. Wilm touched its shoulders with the torch, and it flailed.

Something crunched, but the sound was different from before. My aunt threw the rocks at the feet of the mindless, drawing stones from the boat, hurling them, both handed, from over her head. Wilm swung his torch low to the ground.

The creature flailed its good arm, and sank.

Jillian pushed the boat over the hole, and the ice gave a sound like pain.

I vomited, and apologized to Godiva. Wilm crouched in the boat, packing armloads of snow that Jillian dumped into the hull, and after a while, he squatted higher.

The two of them talked to each other in level voices, short exchanges, the way they spoke when they worked on the cottage. I searched the lake for movement. The feasters' circle had grown small.

The lake cracked, and Jillian and Wilm dropped to the ice. I slid from Godiva, and found the saddle and the rope it held. Jillian yelled. Both she and Wilm spoke fast —to me, I think, but I didn't want to listen. I stepped onto the ice. It creaked louder, so I crawled.

The lake's snow came up to my armpits, and it awoke me to a kind of clarity. Wilm and Jillian hollered for me to get off the ice, but from this angle, I couldn't see where they were. I stood to find them, and they scowled from where they lay.

I stuffed snow in my shirt, and the cold burned. The ice had the smell of water, earth, and blood. The mindless didn't need to breathe, so it could have been sliding along beneath me, gripping the lake as I did. Godiva stood on the shore, as silent as the trees.

Finally I got to my aunt—and I wanted to hug her. Wilm had a burned palm. I looked at my hands, while we fastened ourselves to the line, and I could barely tell what they were.

We crawled in silence. The snow had slowed. Then, within five paces of shore, I made a wet sigh, and my body stopped. It simply quit, as if I were falling through, to sleep.

It was Wilm who got me; I remember how he shoved his hat on my head. He must have run to me, to get there so fast.

chapter 9

NEGOTIATION

Ever since they delivered me to my hanging cell, I've wondered why the Church decided the young ones would serve as my guards. Otto, the prison sergeant, is middle-aged, but the rest of my sentries are a few years on either side of Garfield. And Garfield is so young that when he was born, I was still absurdly old. At first I thought my guards' age was an oversight, something misdirected by an overworked lieutenant who was born when I was at least surprisingly old. Then, as the days went on, the arrangement began to leave me a little offended. You direct an army or two, and you think you might get an escort who's at least out of puberty. Perhaps our armies were actually doing better than I thought, and the young guarded me, because the older soldiers had to move closer to the front. It's possible. And so is my earlier suspicion about how the boys are both brave and expendable. Still, I've begun to fear their worth is also testable. Post them with the supposed witch, and see how they fare. Maybe the Church leaves Otto to assess the boy's progress. Or maybe they use Otto to help the boys prepare for the larger war. And yet I've just noticed another possibility, about how the yellow brick on the altar might be thinning the sentries. Though I still don't know why, I can now say for certain that the ones who approach it do not return to the yard.

Over the last few weeks, Garfield and I have established a kind of barter. After I've told him to make a list of goods, as he calls them, he's begun to recite me an item, in exchange for my answering a few of his questions.

These usually center on my life in the war, and Garfield may have convinced himself that he is conducting some kind of interrogation. As far as possible, I've acted as a simple veteran who is happy to talk about her service. The fact that Garfield believes me is proof he doesn't know many veterans. But I like how his ignorance suggests he is still so untouched by battle itself.

When we've talked like this, we haven't been able to visit for more than little spurts. Otto has stood nearby, for one. And from what I was able to hear from the bridge, the other night, I've remembered how wind can carry voices. And anyway, brief exchanges are how taming works. Garfield and I have fallen into a routine, where Garfield offers his good, and then asks his questions. I answer in a way costly enough for it to be honest, without it taking so much that I collapse. And over time, the rhythm of it all has settled into something like this:

Garfield said, "We went on parade yesterday, and everyone marched, and the sound of it filled the yard."

"And also your chest, I bet."

"Well the drums filled my chest. I got to stand next to one, and I felt that my heart beat right along with it."

"That's good, Garfield."

"Right. So what did you do in the war?"

"A little bit of everything."

"You ever kill anyone?"

"Yes."

"Did you ever kill a lot of people?"

"Yes, Child. But if you ask about that, you'll have to pay a lot more."

"Then what was your worst injury?"

"In fact, I became possessed."

"Esaosh. By a demon?"

"I think so."

"On purpose?"

"No, Boy. Not remotely."

"What was it like?"

"Like? I suddenly felt I should be grateful that anyone could find me worth touching at all."

"Oh."

"Actually it's a little like prison. It's probably worth wondering whether you want your prisons to feed that narrative."

Garfield said, "I was chopping in the kitchen yard, and I split five logs, with one blow a piece."

"Nicely done."

"And now I have a question."

"Of course."

"Did you really serve with the Paleman?"

"I did."

"You knew him?"

"Sure."

"What was he like?"

"Driven. Ridden."

"And where do you think he is now?"

"I don't really know, Child."

"But he can come up out of the ground, right? I mean, that's his trick?"

"Well, you'd have to get him into the ground again first, and I don't think it's a place he'll ever go."

Garfield said, "Bats came to the window, last night."

"That's always nice."

"The moths were out on account of the warmth, and then the bats."

"For your light."

"And the bats bounced against the glass, and I could see their gray and white bellies."

"Well, that is outstanding, Garfield."

"I thought you'd like that."

"So you must have a good question on the way."

"I do."

"Let's have it."

"Heretic Gaelle, I want you to tell me if you were ever in love."

"That's what you want to know?"

"Yes. You're a girl."

"A pretty old girl."

"So were you ever in love?"

"In fact I was."

"I knew it. And are you still in love?"

"I am."

"And is it with someone I know?"

"What, you mean like Otto?"

"No. No!"

"All right, Boy. I'll tell you this. It's someone you don't know yet."

"What do you mean, *yet*?"

"I mean, I will have to introduce you."

"And how are you going to do that?"

"Well, I guess I'll have to win."

"Woman, you're barmy."

"We'll see."

"The war, right? For Visjaes? That's what you're going to win?"

"I don't really think winning is black or white."

"So you're saying you won't win completely."

"I'm saying, Child, that we'll win belatedly, but finally."

"Yeah, keep hoping."

"But I think that for her part, Visjaes has already won without us."

Garfield said, "I've decided I like the smell of ink."

"Goes with the scritch of a pen."

"Exactly."

"I like the smell of skunk."

"Woman, you do not."

"From far away, I do."

"Fine. Barmy. Otto can't sleep, because he's burned his fingers, and they keep knocking into things when he's in bed."

"Then you or another guard should tell Otto he needs cold water."

"But not while he's in bed."

"So he needs a tiny bucket, or a large cup."

"No. Like I said, we're done with the water."

"Garfield. Cut a hole at the bottom of the cup, large enough for him to put his hand through. Line the new opening with cloth, to make a cushion and a better fit. Then let him sleep with his hand in there."

"Oh. It's like those yokes they put on animals, to stop them from chewing."

"Yes. But let's hope Otto's hand can't chew."

Garfield said, "Yesterday, we fried some pork rinds, and we ate so much we got sick."

"How pleasant."

"So we gave some to a stable cat, who got so full that she lay on her side with all of them around her."

"Good on the cat."

"And then from where she was lying, she just opened her mouth, and continued to nibble."

"Garfield, that is almost obscene."

"She was so happy."

"Might you have a question?"

"Yes. I want you to tell me what it's like to voyage by boat."

"By boat or by ship?"

"Ship."

"You get to love a ship like a steed."

"It's why they call them a *she*."

"Well, Garfield, I generally don't like being compared to livestock, but a ship does kind of gallop along. And you find you'll do everything you can to keep it healthy."

"And is there such a thing as a lobster?"

"A lobster? Yes."

"And it wears armor?"

"Yes, Child."

"And it has a stinger tail?"

"No. But some have claws that can snap an oar."

"And is there such a thing as a unicorn?"

"Actually, no, I don't think there is."

"Oh."

"But I haven't seen everything, Garfield."

"But can you really talk with bees?"

"I know someone who did."

"And what do they say?"

"Honestly? I think they're angry we're here."

Garfield said, "Today I got to ring the bells."

"You're shouting some."

"Sorry."

"You rang the bells?"

"The rope is as thick as my arm, and I have to jump completely onto it, and then I let it take me way off the ground."

"That's a big bell, Garfield."

"And it goes Bong. And it's like my whole body goes Bong."

"And will you do this often?"

"No. Once in a while."

"All right."

"Heretic Gaelle, what's your favorite food?"

"Eddle tart."

"What's your least favorite food?"

"Anything that once had more than four legs."

"Can you really fry a steak in a breastplate?"

"Most soldiers can."

"What's your favorite weapon?"

"A shield."

"And do you, at age one-hundred-whatever, think you'll die in prison?"

"Well, change direction that fast, and a wheel will fall off."

"But we could make your tart for a final meal."

"In that case, my favorite meal has seven courses."

"You can't do that, Woman."

"Well, I had to try."

"You're old, Witch."

"Thank you."

"So are you afraid?"

"What, to die?"

"Yes."

"I suppose."

"And do you reckon you're scared of the pain, or of what happens next?"

"Come to think of it, after all my years, I'm afraid of the judgment after."

"Yeah. I reckon this makes sense."

———✥———

Garfield said, "The other night, on guard duty, I watched rabbits joust."

"What now?"

"One rabbit stood, and the other rabbit ran toward it, and the first rabbit jumped just as the other passed under."

"Garfield, you saw this?"

"You reckon it was courtship behavior?"

"I don't know. But I'm glad people don't do it."

"I think the lady leaps."

"Of course she does."

"So, Woman. Does a giant really live in Merrial?"

"In a manner of speaking."

"And the ground there is made of glass?"

"Sometimes."

"And the streams have powdered?"

"And some of the trees have burned bright red."

"Then I don't think I'd want to go there."

"Child, it doesn't feel like part of this world."

"I guess lots of Celd feels separate now."

"War can have that effect."

"And what do you reckon your Riven army will do, now that they're without you?"

"It isn't my army, so I'm sure they'll keep doing what they always do."

"Fight us, you mean."

"Fight the Church."

"And do your Riven really fight your own soldiers, when they come back as mindless?"

"Yes. They ask us to."

"What, when they're mindless?"

"No, Child. Before. In their wishes."

"That would be mad."

"The Church also fights its own, this way. It's one of the kinder things they do."

✤

Garfield said, "I like kneading dough for bread."

"Oh, everything is wonderful about bread."

"And I like rain on the roof, and a feather bed."

"I like waking up cold, and pulling on a warm blanket."

"Yeah, that's probably good for your old bones. And I like sun on my eyelids."

"But only when you have to wake up in the morning."

"And the other day, they shaved all our heads, on account of the lice. And we all stood around and petted each other's stubble."

"One another's, Boy."

"What?"

"If you petted more than one, it's *one another*."

"So you're a girl. Why doesn't your hair grow past your shoulders?"

"It stopped getting long, after I went into Merrial."

"Esaosh."

"Stay out of Merrial, Boy, if you can. Even Treehand is better."

"They say that in Treehand, you climbed down a tree headfirst."

"Yes."

"And can you climb up again, backward?"

"Only for a few feet. It's hard to back up, when you can't see how the tree bends."

"The Treehanded do it."

"Well, they know each tree as if it were part of themselves. The worst thing you can do to the Treehanded is take them out of the forest."

"But that's what your army did."

"Garfield, the Treehanded in my army made their sacrifice."

"Do they follow Visjaes?"

"Some of them."

"And was your mother really an outlaw?"

"Yes."

"Did she follow Visjaes?"

"Not in name."

"So when did you start to follow Visjaes?"

"I was always aware of Visjaes, Child, even when I didn't know it."

"So even when you didn't follow her by name, you still did?"

"Yes. And then I felt lonely for a while. And then, little by little, I noticed that somebody also sat in the room with me."

"Then you've met Visjaes?"

"No, I didn't mean that literally. I've just stood where Visjaes has recently been."

"And what would you do, Gaelle the Riven, if you could get free from here?"

"I'd walk home."

"Walk? Do you think you'd make it?"

"You know, if I didn't, I think I'd still die happy."

chapter 10

RUDIMENTS

part ONE

Saved from the mindless, I slept. In my dreams, cold and silence spread: water like a room with a pale, opaque top. Stillness loomed, something like a loss of senses, something that stemmed from the core of the world—a stasis, a fixedness gone white as a cataract. The dream's water had a spot inside, far off, floating, a spot with limbs and withered skin. It curled its fingers.

It walked now, in place, making currents that jostled it forward, until it bumped a bank, and lifted to the ceiling. It floated supine, uttering the color black, as it spoke with blue lips.

I woke to darkness, tried to sit, but couldn't. The darkness held a heft, like the side of a storm. But it had a point of light, far off—a hole, a warmth—and as I reached for the spot, my life constricted around it, as if the spot were a wound.

The spot enlarged and approached. It was bright. It was fire. I wanted to reach for it, but I couldn't move. I opened my mouth, and nothing came out.

The light neared, and hovered out of reach. Someone put a hand on my forehead, and kissed my cheek. She was here, this woman who was both as annoying and dear to me as I was to myself.

"Teph isn't here," said Jillian.

She spoke about poison and depth perception, and held my hand while I stared at the light. I was like a moth to a lantern, trying to get back home.

part TWO

I spent the next two weeks in bed. The bandages on my hands were like the snow on the ground: something of the winter I'd brought inside with me, and that followed me into the bed, the way the dreams had done. Jillian said two of my left fingers would never be straight again—and the first time I saw her unwrap them, I wept. She insisted the damage was only cosmetic, that I could think of it as scarring. And yet, the wounds enraged me. I hated their meanness, their irrevocability, their sign of how my body was now marked by somebody else's darkness.

It took Jillian and Wilm a week to convince me that, despite my vision of blue lips, neither mindless was Teph's remains. Both Jillian and Wilm stood in my doorway and swore they had seen nothing to suggest him. They said both mindless were too decomposed to be someone who lived only weeks ago. When they found the remains of the blond, they determined he was markedly shorter than Teph. And furthermore, the mindless had large ears while Teph's were small. "Like handles," said Jillian, "on an urn."

As it happens, Wilm and Jillian were right. Neither mindless was Teph the Azman. But my dream did foretell him decades into the future, after Teph acquiesced to the tragedy of becoming our Riven's commander. This is something I'm thankful Jillian never knew.

During the first days after the mindless attack, Wilm teased Jillian about noticing Teph's ears. In my half-sleep, I half heard a conversation comparing the size of an ash urn with a sugar pot, and then with a honey jug. For a while, Wilm referred to Teph as Honey Jug, and at least once, this provoked Jillian to stir her tea with such ferocity that the sound of it had me wondering if she was scraping a crock for whatever clung to the sides. These days, Wilm entered and left our house as he pleased. He kept a bandage on his burned hand. He lay his palm on almost any prominent surface. He stretched more than he used to. He asked Jillian to carry most anything lacking a handle, and she would.

Even on my sickbed, I knew we wouldn't have fared well without Wilm. Not with two mindless and one salted arrow. The blonde mindless likely would have succumbed to its brother in any event. But without Wilm, we couldn't have shut the other one in the ice.

In retrospect, Wilm had been brave as the rest of us. He might have been braver, in fact, seeing how the mindless amounted to his worst fears on two legs, and that he'd also mastered such fear for a girl who was not even his blood. Maybe he just wanted to erase a debt, to make my father's house less hallowed. Or perhaps, in risking himself, Wilm had begun to hallow himself. Whatever the case, we should have paid better attention to what he was doing in his own woodland hovel.

As I recovered, Wilm and Jillian preferred to discuss the mindless only when they were away from me. They would whisper in the front room while they boiled water and jostled the fire. I would pound on the wall until they included me. I threatened to follow them—out of the bed, to the barn, to Wilm's house, to the lake.

Then, after about a week, Wilm brought me his hammock to hang by the fire. He and Jillian built me a bed in it, and I was smart enough not to protest where it came from. They sat in the surrounding chairs while they cogitated. And I swayed, while the snow fell, as if they truly did pack me along with them.

We knew a few things: As long as the ice held, our bottled mindless remained in the lake. It was a powerful creature, but it would require near-impossible strength to break through the ice without any sort of purchase. Lake Kelmer's drop off was steep, and as far as we knew, it would give the mindless no leverage. I asked if either the water or the cold would further degrade the creature, and Jillian said how, on the contrary, freezing would act as a preservative. She'd heard some Azmen even kept their mindless in cellars, as a sort of cold storage.

In the meantime, Wilm had used snow to pack the space between the ice and the outside of the rowboat. And when I saw it later, the whole thing looked square and deep as a crypt. Wilm built an ice pillar in the boat, something resembling a cross between an obelisk and a snowman. He inscribed each side with the celdan sign for danger: a plus sign with the middle hollowed out. People say the glyph was originally used by miners to mark the presence of a sinkhole. And on ice, most folk would probably think it showed a similar hazard.

We also knew we wanted to keep these warnings vague. Even Wilm agreed. Considering how Jillian and I were misleading him into doubting the truth about Lucinda spreading the Treehanded weed, I found this stance ironic. And when Wilm and Jillian told me about our secrecy, Jillian gave me a look to suggest she knew what I thought.

"Do we keep the warnings vague," I said, "because we're worried about drawing attention to Teph?"

Jillian said she didn't think the ferals' mindless had come for Teph.

"He set free two mindless," I said. "He ambushed the people who were supposed to find the mindless. And then we get a visit from what? Another two mindless?" In my hammock, I swung with my worry that the Retrievers might arrive next.

"So while you've been healing," said Wilm, "we've decided these mindless can't actually be from Treehand."

"They're far too intact for such a trip," said Jillian.

One of the mindless had poked bones from its own knees. "They were tattered," I said.

"Yes, but you should have seen the blondie in the ferals, Gaelleda. It's been what? Ten days? The feasters had taken even some of the bones."

"Another sign," said Jillian, "is that the mindless screeched. They signaled."

"But Azman mindless," said Wilm, "are mute."

Their screech was a sound I could still imagine I heard on the wind.

"Wait," I said. "Who says they're mute?"

"Teph does," said Jillian. "And simply put, the mindless obsess him."

They do obsess him. Wherever Visjaes has put him now, the mindless probably still obsess Teph.

Jillian told me that because mindless don't breathe, somebody would have to punch a hole in their cheeks, or insert a whistle, or do something equally deliberate to induce the ability to keen. Wilm said they couldn't tell anything further, from what little was left of the creatures.

"Well, if they made a noise," I said, "they'd be easier to find."

"They're already conspicuous," said Wilm.

"You can ride for six days in all but one direction around here, and not find a road," I said. "You think it isn't hard to lose mindless?"

"What I'm thinking, Gaelleda, is that somebody makes the whistle so the mindless can make terror."

Such an arrangement should have been a clue for us. We already knew of an entity that liked to spread terror.

"I have a friend who hears things," said Jillian. "In a coastal village, in a place near the islands of Bakeet."

"Bakeet the Tail," said Wilm. "It has a tale."

Jillian gave him a look to suggest he pull himself together. "He says another mindless, a female mindless, was spotted near Cadmus."

Wilm rubbed some soot between his fingers. As far as we knew, everyone in the Church Empire still condemned mindless.

"What does this mean?" I said.

"What it means," said Wilm, "is that they're living to our west and coming from our east, while we are the bare-naked meat in the middle."

"Actually, we don't know what it means," said Jillian.

I imagined mindless lumbering over whole swaths of Treehanded weeds.

"What does it mean about Treehand?" I said.

Jillian pulled at her braid.

"Your aunt thinks the way she always thinks. That both the Treehanded and the mindless want my horse."

"It would explain," she said, "why everything ends up here."

"But it doesn't explain the mindless near Cadmus," said Wilm.

I was swinging the hammock so fast that Jillian clutched its end until the swinging stopped.

"Do you have an answer?" I said.

She let go of the hammock. "No."

As it happens, Jillian was right; we'd later see how everyone wanted that horse. And yet, from where we were, it wasn't easy to confirm such a thing. If the events surrounding Lucinda were a tapestry, our orchard was the merest thread. Lucinda was the center holding the entire weave together; this was the first thing we'd have to discern. And the second was how some elements of the tapestry had more than one purpose.

part THREE

In the following weeks, I healed while the other two built. They pried the scaffolding off Wilm's second floor, and used the wood to affix rungs and platforms to the tallest elder nearby. I didn't see them work, but I knew which tree they used: a thick, black one loomed on the other side of the land from the orchard, with its crown rising twice as high as either of our houses. The way its branches curved, it looked like a many-armed demon. I imagined Wilm and Jillian building awnings and windbreaks, a rope ladder we could remove. The news from Jillian's contacts reported no more mindless. But either because we were suspicious of the information or simply afraid, we planned to build the watchtower as quickly as we could.

In the evening, Jillian fletched arrows by the fire, with new tips she'd bought in Ludington. She'd also tried to buy salt, but none of it was the black sort Teph had used. Even the white kind was in short supply. Instead, she bought lamp oil, and soaked the arrows carefully so as not to warp them. The pan was the same one we'd used to force-bloomed the almond branch, and this repetition felt at once proper and inevitable.

Both before dark and at dawn, Wilm made the rounds at Lake Kelmer.

He checked the snow for lurching footprints and the ice for melting and cracks. All of this was a safe assignment for our time of year. Despite its sudden drop-off, Lake Kelmer is relatively shallow, and there are many winters when it freezes solid. Still, I imagined Wilm as a blue silhouette among the twilight blooms of color, peering at where his stars would emerge, and facing away from the unnoticed ice that clouded black.

I pushed the thought away. To think of it felt like a kind of summoning.

I told Jillian she should go with Wilm, or at least take turns with him. She said he wanted to do his rounds alone. She wagered maybe in beating the mindless, he somehow felt an ownership for the thing.

"But if they find him," I said, "he can't call."

We sat at table, and she gave me half her frybread. "He said he'd bang his pot."

Jillian and I never spoke of how I'd called her while the mindless had me treed. Since the moment when we both sat, half-dressed by the fire, we never again spoke of Touch, or toss as she'd called it. I later met a man with a wide sense of time, and he explained how, at one point, the universe combined with everything into the smallest imaginable speck. He suggested Jillian and I retain a vestige of such proximity, and that this is how Touch works. Although not even he could tell me what happens to this vestige after death, I liked his thought of nearness. During all my adolescence, I never told Jillian how much our Touch—our connectedness—among the mindless had made me never want her fully to leave me again. God, even after her death, I still keep my want. But I'd like to think that this winter of the mindless was when I began to become gentler with my aunt. Not all at once, of course, but as we dealt with what closed around us, I started to realize she was my teacher and my lookout and my deepest friend.

I'm sure Wilm saw our connectedness, even before I did. But if he knew that Jillian and I could Touch, he never mentioned it. Wilm was more tactful than I had given him credit for, and he was also savvy. He'd lived in his pastures for decades, while he probably spoke with my mother and my aunts. He might have even watched the Church cart some of them away, or watched Miriamne return with parts of her cut away. Events like these could make anyone keep distance from a family. And if this family's two remaining heretics now wandered their woods and thought at each other, then the less one acknowledged the better. The Church would certainly interpret Touch as magic, and in symbolic stoppering of all incantations, they killed mages by shoving stones down their throats.

So Wilm played dumb. Sometimes he'd watch the two of us the way he'd regard a barely-controlled fire. But when something about us got too strange, he simply found a reason to take his leave. As time went on, he probably had to play dumber and dumber, until this act itself was a sign of his choosing us over the rest of the world. Wilm, who never wanted trouble, who had used astronomy to forecast avoidable trouble, had chosen us. He had chosen the heretics. And I now believe that's because Visjaes had used Lucinda to choose him.

While he and Jillian built the watchtower, I swung in the hammock as something waiting to land. The house sat still, and the sky lay low and pale, as if all of us floated under ice. Such a thought kept me sitting bolt-straight in the hammock, daring myself to talk. In my thoughts crept an image of my speaking, then grabbing hold of what I said, and tearing it in half. It was hard to say what the speaking meant, or what any of this had to do with Teph's blue lips, but even then, it somehow suggested self-desecration.

That winter, a choice had settled upon me. In certain ways, it was the same choice I'd faced with Wilm and Lucinda, and as such, it was the same one Jillian addressed, over and again. Loss could provoke violence. Fear certainly might. And the Imperial Church daily promoted violence through those avenues alone. Then, if you brought in the Church's teachings about strength and reason, it became evident that we celdans were supposed to accept violence, at least when it became rational to do so. Such behavior found reinforcement from instinct, the self-serving Observer, with its door left open for Esaosh. And finally there loomed Esaosh himself, who brought us here through war, who continues to wage war, and who rejects nearly wholesale the so-called weakness of love. These days, as I swing in my cell, preaching both to an improbable bird and any guards who can't help but listen, I suggest how, considering who owns us, we celdans have a proclivity for violence, the way a pig might have a proclivity for mud. The Cadmul award adulthood to a child after his first impressive kill. Our world rings with such applause. And the poison from my ferals snake, this poison that lingers still, is the fact that part of me also applauded when I'd torn the creature in half.

The orchard's two instances of violence—the snake in the ferals and the mindless in the fruit—began to stack as the winter's ill-gotten twins. In these days of truest rest since killing the snake, I had begun to dream that from the elbow down, my arms had turned into serpents. Sometimes they bit me, or I tore them in half. Other times, I marveled at what my arms had become: their fluid reach, how they could have flung the mindless into the trees. It was only during these marvel dreams that I awoke, as if someone had just called to me. I would lie, then, with the cold of spent adrenaline, holding my own hands, trying to retrieve the voice of the caller, while ignoring the pull of the dream's exultation as it crept back to its hole.

I didn't know what any of this meant. But I couldn't address it with anyone else. It was too dark, too violent, too odd, too persistent, too much of a confirmation of the anxiety I had seen on Jillian's face after I told her about the snake in the first place.

So in the meantime, this winter, I did a clumsy cleaning of the house. It helped me to put things in order. I cooked and talked. Although I left out dreams, I narrated the day to my parents. Or like a person in the wind, I sang to myself, as if to reassure myself I sounded like myself. Other times, I tried to say words only with the same syllables, or whose order had increasing syllables. In short, I resorted to poetry. And despite all my muddle, I startled at how so many of those in my extended family have found peace in some form of the word. Certainly I do so now. And even if I overlooked Increase's demands, I'd feel that stopping my tale would amount to a betrayal of that solace.

During my winter recovery, the hammock recitations helped me, but they didn't offer a cure. The dark thoughts didn't bore a cavity into my consciousness. And yet they still poked from a hole that was already there.

On a late afternoon, Wilm found me sitting sideways in the hammock, facing away from him, while I recited every word for *rebel*. His boot scraped the floor, and I turned.

"I'll come back," he said.

"It's nothing."

"You're busy."

"Just talking."

He put a hand over one ear.

"To myself, Wilm."

"Now there is an honorable farm-life tradition."

"Well, there isn't much to do when I can't go outside."

"And that's because your fingers are mangled."

I stood, and the hammock flipped. "What do you want?"

"Gloves." We usually kept the spare ones on top of the parsnip barrel by the door, but somebody had moved them. I hadn't; I still wasn't sure I could wear gloves.

We looked behind the barrel, and in the hanging baskets, and underneath the crockery shelf. Wilm even had me check the folds of the hammock—although I'm glad he had the respect not to rummage it himself. The hair on the back of his head stood up, from where he'd rubbed it in frustration.

I said, "Check your path, I guess."

"And who takes off gloves outside in the winter?"

"Maybe the same one who goes into the woods without them."

He peered behind our carrot crate, and I stiffened.

"That isn't the one you want," I said.

"I'm not picky, Gaelleda."

"It's only one glove. And it isn't yours."

From behind the crate, Wilm pulled a single, cloth glove. A scatter of beans fell out the opening.

He held the glove so that it didn't spill. "You have a varmint."

"It's just a mouse. Or a chipmunk."

"Something has been storing up for the winter."

"Just leave it. Please."

Peering at me over the glove, he sort of pet where the seeds had bundled. His eyes seemed particularly brown in this light. "Can't keep the beasties out anyhow." He lay the glove back in its place.

Both my aunt and I had likely noticed the stash back there. But it was winter already, and it seemed cruel to throw out somebody's savings.

Wilm stood in front of me, and pointed until he nearly touched my shoulder. "You love animals, Gaelleda."

"I don't think you're one to talk, Wilmeda."

"No, I am not." With his rolling gait, Wilm walked to the fire and back. He peered my way, and hummed.

"Don't twinkle at me."

"You're your daddy's girl. And I mean that as a compliment."

"I was going to take it as one."

"It's good to love the land. The creatures." I thought of the elk in his pastures' ashes. "They point to something better." He patted my shoulder. "We see that."

Aside from the hallowed nature of the house, this was another way Wilm and I were the same.

"So is that why you like the stars?" I said.

"Yes." He smoothed the back of his head. "Goodness here. Goodness there."

"My father was good."

"Yes." He tightened a knot on the hammock. "Yes, your father was good."

He took some burlap, and tried to wrap it around his hand. Then he tossed the cloth onto the table. "You know, Gaelleda, you should get your book."

"My book?"

"You of all people must know how to read. You with all your inky relatives."

In my mind, dark words flowed from blue lips. "I thought you didn't like anything related to Teph."

"I don't care for the man. He is a foreigner and he's likely a thief."

"I rest my case."

"But I don't believe he's a mindless, and I don't wish him ever to become one."

"Well, I guess that's something." Considering how, in Wilm's mind, Teph's thievery probably amounted to Lucinda's removal, his concession wasn't entirely empty. "You know, Wilm, I do believe Teph tried to help."

"And you know it's still OK to blame him."

"You can blame him, but I don't."

"You maybe don't blame him for Lucinda."

"Wilm, you can come into the house, and you're welcome to the fire—"

"But I should stay out of your tree?"

I made a fist, but stopped from the pain.

"Gaelleda, the logic is very tidy. Teph brought the idea of the mindless. Before then, you hadn't even heard of the mindless. These are terrible things he talked about—darkness, evil." Like tearing the snake. "But most of the time, a dark worry is different from a dark wish."

Somehow I felt smaller and cleaner. "You mean we all think dark things?"

"Yes, but," he looked sharp. "You missed the point." He brushed a feather from the hem of his coat. "Your dream mindless has blue lips, because of what Teph talked about. Yes?" At the time, Wilm made a certain amount of sense. "But Teph didn't mean to bring you trouble. If he had, he would have just killed you in your sleep."

"That's nice."

"Well, think of all those knives. He could have put you in a stew." Wilm shoved his bare hands in his pockets. "But you're welcome, Dearest." He opened the cottage door. "And you should read a book. Let in some other voices. And you should crack the door some. It stinks."

After he left the house, I lay back in the hammock, and let the fire warm my side. I looked at my hands, held them, and closed my eyes. Wilm showed his affection when he'd tried to address what he perceived as a Teph-related qualm. And although I could never thank him without admitting far too much, what he said in passing did help me in ways he never perceived.

The next day, I entered the cold end of the house, threw open the storage chest, and drew out Teph's book. I lay my hand on its cover; it smelled of his pipe. During those last few weeks of my recovery, I read aloud to myself when I was alone. I sounded out the words I didn't know, using the pictures as prompts. Maybe all this was to assert how I did not blame Teph. Even now, I have trouble blaming him for so many things. But with his book, I began to reason how the best way to protect the world—from myself or from others—is to learn it, to store it up a piece at a time. This way, when the world comes after you, you can recognize that even while it charges, it carries the things you've come to love.

part FOUR

During the winter, I turned sixteen. For my birthday, Jillian had a pendant fashioned from the well of my father's ox-bone pipe. She put it around my neck, brushing me with her fingers, and she gave it a little tug when she was through. The pendant carried the smell of my father's smoke, and I kept it in his old tobacco bin at night, to keep the scent as long as I could.

The days lightened. I came down from my hammock, with full use of my hands. And I began to accept how my little and ring fingers angled out, as twigs. The days brought air warmer than the ground, and the snow cover had only a slightly cooler smell than the rain. The village of Hal's Bride—the one next to Northcraft—held its festival where it burns the winter in effigy. The farmers put in petitions to raze the dead stubble of their crops, and Wilm said they were already making the fire breaks. In these parts, the springtime smells of smoke.

Jillian began to accompany Wilm on his trips to Lake Kelmer. She'd leave before dawn. After my chores, I would brew tea for her return, and while I waited, I watched the steam rise from the pot, as if it were an ascending wish.

Jillian helped patrol again at noon and sunset. She carried the maul we used to split wood, and I wondered if it would be possible to hit the mindless when it was still frozen enough to shatter.

Jillian's Northcraft informants had begun to yield rumors. The mindless talk was infrequent, obscured by distance, and devoid of any sense of the mindless' motives. Jillian said the stories sounded like the common tall tales of troll attacks, unless you knew how to listen for such details as the creatures' slowness and their inability to reason. All told, Jillian had three additional, authentic reports: one from southern Cadmus and two from eastern Holding. One Holden account wasn't far beyond our region, but the other came from near the coast. From such a scatter, we could only presume that the creatures were either tracking more than just Lucinda, or that they weren't very good trackers at all. Eventually, we'd discover the latter was closer to the truth. But those who sent the mindless also capitalized on the way their creatures wandered. Meanwhile, our dread remained as inert and self-sustaining as the thing beneath Kelmer's ice.

One night, Jillian and I heard Wilm's accordion, soaring and pure: not a wheeze, but a kind of aria somehow reminiscent of the glove of beans and millet. The music hung in the evening's softening air, as something of an anti-keening. Jillian did an absent slight-of-hand with her sewing needle. "Helping seems to help him," she said. So at least there was that.

part FIVE

Helping does help. During the present war, when our army rescues prisoners from the Church's dungeons, we set them to immediate work in the rear. They roll bandages and dispense food, and they return to the potency of good use. They are the hardest workers, and frequently the most joyful.

Back at Ludington, in the spring of my recovery, I hadn't returned to the orchard since the mindless found me there. Jillian had given me the chores I could do closer to home, but as the weather warmed, she widened their area so that I seemed to gain ground with the retreating snow.

When most of it had left, she led me to a crate she had hefted into the back of the wagon. In the box lay about two dozen eddle sprigs. Beside the crate, she'd packed shovels and waterskins. "Today," she said, "we're going to repair the orchard."

I pressed my heel into the farmyard's mud. She must have wanted me to return to the line of trees I'd left in my wake. The mindless had laid waste to them until the orchard stood as dismembered as the mindless themselves. Such maiming was one reason I hadn't gone back to the grove at all, and I now considered refusing the trip. An ax lay in the wagon bed. I said, "I don't think I can fell those trees."

"Oh no, we've long since finished the dead ones. You didn't need to go through that."

Wilm and Jillian had amputated the orchard while I dangled beside the fire with my book.

"Gaelle," Jillian sat in the driver's seat, "this will help."

I rode in the back of the wagon with the shovels and the sprigs. Jillian had lots of room up front, but she had enough tact not to say so. I didn't know why I stayed back there, sitting on top of some folded crop mesh. Maybe it was because I wanted Jillian to go first, so as we approached the orchard, I saw it only as I looked around her. She was my point of reference, my home.

At first it was hard to see where the mindless had ruined the trees. I gripped the wagon side, and waited for it all to roll out in front of me. But when it appeared, the path was a stubble of stumps maybe as wide as the wagon's length. Fires had caused much worse damage.

"It's so small," I said.

Jillian had me help her heft the sprig crate. "It wasn't a brutal loss."

Even the sprigs felt lighter than I'd expected. And this was good. The trees could absorb just about everything; they too had escaped with a simple scarring. But that didn't feel like the whole truth—not for the trees, and not for me. A kind of sacrilege had happened here.

Jillian had already started digging the planting holes. I grabbed the other shovel, and it made my hands feel strong to hold it. We dug a dozen holes each. My father and I used to plant trees; he would stand over me while I sprinkled the earth with bonemeal.

Today, Jillian and I would plant the new sprigs next to the old stumps, with the hope that the roots from the saplings would join the community already living there. The winter's cold still rose from the ground.

As I worked, I put my back only in Jillian's direction. She popped her knuckle, and I jumped. That sort of thing can sound like a snapping twig; some soldiers will wake out of a dead sleep, from the sound of a cracking knuckle. Now I squatted over a sapling with the waterskin's heavy bulge. I had brought along the shovel, even though we had finished digging.

I caught Jillian glance at me once. She usually worked faster than I did, but now she matched my pace so she was never far away. I steadied a sprig as I raised it. The planting stood on its own, and my throat tightened.

"We took the sprigs from the dying trees," said Jillian. "That seemed the most appropriate."

"Well." I couldn't look at her. "It cuts down on waste."

That may have been a cynical thing to say.

"Or," said Jillian, "it makes the sprig into less of a replacement and more of a," she stood, "a reshuffling."

"You make it sound like rimstack."

She chuckled, and waited for me to stand. We moved to the next set of holes.

A twig fell from a branch where a red squirrel scrabbled. I'd choked the shovel at the sound, so I held it like a long-handled knife. "I keep expecting Wilm," I said.

"And you expect to lay him out?"

"No." I dropped the shovel. My body expected something other than Wilm.

"He had to shop in Northcraft. He wants paint for his stars."

"Of course." I thought of a path through the stars, waged by somebody fleeing.

"This is our job, Dear."

I wiped sweat from my lip. "Fair enough."

"You have to take your land back, Gaelle." She looked taut where she squatted. She'd brought a kukri. And this meant either that she wanted to share how I felt, the way she shared my pace with the planting, or that she was trying to recover land of her own.

Water trickled to my boot. I said, "Wilm seems better, these days."

"It helps him to help."

I thought of him haggling in Northcraft, smelling of onion and past-prime hazelnut. "Did he ever know Miriamne?"

She sat from her squat. "I suppose. A little." She leaned back on her hands. She said Wilm began to build his pasture after Miriamne had already started writing. She didn't live here then. Nor did Jillian, who was working as an outlaw. "This was first and foremost your parents' farm."

"So Wilm knew my mom."

"Oh, I think he liked your mom." Most everybody did. "You could probably ask him." I didn't want to. "I think he was content to accept that your mother was gentle. Simple, even."

"Dumb?"

"No. Quaint." She adjusted her kukri. "Well-behaved."

"Then he is a git."

"Well, his fields nearly touched ours. So he needed her well-behaved." It was the way, I figured, we all needed not to run. "He needed to rely on her for trade, you know? News, help with the occasional beast."

"The way he did with us." Until his horse killed us.

"The thing is that when the Church arrests a hedgewoman—whether she's a heretic or not—they punch a hole in an entire network."

"And that means people learn to overlook things."

"Sure," she said. "Or at least until the Church makes them feel they'll risk something worse if they don't. And I say *hedgewoman* here, but I also mean your father."

"But women need to be better behaved."

"Do you know that in the prisons, the jailers fear the women more than the men?" I sat still. Jillian never talked about prison. "Our supposed weakness suggests we shouldn't receive punishment as brutal as what happens to men." She straightened her shirt. "It's probably how I'm still alive." I wanted her to stop touching her shirt, so she couldn't show me anything else she had beneath it. She said the Church's same supposition of weakness is what makes them believe a woman's rage is less controllable than a man's. "We're supposed to go berserk," she said. "So they strap us down. They keep us in smaller boxes. And the irony is that this sort of treatment would drive most anyone toward madness, whether they started out sane or not."

I couldn't move, or even look away from her. What she told me sounded like a confession somehow worse than the fact that she'd withheld from me another aunt. I watched the trees now, not for mindless, but the garrison. "I'm sorry."

"No, it's all right. But you see why the Church can never arrest you."

In my later years, I've sometimes wondered if this afternoon was Jillian's Treehand moment, where she let loose a horror she'd saved up, because she needed it to menace someone else for a while. But among the new eddle trees and the stubble of the old ones, I didn't receive her story this way. My father's talk of Treehand was something that dropped from the ceiling, as if one of our herb baskets had finally landed with the weight of a festering nest of beetles. But Jillian's description of prison, and women, was a truth I somehow expected. Church canon described us as deformed males. It made sense the Fathers considered us fragile in every way except malice. And it further held that they feared us, because first, they didn't know us, and second, they liked to oppress us. Wilm, in his hut, had shown such fear when he'd stepped away after he thought he'd pushed me too far. Jillian's discussion of women felt more familiar than Treehand, and in this way, it felt more inevitable. But it didn't leave me horrified. It just made me mad.

I grabbed the waterskin, and set upon the next planting. If anyone could irrigate with a vengeance, I did. "Why didn't they imprison Miriamne?"

"They killed Miriamne."

"But they didn't end her all at once."

Jillian pushed herself to her feet, heavily—this woman who could spring from fenceposts. "You know, it's advertisement, if you walk around bearing the Church's punishments."

"Esaosh, these people."

"And you know why else." She mashed a clod of earth around the base of a sprig. "Because they didn't want to look like they were shutting her up."

"They gouged out her eyes!"

"But they didn't start there. They started by taking off her finger, and arguing down her theological points."

I imagined them doing both with a file.

"What they didn't want," she said, "was to look like they were shutting her up with anything but rhetoric."

"That and dismemberment."

"Well, yes, but the Church takes off fingers the way other people would levy a fine." This is true; many of the Church's own have missing fingers. "There's less to keep track of, this way."

"And less with whom to argue."

"And here's the thing. They couldn't win the arguments with your aunt."

"They couldn't out-reason a woman."

"And they'd try. And she'd retort. And then they'd cut." From where she sat, she flopped onto her back. She spread out her arms. "Gaelle, this day was supposed to cheer you." She slid her arms a bit.

I stood by her shoulder. "You're making a mud maiden."

Her eyes appeared almost green beside the muck. She looked me in the face, and slid her arms and legs into arcs. She laughed. "Snow ones are cleaner." I helped her up.

"You know," I said, "I think today actually might cheer me." I turned toward the eighteen sprigs we had planted already. "I can see why you do it. Why you have to do it."

"Why I fight, you mean."

"Why we fight," I said, and her eyes tightened at my use of the pronoun.

I sort of pointed with the waterskin. Why we plant trees. "Why we take back the land."

part SIX

That spring, as I moved from Wilm's hammock and back to my old bed, I lay awake with thoughts of the eddle saplings that grew in the mindless path. The head of my pallet faced the wall closest to my mother's oxcart, and I imagined the cart's bramble sprouting with the sprigs, so they mingled and grew full. No one should have forced my mother to behave. No one should have minced her sister, because this sister was smarter than a Church full of predatory men. And no Church should be so vile as to keep its people from reporting either a Treehanded horse or the walking dead. I made fists under my covers. It still hurt do so, but I let the pain itself drive my resolve. No mother's child should mangle their fingers, and their mind, and a splendid line of trees, to escape what the garrison should be called to subdue. And the fact that all of this did happen was enough to make me the very opposite of subdued. I would fight. If an enemy came to our farm, they would find two women to fear.

I started to train myself. Jillian had already said she would teach me, and perhaps if I'd thought about it, I'd have realized I was departing from her plans. But all I could see was the need for strength. Farm work is hard work, and I was already lean. But I began to lift water buckets. I sprinted laps in the relative safety of the horse pen. The few times Jillian or Wilm found me, I told them I was making myself healthy again. My progress was a tonic. I developed muscles I hadn't yet seen: the quartering of the thigh, the horseshoe cleft in the back of the triceps. My arms grew too wide for my sleeves. Jillian never seemed to notice, except to ask if I was still finding time to read. Wilm had either long stopped looking at me, or had gotten better at hiding it. I didn't care; I, for one, liked both the power, and the thought that when the time came, I could stop danger. I wouldn't destroy my father's orchard next time, or cause our neighbor to burn his hands. My training wasn't fear, I told myself. It was a kind of control. It wasn't violence. It was a sort of killing to kill violence, an effort to sever the snakes. It was a sort of becoming deliberate, the way Jillian wanted. It was growing up, to carry the fight.

Somewhere on the property, my aunt kept her kukris. She likely stored them with her leather armor, someplace secret. I told myself stories of her showing me how to use them—of my awaking before dawn, to find her sitting at table, with her kukris splayed before her like keys. She did nothing of the sort. The one time I got up enough nerve to ask her where she kept them, she flattened her mouth as if I'd posed the question at least once a day. "I keep them," she said, "as far off as possible."

"I don't want to use them," I said.

"Good."

"But you must figure they're useful."

"Gaelle, they're a failure."

"Or a necessity."

She kept her back to me. She was cleaning out the fireplace, and her hands looked almost dead from the ashes. "Listen to me." She turned. "The kukris are a failure of everything else that should keep a person from using them." She pulled a horseshoe nail from the ashes. As a means of cleansing them, Teph would occasionally burn shoes that Lucinda threw. Jillian set the piece aside for Wilm.

Denied the kukris, I resorted to a hatchet. Everybody in Holding becomes proficient with a hatchet. Wood is how we heat ourselves and how we build our shelters. I've watched men fell a tree and turn it into a canoe, in a matter of days. The hatchet was such a tool that it was easy to forget it was also a weapon. And I didn't remember the point until Wilm mentioned, idly, how a man's ribs had the thickness of a basic plank of wood.

In my lonely afternoons, I started to work. I already knew how to cleave a log with one blow. Now I taught myself to stop the blade halfway through, and to angle it in such a way as to extract it fast. I learned how to throw the hatchet—to sink it into a post, or to toss it in such a way as to smack the target with the blunted end. As a family object, our farmstead's hatchet was older than I. And while I trained, I imagined my targets were mindless, or Treehanded, or self-defensive churchmen. With each throw, I sought to obliterate everyone's regret. I made, in other words, an attempt to undo so many things, and they included events I didn't yet half understand. At best, I worked with the hope for an overturning, or returning, a kind of redemption.

In my memories, these days, I see myself throwing the hatchet with the same expression Garfield had when he watched the spot on my flagstone that signified his home. It's an expression that carries a light from a distant awareness of how we all had been born for better.

On the farm, the evenings got lighter, and my aunt went out later. I made a lot of firewood. Afterward, I made kindling. In a matter of weeks, I'd gotten good enough to want people to see me work the ax. The split of the wood reminded me of my father, and I pictured him sitting on the fence, where Teph had once rested. Then, after a while, I imagined Teph sitting there too. Sometimes I wondered if Jillian watched. And it was these thoughts that kept me, on a foggy night, from noticing I truly had an audience.

"You must take after your aunties," said a man.

I spun around. He leaned into the fence, but I could see only his silhouette. He had an extremely round head.

"I startled you," he said.

The hatchet stuck from a beam, across the yard.

"Are you the grown-up little one?" he said. "The blocky-headed child? Lloyd's girl?"

"It's dark and you're a stranger," I said.

"Yes! Well, nearly dark. It's good you know the Law of Trespass." Strangers were to announce themselves after dark, or lose protection against violence. "I suppose it's also good I'm a lawyer."

"I don't know any lawyers." I thought to Touch for Jillian, but realized I already had.

"Your aunt about?"

"Not now."

"Your father then?"

I blinked. "No."

He looked around the barnyard. "I guess you're old enough to be on your own."

"I'm old enough to protect the farm."

He was quiet for a while, and then I realized, from a soft wheeze, that he was laughing. "You sure don't fall far from her tree."

"I'm especially good in trees."

Now he was laughing, full bellied. "I set you up for that one." He let go of the fence and scratched his head. "It is dark, isn't it?"

"What do you want?"

"What? Oh. I have something for your aunt." He held out a sack. "We pay her every now and again."

"What for?"

"What for? Church work." Of course. "All lawyers are part of the Church. You should know this." The sack clinked.

"You can just leave it." I glanced toward the road. "She'll get it when she's back."

"Which is also when you'll be done with your throwing."

"That's right."

"In the dark."

"Near dark."

He was laughing again, or still. He sounded like the continuous squeak of a spring.

"Actually—Gaelle?"

I hadn't given him my name.

"I was hoping you could sign this parchment for me. It helps, is all, with the record-keeping."

I thought of the Church taking fingers over fines. I Touched again.

"If you prefer," said the man, "I could wait for your aunt. But as you say, it is nearly dark, and inns are far off. And I wouldn't want to put you out by staying the night." Holding had a law about extending hospitality to a churchman if he came to you after dark. In this case, of course, the guest had to pay nothing.

A horse whinnied. "That's Bravey." The man sniffed. "Stupidest name for that horse. She hates the dark, especially in these parts. I've even had to leave my lantern by her. See there?" A faint glow came from the bend in the road. "It'll help you to sign, if you come over by the light."

"Or you could bring the lantern to me."

"Oh certainly. But no. She'd give you so many road apples that you could grow turnips in the thoroughfare." He rubbed his throat, as if he tried to swallow something. "You don't trust me though. I see you don't."

"Nope."

"Fine." He squelched in a patch of mud. "We'll have it your way."

He moseyed down the path, and I walked backward until I got to the hatchet. The horse whinnied. It whinnied louder, and snorted. The churchman jogged back, with the bouncing light of the lamp.

He leaned over the fence. "Best sign fast."

"You could have brought the horse here."

"Not today though. I've a cart."

In the light, he showed his wrinkles. He was much older than I thought, and he was completely bald. He held a quill and parchment. The writing on the paperwork was flourished, but brief. I could read—and I made a show of reading—every part. It was a receipt for 215 talents. It had an obvious place for me to sign, and when I did so, I tried to be fast and careful. And in spite of the moment, I was proud. It was the first time I had officially signed my name.

"Excellent," he said. "Gaelle, I thank you." He handed me the sack. "Use it in good health." He made a raspy roll of the parchment. "Incidentally." He touched his cheek with the end of the scroll. "I did surprise you, and I know you aren't aware of how we're old family friends."

Jillian's Touch answered, like a warm hand on the top of my head.

"We're friends," said the man. "But in the future, you should be careful about threatening the Church, no matter how funny you are. Legally speaking, I could see you killed."

He clapped my shoulder, padded to his horse, and peered back around the corner. "Lucky you! Just three." He waved, and ducked back away. There was indeed the creak of a cart. I must have been so very deep in my work, not to hear it approach in the first place.

A breeze blew the smell of horse, and I discovered I was freezing. Jillian Touched in a way that pressed me a bit where I stood. I answered, and clutched the hatchet. Some part of me yearned to wait in the house, but I didn't want to move. The way the bag lumped made me want to nudge it, but I was afraid something might crawl out. The churchman *could see me killed*. Heaven knew this was likely true. I had a weapon, of course, and I could throw it at any danger. But at the moment, I would have only one shot, and then I'd have nothing.

Jillian and Wilm jogged into the yard. Jillian carried the maul in one hand, and she leaped the fence.

"It's a delivery," I said. She looked around. "Church work."

Wilm stalked to the road.

"The Church was here?" she said.

"They asked for my dad."

"What did you say?" she said.

"That he wasn't around."

She picked up the sack. "Bald man? Extremely round head?"

"Said I took after my aunts."

"That's Mellion." She took my arm, and led me to the house. "Mellion is a deliveryman and a spy."

"He said he was a lawyer."

"Absolutely."

Wilm returned from the road. "They've left a pile of horse manure."

"Let's not get nostalgic," she said.

"Jillian," I said. "What in all hell do you do for the Church?"

She set her shoulders. "I told you what I do."

"And what did you do lately?" I said.

She cast a look over the yard. "It's a salaried position."

"How contractual," said Wilm.

"They keep the advantage this way," said Jillian. "They bring me the money, and they learn where I am."

"And what do they do," said Wilm, "if they can't find you?"

"Then they wait," she said, "with the person they do find. And if that person can't help them find me, they take the person with them, and keep on searching."

"Esaosh on a chamber pot," I said. "Jillian, you have got to stop."

She blew a scoff. "Just all of a quick?"

Wilm said, "No. No one can stop, when they're hooked by the Church's string. Especially not you people."

"What do you know of our people?" I said.

"Gaelleda, I lived on my pasture for twenty-two years. You women." He waggled his hand. "Wild haired, wild eyed—"

"You're saying we didn't know our place," I said. "After all this?"

"I'm saying that some of you didn't know reality, Gaelleda. Your mother would come out and stutter at me—"

"She did?" I said. Wilm scowled. Jillian smoothed her forehead. My mother and I had just shared a joke.

"Gaelle," said Jillian, "what did Mellion say?"

"He said he had money," I said.

"Tell me exactly," she said.

I remembered my surprise, the coil of his laugh. "He came out of nowhere," I said.

"And you were where?" she said.

"In the pen," I said.

"Doing what?" she said.

She knew what I did, and she probably knew why. "I was throwing the hatchet," I said.

"They call it a hand ax," she said, "when you use it as a weapon."

"And I was throwing it well," I said.

"And I'm sure that impressed him," she said.

"He told me," I said, "the Church could see me dead."

I shouldn't have told her so. I'd wanted to make him the villain, but Jillian looked at me as if I'd confessed something of my own. Wilm wiped his face with his hands.

"Why," said Jillian, "did Mellion tell you that?"

"Because he wanted to scare me," I said. "Because I probably scared him." As a woman, I meant.

"And were you scared?" she said. "Did you do something?"

"Do something?" I said.

"Say something?" she said, "Throw your ax, maybe? Threaten his life a little?"

Wilm made a noise in his throat.

"Gaelle," said Jillian. "Did you threaten the Church?"

I lay the ax by our doorframe. "In fact he was trespassing." I got a bad taste in my mouth.

Wilm cursed.

Jillian said, "This isn't how we fight."

"Jillian," I said.

"It isn't." The look she gave me showed she knew exactly what I'd meant about scaring.

"Jillian, it's not like I killed anything," I said. "Esaosh, I'm not daft."

"Most killing is murder," she said. "If you're lucky, it's just property damage." She stood by the door. "But if you try to kill the Church, you can kill your whole family."

"You people," said Wilm. "You're outlaws. You're thieves. But you have never been murderers."

"Why are you allowed in this conversation?" I said.

"Because this whole tragedy started with my horse killing your father." He said that—Wilm—in front of our house's door.

"It's an old tragedy," said Jillian. "Many parts." In his lantern's light, Wilm's ears had gone red. "Now. You threatened the Church."

I said, "I threatened a trespasser."

"And this threat could provoke more notice from the Church," said Jillian.

"To be fairest," said Wilm, "Gaelleda is part of a noticeable family."

"And because of this," said Jillian, "I can protect her."

"I don't need protecting," I said. "That, and not killing, is what all this ax business has been for."

Jillian still looked at Wilm. "The Church still knows she's my dear one." Wilm grunted. "She's worth more to them alive."

She said this with a flick of a finger, but it felt as if something large had brushed me. It was as if Mellion's laugh had heft. In this moment while I stood in a pen, I encountered the realization that I truly could be a target, or that they could use me to target Jillian. Despite my attempts at self-sufficiency, I could also become passively dangerous, if only by what, and whom, I knew. My own identity could be a weapon of self-harm.

"Gaelle," said Jillian. "Pay attention. Mellion's conversation." The way she stood, she still kept us from entering the house. "What happened next?"

"Next, nothing," I said. "He wanted me to come with him to his horse. I said no. He wanted me to sign in the light, but I made him bring it."

"Sign?" said Jillian.

"The receipt," I said. "I read it, Jillian. That's all it was."

Wilm clicked his tongue.

"You signed your name?" said Jillian.

"I do know how to sign my name."

She said, "Did he tell you where to sign?"

The yard began to feel very quiet. "No."

"I was stupid," she said.

"No. Nobody was stupid," I said.

"Gaelle." She leaned against the house, as if someone had backed her there. "Gaelle, it was a test." It was an inquiry, even, an inquisition. "Now they know you can read."

"It isn't outlawed," I said.

"No, but it can be," she said. "And now they will watch you for trouble."

Maybe they'd take my ax-throwing hand. The stars seemed to shift, or to clarify.

"They must have suspected," said Wilm. "I mean, your whole family could read."

"And it's important to read," said Jillian. "It shows you all the shit they've surrounded you with." She grasped my pipe necklace. "But you must not menace. You must not destroy. You must not look so much as sharp-eyed at anything, unless you fall under full attack." The way she held the pendant, it was as if she invoked everyone who counted me as a dear one. "Gaelle. The Church is an organization that devotes itself to deceit."

"I hate them," I said.

"They are professional predators," she said.

"And they make you serve them," I said.

She kept hold of me. I waited for her to shudder. "They are professional predators."

part SEVEN

A week after Mellion's visit, I still talked little with Jillian. Whenever I made mistakes, I became either silent or belligerent, and I had the maturity, this time, to choose the former. I hated myself for how Mellion had tricked me, and I hated our being prey. No person should be prey, as if someone else thought we existed only to fulfill them.

This notion of predation is the hardest thing to teach, no matter who you're trying to turn from the Church. It was likely hard enough for Jillian to teach me I was a target, and I had been raised with the knowledge of a threat from the first moment someone admonished me not to run. But when you deal with a person who's been raised, or trained, to find security in the Church, who finds a bastion in the mouth of that predator, you have to get them to accept a kind of parental abuse. You can't do it directly. You have to show there's more to them than what has so constantly dominated their sense of self. You have to show how questioning such domination is an act of faith in goodness, instead of a lapse of discipline. And what can best let them make such a turn is their love for someone who exists apart from the domination itself. For those subsumed by the Church, love can add another center to their world. It shows them a part of themselves that gravitates toward this other center. And over time—and such a thing requires time—someone raised in the Church can find the god of goodness not in this person's old sanctums, but in the face of their own dear one. As I hang in my prison, I don't preach this point out the window. I whisper it to Increase, who mutters a bit in his throat. If the Church is your enemy, you have to love this enemy, one by one.

During the week beyond Mellion, Jillian continued to teach, as if the man's visit had only increased her sense of urgency. She probably hated herself for not warning me of him, because she lingered more on the Church these days. She told me its branches the way she'd describe the parts of a trap. Back then, she said the head of the Church was the principe, and that he held charge of all matters. The principe's name was Emeric the Gilded, and he presided in Ordinal, just a ways up from where I now dangle. Under the principe, the chancellor of the Church supervised all secular aspects of government. His name was Aldo Gaius, and he also served in Ordinal. At the same rank as the chancellor served the abbot, who presided at the abbey in Holding. This was Lumis Caspar, and he was the one who pulled Jillian into the ruins whenever he found one, or needed to find her. As abbot, Caspar was further in charge of all the empire's spiritual matters, including something called the Sword Potent, which consisted of the knights, who arrested heretics; the inquisitors, who judged heretics; and the exorcists, who treated heretics. Caspar would grow to take charge of far more, but even when I was young, he commanded plenty.

Where we sat at the cottage's table, Jillian ground some of her egg shell between her fingers. She didn't need to elaborate.

"Mellion is an inquisitor?" I said.

"Oh, I think Mellion's been all three, but yes. He visits and inquisits." She dusted her hands.

"Have you known him long?"

"Yes." She rose from the table. "Sort of the way you'd know a trick knee."

"You'd think they'd be able to look for the weeds, or maybe even the mindless."

She turned to me with an open face.

I said, "The Sword, I mean."

"Gaelle." She looked at me as if I'd just signed Mellion's paper all over again. "We don't want the Sword on the move."

She cleared the dishes, as if they were the last remains of the discussion.

She said, "I figured we'd go on a trip today." When I was little, I'd liked trips. "Jan's Rest, for horseshoes."

I thought of the nail we'd found in the fireplace ashes. "Godiva's still got good ones."

"I know." She wrapped her scarf with a small flourish. "But these are for us."

"What?"

"Come on. No Wilm."

"Why do we need horseshoes?"

"Take your cloak." She tossed me the thing.

"What are they for?"

She opened the door, and she stood there with the cold. "If you must know, they're for a game."

Jan's Rest was a hamlet two hours away, slightly farther west of Northcraft than Hal's Bride. It didn't make the best horseshoes, but its smith sold the cheapest ones. In fact, the farrier in Hal's Bride said he practiced his skill by improving these.

Now in the wagon, Jillian would not tell me how the horseshoes were for a game, and she said I wouldn't guess anyway. This was an invitation to try, and I came up with everything from target practice to weight training.

"Now," she said, "we went to Jan's Rest to shoe a pig once." She lit her pipe.

"What?"

She puffed. "His name was Bocephus. He was a very self-important pig. And he had an incredibly round head—which I think you'd appreciate."

Maybe we could shoe Mellion. "Why'd you name him Bocephus?"

"Miriamne thought he should have a lot of syllables. Something like an incantation."

"A heretical pig?"

"Well." She sort of trotted her hands. "He would eat only from a certain bowl. He had a paisley on his rump that he'd waggle around like some kind of decree."

"So a Churchly pig."

"Could be. He'd count the carrots you'd give him." She might have jostled me a smile, but it was mostly hidden under her scarf.

She was trying too hard. Jillian must have known laughter beat fear, but it might have been the only weapon she couldn't learn well.

"Once he sat on a rose stem," she said. "And it got stuck right across," she gestured behind her, "in his hair. And he wouldn't let anybody remove it. Not even your mother, whom he sometimes followed like a dog."

"My mother had a pet pig?"

She shrugged. "And so he just walked through the barnyard that way, faster and faster, trying to get the stem to come off—which, it eventually did."

"I see."

She pulled down her scarf to let out a breath. It was good to see her mouth, anyway. "Every morning, for some reason, he would lick the side of the cottage."

"The pig?"

She chuckled. "Every morning, before dawn, there was this *rasp, rasp, rasp*. And your mother would say, 'B'cephus!' That's how she'd say it. 'B'cephus!'" I thought of my mother, disheveled and irked. "And the pig would stop for a while. And then we'd hear *rasp, rasp, rasp*."

I fetched a laugh. It was funny enough. "Dumb pig." Jillian rubbed her knuckles, as she did these days. "So this is when you lived with them," I said.

"The family."

"Yes. For a little while." She peered at her feet. "For a little bit, we all lived here."

I wanted to ask when, and for how long. I wanted to know what dissolved it all, but asking about any of it felt as if I would dissolve something else.

"So we shoed the pig," she said, "because he was a big pig."

"How?"

"Well, we got him drunk on fermented eddlefruit, which is something he loved to do—"

"But why would you shoe—"

"Because he was so big, that your dad would use him to haul things to town." She squared her hands. "Gave him a little cart."

"Jillian. You have to be making this up."

She held up her hand. "People knew him. Bocephus the Peddler Pig. Sold apples and plums."

"Oh get off it. He peddled things you'd serve with pork?"

"Well, he didn't know about pork servings. And he wouldn't think it pertained to him anyway, which, of course, it didn't."

We waved to a herdsman and his sheep.

I said, "I'd never heard this story before."

"Ah."

"It's ridiculous."

"Well. I think of it whenever I come here." And with Miriamne disclosed, she had more freedom to tell me these things.

My father had described my mother, of course: her warmth, her humor. But I'd heard little from Jillian, and I'd heard nothing about Miriamne. And in spite of, or maybe because of, what happened last week, it was good to see Jillian smile. It was better to imagine them all smiling. "You should tell me more of these things."

She sat up straighter, and pulled her braid from her scarf. "All right."

She chucked her chin at Jan's Rest. The village appeared as a lopsided circle within a single-layered palisade. It had houses of cob, wood, and moss. Oaken planks lay in the road as a means of mitigating the mud. The smithy itself was a lean-to with an anvil, and a bellows, and a few ragged tanning racks. Stumps stood in a circle by a wagon whose side had a drop-down counter. The cooling troughs held clotted water, and not a single one was full of oil. An old man with scarred forearms peered into the nearest one. An older man, with torn breeches, squatted by a few cords of firewood.

I asked Jillian if either one was the man who shoed Bocephus, and she said no, that the smith by the trough was his son.

The smith drew a crooked nail from the trough, and wiped it on his leg. Jillian handed me the reins, descended from the cart, and talked with him. He nodded, pointed to the stumps, and told us to wait.

He had three shoes for sale, but he needed to make one. Jillian told me this, as we settled the cart. It was good to stretch, especially in the forge's heat.

We sat. The older man nodded to us, and he fed the fire. He was missing two of his fingers.

"You have a look to know things," he said to Jillian. His voice hitched, as if he spoke some during his inhale.

Jillian clasped her hands on her knee. "I just know I need horseshoes."

He glimmered at me, and I looked at my own maimed hands. "I have a look at the fire every day." He pressed his chest. "I let it breathe into me. The fire wants to come in." He breathed, and coughed.

The smith started to hammer. "Be good to the company, Albert."

"It likes to live inside," he told us.

"You don't have to say any more," said Jillian.

He had a touch of soot in his nostrils. "What's the Sword going to do to me? Send me into the arms of my friend?"

"Then maybe think of what they'll do to us," said Jillian.

He waved his hand at her. "Then you don't need to overhear anything I have to say. Not announcing it's for you, anyway." He shuffled to the flame, and fed it. "The fire is alive, is all I say. It eats, it breathes, it casts waste, it multiplies." He touched a burn scar on his forearm. "It's soft if you pet it."

"No petting, Albert," said the smith.

"The Church knows you need to build a ring around a fire before you summon it," said Albert. "That's Church teaching. Sanctified. Otherwise, it gets out."

"Gaelle," said Jillian. "Maybe go sit in the cart."

I didn't want to go anywhere.

"We aren't here to talk theology," said Jillian.

Albert said, "The Church says a heretic might tell you that although we need the Church's light, we also need the fire's warmth. And the fire just gives it away, you see, just by being."

"The Church would teach," said Jillian, "how warmth begets passion, and that passion tempts Visjaes."

"And the Church would also teach how some heretics know that without passion, none of us would be here." Albert licked his lips. "And without warmth, the world would freeze over."

Jillian spoke a little louder. "But you don't say such things."

"No." He rubbed his scar against his face. "Only if I were a heretic." He got close enough to the fire to make me fear he'd hug it.

The last of our horseshoes hissed in the clotted water. Jillian fished coins from her purse, and yanked hard the drawstring. From a nearby house, waddled a single sheep.

The smith handed Jillian the horseshoes, and also gave her back some coins. "We're sorry for the mess."

"You know," she said, "he could risk you by implication."

"Well, he's wily by how he talks in what the Church teaches."

"And he's your family," she said. "Some cousin or uncle."

"Look," he took a step toward her. "Most of the town just tells folks he's daft."

Jillian took the shoes. "Keep him quiet." On one of the stumps, she placed the money the smith had returned. "It's worthwhile, to everyone." She later told me she wouldn't risk appearing that she took a bribe to shelter a heretic.

In the wagon, I held the horseshoes' nobbled heft. They were thick, weighty, and not at all even. I asked if the fireman had left us somehow implicated, and Jillian shook her head. The Church could convict you for not turning in a heretic, but the fireman had spoken enough in hypotheticals to keep us safe enough. Besides, if the smith was right, the Church would have to raid the whole town. And this was something it rarely did, because the move hurt the Church's revenue. "You can't tax deadmen," she said. "But," she wrapped the scarf, perhaps to muffle her voice. "The problem of implication is why I am always so careful about the information I give you. Do you see?"

"Jillian, I'd never report you."

"I know." She grasped my unscarred forearm. "Exactly."

The horseshoes jangled on the seat, and I spaced them so they'd stop. The wind raised the road dust like ghosts. "So does he, hypothetically, worship the fire?"

"A hot light instead of a clear one?" Despite the cold, Jillian wiped sweat from her face. "Hypothetically, I think the fireman worships enthusiasm." This seemed like an odd choice. "Of course, if that's what he does, it's absolutely damnable."

She told me *enthusiasm* is an old term derived from *en theos*, which essentially means *possessed by God*. And because Esaosh is the god of the stalwart rational, a *God* infusing enthusiasm implies someone else. This is the first time I ever heard of Visjaes in a way that emphasized Visjaes' godhood over Visjaes' villainy. And it didn't escape me how the pairing occurred in something as ancient as a word.

Our cart rolled along. The sun rose higher, and it made the ground exhale its cold. From the road, I watched a boy beat a rain barrel with a stick. Water splashed from the top, and he shrieked.

"So what you meant back there," I said, "is that enthusiasm is demonism?"

"Well maybe the Church would say so. Passion and all." We pulled up to the cottage, and Godiva stomped. "Other people might say the fireman worships love."

"Love."

"Oh, love can be terrible." An accordion aria through the trees. "Love is awe-ful, you know, as the center of things." Jillian squinted at me, and set her feet against the wagon's floor. "You must know that love isn't tame."

I nodded then, because I figured it was the mature thing to do.

Jillian wasn't good at comedy, but she was a grandmaster at devotion. Not discipline, not duty, not anything so trainable. But she had an instinct and a resilience I've tried to emulate as, throughout my career, I've attempted to turn potential allies to our cause. I don't know if my aunt ever outright worshipped anyone; she might have been afraid to imagine herself in relation to a god. But I believe her alarm over the fireman was not just in how he spoke heresy around us, but that he spoke a heresy she, herself, embodied. Love, in the form of either Visjaes or Jillian, is not tame. In fact, Jillian's whole house was ablaze.

We never saw the fireman again, but I remember the hitch in his voice and the mark on his arm. He had been touched. He certainly wasn't the first heretic I'd met, but unless we count Wilm, who was still becoming, the fireman was the first mystic I'd found. Albert had met a divinity who called to him from the pine needles and the fallen wood, who started with smoke like a whisper, who warmed his crotch and his belly and his face, who made him tear, and who lifted his eyes skyward, until divinity's light arced away like a bird. Albert the Fireman was the first witness I met who pointed to a center of the world that made us larger simply by bidding us near.

In the barnyard now, Jillian lay eight horseshoes before us. Four were the ones we'd bought, and the rest were a lighter sort she'd pulled from storage. She threaded rawhide strands through each of the holes, and she tied the lines until they resembled necklaces with huge, horsey pendants. Then she looped the strands so they dangled the horseshoes from just above her elbows and knees. They swung with enough give that unless she moved very carefully, the horseshoes clanged.

"This game is called Silence." She fitted me the same way. "It can be a race. It can be a sort of hide and seek. It can even be a climbing game." She checked that the lines weren't too tight. "But today, we're just going to play without keeping score."

The idea was not to make noise. Jillian outlined a course taking us around the house, and along the top of the horse fence, and then under my mother's oxcart, to the cottage door.

I blustered. I didn't know if I could do the fence even without horseshoes.

"It's good to be strong, Gaelle. But you want to be lithe."

I walked, and clanked. The different weights in the horseshoes were both noticeable and random.

"Jillian," I said.

"You can't hold the strings."

She stood with her knees and elbows bent, as if she walked waist-deep in very cold water. She took long, measured strides.

"You look like a water bird," I said.

"Yes," she stopped. "That's right. They try not to make ripples, to not startle the fish."

"You'd startle a person."

She took three smooth strides. "In real life, you'll be without horseshoes, and you won't have to walk like this." But, she said, this exercise taught muscle control. "Try again."

It felt ridiculous to stand the way she did, but I spread myself, as if the horseshoes dripped. She watched. I dropped my arms, and I clinked. She splayed herself again, and stood on tiptoe. There was no way to keep from noise without imitating her exactly.

I set my stance. Something about it forced my eyes wide. I opened my mouth.

Hers twitched.

"Don't laugh," I said.

"I'm not going to laugh." She spoke without moving her mouth. "If I laugh, I'll make noise." The horseshoes swung.

"What happened to the pig's shoes?"

"Oh, he learned to throw them."

"Now you're trying to make me laugh."

"It turns out he hated both the honk of geese, and a particular peddler who played the harmonica. So we had to stop taking him to market."

I clanged. She clanged. "Stupid pig," I said.

The Silence game made us sweat. We huffed and muttered and swore. In the next morning, despite my conditioning, my sides would ache from all the slow balancing. On this first afternoon, we did walk on top of the horse fence. I moved along the rail while Jillian kept by the side of it. The water-bird stance made the fence easier than I thought. And when I did fall into the pen, Jillian told me my job was to climb out without clanging.

We played, and then Jillian stopped. Wilm stood at the edge of the yard, with his hands loose at his sides. He just stood, then backed up the way he came.

"Drat," she said.

I climbed from the pen. "He probably thinks he saw a conjuring."

She strode after him, clanged a bit, and stopped to unfasten the shoes from her legs.

"Tell him about the pig," I said.

part EIGHT

A month later, the heat opened like a hand. The horseshoes warmed in the barn, and I figured that if the man in Jan's Rest ever worshipped this kind of intensity, then he was a demoniac after all. The heat expanded and flattened. It steeped. Jillian and I played our Silence game. I thew my ax. One night, Wilm sat the accordion in my lap, and told me it was like hugging the music with all your might. In the evenings, Jillian and I heard his songs become longer, more complex, and occasionally intricate enough to match the business of growing. The problem was that what warmed this year felt like our own dread. The torpor turned to agitation. The eddlefruit blossoms bloomed red, but they only gave the spring the look of violent birth. The season was the death of our reprieve.

The lake ice thinned. Jillian had long since found the man who owned the mindless's boat, and she'd given him money for a new one, plus a significant portion of our fish stores. I don't know what excuse she gave for what happened to the boat. Wilm said she blamed me for attempting a prank, but honestly, I didn't care. Most of the time, I spent my solitude listening, however impossibly, for the shatter of boat wood, the buzz of a fly, or the creak of a cart.

When the lake mindless did get free, it happened just before dawn. Perhaps the creature had the help of the full moon. I heard Jillian's feet hit the upstairs floor, before I heard the baying through the trees. The sound of the mindless made me curl over myself, as if I'd been punched.

Jillian found me doubled over with my hands on my knees. She led me to a chair, and I slowed my breath while she pulled on her armor and her boots. She grabbed a wooden vial she'd bought in town two weeks ago. Now she gave a brief rub to my head. I'd been trying to Touch with Wilm.

I straightened.

"You stay," she said.

"No." I had trained too much for this. "No, I'm sorry. You don't have time to keep me out of this. And you need my help."

She had a look I couldn't parse. It had more pain than surprise.

I left with her, squeezed the ax, and entered the yard. The howl of the mindless came high and wet. Beneath the noise beat the din of Wilm's pot. He knew to drum a code that told us the direction to run. The mindless had gotten to the east of the lake, which was also the direction of the road.

My weeks of training had made me fast enough to outstrip Jillian who, I later learned, had gone to fetch a shield.

I stopped, now, in woods that held a towered stillness. The mindless called, with a lurching sound, while Wilm's pot noises kept regular as his heartbeat. I squished through mud and avoided patches that would pull. Spots of snow remained in the forest, and they glowed in answer to the moon. Everything smelled like the lake. Wilm's pot ringing had stopped.

The mindless keened, loud and close. Its cry finished in a gurgle.

Now I caught movement to the side of me. The mindless stood to my left, with its back turned, about fifty paces off. I'd mistaken it for the dark of a tree trunk. One arm hung lower than the other, and its ears were gone.

Snapping turtles lived in the lake. I counted—one, two. The creature turned in profile, and its nose was gone. Three. This was good. It was. It explained, in part, why the mindless hadn't picked up my scent. I crept forward; I'd trained myself for this. The mindless whined, walked into a tree, and flailed. My out-angled pinkie chafed in its glove. Nobody deserved a blasphemed existence.

I readied the ax.

It felt too heavy.

I pictured the ax leaving my hand, the blade cleaving the back of the neck, ending the creature with a blow. I thought of Teph.

The thing lurched two steps. I drew back the ax, but—I couldn't let go.

The mindless turned my way, with holes for where its eyes had been.

I pushed myself, told myself *now*, but it was as if I acted in a dream. The mindless shuffled toward me and I fell to the ground.

Wilm stood above me with the branch he'd apparently used to take out the back of my knees. He shoved a shield into my arms, and it bloodied my lip. I'd dropped the ax.

Metal whistled. Jillian's kukri landed in a tree to the left of the mindless. The creature backhanded the tree trunk, and the tree shuddered.

I threw off the shield.

A second kukri whistled, and it made a wet smack.

The mindless rasped, bolted upright, and fell face-down.

Wilm had my ax.

"Give it!" I said.

He puffed his cheeks at me, and his beard bristled.

Jillian stood over the mindless. The second kukri protruded from the mindless's chest, while the creature lay still.

"I could have done that," I said.

"Go away," said Wilm.

"You ass," I said. "You stole—"

"Gaelle," said Jillian. "Go away."

"I could have killed it," I said.

"What do you mean *kill?*" said Wilm.

"I could have hit it the first time," I said.

"You're bleeding," he said.

"Gaelle." Jillian held a kukri that was long and serrated. "Get home."

In a world of violence, Jillian's great act of devotion is that she tried to keep me from violence. The mindless twitched. Jillian stabbed it in the thigh, and the creature went rigid.

The wound didn't bleed. "What did you do?" I said.

"Black sap," said Wilm. "Begone."

"Black sap?" I said.

"And you didn't have any, Smarty," he said.

"We have very little time," said Jillian.

"What is black sap?" I said.

"It's seasonal. Expensive. Contraband." Wilm loomed slightly over me. "Get your stubby self home."

"You aren't my father," I said.

He muttered something to Jillian.

"Please go home," said Jillian. She spread the mindless's arms, and hunched at its elbow.

My gut tightened. "What are you doing?"

Wilm readied my hatchet—my hand ax. I didn't know if this moment made the thing a weapon or not.

"Is it paralyzed?" I said.

Wilm spoke softly. "You said they said twenty minutes."

Jillian made a face, and pressed the blade at the creature's elbow.

"You have twenty minutes to chop it up?" I said.

"Look away," she said.

I lifted my eyes, and I wanted the rest of myself to follow, as if I could rise out of here, to arc like a fire. Above us, a chickadee washed himself in a spray of wet pine needles.

Jillian gnashed her teeth, while she and Wilm started to saw. Or at least I think they did. The chickadee pecked the branch.

"Can it feel?" I said.

They worked.

Wilm breathed heavy. He said, "We can roll it to get at the joint."

"Gaelle." Jillian huffed.

"Not on me," said Wilm.

She retched.

I walked away, through mud and clots of shining snow. Jillian had been right about my not being ready. Both this realization and I floated our way home.

I wasn't ready. I'd like to think that the people who ever become ready are those who occupy the opposite side of our war. And even then, I'm not sure if they truly are prepared to absorb the cost of ending a life, even a go-lemized one. If killing doesn't take a toll from you, it usually means you have nothing left. It's why I love Garfield, who still gets excited about saying *whore*.

part NINE

The night after we dismembered the mindless, we went to bed early. I don't know about Wilm, but that's what my aunt and I did. It's hard to say how much she slept; I managed very little. But it seemed necessary to lie there, to go to bed before sundown, and essentially kill this day.

I never asked what Wilm and Jillian did with the mindless's remains. I assumed—I had to assume—the creature lay inert throughout the entire operation. During my hours without sleep, I imagined it feeling nothing, or better, I imagined it feeling the relief of finally floating, piecemeal, to nothing.

In light of what Teph had told of the mindless on their farm, Wilm and Jillian probably had to do more than cut, if they'd wanted to destroy the creature outright. Burning was the likeliest tack, but under the circumstances, cremation would have been both extremely difficult, highly illegal, and potentially toxic. I imagined the mindless burning on a pyre of Treehanded brush. Jillian had long suspected how both the mindless and the Treehanded were a conflagration that spread after the horse, and by extension, also her rider. We would learn she was right. She just forgot Mellion, our third visitor. His return would lead us to realize the Church sought Lucinda too.

During the first days after the mindless, time ran together like a rotten soup. At some point, Jillian described how the black sap itself is Treehanded. It comes from the alarmingly-abundant moaske shrub, and a thimble-full can poison a grown man. Black sap has been used both by physicians and torturers alike; it keeps the body still, although it does nothing to block sensation. Most often paralysis sets in, even if the sap has merely been absorbed through the skin. The timing of the effect is unknown, but sap is sap, and it is hard to remove.

It felt stuck to me, somehow, what I had seen with the mindless, what Jillian had bidden me not to see. I wasn't paralyzed, necessarily, but something in me had stopped. It would be fanciful to say it was my childhood; most of us never had such luxury anyway, especially after losing both parents. And in this thing's cessation, I realized Jillian had done so much to protect me not only from the Church but also from the occasional cruelty of simple necessity. She wanted me to keep living as much as possible without perceiving the cost of it all.

Out of necessity, she had procured the black sap. Out of necessity, she had a contact who knew how to use it. Furthermore, this same person, or at least some person, was very good at guessing how to handle mindless. And out of necessity, Jillian had not told me these things, because among all else, she was also protecting that person as well. It took me years to learn who this person was. And by then, it was too late.

part TEN

The years passed, nearly six of them. Compared to what had happened when I was sixteen, they felt like a non-time, when I grew, but not as much, when we dealt with the mindless, but not in person. The Church had started to make daily pronouncements against the creatures. Judging by what I saw in the next few months, this was a deep and secret hypocrisy. But all we knew at the time was that the Church didn't talk directly about the mindless who'd come to us. Instead, the Sword Potent started a great purge against necromancy, in general. Its inquest, so called, apparently started from mindless sightings throughout Cadmul and Holden townships. The investigation put most of its weight on the coastal parts of the empire, but it was pressing west. And as it did, it already began to squeeze out money and food for the soldiers who interrogated the very people who provided those things. We didn't know then, but these were part of Holding's preparations for the worldwide Reordering War, just as we didn't know the Treehanded prepared for the same.

During these years, while the Church used the mindless scare as an excuse for martial law, the Treehanded invasion seemed dormant, small, or at least unnoticed. None of us knew where either the Treehanded or the mindless had come from, or why, and even I wondered if Jillian had been too facile in pinning their nexus on a meat-eating horse. We heard nothing from Teph. I still hated the sound of flies, and I killed whatever I could, but it was as if our actual Treehanded corpse had fallen from the sky, and disappeared into fire. The inquest said nothing about either the Treehanded or their plants. And in some perverse way, this made me feel all the more alone. Wilm was proof of what we had seen of the Treehanded; his very cabin was proof. He continued to call Teph a charlatan, but he never forgot Lucinda. He drew her picture, in dark lines and heavy angles, then in soft swoops as if she comprised of air. And at times, in fact, his love for his horse is what best helped to keep that part of the past a reality.

We still found a few Treehanded plants in the horse pen. But we burned fewer each year, and we began to suspect Lucinda really was the only agent from that forest. It was as if she had left some trail only we could follow, if we only had the authority and the resources. Maybe the weeds had so well disguised themselves that we were the only ones who had discovered something wrong. But the possibility seemed to shroud everyone else in such damnable ignorance. Or at the very least, they suffered the inquest's equally-damnable distraction. So in the meantime, we waited. We scorched the farmyard every summer. Godiva, decrepit and mild, watched from her tether. She died when I was seventeen, a few years older than I. We bought another mare, Tasha, who was blue-eyed and dainty and had brown and white spots, like a cow. We let Wilm keep her; he actually owned half. He loved her, I think, but as far as I know, he never drew her picture.

Wilm raised his tower: a two-floor cottage with a third-story lookout. His was the largest building in the fields, three times the size of what he'd had in his pasture. He worked the house out of forest and earth; he didn't even request glass for a window. And after a while, I started to figure the construction was good for him, that he liked the idea of cutting to build.

He spent more and more time in the forest. I'd glimpse him deep in the trees, as if he, or my aunt and I, lived behind bars. We'd sometimes hear his accordion, which sounded less like an aria now, and more like an ascending gyre. We also began to see the watchtower by his hut: a shingled column with dark window holes, that rose to a height where Jillian finally had to ask Wilm not to build taller. She suggested the thing could attract curiosity from the road, and he acquiesced. Wilm had been so cantankerous before, that his compliance felt like an attempt to keep distance between us, or at least to limit the exchange. We'd call Wilm out each week, to ask if he needed to replace his supplies. He'd tell us what he'd seen from his rounds: a feaster carrying a bobcat, a traveler who left a road-hole filled. Wilm didn't stay long. Aside from discussing business, he spoke a flailing sort of small talk. This might have been Wilm's nature regaining its equilibrium. And yet it might have had something to do with how both trapping and carving up the mindless had changed all of us. It created an intimacy of brutality. And with the inquest likely also committing brutality in the face of the mindless, we couldn't keep from wondering if we shared the inquest's side. We didn't talk about it. Not even my aunt and I talked about what had happened to the lake mindless. What we'd done had been both necessary and shameful—something that made us less than people by forcing us to treat someone else as less than people. Frequently I thought of Teph on the plantation where the mindless chewed the ground. I feared the mindless still; it would have been foolish not to. But I also understood how Teph had become a fugitive for their sakes.

As the inquest ground along, the Shield Potent—the Church's secular constabulary—posted sketches of the mindless in every church. We laughed at this, as if somebody would need to consult a picture before they ran from such a thing. But the portraits of the so-called necromancers became less absurd. These pictures came from Lumis Caspar's Sword Potent. This is when the knights started their house-to house-searches. The Sword proclaimed, early and often, that the mindless came from within the eastern kingdoms, that Azmon was faultless, that Treehand, though ever-infested, had kept to itself. The pictures went up. Jillian came home with rumors of people who were taken away: individuals mostly, hermits. Certainly not people whose demise most anyone protested.

Emeric—the Empire's current principe—declared from Ordinal how the war on necromancy had already achieved results. And occasionally I found this soothing. Innocents aside, the Church finally hefted itself against a true enemy, an enemy to both us and the unfortunate dead. I said this to Jillian, when I was eighteen. She pulled the sides of her eyes until her crow's feet disappeared.

Then, on the cottage table, she emptied the wooden cup from which we never drank. Out slid two bone rings that were about the size of the hole I could make with my thumb and forefinger. Jillian said she and Wilm found one in the front and another in the back of the lake mindless's neck. The bones were avian. Just as she and Wilm had expected, somebody had indeed implanted them to allow the mindless to make their sounds.

I told Jillian to notify the Church, to send the rings with a written explanation. She told me of an elderly man in a coastal village who had volunteered to do the same with a mindless corpse he had found. He gave his dog away. He bequeathed his boat to a neighbor. He sent his letter to the Church, and he disappeared a week later. The Church's suspicion was as depraved as its ham-fisted defense. And this wasn't to mention the depravity of grafting a dead man's throat with a bird, in such delicate offense.

I continued to run in the safety of the horse pen. If Tasha was around, she sometimes followed. I avoided the hand ax. We still kept the thing; it was too expensive to replace. And yet I kept it as dull as its own filth. In time, Jillian did make me use it. She urged me to throw it, and to split the wood. The idea, she said, was to make it ordinary by cleaning it with use. I couldn't ever throw it as well as I once had. The weapon reminded me of both the mindless and the snake. And in fact, both of those things were a claw on the same hand. They are perhaps another reason why, although I still believed peace was sometimes weak, I preferred it to the shame and pity that came from even the most necessary brutality.

In those years, my aunt looked older. She was older. But I think I also noticed more of her strain. Jillian had a brown spot on her hand, as if blood had dropped and dried there. She had a stiff walk in the morning. Her braid streaked gray. In terms of height, the years had evened us out somewhat, as if becoming a young adult pulled me up beside her. I could see Jillian's terror of what must still have felt like sudden motherhood: her attempts to raise me as a functional person; her mistakes; and mine. And this realization allowed me, sometimes, to see her patience.

Jillian was the only one of her sisters to live into her sixties, the only one of our family, in fact. She must have felt that. I did. I caught myself imagining how different she would look if, instead, she were Miriamne, or my mother. And then I wondered, but never truly wished, at how different I might be.

Of my family, Jillian told me more: how Miriamne was tall, and dark, and strident. She was the eldest, and she enjoyed the eldest's authority. She had a frequent laugh, and a pipe redolent of myrrh. And although Miriamne braved the Church to the point of provoking them, she wouldn't go into even the smallest clump of trees without waving a stick in front of her. She hated spiderwebs, said Jillian. Not spiders, but the webs, their feel. My mother—shorter, the middle child—would walk in front of Miriamne, if they went into the orchard together. But because Miriamne was taller, Barbara sometimes missed the webs, and this was why Miriamne carried the stick. Barbara had a round face and steady eyes. She spoke in a way that was slow and matter-of-fact, which sometimes let her say the most outrageous things without initial notice. She was the one who made Miriamne laugh the most. And during all the time when she seemed most suited of the three to live the orchard life, she was always Miriamne's editor.

Jillian taught me of my family in passing, but about other things, I felt as if she filled my hands as fast as she could. Sometimes she was direct. Other times, she'd try to make the training into impromptu games, or even unacknowledged repetitions. Maybe she was indirect because she didn't want to scare me. Other times, I wondered if she was self-conscious about how teaching was part of her own love's currency—that in this way, she, so careful and stern, was as lavish as Wilm's showering his affection on Lucinda.

Jillian had me practice the Silence game and the counting exercise. She taught me how sleep is valuable, even when it doesn't come. Mere shuteye will recharge a person, even if it can't do sleep's healing. Jillian showed me how women can get most places by acting innocent, or lost, by never looking a guard in the eye, and by asking about the men's wives and children. She said that outside the cities, whiskey isn't as good a gift as fresh water, but that in many places, the best offering is fruit. Watermelon, the so-called mid-Holden ham, is best for dehydration, because in addition to water, it carries sugar and salt.

She showed how, in a pinch, you can gather water from a field by tying cloth around your ankles, stomping in the dew, and wringing the cloth in a pan. She said that by pouring boiling water in a toughened wineskin, the skin will serve as both a heater and a source of pure water. She told me about packing a wound with cobwebs, and showed me how to lance an infection. She told me to watch the treetops for wind direction, and to consult birds and smoke to see if they hover low to the ground, as they will before a storm.

She said to watch a town's peasants, where if they disappear from a common area, I should too. She told me that if I ever found myself in a mob, I should also riot until I got to safety, that this participation would make me less conspicuous than any other activity. She told me never to take an inn room on the ground floor, to carry a wooden wedge as a means of securing my door, and how if pressed, an average person can survive a jump of three stories. She said to look for prostitutes, that where they stayed, it was reasonably safe for women. But she also told me how to lean in toward a man, and use an open-handed strike on his throat, if it became clear I had to fight.

She offered honey as a sealant for a wound, raw egg as something to soothe a minor burn. She taught me to sing loud and bawdy songs, as a means of befriending a crowd. She told me to take as much care correcting a strange man in public as I would reaching into an unattended sack. She showed me to control my fear with distraction and jokes, how the humorous and the frightening operate along the same mechanism of timing and absurdity. She told me to sit, if I trembled, that I could press my feet into the floor to stop my legs from wobbling. She taught me to quell worry by focusing only on what I could affect, and to make the rest as negligible as possible. She continued to urge me to seek the good: the man giving his life to write to the Church, the defiant hen hunching over her brood. Goodness pointed to hope, and hope led to productivity. She made me love my body as an ally, as an animal that both kept me warm and regulated my effort, that fought for our survival to the point of its own partial obliteration. The passing years gave me strength and speed; tapered (if crooked) fingers; ever-keen vision; and apparently something similar to Miriamne's voice. Where I caught myself looking at Jillian, she may have caught herself looking at me. Imagine your body, she said, as your family both fused together and living on, so they can protect you.

chapter 11

Soot and Portence

When I'm in the Bell, my hanging gaol, the worst part of the nights is the sound of the mindless pens. In my childhood, Jillian and Teph might have been right when they claimed the mindless don't move around at night. But just like every other weapon in this war, the mindless have evolved. In the months before I came to the prison at Ordinal, our spies discovered how the Church golemancers worked to develop a breed of mindless that functioned in complete darkness: cadavers with fine bristles that sense movement in the air.

The mindless in Ordinal's pens keen too much for them to be the kind to rely on air currents. And anyway, you'd think a crowd of bristled mindless would jumble themselves berserk. But this is the sort of thing I consider when I dangle in my cell. These days, people see my crooked fingers, and figure I just warped with age. But the Church that hangs me here knows my history with the mindless: how I've hidden as they've stumbled over the trenches above me, how I've pushed them into lye, and how I've watched them dismember some of my companions of nearly all the goodness they had. The mindless aren't the Riven's worst enemies. But as harriers and shock cavalry and even a form of execution, they embody everything we fight against. They are the walking fact that in the name of so-called holiness, the Church will devour a person, and spit up whatever's left, just so it can remake her as a weapon for use in a war for domination. It's the truth. If you can get yourself to treat other people as things, you can aspire to demonic efficiency.

These days, Increase snoozes by a candle I keep for him. He huddles so close to it that I wonder if he'll singe what little down he's got. But he coos by the fire, and I try to listen to him, over the pen's howls and the thrashing. Wherever he's from, the bird keeps me sane. He's what keeps me talking, sure, but, aside from Garfield, he's also the one who allows me to spend my warmth on something. One of the most lethal parts of solitary is that you don't usually get to do such a thing. I'll never forget how the man who scrawled his dungeon had become nearly violent with his need to spend himself. Most days, I reckon how such a need, and its denial, is one reason the jailers hoisted me into the Bell, to begin with. They couldn't have foreseen Increase, of course. And on account of how they usually treat one another, they probably couldn't have anticipated the gift of Garfield, either.

The boy arrived at my cell, last week, with shined buckles on his boots.

"Were you around for the Battle of Ketch?" he said. This was the engagement for which Garfield—named literally *plain of the spear*—was called. "Come on. I bet you were there. I bet you were everywhere. Were you?"

"I was. At the battle."

"My mom said she saw us beat you. She told me she watched it all."

If his parents had seen it, they'd named him *Garfield* to perpetuate a myth.

"Is this on your happy list?" I said. "Being named after a Church victory?"

"My List of Goods."

"Yes, you're very proud."

"I'm proud of our win." He straightened with his halberd. "Light and Allegiance!" This had been the Church's motto since the start of the war.

Garfield smacked a fruit fly against his temple. They live in the castle refuse, year-round. With all his gloating, I couldn't tell if Garfield was baiting me, or if he'd just heard somebody's particularly enthusiastic lecture.

"You seem very up today," I said.

"We had a new dean in history." His voice cracked, and he just let it.

"Brother Wegman has the grippe, so we got Brother Helbor instead. And it sounds like he would be a bore, because of, you know." He sort of rolled his hand.

"I see."

"But he isn't a bore. He's got a withered hand all grown over with fingernails. And it clicks when he uses it to point." Some curses could do that.

"So did he fight at Ketch?" I said.

"No, he got in the way of one of our choirs." The Church choirs still sing, but Caspar's magic has blasphemed them into a kind of artillery. "Have you ever heard a Church choir?"

They were at Ketch. "It's not on my List of Goods."

"Oh." He grasped the bars between us. It looked as if he couldn't decide whether I had heard a choir or not, or if he should ask further. "Helbor's good. Really deep voice." He held to the bars, and despite the Bell's height, he leaned back. "Dean Wegman is way too fat, and if he meets someone he doesn't like, he offers his finger for him to shake, instead of his whole hand."

"Really?"

"My friend, Martin, saw it. Said it reminded him of a ding-a-ling."

I gave him a laugh, and he jostled his elbows while he leaned. Boys his age will run hot and cold. But I was still amazed at how Garfield had just walked in, and started telling me about his day.

"Hey," he said, "did you ever go to Pegrum?"

"No." Pegrum is a prison that's also a training academy for the Sword Potent's elite.

"Helbor says the choirs rehearse there."

"They do. But now, it's my turn to ask."

From where he leaned, Garfield puffed his chest at mock attention.

"Tell me more from your List of Goods," I said.

"Martin and I stumped Otto." I wondered if this was hard. "We were in the buttery, and we asked him what's the difference between egg whites and snot."

"You asked him this?"

"What?" He stopped leaning. "You think I'm being impolite?"

"No. I'm just surprised it stumped Otto." I rubbed a stiff elbow. "Everyone knows that snot is saltier."

Garfield let go of the bars. He glanced toward Otto's guard alcove, and when he turned back he looked almost proud. "You're gross!"

"Tell me I'm wrong."

He made eye contact with me for a moment, a little chip of light.

"So let me tell you something from my list," I said.

"You had a good thing happen?"

"It was a cat." This was true. "Ran along the bridge, after a finch, and stopped nearly just where you're standing."

Garfield nodded as if he read a sign. "We get a couple of cats."

"Well, I don't."

"What color?"

"Black."

"Naked or not?"

"Naked? You mean, did it wear a little frock?"

He pouched a sidelong smile. "Soot has fur. Portence has only half."

"It was a fully-furred cat."

"Soot."

"What happened to Portence?"

"Nothing that we know. The herbalist just says she's unfortunate."

"That's the diagnosis?"

"And she's blind."

"How old is this cat?"

"Hey! What's with all the chin wags?" Otto had called from halfway along the bridge. "And Porty's younger than you!"

Garfield put his back to me, and broomed his halberd.

"Hold it right," I said. Garfield fixed his grip.

The wind was too unpredictable with sound, at this height. We'd have to remember to whisper. We waited for Otto to cross the rest of the way to the Bell, but not even his torchlight moved.

"Sometimes he naps," said Garfield. "And he's a grouch when he does."

I stiffened. I touched the boy's shoulder, and he stepped away with a glare. Garfield likely knew how dangerous it had been for him to tell me about Otto's naps.

Otto started his return to the alcove, and Garfield wiped the sweat from his own neck. He knew what he had done. I held the wrist of the hand that touched him. I knew what I'd done, too.

"I'm afraid," I said, "that while she was here, Soot ate most of Ketch." The remaining bits of the cricket lay on the flagstone.

Garfield turned his back to me. "I bet that's in your good list, all right. Some beastie eating half the battlefield."

"Actually it isn't." In a way, a devouring is exactly what happened the first time.

Through a grate in the cell's far corner, a stink rose cold from the mindless pens. Garfield and I didn't speak for the rest of the night. And really, this was for the best. The first rule of any sort of resistance work is to remember who you are and who you're talking to. For a moment, Garfield and I had forgotten. And yes, he wasn't part of the resistance; he would swear he wasn't. But yes, in spite of our little lapse over naptime, he would be. He had shown me that when he met my eyes, after we divulged to each other we knew the taste of snot.

It's ridiculous, this shared and ordinary secret, but it's how trust builds sometimes. Over the next few months, Garfield likely will trust me more. And I will have to live with the fact that by turning him, I might see him killed, either at the hairy hands of Otto, or from a standard-issue mindless snuffling in its yard. When the jailers walked me here, I saw the remains of cassocks that some of the mindless still wore.

And here is something I will not tell Garfield, no matter how close we get: what made the Battle of Ketch infamous was not its spears, but its dead. In what might have been an antecedent to the mindless type with hairs, the Church had learned that if they transfixed the mindless on javelins, the creatures could use the vibrations through the shafts to detect the approach of intruders. Over half a day before we marched on the Church's holding at Ketch, the mindless keened from their poles. The Church was waiting on the battlefield, and either from the horror or the ambush, our forces broke into a rout. Back then, the Church wasn't entirely shameless about its atrocities, and it spread word that its elite spearmen were the ones who had mastered the day. Loyal peasants had babies in celebration, and children like Garfield got their names. And yet if the boy's parents had lived nearby, they must have known the truth about Ketch. They must have spoken it to each other, the way my father had told me about the Treehanded bundles. If they'd wanted to be honest, they should have named their son Wightfield. This, of course, is what I will never tell the boy. Just as I won't suggest his parents probably named him after a lie, simply to keep him safe.

I still remember the smell of smoke from our army's retreat. The Church had burned the ground as an attempt at erasure. It's what they did after each battle they won, ostensibly to remove our taint from their lands. But I guess they also relocated witnesses, the way we had done at Wilm's pasture. Garfield is not the first child I've trained to fight on our side of the war, but he might be my last. So I want to do him right. By neglecting to tell him of his name, I'm resorting to Jillian's old trick of parceling the facts. But you have to dose truth sometimes, like a medicine. You have to, if you want the child both to live as long as possible, and to die for the right good. After all this time, I have mostly stayed reluctant to kill. I hate how Garfield will die in some war and I hate how I will too. But a death resulting from a life against Esaosh, is a death that will set the boy free.

chapter 12

INHERITANCE

part ONE

On a summer morning when I was twenty-one, I awoke to something sounding like a scream. The noise disappeared after I came to, but part of me remembered what I'd heard. And that part had me sitting up in bed.

The cottage sat dark and cold. The fire must have ebbed, and this meant it was early morning. The mosquitoes hummed through the outside walls.

I opened my hands, and the air felt cool on my palms. Tasha stomped in her pen. Another horse whinnied, and I shot to my feet. This noise had been the screaming sound. Now something out there creaked and jingled. I Touched Jillian upstairs, but I either received or imagined something like an answering fuzz. Jillian had been ill yesterday; she'd gone to bed before dark.

After dressing, I moved to the cottage door, and from the mantle, I grabbed our loose-handled carving knife. I hoped Teph had returned. I whispered for Jillian, but the sound was futile. And I knew this the way that I knew the Teph wish was futile. Someone's boot squelched in the puddle that collected in the front of our entrance.

I clenched the knife, and slammed open the door. Something crunched metal and wood. Another thing slammed my wrist, and the carving knife fell.

Two suits of armor—two, red-caped guards—settled themselves on either side of Mellion. He squeaked from within his traveling cloak. The guards had square, iron shields, and one of these sentries held the knife.

"You and your weapons," said Mellion. "You carry them along, the way a lady carries her flowers."

Everything I wanted to do in this moment was far too dangerous. Mellion made a kind of sucking smile.

"My aunt is indisposed," I said.

"Do you know," he said, "that when I was a child, I thought *disposed* was a euphemism for the privy?" He aped a woman's voice. "'Where's your father?' 'He's in disposed.'"

"She's asleep," I said.

"Well, you know our Lord Esaosh." He clasped his hands, as if to recite. "His agents descend upon thieves in the night."

"Around here," I said, "it's the thieves who descend in the night."

"Then you come from a pagan place. Because I was quoting scripture."

I shouldn't have confronted him; the people beside him were head-to-foot weapons. And yet, something inside of me couldn't help but confront him.

Mellion took my knife from the guard, and offered it to me over his forearm as if he were a valet with a utensil.

"Get your aunt, Gaelle." He dropped his smile. "You both are going on a trip."

He said what I'd somehow expected.

"It's an astonishing place," he said. "I assure you. Abbey Holding is a true wonder of the world." He made a slow point for me to go.

I wanted to do exactly what he suggested, but I didn't want to obey.

He said, "I can ask Rudyard to fetch her, if you like that better."

"No," I said. Rudyard sounded like *red guard*.

"You can take the knife with you," he said.

I headed for the stairs, before I realized what I was doing. I'd gripped the knife as if I hoped to plunge it into a stump.

Jillian, fully dressed, waited at the top landing. She brought me into the upstairs room that she'd long since enlarged by taking down her and my father's partition. Now she wrapped me into a loose-limbed hug. "Keep your temper."

"They're in armor."

"Yes. And when they leer at you, do not look them in the eye."

For a ridiculous moment, I wondered if this morning was one of her tests.

I said, "Why are they here?"

"It's likely just a job."

"They don't do this with your other jobs."

"You haven't seen all my other jobs."

"Jill—"

"I know." She looked tired, as if, for one moment, she let me see she was tired.

"Tell them you're sick," I said.

She showed me a deep breath. "It's just a cold."

"Tell them it's worse." She was shaking her head. "They've come for us both."

"Both." She spoke to the room, which used to be my parents' room. "They've started to think you're old enough."

"For what?"

I saw her try not to look tired. "To be noticeable."

I should never have signed my name. "I'm sorry."

"No-no." She reached for my face, and drew her hand back. "You make me proud." She peered at the floor, as if she could look through it. "Try to remember what you've learned."

On her nightstand, she placed the old black-sap cup, with the mindless whistle inside. The cup was for Wilm, she said, so when he saw it, he'd know who had come.

I thought of Wilm going through our house, of the sweat growing around his eyes, of how wrong things would have to go for him to venture upstairs in the first place.

Jillian knelt by the table. It was older than I was; it stood like an age. The cup was contaminating an age.

From under the bed, Jillian had drawn out a sack I thought we'd lost. It held clothes: a new tunic and breaches, new boots.

"We'll call them Church clothes," she said. "Whenever you're with the Church, you'll wear them. When you're away from the Church, you'll wear something different."

"You make it sound like a uniform."

"Good enough. When you aren't wearing it, you'll be harder to spot."

She gathered her things. "Where is your uniform?" I said.

She massaged her shoulder, the way she did in the morning. "They know me too well." She tidied her breeches. "I'm sorry you look like me."

"No, that makes me proud." The words just slipped out.

She made some quick blinks, and stuffed my necklace into my shirt. Then she started down the steps, not quite slowly, but as if she would receive someone, as if she too were unsurprised.

Voices rose from downstairs. I glanced at the room—the box of knots, my father's two leather belts—all of these things meant to fasten.

"Our condolences," called Mellion.

"Gaelle," said Jillian.

She stood at the bottom of the stairs.

"Your father's accident." Mellion appeared beside her. "Poor simpleman."

Jillian held my gaze. We'd long decided that if he ever asked, we'd tell Mellion our dead mare, our ever-peaceful Godiva, had thrown my father. I stepped down the stairs in the manner of my aunt, and unlike the first time I was born, I descended deliberately.

part TWO

The soldiers had driven six horses. All of them were brown beneath the mud their teamsters had smeared on them to repel the mosquitoes. The men had harnessed the horses to a wooden globe on high wheels. I'd never seen a carriage before. Jillian took my hand, and I let her hold it.

The wagon wasn't an exact sphere; it was more the shape of one of those full-faced helmets that widens for the brow and tapers toward the chin. In the way of such helmets, it had only a slit at the top where the eyes should be. The Church symbol, the stick-depiction of something resembling balance scales, ran down the entirety of the coach's side, adding a sort of face to the helmet.

A soldier—maybe Rudyard—opened a door that split the face down its nose. He gestured us inside.

"Let's go, Dear." Jillian tugged me toward the carriage.

I tried not to balk. The trick was to comply, so as to avoid notice, but even in these circumstances, I did not comply well.

The mosquitoes whined. The inside of the open carriage sat dim and quite small. Jillian was telling Mellion how I still didn't like the dark, and how I'd never seen a carriage. I stepped inside the cart, to a sour smell. Aside from another visor slit in the opposite face, the coach lacked any windows. Jillian slid in beside me, but we had little room. She took the seat across.

"There," she said to me. "You see?"

I looked at her, and she patted my knee.

The coach jostled with a soldier taking the driver's seat. The carriage bounced again when, I later learned, the other soldier stood on a runner in the back.

Mellion squeezed into our compartment.

"Gaelle, Honey," said Jillian. "Come sit by me." She grabbed my arm, and pulled me to her. I sat, rather hard, on the side of her thigh.

"Gaelle," said Mellion. "Daughter of Barbara and Lloyd." He shut the door, and the carriage cut off almost all light. "I'll just sit here for a while, before it gets too hot." The carriage lurched. We bounced, and I looked for something to hold onto. "Barbara died quite some time ago. A bit over twenty years, yes?" He counted under his breath. I gazed through the window slit, and tried to put all my awareness out there. "So, Gaelle, I wonder why your aunt is treating you as if you are younger than you are." He bobbled a stare.

"I'm not sure I follow," I said.

He laughed. "I'm sure you don't follow much anyone at all, anymore." Jillian Touched like a feather. "I remember your time of birth, generally speaking. Your aunt must think at least one of us is a simpleton."

"Does this trip concern her?" said Jillian.

"No," he said. "Not other than the fact that we want to keep her where you are."

Jillian said, "She's done nothing—"

"Our concern is not with her, Yeomen. We suspected she had reached majority. But your pretending her youth makes you appear as if you wish to protect her from her own standing."

"We're not hiding my age," I said.

"That's good," he said. "And welcome to it. A young woman is capable of practically anything."

"Mellion, she knows not to trust you." Jillian spread out beside me, and I tried not to budge. "In fact, I don't imagine even you trust you."

"Liars," he said, "lie to protect themselves until all things lie with a look of falsehood—including the occasional truth."

"You would know," she said.

He wiped his mouth. "The dawn promises heat today." We hit a rut, and I braced myself against the ceiling. "It will take a little more than two days before you hit the monastery road. Then another one before you come to Abbey Holding itself." The dark of the carriage hid his face. "We are in a bit of a rush these days, so they'll just switch out the horses and the soldiers, instead of much stopping." He kicked at something that rustled on the floor. "We did lay some straw for you though."

I straightened, as if everything inside of me went rigid. Jillian Touched a steadying Touch, but the reassurance simply confirmed the worst of what Mellion had said. I imagined Jillian and me with our mouths against the door slits, breathing through a crack.

Jillian said, "It's a familiar shame, isn't it?"

"What's that, Dear?"

"That you have to give us food and water. That you always have to take us alive."

"Oh, well, I have to take *you* alive."

"You have to take us both alive," said Jillian, "or there won't be anyone in this carriage left alive."

"Jillian." He laughed her name. "As far as your family's malice is concerned, it's best you do not model the trait." He made a stretching noise. "Besides, you and I both realize how the deaths wouldn't stop here."

"We are all prepared to make sacrifices," she said. "Though I'm not sure your abbot is."

Mellion said, "Everyone wants to be free, my dear, but don't give yourself away."

"It's all right," said Jillian. "It's a shame we can't kill you either."

"Isn't that always the way?" From the sound of it, he scratched some part of himself. "You know, until the last die rolls?"

She lay her hand on mine. I'd expected it to be cooler.

From Mellion's side of the darkness, came the sound of skin on skin. He could have been rubbing his hands or his neck or his face. He could have been hot, or amused, or just trying to stay calm.

"Gaelle," said Mellion. "Speaking of monasteries. What is the Church's core mission?"

Jillian's hand slightly flexed.

"The Church's core mission," I said. "This mission is to stand as a citadel for Esaosh until he returns. To bring all the world to him, so he can welcome his own and crush his enemy, Visjaes."

"Ah," said Mellion.

My father taught me the credo. He recited it every quarter, at the fair, when the market-stall vendor asked for it along with his money.

"Then it's true, my dear," said Mellion, "that you have seen the alternative to heathenism?"

This was a test; the Observer told me so. Mellion knew heretics raised me. It would arouse suspicion, if I behaved as if I had faith. And yet I would implicate my family, if I said anything to counter the teachings of Esaosh.

"Gaelle," said Mellion, "have you seen this alternative?"

"Honestly," I said, "I'm so young, I haven't seen much." Jillian shifted and relaxed.

"I see," he said. I touched my necklace. "So tell me, Young Lady." He leaned forward, almost as if he wanted me to feel his nearness. "Have you ever seen a crime?"

"Not really. Not that I'm aware." I slid my finger through the necklace's pendant, as if it were a magic ring.

"You know, my dear, if you witness a crime and do not report it, you yourself fall guilty of the crime."

I breathed the scent of pipe smoke.

"Do you have a crime in mind?" said Jillian.

"Yes," said Mellion. "For instance, Gaelle, if your aunt commits a crime, your first outcry would have to be against her."

"That wouldn't happen," I said.

"Which part?" said Mellion.

"My witnessing a crime. My aunt works the farm and she works for you."

I hoisted myself up straighter; I had to portray innocence. And in the moment, this meant I had to be like my father.

In a strip of sunlight, Mellion wrinkled his nose, and gave a short, toneless whistle. "There was a law here, long ago. It said you could plow your fields only east and west." He gestured toward the window. "The rule was to go along with the roads, which also went this way, so that everyone moved in the same direction."

"In case you decided to snatch a field and make it a road," said Jillian.

"Wartime, sure," said Mellion. "And if the fields went the other way, you'd always get the one soldier who'd go *buh buh buh*."

He laughed to himself. He'd probably told his joke a hundred times. "Tell me, Gaelle," he said. "Do you know of the Clearing Wars?"

I thought of pulling the Treehanded corpse from the grass. "I know some," I said.

"What were the sides of the Clearing Wars?" he said.

"The Church and Treehand," I said.

"Now what if I told you there was a messenger captured by Treehand?" said Mellion. "He had to deliver orders from Ordinal, and he swore to his captors he would die before he gave up his silence." From out of nowhere, he touched my knee, and I jerked. "He was a heroic man, most anyone would reckon. Loyal to his cause."

Jillian inhaled, as if to say something, but I never heard her breathe out.

"Do you know the story? Yeoman?" said Mellion. "My wheezy firebrand?"

"She answered your catechism," she said.

"The Treehanded," he said. "They brought the soldier to their wormy huts. And there, in a stick crib, they kept a Holden newborn." Jillian Touched in a way that pressed. "Treehand keeps having issues with children. Theirs, ours." I moved my knee, and he let go. "Anyway, they said to the messenger that if he didn't disclose his intelligence, they would break the newborn's arm, right in front of him."

"That's enough," said Jillian.

"What followed," said Mellion, "was the Oading Rout. The messenger's capitulation—and his need to save the child—brought catastrophic losses for the Church. We had to retake the same land, months later, where the bodies of the old battle still moldered in the leaves." This was a terrible thing he told me. I apologize for telling you. "So now then, Gaelle. Gaelle? You must listen carefully. You must understand, my maybe-knows-nothing—my young-lady-ax-shot who is so very capable of anything." He rapped on the carriage door, and I jumped. "The worst treachery, the very worst, lies in your simply choosing the wrong good."

The carriage had stopped. Mellion opened the door, and the outside offered the green of a rainy morning. A hayward chased his cattle, noticed us, and looked down.

"And now, Jillian," he said. "Suddenly so very protective."

"Go home," she said.

"Yes, I intend to depart your trip presently." He took a dramatic sniff of the outside air. "You'd best not let motherhood make you desperate, Madam. Remember what else you've done when you've been that way." He half shut the door. "Better to stay as calm as you were when we had your sisters."

part THREE

Something had struck me in Mellion's mention of desperation and sisters. It was like a pin to mark a place, or it was like a needle prick. I couldn't look at Jillian, as the carriage started its trundle. The pin was sticking from her.

"He is a pathetic man," said Jillian. "He has no spine, so he tries to steal other people's."

The carriage felt way too small, as if we sat in a sinking container, falling deeper than air.

"Gaelle."

I shuddered.

"Gaelle, he will not torture us. He needs us in good condition." She touched my knee, as if she put something next to what he had placed there. "Gaelle."

"It's fine."

"He will make us uncomfortable. He's learned his greatest gift is in making people uncomfortable. Still." She spread her fingers outside the window. "We have been through much worse."

She pressed me with more reassurance, but I half heard it. I watched her fingers and tried to picture what I would do if Mellion wanted to cut them off. I wondered what she would do if he had held me, as a baby, hostage for her secrets. Mellion had mentioned *sisters*. He'd said the word as if it held a trap door.

"What would you have done?" I said. Jillian drew her hand from the window. "About the baby?"

"In the story I heard, it was the Church that threatened a Treehanded baby."

"Either way," I said.

"Gaelle."

I'd asked an unkind question. But over the years, I would answer it myself.

"Mellion tells the story," she said, "because Mellion gave up his younger brother."

The trap door. "He killed him?"

"He fed him to the Church. But yes, the brother's long dead."

The killing could have stilled or increased Mellion's laugh.

Still, the pin stuck, as if Mellion had inserted it like a curse. "So what would you have done?" I said.

The way the sun came in, I could see her grasp the crown of her head. "It's too much of a hypothetical."

The past five years lay in my memory like a spill. "I don't think it's so hypothetical."

"Well, Gaelle. I've never had to sacrifice a baby."

"But would you?"

She blew out her breath. "I don't know. Do you?"

It wasn't hard to imagine two armies in the woods, dying to protect their own infants; of my mother dying to preserve an infant; of Mellion accusing my aunt of motherhood.

"This is what you need to know," she said. "Mellion is right about betrayal."

"What do you mean he is right?"

"Well, in fact, sometimes he's right. That's what makes him so horrible." She looked at me, as if she were determining where to land a blow. "Gaelle."

"I don't want to talk about it anymore."

"Gaelle, if it comes down to your life–"

"Don't."

"Your life."

"And you also have a life."

"And I'm telling you now." I Touched her hard, and she sat back. "You sacrifice me," she said. "You do it. In less than a heartbeat."

"No. And never. People don't do those things to family."

"Actually. Some would say it's the prerogative of family to sacrifice itself."

The way she said this—the way Mellion had said his piece from outside—the pin stuck. I didn't want to think of it; he was making me think of it. He'd set a marker in time, a marker that pushed through to another moment that somehow still bled.

"Jillian." My voice was so small. I couldn't see her face. "Did you sacrifice your sisters?"

part FOUR

In the shadows, all I could see were her hands, and they lay still and flattened. She said, "I absolutely did not."

I should have stopped. Maybe she'd have kept telling me about the family in her own good time. But I was young, and I was scared both of having information and not having enough. And in many ways, Mellion was a goddamned assassin.

Jillian had clasped her hands, and now she put them between her knees.

"So," I said, "none of this is what Mellion meant about your calmness and your sisters?"

"Gaelle. No."

"Because you seem very afraid right now."

"Now you listen." Her feet scraped the straw. "I am afraid of things you don't even know about."

"Yes! That's true! Because you won't tell me."

"There is too much to tell you."

"And you were calm at some point." That's what Mellion had said. "Right? Jillian? You were calm when the Church *had your sisters?*"

"Stop it."

"They had Miriamne? Whom you kept from me? They had my mom?"

"She sacrificed herself!"

The carriage bumped, and I welcomed the pain of the blow. It was as if something lay on the floor between us, now, something we'd have to kill. "Who sacrificed?"

She rasped.

"Who?" I said.

She had hidden her hands.

"Are we talking about Miriamne?" I said. It was the better answer. "Miriamne?"

"Miriamne," she said. "Gaelle, her life was forfeit already."

"Forfeit?"

"I have told you all of this."

"No, Jillian. You only told me she died."

"No, what I told you is how the Church made her die."

"Stop lawyering!" I half stood, and I bumped my head. "Because what you didn't tell me, Jillian, is that you wouldn't let *sisterhood* make you desperate."

Her face, from the darkness, was in mine. I sat, and she leaned over me. "You will not put Mellion's words in your mouth."

Her breath smelled of sickness and sweat. I wanted my father and mother. I wanted to be like them, especially my mother. She would know how to handle this sister of hers, this person whom I so damnably resembled, this person I was *proud* I resembled.

Jillian sat back down.

I said. "So, unlike what you'd said to Mellion, you didn't vow to kill everyone to protect your sister? Right? You reserve that for me?" With all her anti-killing talk, this threat especially stank. "You didn't promise there would be nobody left alive in a carriage, if they hurt your sister?"

"Gaelle, I am asking you, please, to stop."

But I couldn't stop. This was a big lie: something far beyond her not telling me of Miriamne at all. "You said you would do that for me—die outright for me—"

"I accompanied her!" She hunched on her toes. The carriage lurched, and for a moment, I thought she'd fall on top of me.

"I went to the abbey" she said. "I signed the agreement." Her voice broke. "And I was there, hale and watching, while my big sister was burned."

Something slid along the top of the carriage. I had doubled over in my seat.

"You don't have a sibling," she said. "You will never have to watch her, to denounce her."

"You denounced her."

"Yes! I denounced Miriamne. She told me to." She spoke with a little gasp, and for a moment, it reminded me of the fire heretic. "This calmness you throw in my face? My calmness was so they didn't burn her alive."

"I don't—"

"It was part of the deal. And of that torture—that hell—I thank God you know absolutely nothing."

I shuddered, the way she'd done when she pushed me into a wall. "They make mages swallow stones. You said so."

"And they do so, yes. Most of the time."

"Most of the time? What? Except when they run out?"

"When we got them to run her through."

My knees sagged, while I sat. They went weak for an aunt I never met.

"It was part of the deal," said Jillian.

"What sarding kind of deal?"

"To spare her pain! To keep the rest of us safe!"

"The rest of who safe?"

"Everybody safe! All the loved ones. All the family, all the friends—"

"And this was the deal? She died quickly and you lived?"

"Many of us lived."

She put herself completely into the carriage's shadow. Some part of me—the Observer, maybe—made its brutal and necessary calculations. I started to cry.

"Miriamne denounced her friends," said Jillian. "She denounced her work." The recitation came without parceling. "We denounced her. They ran her through with a spear. They burned her on top of her books. And afterward, I began to serve at the pleasure of the Church."

A swatch of light fell onto Jillian's elbows, which she was digging into her thighs. She bowed into herself so tightly that it looked as if she tried to keep something from escaping her. And maybe she was; maybe she fought to contain both the pain of this sacrifice, and what had to be years of rage.

I sat with what I'd learned, for a while. At first I hefted my silence as a kind of punishment. But it started to lean against me with a weight that taught the burden of Jillian's own silence. For years, she'd kept silent, the way she did now, while she must have felt me fume. Suddenly I wanted to reach for her, to brush something off her, to help her stand by the windows, so she could breathe good air. Maybe I could help us find the good, to shuffle us remaining loved ones together like feet. But I didn't know how. She'd never asked me to do such a thing for her.

So I stood in the carriage's dipped center, and peered through the carriage door, as if I were a soldier in his helmet. For hours, I stood, seeing nothing—and I wanted to see nothing. Then I hoped a roc would carry off Mellion by his very-round head.

Jillian wept, and I wondered if I should hold her hand, to fill it. The shadows had lengthened along the evening's yellowed land, and the forest stood in back of the fields, leaning from green to darkness. We passed a tree stump, crooked and pale. On the ground, another tree had cast its shadow over the stump's silhouette, and this shadow completed the other, until the outline of the first tree looked full-grown.

The image was so at odds with what we'd last talked about that I simply sat down. My foot brushed Jillian's, and I left it there. I reached for her hand, and couldn't find it, but she slid hers, cold, beneath mine. The light passed above us, and I lifted her hand off the carriage seat, into the air.

part FIVE

The carriage creaked and bumped as we passed through some farmstead's smoke. The smell reminded me of my father, and now his pendant still hung from my neck, as an insistence.

"So, during this whole execution," I said. "Where were my parents?"

Jillian let go of my hand.

"Please tell me," I said.

"They were there, of course."

"Right. So now tell me what the Church made them do."

"Them?"

She used to say my mother was the biggest heretic of them all.

"Jillian, you know I'm not stupid."

"I wish you were." It would have been easier. "The Church made them vow to raise you as a fully-claimed servant of Esaosh."

I felt slapped. "What—"

"So your father took you to your Claiming ceremony when you were an infant. You lay on the altar of the priest, and he gave you to his god."

"Lloyd never taught me of Esaosh."

"And then when you went to the fair each season, the vendor gave your father catechism for you to overhear."

"The vendor—"

"His name was Benthem. We gave him extra to do it." She chuckled. "Today it paid off."

For the first time, I felt sacrificed. "I'm Claimed?"

"Gaelle, everybody's Claimed. It practically happens when they change your first diaper." I tried to remember lying on a slab. "I was Claimed. Your mother was Claimed. Miriamne was Claimed, when we were girls. A while later, she wrote an essay, 'Disclaimed.'"

I leaned against the carriage's seat. At least my mother had been spared the sight of my lying helpless in a church. The wagon jostled, as if it shook something loose. "Wait." This was the loose thing. "How did they know my parents would have me?"

"Well, easily enough, I guess. It's reasonable to assume a young couple will eventually have children." Some people were encouraged to have children, though I imagine we were not. "You know the Church is in the business of meddling with children."

The day's old, unseen thing still lay on the floor. "So that's it? That's what my parents had to do?"

"Weren't you just devastated about being Claimed at all?"

"And you just said it was nothing."

The carriage wheels ran through a puddle. "If you had been a boy, I suppose it's possible the Church would have taken you."

"As a monk."

"That's a guess, Gaelle, but it does raise an important point."

"Would you have let them take me?"

"No. But listen." She sat next to me. "When we get to the abbey, you need to remember that the people there were also taken."

"Like Mellion? You're telling me he was taken?"

"No. Not all of them. And even the taken ones usually turn."

"How tragic."

"It is tragic." It is. "But not all of them turn. And you cannot hate them wholesale."

"Well, I do hate them wholesale."

"Then you will sacrifice both of us for your hatred." She didn't move, and in the half-light, I imagined her staring at me as hard as she could. "At the abbey, you will have to be respectful. All I just told you, all that I have kept from you, is because they wanted this to unbalance you."

"Then Mellion did his job." He had. And every time I find a way to love someone like Garfield, I picture Mellion shrinking a little more.

"I think," said Jillian, "that you'll have to try to be pliable."

It was like she'd asked me to try to be a fish. "Jillian, vow or not, they know you raised me."

"No. They think your father was living until a very short time ago."

Jillian had denounced Miriamne. Miriamne had denounced her books. "So you want me to play dumb."

"You know the key to sleight-of-hand, how you play to match your watcher's expectations."

"You mean like not correcting a man."

"I'm sure you've seen how women can play dumb very well."

"It's a betrayal to act dumb."

"To whom? Miriamne?" She put her hand in the crack of light. "She would tell us to save our own lives." Such life saving was Jillian's prerogative. She had chosen it before.

part SIX

I slept in the carriage, but it was a dark, twisting sleep. Somewhere along the night, Jillian slid her sack under my head. She could have used my bag, but she might given me something of hers because she knew I needed it. Beneath my anger and hatred, there spread bewilderment, and terror, and a sense that Jillian's disclosures, no matter how belated, felt far too early and far too large. Jillian had been shielding me from my family's own cataclysm. And in the carriage, she may have known some of my terror was for her.

This was the whole tension of Jillian's later life: her desires to both protect and involve me, to embrace how I was like her, and to regret the resemblance. Our similarity marked me as part of our family, and yet it also marked me as utterly divergent from the rest of the empire. Mellion, in the way of his feints, had already made the point when he compared me to a lady and her flowers. In the moment, I hadn't caught what he'd said. In fact, he'd annoyed me because I thought he implied I was like a lady in the frivolity of her flowers. What he'd meant, however, is how I wasn't a woman; I was a non-woman among a family of non-women, within a class of people who could barely be women, no matter how pious they were.

Celdan women, the Church would say, are essentially a liability. They tempt. They coddle. They dilute strength. This is why they aren't allowed to enter the Church's bastions and monasteries. It's why, except in time of great duress, they aren't allowed to participate in warfare. Exceptions exist amid the soldier class; if a woman has the strength and (often) the ruthlessness to fight her way into the military, she can advance as long as she fights for her post. She becomes, however, both a curiosity and a target. And regardless of whatever rank she achieves, her mannish skills and clothing mark her as lower-class.

This is because the celdan countryfolk lack the luxury of stark gender assignment. Everybody labors according to the wild's demands. Women in the fields grow strong from their work. They learn how to use an ax. They wear pants. I didn't see a woman in a dress until I was nine and at the Northcraft fair, when a noble's servingwoman came to procure the best goose for her house. Dresses were frivolous garments, and we owned few garments. Even the prostitutes wore pants. If they wore anything else, they committed the crime of dressing beyond their station.

The women in my family were weapon-wielding, trouser-wearing non-men. We were large in our passions, strong in our convictions, and unreasonable in what Jillian displayed as an abrupt sort of compassion. And in the meantime, the most innocent adult among us was a man, of all things, who happened to possess a disturbing knack with plants.

Our abbey trip continued into the night. In the morning, I awoke, and amid the growing stink of the carriage, a passing shower smelled fresh. Jillian handed me the shirt from my bag. She'd dangled it out the window, during the weather, and I pressed it to my face. From all I'd considered, I wondered why she hadn't furnished a dress as my Church clothes. But seeing how Mellion had treated us, a dress may have been a garment beyond our station, too.

In the carriage, I stood with my feet braced against each of the benches, and I looked out the slit. Despite the rain, the morning light let us see better, both outside and in. The pines crowded thick and close, and where I stood, I couldn't see the tops of them. They reminded me of the tree jumping I had done with the mindless, and of the cup waiting upstairs for Wilm. Behind me, Jillian lay on her carriage seat with what looked like a smile.

"How long do they keep you?" I said.

"It really all depends."

"And I'm just supposed to be helping you?"

"Well, I'll make you read books."

"And what will you do?"

"Just advising, mostly. Looking at a tomb or a hallway."

"You mean you'll be looking for traps."

"It's an old abbey. They have renovations, excavations."

"You mean for traps."

"But old traps. Rubbled-over murder holes, mouse-eaten lines."

I gave a blunted Touch. "I don't think so."

"Gaelle. Yes. "

"If it were so easy, you wouldn't be this valuable."

"Well, mostly it is so easy, if you know what you're doing."

"And just how exactly is it that you know what you're doing?"

I turned to her, and she sat up on her elbows. Somehow I'd never asked her before.

"I learned my trade from a friend of the family," she said, "long dead." This person was my trainer's trainer, a grandmaster. "He gave me the armor, in fact."

A man had given Jillian something to keep her safe. "Was he an outlaw?"

"He was a Bakeet pilgrim."

"And the traps killed him?"

"No, the ice killed him. He went too far north." She was parceling again.

"Did he make it for you? The suit of armor?"

"Actually, he made it for his wife."

I thought of Teph kissing the palm of her hand. "And where was his wife?"

"Even longer dead."

She lay on her bench, playing with the laces on her shirt. "She died," I said, "so he gave you the armor?"

"I was the best student he had."

"His student."

"After she died, we met in prison."

So it was that part of her life. The few times Jillian mentioned prison, it felt as if she mentioned a war.

Jillian had made a little knot with her laces. Now she gazed out the window, and her eyes moved with the passing trees. "You should know the prisons are the heretics' great universities. You see? During all the worst times, friend after friend can be found in the prisons." Jillian had adopted the tone she'd take when she was teaching, but I knew her face well enough. She'd withheld. "So my teacher befriended me," she said, "and his friends befriended me. And we were friends for a very long time. And some of them are still the people I go off to see." She spread her hands on her belly.

"There is something you aren't telling me."

"There are many things that are personal, and I keep them to myself. And I have the right." She tugged her braid. "But in the meantime, you aren't hearing what I am telling you."

"Maybe it's because I'm seeing your tells."

"But what I'm trying to tell you, Gaelle, is about the resistance."

The word seemed to fill the carriage, as in fact, this was exactly what the carriage sought to contain. "The resistance? The ones you give some treasure to?"

"It works against the Church, and you should know it tries to be everywhere." I'd heard of her resistance work before, of course. But this was the first time she even obliquely mentioned this resistance in terms of where they were. I felt a little warmer. Everywhere felt warmer.

"Will we see them?" I said.

"I hope."

"At the abbey? Even there?"

She knit her fingers together, as if she showed me how she hoped. I'd so seldom seen her hope.

"Is that," I said, "why you've been smiling?"

She put a hand to her mouth.

"You're smiling again."

She moved her hand, and I looked away so she could have the smile to herself. All these years later, I still keep hold of the happiness she found in the carriage. She'd been shuffling her loved ones back and forth while she counted, and in a few days, another one of their number would reach for her.

A breeze washed through the cart. Despite the peril of this trip, this part felt good, this excavation. But at the same time, I caught a whiff of sleight-of-hand. Jillian had given me information about the resistance, but she hadn't answered much of anything I'd asked.

"Jillian." I put the armor sack next to her. "I know it's going to be dangerous."

"What is?"

"You know what is. This trip. Your task."

"We don't—"

"Otherwise, they wouldn't have dragged you away in a prison wagon. They wouldn't have taken me as collateral. And you wouldn't have a way to help the resistance." I'd made her smile leave her, and I hated that. "You're an expert at what you do." With a dead woman's armor. "And I imagine they use you in very deadly places."

She looked out the window, and her nose was hawkish in the light. "Gaelle, you know you are my very best friend." The truth of her confession opened a space in me. "You are part—in fact, you are the very core—of my resistance. And all you need to understand is that since Lind and Harwell's passing, I am the very best intrepid there is."

part SEVEN

We endured our trip. Through the window, the soldiers handed us yams and waterskins. We petitioned Rudyard to accept that if one of us stayed in the carriage during a stop, the second could go out. Half of us wouldn't dare to run without the other; the Church used us as collateral, because they knew as much. Rudyard, who looked about my age, appeared doubtful, until he stuck his head into our carriage, and coughed. During the handful of stops afterward, he let one of us sit with the carriage door open while the other crouched in the fields. There wasn't enough time for both of us to go during the same opportunity, but we made do.

The rest of the trip, we stood as long as we could. The stance was exercise. We pressed at the door slits, as I had imagined, but we didn't gasp. The cross breeze was enough that if I tilted my head, the air blew along my face, into my nose and through my hair. It made me consider the shape of the day, how it opened around us and closed again. And somehow a sense of freedom came with the thought. Even now, in my hanging cell, I remember how a sense of vastness is a prisoner's friend. It pulls at your confinement, even if it's only the vastness of death.

Sometimes Jillian placed her hands on her knees and kept a far-away look. In the meanwhile, we read. That's what it felt like, as we peered out the slits. We watched the countryside roll by as if we opened a scroll. A line of smoke rose and flattened from the chimneys, and we waited for its promised rain—the air's cooler fit, how it would let us sit together. And as we read the landscape, the carriage became an eye that rolled through it all.

part EIGHT

On the second afternoon in the carriage, we slowed to hooves and voices. Outside, passed a train of at least three wagons, with a team of horsemen in studded leather. They traveled north—we were at a junction—and their headsman spoke to our driver. Jillian said they were a merchant convoy, probably transporting luxuries, such as dyes and spices. The retinue was likely part for security and part for show. The better you guarded your goods, the more valuable they looked. This was, incidentally, why the Church gave us such a small escort. The worse the Church treated you, the more they feared your power. This fact resonated through both the prisons and the poor.

The merchant train crossed our road. We turned left onto their same path, which was the monastery road, and we gave the right of way. Jillian said the surrender was political: intimidation, security. By keeping all traffic in front, the Church could hide what might happen behind. Imperial transports had been known to pull over, to urge bystanders to pass. Travelers had since learned to keep their distance.

The dark came, and I tried to remember Godiva, as I felt the pull of the horses. Our carriage team whinnied, like the first sound of the morning when they'd arrived at our farm. That was nearly three days ago, but it all seemed farther apart, as if those three days bookended the history of my mother and my aunts. The carriage horses had the sound of Lucinda, who seemed both older and more recent than my family's history. I imagined her pulling our carriage, and I sat up.

The Church must already know. They must have found that I had spared Lucinda's life, and that we burned weeds in her horsepen. Teph might have confessed to Mellion while they threatened a baby.

Jillian put her hand on me, and I whispered what I thought.

She shook her head. Her people had heard nothing. Her abbey friend had heard nothing. She said that if the Church did know about us and Lucinda, they would kill people at our farm and not stop until they got to the eastern coast. Their own crack-down against necromancy showed they didn't know. They occupied themselves with the mindless, and not with the plants.

I asked if Jillian thought they suspected us of necromancy, and among all our whispering, she startled me with a laugh. Miriamne, apparently, had inveighed against necromancy. It was one of the few places where she and the Church overlapped. In fact, our practicing necromancy would be a larger denouncement of Miriamne's work than any stake-side coercion could possibly achieve.

The outer darkness was so complete that I couldn't see a shape of what the carriage passed. "So if they knew she hated necromancy, they must think she used magic of another kind?"

"Oh, of course. There's supposedly magic to transmute metals, or magic to tell the future. By the way, it's a capital crime to foretell a churchman's future."

"You'd think they'd like divination."

"No, not nearly. If you're wrong, you've lied to them. If you're right, you've consorted with Visjaes."

She'd once confounded me with her belief that magic might be real, the way demons might be real.

"The Church must think Treehand has magic," I said.

"Magic to influence plants." Maybe the Treehanded practiced such a thing. "And then of course there's magic to summon."

I thought of the fire man. "To summon demons?"

"And storms, and plagues, and boils."

"So basically anything."

"Magic is the arrogance to demand the universe give you precisely what you want, exactly when you want it."

"Well. That sounds like nobility."

"Imagine drawing a summoning circle with your own arcane entitlement."

"Or your own arse."

She tapped the side of her head, and I laughed.

"But you should know," she said, "the Church occasionally does manage to work a miracle."

"They get their miracles through magic?"

"They heal, of course. They say it's divine power from Esaosh, but once you hold no confidence in him, you start to look for something else."

"They don't just use herbs?"

"Not like any I've ever seen." And Jillian knew at least enough about herbs to procure the black sap. "The fact that they do heal is one of the reasons they keep ahold of the people."

She once told me the Church tried to cast magic, but I hadn't ever thought they'd actually gotten off a spell. "Can they raise the dead?"

"No. That is necromancy."

"Necromancy is raising the dead like the mindless." Rudimentary. "But nobody does anything like resurrection?"

In the moonlight, she looked me over, from my pendant to my lap. "I've seen no signs anywhere of resurrection." Despite all our losses, I considered this just as well. "The Church can restore limbs. Occasionally. Either by skill or by luck."

They probably lay someone on the claiming altar, and fit them with a leg as if it were on loan. They probably chased hedge healers, while their priests tried to press worse healing on their people. In my lifetime, as the Church approached war and then entered it, they would improve how they healed. Maybe such a thing was part of Celd's accelerated evolution of warfare. But at the moment, as Lucinda and the mindless wandered, and we approached the rim of my adulthood, the Church also accelerated toward other magics, other warfare. Some of their progress came from audacity—absolutely. And it also came from an entity that hollowed out part of the ground beneath them.

"You remember Abbot Caspar," Jillian said. "He lives in Holding." He was the Church's highest abbot, the one opposite the secular chancellor. "You should know he is likely the one we are going to see."

I glanced outside, and felt blind. "We're going to see the abbot?"

"And he will try to impress you."

What I imagined, for a moment, was killing him.

"Gaelle, he is sharp and he is captivating."

"So we're going to see the Church's third in command?"

"Second, essentially. He's far more ambitious than the chancellor."

"Well, maybe Caspar likes to draw circles with his arse."

"What's certain is that Caspar will become far more powerful, if he ever becomes a martyr."

I closed my eyes, answering darkness with darkness.

Jillian told me Caspar was the one who harnessed her when she accompanied Miriamne. He was the abbey prior, then, the second under the abbot.

Jillian had been wanted as an agitator; he knew her feats. And he suspected if he stuck her in dark places, and twisted her this way and that, he could use her as a kind of key.

Maybe from her cold, she coughed then. Over these past few years, her cough had developed a reediness.

I said, "Do they want me to replace you?"

She huffed. "How old do you think I am?"

"No. Do they want you to train me to replace you?" Jillian, the grandmaster.

"Gaelle." She put her head in her hands. "If you act mostly harmless, they will think you're mostly harmless."

"If I act dumb, you mean."

"If you act pliable, which can sometimes be very smart."

One of the horses whickered, and I remembered her weeping upstairs, on that first night.

I said, "You want me to get out of this."

"No. Dear. You can be less visible than I am. You can. But you can never get out."

part NINE

During our ride, Jillian described how every province but Treehand and Merrial has at least one seminary. Ordinal's halo in eastern Cadmus has the most. Farther out, the frontier seminaries function primarily as keeps against both the nomadic Tonn and the Treehanded settlements. The most prestigious seminaries are Ordinal Cathedral, where the Bell is now, and Abbey Holding, which is where we headed in the carriage. The first is for men who study the military and the bureaucracy, and the second offers the more treacherous path of theology. Ordinal is the largest seminary, but Holding produces the most Church leaders. Merit, heredity, politics, and money all play a role in which aspirant gets to go where, but all this may fall secondary to the conscription—

the *recruitment*, so called—that collects boys like Garfield.

An even darker form of recruitment happens in the heathen lands, such as Treehand, where the harbingers—that is, the missionaries—kidnap promising children to raise within the Church. The practice is rare, because despite its grabbiness, the Church has a deep distrust of foreigners. And yet, during our carriage ride, Jillian mentioned a rumor that Caspar himself was part Treehanded. The peasantry said he had a private chirurgeon cut out his spines.

I didn't want to know these things. They were dark things I could do little about, and they possessed the same seedy intricacy as their attendant economics and politics. When Jillian explained them to me, the cart felt stuffier than it ever had.

"They depend on this," said Jillian. "They depend on how it's hard for the uninvolved to think about these things."

"Well, then they're smart."

"Oh very. The elements they want us to watch—the alarm over the mindless, the malice of the heathen—it's all threats and postures, hues and cries. But the real danger exists in the vanishings, the sermons, the bureaucracy, the writs." She swatted a mosquito. "I will tell you, I'm not the only master of sleight-of-hand."

"I think there's danger in the mindless."

"Of course there is. And danger also comes from the Treehanded. But they aren't the only infestation. Not by far." What she said is so true, that I wish I had the chance to tell it to Garfield. The danger is almost always in the small.

The carriage stopped. Outside, a man waved to the driver. The cart creaked, and the wheel sound changed. We'd moved onto cobblestone. Jillian groaned at the rumble, and she stood. Out the window, far below, appeared a shining strip of water.

We moved along a bridge. The water was the Haft River, which feeds Ordinal and Holding before emptying to the sea. As with most every waterway except Treehand's Ariadne, it is the safest and fastest way for travelers to get anywhere. We would cross it again before we reached the abbey.

I peered as far as I could along the valley. The trees here had more variety among the pines; we'd gone that far south. We made a slow turn, and I pressed my face to the window slit. On the horizon, loomed a mountain with a white, square outcroppings along its middle and top. Just to the right of the center peak, rose a spire.

part TEN

We watched the abbey for hours. When the wind blew from the east, it brought the stink of sewage, butcheries, tanneries, and the waft of something darker. Jillian said the abbey kept close to 8000 servants to support 130 monks. Many of the workers served as lay farmers and craftsmen. They tithed their wares to the Church in exchange for protection, or inspiration, or forgiveness, depending on their lot.

Jillian told me we would not be able to see most of the abbey. Through the western village, which we approached now, we'd cross a bridge to the settlement's pastures that housed the goats, cows, swine, and their keepers. On the east end of these yards, stood the first of three granite walls that circled the abbey and rounded back until they hit the mountainside. A balcony jutted from the center of the third wall, and this was where the priests would address the people. No layperson was allowed beyond it without invitation, such as would come during an invasion, for example. No monk was allowed outside the wall without dispensation.

Now the dark stink grew aggressive. It reminded me of the mindless. The horses balked, and I looked to Jillian. The carriage leaned with a guard's dismount, and he trotted off to the side, toward the garrison.

"Cities stink," said Jillian. But in the dark, she sat very still. We pressed forward to more roads that spread from the bridge in all directions. Two-story buildings lined the side streets, leaning across to one another, until I figured a squirrel could jump from one to the next. So, apparently, could fire. Tubs sat in front of every other building, water basins the size of wagon wheels.

Jillian guessed some of the stink came from the basins themselves; the water could become so foul that it sometimes actually fed flame.

Beyond the stink, drifted market smells. The bottoms of buildings held shops. These had pull-down shutters that offered all manner of wares—farm tools, shoes, bolts of leather—enough wares to make the shutters sag. The spread of goods was like the Northcraft market, but it went in all directions, as if it were a flood of a market that washed its items along the street sides.

Among the crowd, as a kind of un-quelled blaze, lived the crimson of the Church. Banners hung from lantern posts, with the red, scale-like emblem of Esaosh on a white field. Soldiers marched in their crimson tabards. We approached a gatehouse where there stood a monk in robes of the same red, with a cowl down his back. Along his head and his neck, he had a skin-tight hood that, from a distance, looked like the shiny skull of living bone. He was old, and he spoke to the gate master in a feathered voice. He stopped as we passed, staring into our window slit as if he were making eye contact with a single entity.

"Do you know him?" I said.

Jillian said she didn't, but that he was of high rank. The color showed it; the hierarchy moves from blue (at the lowest), to brown, to white, to red. White is for purity, and red is for the power that comes after such cleansing. Red is also the most expensive dye in the world.

"It's the color of what they suck," I said.

"But you'll find it makes them easier to spot." Maybe they were like the mythical redcap imp, starting off white, and then drinking blood to fill up.

The light in the carriage changed, and the sound of the wheels turned softer. We'd crossed onto another wooden bridge, traversing the Haft again. Below, the river looked nearly clogged with ships, and the shine of the water didn't match with the smell. This was a metaphor for the Church I would have happily shared with Jillian, if she hadn't been sitting with her head bowed.

I'd never seen her do this before. The light changed again, as we came into the shadow of what would meet us on the other side of the bridge. Presumably we headed to the monastery. I couldn't see anything except the pull of the river and the occasional flashes of red at the docks. I imagined a monk leaping from roof to roof.

Jillian still had her head bowed, as if she was ill, unaware.

"Are we supposed to be praying?" I said.

She raised her head, and rubbed her eyes. "The quiet's just helpful to gather yourself."

She adjusted her braid, and she sat straight. She lowered her gaze to her lap, and I felt as if I'd taken something from her.

Something buzzed, and a bee flew in through the carriage slit. We both watched its activity and its freedom. It lighted on my knee, and I got it to walk on my finger.

"I tried to pet a bee once," said Jillian, "when I was two."

The bee lifted off. "How'd that go?"

"Frankly, I felt a little betrayed."

The blast hit me before I heard it. I landed on my knees, in the straw, with my hands over my ears and my aunt crouched over my back. The horses had screamed. Dogs barked from behind and below. Jillian pushed off me, shouting at the driver.

Somebody up top laughed. "Ain't you heard of a cannon?" he said. It both marked noon and declared that the Church had something called black powder. We'd later learn how this powder was the racing spark of war's acceleration.

Jillian leaned against the carriage wall, as if the pound of her heart had pressed her there. "Gaelle. Be pliable."

chapter 13

MINTING

The snow falls in straight lines out my Bell's window. The flakes land fat and soft, in a way that makes the Cadmul say *the old woman is plucking her geese.* I imagine the snow hushing Ordinal's spear tips and palisades, as if the earth itself could hush a war. Well. This old woman is washing her face. Goose-down snow is best for such things, with apologies to Increase. The rinse makes my eyes widen and my face ache. Increase sits away from the window, next to the candle I keep for him. A blotch of snow has landed on the bird's head, and he wears it briefly, like a little doily.

Lately, I've tried to touch him. I lay my hand on the flagstone, beside his candle. Sometimes I offer a dead spider from the floor cracks, or a runaway pea, or a piece of pork fat. It's hard to say what Increase eats. He gives it all a once over, and he angles his bill. Most often, my hand makes him toddle to the next flagstone. The other day, he lowered his head so I thought he wanted me to scratch him, but it turns out, he just watched a yellow centipede. After my misstep with Garfield, I haven't touched anyone in weeks. I've even Touched into nothing, for people I know I can't ever reach.

After he scared me by mentioning Otto's naps, and I scared him by grasping his shoulder, Garfield and I have exchanged only pleasantries. We've done this for the better half of a month. The boy has started to bring a book to read at his post—a tome with the ornate bramble of Profundus, which is the Church's holy language. The book wears a little manacle on its cover, from where the librarian usually chains it to a shelf. For a week, Garfield has squinted at the manuscript, and hooked his elbow around his halberd as if it were some kind of chum. Once he did tell me the weather had stopped sleeting, but I didn't have it in me to ask if this was part of his List of Goods.

It wasn't until yesterday's minting—an end-week, re-dedication service—that Garfield arrived half an hour late from what sounded like a skirmish in the yard. He stood at his spot beside Mama, trying to slow his breathing through his nose. By what I could hear from the alcove, Otto hadn't menaced him for his delay. And such restraint was remarkable. Otto occasionally made a late boy sprint the bridge to his post.

After Garfield arrived, I sat by my pallet, with my stone. "Did you have to run here?"

"No," said Garfield.

"It sounded like a festival outside."

"Do you know what, other than willow bark, works for pain?"

"Are you in pain?"

"No." His breath had almost returned to normal, so he probably wasn't.

"Aspen bark works. Or birch."

"There are no trees around here." He shouted a little. "And the herbalist left."

"Garfield, what kind of pain?" I stepped to the bars.

He held to Mama, and put his back to me. "Martin hurt his ankle." I bowed my head, and gave thanks that Garfield couldn't see my relief. "I know it's just an ankle. Otto says as much."

"But a soldier has to care for his feet."

"And Martin loses his breath if he gets scared."

"I see."

"And pain makes him scared."

"Well, of course."

Apparently, after the minting service, Martin was carrying the sac of dedication coins, when he decided to jump down the cathedral steps. The problem was that the bag was open, and the coins flew out, and while Martin tried to catch them, he made a hard landing on his ankle. At first, the boys around him laughed. Even Martin laughed. He's thirteen; unless somebody dies, boys his age think physical injury is hilarious. But Martin and his friends couldn't find one of the coins, and as Martin's alarm increased, the swelling in his ankle did too.

"We found the coin," said Garfield. "It was under a shrub. But Martin thinks Esaosh has punished him."

The Church uses corporal punishment for financial crimes, so I suppose their god would too.

"You need to see to an ankle," I said.

"I know."

"That said, even Otto calls it a minor wound."

"He means the punishment is light."

"Then he also thinks it's punishment." We whispered now. The wind blew in all directions.

My mouth had gone a little dry. My next question would risk far more than a thoughtless grasp of the boy's shoulder.

I said, "Do you believe Esaosh is punishing Martin?"

"I don't know." He's answered the question so quickly that he'd evidently asked it himself. "But he needs to feel better."

The torchlight flickered on the back of Garfield's helmet, as a little fire that betrayed itself there. Guards his age can cleave to one another as brothers united in their orphaning. The bonding works well enough until ambition starts to compel them toward rivalry in their late teens. What I look for, in the meantime, is a boy who will likely refuse such contest. That's not because I want them feckless; in this world, you usually die if you're feckless. Instead, I've discovered these boys can grow to rival the Church itself.

Garfield had bowed his head, perhaps in prayer. When he looked up, he scratched under his helmet.

"Garfield," I said, "has Martin tried his mind?"

"Tried it?"

"You can tell him to imagine the pain running out of his foot."

He turned to me, as if I'd touched him, and he searched my face, the way he might try to read a field. "We don't do your magic."

"It isn't magic. It's imagination. Does Esaosh forbid imagination?"

Garfield stood halfway in his turn toward me, and he looked as if he wanted to go ask Otto.

"Go ask Otto," I said. God willing, he wouldn't.

"Your pain trick sounds stupid."

"And chewing on a piece of bark makes you look like a goat."

"Goats don't eat bark."

"A goat will eat anything. We had a group of siegemen who would use a goat to eat through an apron wall."

He turned all the way toward me. "You did?"

"No. No." I motioned for him to turn back around. "But try the pain drip or don't." My heart fluttered. "One day I'll tell you about a pig."

"I don't like pigs. They have demon teeth."

"Fine. I won't."

He sighed. In his worry, maybe, he'd forgotten to bring his book. He jostled one of the bridge's rope railings, and watched the day's slush fall below. "You mean," he said, "Martin just thinks about the pain leaving his foot?"

"He can imagine it dripping out."

"Like blood?"

"Is he tidy?"

"Yes. He likes to clean the dust off the mirrors in the chapel." Esaosh's churches have at least a scatter of mirrors.

"Tell him to imagine an urn for the pain."

"An urn?"

"Yes. Let him fill it, and then decide where to break it."

Garfield stepped to the salt-chalice wall, and faced me. "Who taught you this?"

In fact, I think it was long-dead Miriamne, but I wouldn't tell him so. "It was my mother."

Garfield shut his mouth, and the torchlight made his face look long. He probably kept forgetting I had a mother.

"My mother used to give us spirits," he said.

"That's a good way."

"When I was really little, she would stir it in with some oats. Once with a raisin."

"How lucky."

"But then I'd get dim, and climb into my grandma's lap, and jiggle the fat under her arms."

I laughed so fast that, to keep it quiet, I had to send it into my elbow.

"I don't know why I told you that," he said. "I was such a kid." He cracked his neck, and looked around, perhaps for something to say beyond his fat story.

I had to be careful when we talked about mothers. I was wooing Garfield, as a mother. The Church declares how, in addition to being weak, we women are seductive. They teach we're most dangerous as lovers, but in fact, regarding these boys, we reach them as mothers. The children miss the person who taught them the first, impertinent truth about how love removes economy. The Church points to maternal spendthrift as the way love belies its own weakness. But what the Riven teach our soldiers is that if they find themselves at the mercy of young churchmen, they might stave off atrocity by asking them what their mothers would think.

Now I settled to sleep. Although I usually waited all day to speak with Garfield, he'd trust me more if he watched me sleep. He'd also likely trust me less, if I didn't sleep at all. I propped my feet on my chair. The posture keeps them from swelling so much at night.

"Portence," said Garfield. "The cat. She tried to jump onto the back of Wegman's chair, but she missed, and landed on his head."

I managed to keep from opening my eyes. "He's back to teaching your class?"

"Yes. He called her a half-haired demon."

I clasped my hands on my chest. "Maybe he should see what she does if he offers her his finger."

"No, Wegman's mean. He sharpens the stick part of his holy symbol, to give it a little spike."

I opened my eyes. "On his necklace?"

"Yeah. On the stand part for the scales."

"Is that allowed?"

"He says the Sword does it, to use on pressure points."

I closed my eyes again. From the sound of him, Garfield had faced away from my door. Then I heard him lean against the bars. "I heard an old washwoman when we visited the stocks yesterday." The stocks are just outside the main gate, where the victims looked caught in the Church's teeth. "She said something you'd like. You want to know what?"

"All right."

"She said, when she saw me, she said, 'When I die, I'm going to stomp all over Esaosh's hat.'"

I sniffed in a way that sounded too much like a gasp. What the washwoman said could have increased her sentence to amputation. "What did you do?" I said.

"Nothing." He lay his palm along the bars. "She just reminded me of you."

I didn't say anything. I hoped he'd assume I was drifting to sleep. I watched him, though, through my eyelids, the way I did on the morning when Jillian introduced me to Touch. Garfield hadn't meant what he'd said as a threat. If he had, he would have spoken it loud enough for Otto to hear. In fact, I think what he said came from the opposite impulse. What I wanted to ask, more than anything, was if this washwoman—and her comment—registered on Garfield's List of Goods.

chapter 14

CASPAR

part ONE

Upon entry to the abbey grounds, our prison carriage passed beneath an arch in the second limestone wall. Far below, a road stretched beneath us. And from what I could see, another passage ran above us, along what were now clearly battlements. We passed stalls that were freestanding now. A leather vendor sold only coin sacks, some the size of my fist and others as big as wine skins. These, apparently, were ritual sacks the congregants held over their heads when they offered their wealth to the Church.

Beyond this stall, hung a watchful energy. At first I thought I would find the abbey guard, but as we rolled past, there stood a figure in a black cloak and a white, stiff collar. He had something of a dark, felt sunhat, and around him, in cages and on posts, roosted birds. They were messenger birds and racing pigeons. A falcon, hooded, loomed on a post. The man was a domino in a sea of color, a compass on a map. His clothes were immaculate, as if the creatures knew what not to defile.

"Is he your friend?" I said.

Jillian put a hand on the top of her head. "I don't know who that is."

Sometimes, in my hanging cell, I wonder if Increase will grow to resemble some bird-like iteration of this domino man. These days, if such an iteration sat on my sill, I wouldn't be surprised at all.

Our carriage rolled through the final arch. To the right, stone buildings stood along a path. A blacksmith whetted a blade and wafted his smoke. To the left, the road opened to gardens dotted with white boxes that apparently housed bees.

The carriage stopped, and the soldiers rattled and clinked. Jillian grasped my wrist. Her hand had gone cold.

The guard, Rudyard, opened the door. Blinking, we stepped from the carriage, and the abbey rose, as something leaping at us. It was white as the mountains, as if it had possessed the mountains. I had to back up to see its top. The abbey hefted arches and spires. Steeples in cinnabar tile pushed up and out. The whole mountain wore a crown, of sorts, as if the peak were a monarch both reaching in every direction and protecting against them, appealing to its god and fending away his oppressor. A gold symbol of Esaosh glinted on the tallest tower. The breeze blew, and the post banners flapped, but the scales in the sigil hung unmoved.

I backed into Jillian. She handed me my sack. Rudyard watched, and Jillian asked if he was happy to be home. He brushed his nose while he nodded. He had likely forgotten the stink.

A young man approached in brown robes. He had a white stripe on his scapulary, and he walked as if it squared his shoulders.

"Brother Laird," said Jillian. "You're looking well."

He nodded her a bow, looked at me, and looked away. He asked if Jillian remembered where the guest house was. She said she did. He asked if he could take our bags, and Jillian declined. "I'll spare you the burden," she said. "If we don't hand them over, you can honestly say you didn't have a chance to search."

He looked at her with a kind of gratitude.

"Tell me about the boom," she said.

"You haven't heard it then?" he said.

"I heard it just now," she said.

"But not before? They said you could hear it for miles."

"Well, we've traveled for miles."

"This cannon." He talked with both his hands. "We got it from Cadmus. Black powder burns, and then it explodes into a tube. They say it can shoot where they want it to."

"Like a bow?" I said.

"It hurls a ball," said Laird. "Metal and black. About as big as a pumpkin."

Jillian stepped on a stone, and nearly lost her footing.

"It's like a noisome catapult," he said. "Only more straight ahead."

"That's a weapon," she said.

"I guess they'd like to use it on mindless," he said.

"I don't want to be near it," she said.

"Of course not, my—Yeoman. We'll take you off to the infirmary." He held his arms straight at his sides, as if they should be dangling bags. "And what of your charge, then?"

"She'll come along," she said. "She's my best amanuenses."

Laird bowed again. He waved to Rudyard, and walked us down the building path.

"What is an amanuenses?" I whispered.

"You'll take my notes," she said.

"What is a yeoman?" I said. She turned to me, as if I'd belched. "It means we own land."

I never deeply considered how other people didn't own land. It wasn't until later when I learned how most folk around the abbey were tenants on the abbey's land. They weren't slaves. But by calling us yeomen, the Church implied they didn't leverage us through land, but by something else.

We passed limestone buildings with porches and awnings: a blacksmith, a brewer and a baker, a saddler, and a turner. We ambled along barracks and granaries. This deep into the abbey the churchmen ran each of these posts. We had walked for five minutes, and found no women here.

We passed a large building's herb garden, and Jillian slowed to look.

When I stopped for her, she put her hand on my back, and we kept walking. Then we reached a whitewashed building with bars on the windows and guards at the door.

Our escort, Laird, lagged behind. Finally, he licked his lips and pointed to the entrance. "Esaosh keep you," he said, either in goodbye or in warning.

From where she stood, Jillian studied the building. She reached for Laird's sleeve, and he pulled away.

"What's in there?" she said.

"Just a patient," said Laird.

"Contagious?" said Jillian.

"Not that kind." He walked away.

Jillian approached the door guards. "How dangerous," she said, "is the person inside?"

The guards stared straight ahead.

"Will he threaten my niece?" she said.

One of them spread his stance. "Likely not, Mum."

Jillian motioned me behind her. I wondered if the guards would help us if the patient became unsafe. Jillian opened the door, and the light startled me. It came from overhead, lots of it, white enough to appear almost blue. I thought the building had holes in the ceiling, until I saw they were a pair of windows. The panes had etched glass, roughly the shape of scale pans. Esaosh's symbol made sense in this place; in fact, it was everywhere. But the ceiling here appeared as if the plaster was bone and the windows were light-giving eyes.

Jillian leaned over a young man who lay on a pallet, under the windows. He sweated, pallid and inert. Someone had balanced a brass bowl of water on his chest. Jillian showed me how the water moved when his chest did, that this was a way to tell he was alive. This building was obviously the infirmary. To this day, the Church's first curative is light.

The infirmary's door opened, and a large man in red robes strode to Jillian, with an outstretched hand.

"I told him you were coming." He took Jillian's hand in both of his. "I told him how what he had found had actually called Harwell's own student."

"And Lind's," said Jillian.

"Yes." He shook her whole arm. "He didn't know who I meant, of course, what with him being so young."

The large man's hair was either blond or white.

Jillian said, "You haven't told me what he found."

"Oh!" He turned to me. "You have a protégée?"

"She's my niece."

"Father Felderan." His hand was warm. "Chief Exorcist." He was a member of the Sword. "I'm a healer." He turned to Jillian. "I've come back from a call, or else I would have been here sooner." In his hand, he scrunched the rope around his cassock. "It seems they've found more corpses."

"Mindless?" I said. The word had just jumped from me.

Felderan had crossed his arms, and a tendon stood out on his neck. "She would make a good protégée."

"What corpses?" said Jillian.

"You'll hear the bells. They'll call the villagers to see if they can identify what's washed up." He looked at us back and forth. "Not mindless, no. Old bodies. Only the seniors will be able to recognize them, if they're recognizable at all."

"I'm sure you'll have a busy constabulary," said Jillian.

"Well, the abbot," he said, "he'll tell you where you'll come into the situation. But Jarek," he adjusted the covers on the patient's feet, "he found the first bodies rising out of the north-field well. One after the other," he tsked, "like something squeezed from a tube."

I thought of a demon in a well. "Dead?" I said.

"Yes, dead," he said. "Four of them. Poor Jarek's been unable to drink anything since."

Jillian put a hand on the boy. "So you put a bowl of water on his chest?"

Felderan bared his teeth. "I guess that's a little grim. But I can't strip the chapel of one of its mirrors, and we want him to have water whenever he wants." A bell pealed. "As I said, sometimes I'm away."

"You're the chief exorcist," I said, "you must have servants who—"

"Tell me why we're here," said Jillian. I had not been pliable.

"Well." The man grasped Jarek's leg. "We actually hoped you'd rouse him."

"Me?" she said.

"Sometimes," he said, "the young ones miss their mothers."

"Oh, for pity's sake," she said.

"Not to insult you," he said.

"And don't you have somebody else who can do that?" she said.

"Well, you were arriving anyway," he said.

"I see," she said.

"And," he fiddled with a lancet, "he hasn't seen her much."

"She's the only woman allowed within a mile of the abbey," she said. "I think we can bet he's noticed."

"Yeoman." The lancet clattered. "To be frank, I didn't want her to scare him."

Jillian pushed her tongue into her bottom lip. For a moment, she looked like she'd spit.

She said, "I want the water off the boy."

Felderan sighed, and complied.

"Get your tools out of here," she said. She kneeled next to the bed, and leaned over it. "Jarek." She whispered something to him. She rubbed his brow, and kissed it. She offered everything she had given to me after the mindless chase, and I realized I was jealous.

What Jillian offered didn't help. Jarek moaned, and thrashed his wrist. She lay her palm on his forehead. Then she stood.

"He was in shock," said Felderan. "He's stopped drinking." He peered up at the windows. "I believe what bedevils him is as strong as he is."

The abbey bells chorused now, in three different tones.

"The surfaced bodies are from necromancy?" said Jillian.

"Now that's what we don't want to say," he said. "A claim of necromancy would push the chaos completely out of hand." He opened the door, and the outside looked yellow. "We had a murderer long ago. You may have heard of him. There's a song."

I let the sun close my eyes. At least a murderer was mundane.

"And you think you've got a copycat?" she said.

"Oh no." He stretched in the sunlight. "We think we found his lair."

Father Felderan told us the well bodies appeared a week after Church excavators had opened a buried part of the old abbey—the Lowers, as everyone had come to call them. The bodies were cadavers, disemboweled and occasionally sewn shut. They showed signs, in fact, of outright surgery, a mutilation beyond basic bleeding, that was an abomination in the eyes of the Church. The guards kept pulling up more remains, until the pieces from the well alone assembled nine different corpses. The bodies were old, but surprisingly intact. The deepest ones had nearly frozen from the water they'd steeped in, but now it was summer, and they were out. Then a local catchpole reported how more bodies appeared in the fields.

The villagers scrambled to find them all. They raced against wildlife and disease, but also the possibility of the mindless. The abbey had declared that any corpse that lingered on a local farm for more than a day would cause the farm to be razed. The peasants searched the fields and fens with scythes. They searched their neighbors' land. Others simply burned what they could at the outset. They were afraid of the Church, and they were afraid of necromancy, and they were afraid that all of this catastrophe spoke of invasion. It wasn't the most unfamiliar tale.

So the abbot had addressed his people. On the day before we arrived, he declared with thanksgiving how the recent opening of the Lowers had indeed released the corpses. The exact mechanism remained unknown, but certainly a clog had dislodged somewhere. Equally clear, said Caspar, was that the bodies were not those of monks but of lay people. They didn't, for one, bear the Church's tattoo. Further, he suspected the bodies had been dead for thirty-six years. In fact they were likely the long-recovered victims of Ambrusso the Heretic Vivisector: a scriptorium monk turned apostate, who murdered to supply his rites. The previous abbot, Olvin Niels, had tried Brother Ambrusso, and executed him by oubliette. And now Caspar had declared, with only partial success, how the current emergence of the cadavers was a gift from the Lowers, insofar as Ambrusso's victims could finally find rest.

For almost the entire week, the Church burned an ongoing funeral pyre, which some of the older monks volunteered to tend. Ambrusso had been their brother, their sub-chief illuminator. Apparently, in his off-time, he liked to carve ice. Once the corpse fire had gone out, said Felderan, the ground stayed so warm that dogs would sleep beside it.

part TWO

Now more bells stirred the people. Outside the infirmary, a number of peasants moved toward the exit from the monastery yard, presumably to find the corpses or their families. A few of the folk looked up, and a few of them looked down, depending, I guess, on where their best help was.

Father Felderan led us through the yard, dodging dung piles and mosquitos. The insects numbered fewer than I expected, perhaps on account of the walls. But all these years later, their whine still reminded me of the Treehanded flies. As we walked, Jillian peered through the peasant crowd, but when I tried to look too, she nudged me to keep going. We passed the lay chapel, where its door was open to release the heat. The sun glinted from the ribbon of sanctuary mirrors. Beneath the sound of the bells, the priest recited in a measured tone. The Church scriptures are either poetry or proofs, and the poetry is the oldest.

Felderan left us in front of a white-washed building that had a dark door and shutters. This was the guesthouse, and the inside looked just as dim. Inside, the walls had the same color as the door, and instead of windows, there were holes, about the size of my fist, that made the house look punctured over and again. I had no idea how anybody could keep such a space warm in the winter, until Jillian showed me a bucket of corks by the door. Each one could close a hole, but the room itself revealed a theological exercise. Esaosh espoused light, cool-headedness, clarity. In the winter, the devoted shunned each stopper as something that plugged an emblem of all these virtues. Jillian said she once stayed here in the month of Zappion, curled in a ball, while a pilgrim hopped, half-stupid, in his traveling cloak.

This exercise, so called, is a sinister and persistent ritual. It probably informs how Ordinal's engineers built my hanging cell. In the guest house with Jillian, I picked up a cork, and tossed it.

"It's the religious impulse to offer oneself," said Jillian. "You can try to direct it, but it's nearly impossible to, well—"

"Plug."

"You need to know something," she said. "There are good men who offer themselves to the Church, even if, ironically, it's at the expense of their own reason." Jillian was the first person to tell me this. Whenever I tell it to somebody else, I hear her voice.

Outside, somebody wailed. They'd identified a body, perhaps. Or maybe in places like this, somebody frequently wailed.

Jillian crouched before one of the holes. She turned from it, and rubbed her face. "I guess they just live with how these make excellent spy blinds."

Before we changed for the abbot, we plugged some of the wall. I pounded the corks with an exertion that felt both good and needful. Jillian donned her armor.

"The other woman you mentioned," I said. "Is she your friend?"

"Summer in leather armor," she said. "Starts to feel like the inside of somebody's mouth."

"Can't you please at least tell me?"

She plugged another hole while the bells clanged. "She is a very good friend."

Jillian wiped her face, maybe to hide her smile. I stood taller, and thought of a woman hugging Jillian, until they resembled one larger thing.

"Why is she scary?" I said.

Jillian yanked a drawstring. "She isn't, and I won't discuss it."

"Well, will she scare me? I mean, that could make me insult her—"

"They've maimed her some." Perhaps like Miriamne. "You can handle that."

Jillian creaked in armor given to her by a dead husband of a dead prisoner. Her smallest kukri shone from her boot. I thought of a disfigured woman leaning over my aunt, as Jillian lay senseless under a water bowl.

part THREE

My new clothes were simple: coarse breeches, wool tunic., no dyes. Jillian made me take off my pipe-necklace, because if someone asked about it, she didn't want me to say something to remind them of my family. I rolled my outfit's pants and sleeves. I looked like Jillian's squire, which was somewhat in keeping with the act. The clothes hung large enough to make me appear much younger than I was. That was in keeping with the act as well.

The bells had stopped. We saw Brother Laird pass by the holes before he scratched at the door.

"She's in the blood-letting room," he said. I pictured a maimed woman standing in a pool of the stuff. "I reckon you've got an hour."

"Just an hour?" said Jillian.

He said, "I wasn't supposed to tell you for another twenty minutes."

With her fingers trembling, Jillian put the heel of her palm to her eye. She said to me, "Run some fingers through your hair."

Brother Laird had gone by the time we left the hut. Jillian told me to walk directly behind her, to keep my face down, to talk to no one. If I got lost I should just stand, with my head down, until she returned for me.

"We're going to see the woman," I said.

"You are invisible," she said.

"So I'm invisible with straightened hair."

"Child, believe me. Now is not the time." She straightened her leather the best it could straighten. I told myself that when we met Jillian's friend, I would keep eye contact, assuming the woman had eyes.

We walked in the shadows of the buildings and walls. The scent of pent water arrived on the wind, layered with the other stink.

Before us, bees buzzed. An aroma of herbs washed over the stench, and I nearly stopped. Here stood a garden in every shade of green. It raised my chin, this impertinence against the red. Lavender bushes rose up like stones, and they reminded me of my father.

A yellow-robed man emerged from a squat, slate building. He had fine fingers and full lips, and as he clapped his hands on his head, I realized he was a woman.

She was tall with grayed-brown hair. Along her right cheek, she had a burn that was thin, raised, and white as a seam. Someone had cut a wedge from her left nostril, and they may have also cut off her breasts. Or maybe she'd bound her breasts. She had a tonsure. She looked at least ten years older than my aunt, and tears stood in her eyes. "There are guards inside." She shut the door behind her. "They think that in private, we'll find some plot to hatch." She stood in front of Jillian, and she held her own arms.

"I wish I could hug you," said Jillian.

"You always wish, and it would always give them an excuse to hit you." She gazed at me, and her eyes were gray as the elks' ash. "I wish I could hug you both."

"Who are you?" I said.

"Gaelle," said Jillian.

"I'm sorry," the woman said.

"This is Eleanor." Jillian swayed a step forward and back. "She is my stalwart friend."

"An old family friend," said Eleanor.

"Very old," said Jillian.

Eleanor feathered her stubble. "If they let me grow it out, it would all be gray by now."

"With a little white." They both laughed, and the laughs tumbled on top of each other. All my adulthood I have tried to recall those laughs. For much of my life, I would have one of these women with me, but never both.

"You look no worse for wear," said Jillian.

"Well," said Eleanor, "I think he finally cut away whatever enticed him."

A creep of dread came from what she said. Jillian spoke something, but caught her mouth with her hand.

"What say?" said Eleanor.

"I said I suspect," said Jillian, "that something else might have him occupied."

"Now such a thing, I can't wish for," said Eleanor.

"Well, I do," said Jillian.

"No," said the woman. "First it was the black powder. Now it's the digging. He's always wanted to be principe, and I'm afraid he's gotten so he'll use every threat to gain his advantage."

"All right," said Jillian.

She said, "You know he'll even pit his allies—"

"Don't tell me any more," said Jillian.

"Well." She lavished me a look. "It would all be guesswork anyway."

"He'll tell us at dinner," said Jillian.

"I doubt he's a slave to telling the truth," she said.

"Miriamne would say he's a slave to other things," said Jillian.

"Of course she would," said Eleanor. "I think of her saying so every day."

"Few people, these days, have even heard of her books," said Jillian.

Eleanor tilted me her head. "I love how you have your father's nose."

"You knew my father?" I said.

"Aye. The goodman. I did."

"Eleanor is the almond-plant herbalist," said Jillian.

I looked at the garden, this little patch of ground that tried to clean the air.

"You and Dad," I said. "You had things in common."

"Oh, many," said Eleanor. "I loved your father. But your mother's the one I knew better."

Somebody knocked against metal. Our escort, Laird, stood with his hand on his shield.

"It hasn't been close to an hour," said Jillian.

Laird looked wretched.

"No," said Jillian.

"You know, I think I dropped my dagger." Laird searched nowhere particular. "In the bushes, maybe." He jogged to a clutch of hosta. Every now and then, I wonder what happened to Brother Laird.

Eleanor had grasped Jillian's elbows. She looked deep into Jillian's face, and Jillian kissed her cheek.

"So things are the same these days," said Eleanor. "My plants are slow-growing as always, and the horses are familiar and slow, and we've seen lots of dead bodies." Jillian sort of slouched, and Eleanor held tighter. "Nothing really marches along, except the seasons and the abbot." She let go of Jillian, and she looked at us both. Laird was squatting in the other direction. "You know I love you."

Jillian took my hand, and she pinched. "They didn't give us enough time."

"I love you both." Eleanor moved to the doorway. "So another time."

Jillian shuddered, and Eleanor went inside.

We moved to Laird, and he made a show of discovering his dagger in the bushes. Jillian swayed, and I held her hand tighter.

part FOUR

Laird walked us deeper into the grounds, and the swamp air cleared some. We came to a fourth wall which was so shiny and white that it showed a smudge of my reflection. The slabs resembled hard-packed snow under a layer of ice. Jillian said this stone was alabaster, and I was glad that she could talk about something in the wake of our departure from Eleanor. I wanted to look at something, and alabaster was fine. It was solid and clean, and a heavy cover for what I had to bury for the moment. We could not talk about Eleanor now.

We came to a second preaching balcony that jutted without railings, and stretched maybe ten paces wide. When a celebrant spoke, he must have appeared to float.

Laird had taken us to the wall's northern corner, which had a seam where a door should be. He pulled a white cord I hadn't seen. A door opened within the wall, and Laird stepped through. He didn't even have to duck.

We followed Laird, and he apparently stopped. I bumped into Jillian, and she let go of my hand. The ground looked the same here; we weren't in the cloister. But now we faced the side of a mountain that had curved outcroppings and squared feet. Windows in the stone stood tall, lead-latticed and thin. They reminded me of trees; they were a forest of windows.

This, said Laird, was the Mountain Face of the abbey. The fortress also had the River Face and the Palace Face. Judging by the horizon, the Mountain Face rose high enough to make the sun set faster, as if—perhaps ironically for the Lord of Light—Esaosh's abbey shortened the day.

Now we waited by the Face's entrance. Laird had jogged away. Jillian had flattened herself against the alabaster, either because it was cool or because she didn't want to be seen. I must have stood out like a knob. In the silence, at least to show my sympathy, I wanted to say something about Eleanor. But I had no idea how to start, and I didn't know if we'd be able to finish. Laird returned with yellow robes, and he motioned for us to don them over our clothes. I later learned the yellow meant we were aliens to the order; the color reminded me of a quarantine flag.

We walked along the wall, parallel to the Mountain Face, through an arboretum that had a footbridge and a wooden stage. Then we stopped at a building that appeared as if someone had bricked four cottages together. Its windows, white trimmed, looked darker than light. The door was red and the shutters were red, and all of them had the shine of polished stone.

"Stone shutters?" I said.

"I always thought them ghastly." A large man in red robes stood next to one of the nearest windows. "A man's house should not match his habit." He raised two fingers, and Laird left with a bow. The man had dark brown hair and dark brown eyes. He gave a close-mouthed smile, and long dimples furrowed his cheeks. "Come in." He opened the door. "And take the robes off. Against the white, they look like a dog's been out in the snow."

Inside, he held my robe while I slipped from its sleeves. "You must be Gaelle." Maybe Mellion had told him about me. "I am sorry." He touched the air around my elbow. "You never get over losing your dad."

"No," I said.

"She's already had an ordeal," said Jillian. She handed her robe to a servant.

The man in red led us down a white-plastered hall that had red and gold tiles on the floor. He stopped by a doorway, and I smelled pork. "I won't ask you how the trip went, because I know it was terrible." He showed us to a room with a long, wooden table decked with more food than I had ever seen. "But at least I can feed you."

The table held a part of a pig roast with raisins and cloves as dressing. Someone had baked a tart of apricots, and left more of the fruit in a basket. Almonds piled in a silver chalice with a duster of both sugar and what I later learned was cinnamon. Peas sat in a pot of cream. A servant poured white wine. And the bread was white. It wasn't even harvest time, and as for the apricots, those were out of season.

This man was surely Lumis Caspar. He held part of his cassock as if it were the edge of a vest. "So far, Gaelle, your reaction is one of the best parts of my day." He pulled out a wooden chair. "Do sit."

I sat. Jillian gave a half smile. "It looks like some kind of last meal."

"Or a first." He pulled out her chair. "Please."

She leaned against the white wall, and then sat beside me

"We had to get you here. And quickly." He winced. "Discreetly." He turned his wince to a grin. Jillian flashed a thin smile in return. He shrugged, and crossed to his own seat. "Jillian, all of it's true, now more than ever. You are so incredibly valuable."

She put two fingers to her mouth, pressing her lips. Such an odd choice of words—*valuable*—as if Jillian were something in a case.

The abbot grasped his cassock front again, and he rubbed it between his fingers. "I know that Mellion is as unpleasant as they come."

"I've always dealt with Mellion," she said. "He wasn't the worst part of the trip."

"Nope." He straightened a carving knife. "The prison carriage. The not stopping."

"The fact," she said, "that I saw Eleanor for ten minutes."

I watched Caspar's finger reflect in the knife. Jillian was not being calm.

"It all falls into the same round of insults," he said. But none of his comments really amounted to an apology. As she sat, Jillian leaned over her knees, maybe to press her feet to the floor.

"What I thought, in fact," said Caspar, "is maybe Gaelle could stay with Eleanor while we did our work. Make it a good visit for both of them."

I felt a warmth, something reminding me of home. Jillian rested her elbows on the chair's cushioned armrests.

"I'll have to see," she said.

"Well, it's either with her or with Felderan," said Caspar. "We can't have your niece living among the boys."

"I would like," said Jillian, "to spend some time with my friend."

"And I meant for you to have it," said Caspar. "Jillian, before you go home, you should certainly have time."

Jillian's chest heaved.

"But you know that right now, we're in a crisis," said Caspar. "You've seen the bodies?"

She said, "I've seen a boy in the infirmary—"

"Jarek." He plucked up an almond. "Hails from Marmarth. Talks a lot about his sister." He touched my teacup. "Gaelle, please start eating. The look on your face is breaking my heart."

I tried to blank the expression on my face. It didn't come from hunger.

Jillian spooned some peas onto her plate.

I tore off a hunk of bread, and the smell of it made me weak. In three days, I'd eaten so little.

"Use utensils," said Caspar.

I wiped my hands on my thigh.

"Gaelle has the right idea, anyway." He chuckled at the room. "Time is short enough that we can't do a proper job of eating in courses." I didn't know what a course was. Caspar used the carving knife to thin-slice the meat. "I gave the footmen the night off for this very reason. And it's also one of their birthdays, so please let's leave them some of the tart." He put some pork on each of our plates, and drizzled the juice. "Honoring your opponent also always honors yourself." He bowed his head, either to the boar or to someone else. "Now I know I said we were in a hurry. But everybody has to eat. Even the guards." He gestured to a corner. "They stand in the shadows with all their heavy weapons and heavy armor, watching us eat while they maintain our peace."

Without turning my head, I spotted two guards in a curtained doorway.

"Tell me about the murders," said Jillian.

Caspar pressed his napkin to his chin. "Bodies came up through the well." He stabbed the meat with his fork. "Vivisected. Awful. More in the marsh."

"You have the Shield and Sword," she said. "You have your own considerable prowess."

"Oh," he said. "Well, I don't run around much anymore these days." He rubbed his belly. "Parts of me jiggle that shouldn't."

"Tut tut," she said. I put a finger to her forearm, and she twitched.

"The bell has been ringing nonstop." He pressed the far corners of his eyebrows. "I have old ladies weeping over the corpses of their old, new husbands."

"Well, Caspar," Jillian chewed her peas. "I'm waiting to hear what you'd like me to do about it."

I Touched. She behaved as she did before we burned Wilm's field. And once again, if she had a plan, I'd missed it.

"You can call me Abbot Caspar." Caspar sat still while he looked around the room. "And you can help me uncover the killer's lair."

Jillian glanced at me, and I grasped for a necklace that wasn't there. "If this is what the Church demands," she said, "you know I'll—"

"Acquiesce. Look, he's an old murderer," said Caspar. "He's from way back from when I was a boy. The Church dealt with him. He's long dead. But he has more victims than anyone thought. Gaelle."

I started.

He said, "You do a good job of enduring grisly conversation."

Jillian Touched in way that knocked into me.

"I grew up on a farm. I've seen some violence." Maybe, somehow, the food was something I'd fallen for.

"Violence." Caspar turned to Jillian. "You wouldn't believe me if I told you I'd grown tired of it."

"Oh, I wouldn't," she said.

"Jillian," I whispered.

He bent his gaze toward his lap, and he shook his head, hunched that way. "Boy. You know, you grew tired of it once. Remember?" He sat up, with a slight flush. "You let the flames of it burn out, after they'd done their work."

"Enough." She slammed a Touch. "If you want any sort of peace from us, you will not mention that."

Caspar glanced at me with a glint as sharp as a pin. Outside, the bells had stopped.

"We brought you here in the prison carriage," he said, "because we couldn't let anyone see. I couldn't let anyone think I was importing a specialist to deal with the problem, until I was absolutely ready to deploy her at the problem."

Jillian seemed to work to relax her face.

"All it takes is one to start a rumor," he said. He bit an apricot. "And rumors, these days, are what we're trying to contain. You can understand this."

"Your church," she said, "is what started talk of the mindless."

"Well, the mindless aren't a rumor," he said. "But they aren't coming from here. And I'm afraid what *is* starting to come from this place is old-fashioned hysteria."

"And you like that only when it serves the Church," she said.

"Jillian," I said.

"We prefer armies to mobs," he said a little louder. "The major difference between the two is discipline. But we'll talk more of such things later."

She exhaled until her cheeks went hollow. "Please continue."

"The lair seems to open to an underground structure," he said. "Part of the abbey, old. Maybe even older." Likely despite herself, Jillian squinted. "This place was where we first established a major foothold, once Visjaes left." He watched her. "I think it's rather raw down there. As ancient as the Church has ever been."

Jillian gazed at the black-oak rafters, and in my mind, I appealed to every dead family member to help her keep a blank face.

"Help us, now," said Caspar. "You'll receive an honorarium. You'll uncover abbey history. And you'll keep people from killing one another. I'd say it's all a win."

Jillian looked back at him with that same emptiness.

"You don't really have a choice," he said. "But I like to believe this would actually be your choice."

He knew her. It might have helped if I better noticed how well he did.

"So now," she said, "you can tell me why you brought my niece."

She could have just as easily dangled me before a dog.

He looked to me as if to share my surprise—and I tried to look unsurprised.

"Well," he said, "We are interested in Gaelle. We are interested to see if she, in fact, is your apprentice."

I held very still.

"I can't imagine," said Jillian, "that you'd like us to continue the family business."

"Actually," he said, "despite our differences, I like working with you folk."

"And what's the motivation you'd use," she said, "to start her working?"

Caspar finished chewing part of his meat. "I'll say this once, and I mean it." He gave a soft clap of his hands. "I was hoping we could just make our case."

Jillian Touched, hard.

"You'd have to find some excellent teachers," she said.

"Yes," he said. "It would be vastly better than improving with trial and error."

I thought of the escort, Laird, lying on a ruins' spike—of myself lying on a spike.

"What if she doesn't want to do this?" said Jillian.

"Then she won't do it," he said. "It's that simple."

The pork juice had smeared on my plate. I didn't want to do anything for this man.

He finished his apricot, and lay its stone beside his knife. The flesh around the pit was red and demolished.

"We can't force you," he said.

"No, you can't," said Jillian. "You can force me, but not her."

"As much as we're interested," said Caspar, "we simply thought that bringing Gaelle along with her aunt would be a way of holding two birds with one hand." He shrugged in my direction. "I hate the other expression."

He settled in his chair, to eat. His shoulders were as well-cut and purposeful as his fingers. He had a black spot on his thumbnail, where he must have banged it. He looked older than Jillian, but it was impossible to tell by how much. Maybe, in some sense, he'd broadened instead of sagged; some people do such things.

All this smacked its comparison with Eleanor, and how, when she'd held her elbows, her hands had completely covered them. She'd said she loved us.

"I don't think I want to work for the Church," I said.

Jillian touched my wrist, and either she or I began to tremble.

Caspar watched us with his chin propped on his clasped hands. "Might I ask you to give it more thought?" I imagined the cannon boom. "Just for the visit."

"I don't think her answer will change," said Jillian.

"Well, all right," he said. "We'll see." He pushed from the table. "But for the moment, would you please stand with me?"

Jillian stood so fast that we all likely saw how she wanted to change the subject.

Caspar spread his arms at us. "*The difference between faith and conditioning is thought.* Guess who said so."

"Actually," said Jillian, "my father said it. He just didn't put it in a book."

"Both devotion and depravity depend on reflection," said Caspar. "This is why unguided thought is so pernicious."

Jillian shifted her shoulders. She and Caspar played a game of balance, or rather, unbalance. The contest was the opposite of the horseshoe's Silence.

Now Caspar led us from the table, into a triangular solarium with light-blue paint on the walls. A center floor-tile gleamed, white and polished. Wooden chests stood along the walls. A doorway opened to a dark-stoned room that looked to house a trough around its edge. By the fire, sat a glass vial as high as my waist, with what looked like smoke inside.

At first I thought the walls' plaster held colored designs. Then I realized the lowering sun came through the ripples in the glass in such a way to throw the light, in curved bands, onto everything. The room suggested we steeped in twilit water, or maybe under ice.

Caspar let the bands drape him. "Gaelle, have you seen much glass?"

I told him I hadn't.

"It's a valuable thing," he said. "A beautiful thing. It's like light slowed to let in more light." Such was Miriamne's monument. "Now if I had my way, I would build Esaosh a whole monument in glass." Where she stood, Jillian shuffled her feet back and forth. "Actually," said Caspar, "my cannon might upset a glass monument. Did you hear the cannon?"

"Was that what I heard?" said Jillian.

"I guess it makes sense you'd be ignorant of these things," said Caspar. "There aren't many cannons in the places we stuff you."

"*Stuff* is such an attractive verb," she said, "when you're trying to recruit my niece."

He barked a laugh. "Still, the cannon is more expensive than either of you. And more beautiful, in its own way." In all my life, I've met only two people who call artillery beautiful.

Now Caspar sat in the room's only chair. "I wanted to talk about my reform," he said, "but the cannon is part of such changes, so we can start there." From his pocket, he produced two round pieces of glass that sat in a wooden frame. The frame had long hooks he placed behind his ears, while he settled the frame on his nose. His eyes sat large behind the first spectacles I'd ever seen.

"So the cannon," he resembled a bug. "It has to use black powder. And we have always had black powder, but only in small quantities, and in inferior quality at that. But from a source I won't tell you, and from a formula I also won't tell you, we have been given the means to make it nearly as often as needed."

Jillian's knee bent a little.

"It is truly a gift from God," said Caspar. He held the pendant of his own necklace—gold, in the shape of Esaosh's balance scale.

"Jillian," he said.

She was looking at me; she might have seen the war in my future.

"Jillian." He half stood, and she turned to him, the way she'd turn toward a storm. "Now a cannonball hits the mindless." He snapped. "It dismembers a group of them." He clasped his hands. "Or it does that to any army." He pulled his hands apart, and spread his fingers.

He might have meant the mindless, the Treehanded.

"And yet," Jillian shifted her feet, "you continue to hunt those making the mindless."

"Well, the cannon is just a weapon in an arsenal. We still have to search," he said. "Not every enemy is an army. And, to be fair, we still face the issue of making the cannons, and of making sure they don't explode when we don't want them to." He took off his spectacles, and his eyes seemed to retreat. "Let me make an assurance, my friend." He blinked. "We will still need you."

"You do need me," she said.

"And in fact," he said, "with the lands we hope to open up, we will need people like you, now more than ever." He leaned far toward me, nearly out of his chair. "But maybe you've already made your decision."

I had to look away from him. The glass vial sat by the fire, as if it could explode.

"Naturally," said Caspar, "we will make it a law that no member of the Church can be killed with black powder. I believe a grant from Esaosh should not be used against the people of Esaosh."

"And in the meantime," said Jillian, "you horde your weapon."

"Of course!" said Caspar. "In the same way we safeguard our finances, and our land. And our knowledge. But I prefer the word *conserve*, my lady. We are *conservative* with our wealth." He scraped his chair, and the sound echoed. "We hold, you see. We safeguard. We build. We protect from the foolishly curious." Teph had once foreseen such a thing, when he told me about the wall of students. "Of course, the carefully curious are another matter entirely." Caspar put his glasses back on. "Isn't curiosity what you had a touch of when you started your work? Isn't it what pulls you now, in spite of all, when you investigate the places I send you?"

"You confuse me," she said, "with a pilgrim."

He laughed. "I think you are a pilgrim! At least I hope you are." The vial I studied held his reflection. "Curiosity is the pilgrim's path, if not his staff. It is our desire to uncover and recover. It's the calling we have to worship with wonder." He turned to me. "A scholar is a pilgrim. A reader is a pilgrim. It's how you take after both of your aunts." The comparison chilled me; I was his enemy before I could walk. "Yes?" He was asking me.

"Yes," I said.

"But a question is a literal type of asking" he said. "It's a request. And what all of us have forgotten, both pagan and faithful, is how nothing comes for free." That line, right there, could be the Church's motto. "A gift by any other name is a trap. It sets up obligation. It cheapens discipline itself by denying its necessity. And in the case of knowledge, this 'gift' and obligation are truly demonic. And that is because, truth without toil leads to confusion and self-delusion and ultimate apostasy." Jillian's eyes darted. "Now the steps toward knowledge," said Caspar, "are what tame knowledge, you see. The steps toward knowledge are how we've earned the right to approach knowledge—to finally seize hold of it, and keep hold. And with Esaosh, who dispenses the light of all knowledge, one must consistently earn."

Every part of me itched to look to Jillian, but I figured this was exactly what Caspar wanted me to do.

"You think I'm in error," he said, "for holding close the Church's riches." He sighed through his nose. "That is how much we've forgotten." He bowed his head, and he seemed to pray. "The beasts earn their food, or they go hungry. They develop their strength, or they die. Nations muster their soldiers, their farmers, their masons, their *powers*, or else they crumble to destruction. And in that ruin, that self-inflicted burial, they will sit, until another nation with stronger children tills the soil, until it takes what is theirs from those who couldn't keep it, and builds with the weak ones' bones.

Jillian watched his hands. She pressed her own into her thighs, as if she didn't want any part of her to fly away.

"Of course, what I've just described," said Caspar, "is death, and burial, and resurrection. It is simply the natural order of our lives. And Esaosh, my ladies, Esaosh bids we flourish with our lives. Esaosh bids we succeed for all our lives. He wants us to offer both our good and our goods to secure his aid in our success. And the best success, the one that benefits both self and others, is for us to live on our own, to produce on our own, to grab hold and keep hold of as much self-determination as anybody possibly *could* own." I thought of Jillian in a ruin, standing on a greasy floor. "Esaosh is the god of freedom. Esaosh is the god of reason. Esaosh keeps a torch not for its heat but for its light. And Esaosh cries that altruism is heat *without* light. That it is warmth without reason. That it steals. It softens. It weakens. It rots away at what so many of us have toiled to grow." He offered his hand to me, as if he wanted us to dance, and Jillian took a step toward the space between us. "And this is hard." He tried to meet her eye. "It is hard to hear these things—I know. You love your family. You love your friends. I love mine too." I thought of him bending over Jarek. "But because I love them, I make myself stand beside them. Because I love them, I demand they stand too. And I love them most when they are most sublime. And I love us both when we shine in our strength. And I love us all when we divulge ourselves as God's own champions, recovered and uncovering. Plowing the earth. Revealing his splendor. Taking our stand and our *right* to stand as a nation of princes, of powers, awaiting nothing other than our king."

Jillian stood so straight that she could have risen on tiptoe. I held my hands loose, open and empty, not owning anything.

"Now magic," Caspar stood behind his chair. "Magic rejects our inheritance. Magic offers our claim to somebody else. It bases itself in passion, insofar as it produces illogical wants. It bases itself in wishful thinking, insofar as many breeds of it attempt to contact the dead. Necromancy, in particular, bases itself in filth, insofar as it creates mindless. As a means of giving fealty to something other than the natural order, all magic leads away from the god who created all order. And what it invites in its place is the passionate trickster, the imprisoning giver. The seed of all weakness—who is Visjaes himself." The sky had turned gold behind him, as if he'd timed his speech to meet it. "Magic is what reaches for him."

Caspar sat, and the chair creaked. Maybe we were supposed to applaud, or maybe he was attacking Jillian by attacking Miriamne. Maybe he was calling us weak.

Jillian stepped next to me. "I'm afraid I don't see your point."

"Oh, I think you do," he said. Jillian might not have known that Caspar prepared for what became the entire Reordering War, but she had her knack for knowing the stakes. "My lady Jillian," he said. "This pertains to you in two specific ways. The first is that I have reason to believe the vivisector's lair belongs to a murderer who most certainly used magic and may have been actively worshipping Visjaes. You will do the world a service by going to the underparts of the abbey—to the Lowers—and seeing what's down there. You will also do the Church a service by providing it more information about its past, as a means of helping it toward its present reform."

"Does Ordinal also possess the black powder?" said Jillian.

"Lands," he said. "You always were smart." He turned to me. "Isn't she smart?" I had no idea what to say. "Ordinal utterly must have it. As the Imperial capital, it should possess the most." To this day, it does. "And this stipulation brings me to the second way my lesson pertains to you. And you, young lady." I swallowed, but I wanted to spit. "As captain of this reform, I will be partner, with Ordinal's Principe Emeric. He and I will make the order of the world more clear. It will be easier, in the coming weeks, for us to work together, to find our roles and our best behavior. And to see what works against us." Caspar gazed at the fading light on the floor. "We will have faith that Esaosh wishes us to prosper. We will expect prosperity as commensurate with our individual worth, as people of productivity and as people of faith. According to worth, we will regiment our communities. We will drive back the mindless. We will drive back any and all who even dream of opposing us. All the mages. All the heretics. In driving them to the ground, we will return the world to balance over laxity, to trade over altruism, to holy transaction in every stall, home, and heart." A bird's shadow crossed the room from where the creature flew overhead. Up again, crossing the room, Caspar moved his foot, to trail where the shadow had been. "And here, my ladies, finally, in a stable Celd—a united Celd, a balanced Celd—will have peace."

We should have killed him then, even if the attempt killed us too. Caspar leaned his forehead near Jillian's shoulder, as if to whisper in her ear. "The past has been a brutal tutor," he said. Just slightly, she wrinkled her nose. "It's made us suffer. It's made us bleed. It's shown how we've done things unworthy of our nature, to ourselves." He sighed through his nose, and one of Jillian's loose hair strands wafted. "We've been unworthy to ourselves, and to others." He sighed again. "But tomorrow—Jillian. You get to help me start us back from all that."

The skin around her eyes trembled, and she let out a shudder in a laugh. "Well. That's the longest, most half-arsed apology I've ever heard."

I Touched as hard as I could. He flinted his eyes. "You will hear what you have ears to hear," he said. "But you are going down there regardless."

"It's almost as if you do need me," she said.

"Gaelle," he said. "You were looking at Alder." He brought the glass vial to me, and offered me to take it. I thought of tearing the snake. "It's all right, my dear. You don't have to." He lay the vial at my feet. "It's a little heavy."

This close to it, I could see how the thing came only up to my thigh. The glass had a greenish tinge, and it wasn't filled with smoke at all, but with hair. I backed into Jillian. Blue eyes lay at the bottom.

"That's Alder," Caspar said. "My departed hound."

Jillian said, "Esaosh on a chamber pot."

"Aaht!" Casper held up his finger. "You will not use profanity in front of my god or my dog. That's a forehanded and backhanded prohibition." He lay his hand on the glass, and met my eyes in the vial's reflection. "Those are marbles, my dear. To complete the look."

The vial was like Miriamne's box, but it entirely wasn't.

"Alder used to shed all over the residence," said Caspar. "So after he died, I just collected what I could find." He squatted by the vial. "He never liked to go outside. But he liked the fire." He stroked the glass, and it made a little squeak. "For twelve years, while that dog lived, he would sit next to me, in this parlor or on the private balcony. And he would listen while I practiced my oratory." I felt a little sick. "Believe me. Oratory takes practice." Caspar has become a lethal orator; he leads the choirs. "Actually, I made him bark once, right while he listened." Caspar seemed to study me. Then his eyes went distant. "You know, I always wanted to do that again. I always wondered if I could get the rhythm, the energy, if it were maybe possible to make him howl."

"And did you make Eleanor howl?" said Jillian. "Imprisoning everything you care about?"

Caspar snapped back to himself, and I glanced at the guards' corners. He said, "You've begun to push me far enough."

"No, I haven't," she said.

"Jillian," I said.

"No. Not nearly," she said. "This is disgusting." She clawed her fingers. "This is how you are." She strode to the vial, and I thought she'd smash it.

"Pieces of your supposed beloveds. Ruins. Making the dog howl." I touched her hand, and she threw me off. "You and your black-powder cannon. You and your plow-the-earth speeches."

"Jillian," I said, "be pliable."

"Oh!" She threw her elbow, as if she batted something down. "Pliable! Caspar is the weakest criminal I know. Caspar learns to talk a pretty line, all because he has to convince himself he is right. How his murders, his tortures and his thefts—"

"Enough!" he said.

"Jillian." I had hold of her shoulders, and I stood between her and Caspar. "She's tired," I said to him. "She misses her friend."

He gave me an assessing look, and settled the jar closer to the fire.

"Did you shave its fur?" she said.

"Stop," I said.

"Did you mutilate its face?" she said.

"The glass reminds her of someone," I said to him. "Somebody other than Eleanor."

He squinted, and I glanced toward the door.

"Did you chop off its member," said Jillian, "so you wouldn't be tempted to sleep with it?"

"You will leave me!" said Caspar. In the dining room, a nectarine fell from its bowl.

He pushed in front of her.

I stretched out my hand, and almost touched his chest.

He looked as if he wondered whether I'd do it. I still remember his eyes. Sometimes I imagine him under my hanging cell, looking up with his same expression.

In the priory, he said, "I will send for you both in the morning."

Jillian said, "He shouldn't—"

"Count," I whispered to her. Count the people she loved—the people whom anger like this could outright kill.

Caspar said a guttural word I didn't recognize. He beckoned over our shoulders, and two guards emerged from somewhere I hadn't seen. "Take them home, and walk slowly. She's been in her cups."

We passed the food, largely uneaten.

"Gaelle." Caspar pursued with a brown shape in his hand. It was a book. "This is for while you wait." He thrust it in my palms. "Botany. Like your father." The tome felt heavy and fat. "You keep taking good care of your aunt."

Jillian grasped my shoulder and gave a haggard breath. Caspar's door shut behind us. She leaned her head toward mine. She held on, and for the two of us, I took a step.

chapter 15

Arafel

Garfield is gone. I haven't seen him in five days. Otto stands at the Bell post now, and we do not speak. When he's here, I remove the stool from the north window, and I stand before the sill. The wind makes me tear, and I let it.

Six days ago, the guards thundered as they marched. They sounded older and more numerous than usual, and it turns out the young ones had accepted squads from elsewhere, into a kind of ongoing parade. The pomp and the noise likely meant the execution of a noble, and then the trumpet of an elephant confirmed it. Under Church rule, an aristocrat who acts above his station is said to *have a head wider than the world.* The penalty for such behavior is for one of the cavalry's bull elephants to reduce that head by stomping it. Still, elephants are rare enough to make death by one a spectacle. So on the morning of all the parades, the commotion rose with the sun. Then around noon, a cheer rose, and fell to silence. From the Bell, I watched the portico's torch flame stand straight up.

The execution's clamor had died instantly, and the marching stopped soon after. The trouble with the elephant kind of execution is that it's over fairly quickly, and it makes everyone feel a little fragile. The elephant does show the might of the Church; it literally treads an enemy underfoot. But except for the most fanatic cleric, such a thing is far too sobering. As for the boy guards in Otto's halo, I expect that after this day, they couldn't joke about a squashed head anymore.

Later in the evening, Garfield arrived at his post on time, and he cast a disconsolate glance at my half-empty bowl of gruel. "You want what's left?" I said.

He swallowed. "No." He picked a scab on the back of his hand, and he stopped.

I wanted to talk to him directly about what he'd seen that day, but Garfield was like Increase in how I had to get close to him without anyone seeming to notice.

"You had to read scripture yesterday," I said. From what I could tell, this was the first time since the other day's misreading. "No howling, this outing?"

"No." He watched me move the gruel out of sight. "Martin read before me, and he'd forgotten his scroll in the back of the chapel, so he had to pull whatever he remembered out of his," he gestured.

"Ex nihilo?"

It was telling how he couldn't curse around me anymore. "I mean his behind."

I nodded.

He said, "Nobody paid much attention afterward."

He jiggled a knee. From all the parading, he probably wanted to sit.

"How is Martin?" I said. "With the ankle."

"He's all right." Garfield's eyes had a sunken look, as if maybe he hadn't eaten all day. "I didn't tell him your pain trick. I figured he'd call it magic."

"Well, you are the one who knows him."

"I did it, though." He stood against the chalice wall, with his hands behind his back. "I tried to imagine it for him."

I held to my wrist as if I tried to hold my entire body. "You did?"

"Yes. Because it isn't magic."

"It isn't." Applied this way, it's love.

"I even imagined him a little pot." He acted to hold one. "I made it a honey pot, because they make good noise when they break."

"I'll take your word for it." In their circle around my wrist, I pressed my index finger into my thumb. I wanted to tell Garfield he was a good friend, but such a thing can sound too much like love. "How are things, otherwise?"

"Fine." He gave me a look, as if he'd just shut a lid. "Service was long."

"Because Martin couldn't remember his lines."

"Right." He glanced toward Otto's alcove. "The rector said how in death, all the righteous will become one, as soon as all their sin goes away."

"Light and Allegiance."

Garfield scratched his mustache fuzz. "That's what they say."

This could become a dangerous conversation. "Listen to Garfield," I said, "preaching to a heretic."

I tried to keep eye contact, as long as he'd let me. He'd left a kind of door open, behind his gaze, and I could see him walking around in there.

"Anyway," he said. "That's death."

My heart fluttered a little. Garfield likely fluttered a little, in the wake of both an elephant stomp and a promised reward of eternal sameness. Leave it to an authoritarian church to preach how paradise amounts to falling into lockstep.

"I should let you sleep," he said.

"It's early yet."

"But you aren't talking much." He rubbed his forehead.

"Then suit yourself," I said.

"You know, Gaelle, you shouldn't be afraid of what happens after."

I said, "After?" This was the first time he'd addressed me without using a title.

"Of what happens after death."

"Oh, I think it's mostly an accepting kind of fear."

"The rector said it. Sameness is what we get."

He looked up in a way both defiant and haunted.

"I reckon you have a long way yet to live," I said.

"And all my living, just so I can go away."

I counted a little. I wasn't ready for this. And by the way he'd spoken so abruptly, he likely hadn't been ready to blurt what he did. Now he sniffed, and brushed his nose with the back of his hand. Neither of us had expected an execution by elephant.

"Garfield."

"You're lucky to live so long."

"You can tell me so when you're my age."

"I mean, you're still here. You're still yourself." He wiped his eye, and my knees went a little weak. "Caspar too. He's managed to live even longer."

"Now don't be putting me in the same barrel with Caspar."

"But we're all in the same barrel, right? Or at least the righteous are."

Perhaps he considered me righteous. "That's what they say."

He rubbed his birthmark with his thumb, the way his mother may have done. I thought of Jillian, during the loneliness of my adolescence, of her wondering when to tell me there was a community that agreed with us, that in the resistance, we did have friends.

Now Garfield sat. He sat. I'd never seen him do this before. He said, "If Otto sees, we can tell him I'm tired."

"Garfield, you know you can't sit."

"Don't worry. I won't sleep." Above his head, he tugged Mama.

He sat with his legs splayed in front of him, like somebody who'd spent all day in a rout. I held the stone I'd found in my cell, trying to feel some wisdom from it. If I let myself ease the boy with what I thought, it would be like the first time a person touches a stray animal. That contact—that permission—changes everything.

He squeezed shut his eyes.

"Garfield. You need to get up."

"I'm not sleeping."

He wasn't. He was likely trying to banish what he'd seen. "Garfield." The day's execution probably hit him the way I'd suffered Jillian's carving the mindless. "Garfield, I don't think it's really like porridge." I clutched handfuls of my robe. "You know what I mean?"

He made his mouth small. God would have to help us if Otto bounded across the bridge.

"That's all," I said.

"All what?"

"Never mind. Stand up."

He stood, and I breathed a little. "You said something," he said.

"I'm not sure—"

"You talked about porridge."

He'd seized it like a scrap. I Touched for Patrick. Garfield reminded me of Patrick, our church father.

"Tell me," he said.

"Porridge is the same, you know, once all the lumps are gone." Maybe his mother knew this, when she gave him the treat with the raisin. "That's all I mean."

Garfield approached my door. "So the rector is wro—"

"Some say that if we all become indistinguishable in our perfection, then the only thing that made us singular in life was our deficiencies." I stepped from the bars. "Now stand your post."

"So about death, the rector is wro—"

"Some heretics say that a monolith might be the most efficient, but that it isn't really the most lively."

Garfield scrunched his eyes.

"That's all," I said.

I sat against the far wall. He clasped the bars like a railing. We should have stopped there; he didn't know what he was asking.

"Esaosh," he said, "is the lord of reason and clarity through strength."

"Oh yes. Of course. You preach very well." I said so loudly.

"But you think it's wrong," he said.

"And I am a heretic."

"It's wrong."

I crossed to him, and lowered my voice. "This is what heretics think."

He grabbed his helmet, and for a moment, I feared he might take it off. "I don't want to live like this."

"You don't want to live like a heretic."

"I don't want to die like this."

"You mean, as a heretic."

"It isn't heresy!" He half shouted. "Is it?"

"Child." I'd clutched his hand. "You have to stand post, and you have to keep still."

"They squashed him like a cherry," he said. "Right there, as they beat their drums."

"Garfield."

"What kind of people use an elephant, in front of a family—"

"Hush."

"And then they say how in death, everyone will become like them?"

"Will become like the Church, of which you are a member."

"That's disgusting. It's disgusting. It disgusts me."

"Boy, you turn around. Turn around, and you shut your mouth."

"I don't want to shut my mouth."

"You will shut your mouth." I spoke louder than I wanted. "Shut it, and I will tell you." It was all I could do to end his rant. "I'll tell you everything we think. But you have to stop your yap." He sort of gulped at me, and I drew a ragged breath.

I would be the speaker, then—the preacher. Such a role would shield him some. He would be the quiet boy, simply ordered to stand his ground.

He turned his back to me, and held the cell's crossbar. The little tendons stood out on his wrist.

"Garfield." I bowed my head on the bars. "Some say it's variety, individuality—these little gaps between us that we open and fill—that this is the completion." He rested the back of his helmet against the bars. "They say clarity is good, even sacred, but that true splendor comes from the maker's endless and attentive creativity."

I was evangelizing now, both-handed.

"So," he said, "it's all Darkness and Divergence?"

"No." My God, he was fragile. "No. It's Mystery and Unity." I caught my reflection in the helmet. "In our uniqueness, in everyone's variety, we mean more to one another, and are part of one another, in ways we can't even comprehend." He turned around, and wiped his eye. I tried to remember he was fourteen. "You know, it's too broad to catch in a motto."

"You make it sound full of shadows."

"Garfield, it is shadowed. And it's messy." I looked up, and he was so close that we likely appeared as if we carried something. "I think it's a crash at midnight, a truth living enough to confound all the sages. And this truth walks the plain at night, howling in its grandeur." No. The metaphor sounded too much like the Reaching Man. The boy wasn't ready for the Reaching Man. "What I believe in is a truth that a herdsman finds standing among the din of his sheep, or that lives in the unsee-ably small, or that comes to everything and everybody, even if it has to destroy its way in, like water."

"Destroy?"

"Or correct. Or open." He shook his head. I was losing him. Here I tried to describe a life of encounter, when he'd been busy studying a religion of transaction. "Your cathedral, Garfield, with all its mirrors and its scent of coin. Imagine it in the dark, when the mirrors show something different."

"But it's the same—"

"Halves of things. Glimpses. Uncertainty. Fog. We call it arafel."

"You mean Visjaes?"

"Holy dark." And yes, I meant Visjaes, but not his version of Visjaes. "Garfield." He leaned toward me, and watched my mouth. "Your cathedral, and every faith's cathedral, has ancient rooms you have never seen. And something moves around in them. And if all of you chanted in the night, and then if all of you stopped chanting, you'd hear someone in those rooms who was still chanting, in words you couldn't understand, because they'd never been uttered before." I held to the bars; I needed to sit. "But such chanting is constant. Such love is constant. The attention, the variation, the correction, the creation—it is a continuous act of love. And it is not economy."

"Garfield." Otto stood with a mace in his hands. "Into the castle."

Garfield grabbed his halberd as if he'd spin it like a quarterstaff. "She didn't—"

"Didn't what?" The bridge still bounced from where Otto strode. "She didn't give you a five-minute speech in a language you don't understand?"

Garfield lowered his halberd on loose arms.

"Because I heard it myself," said Otto. He slammed my door with his mace. "Foreign language? Maybe a spell or incantation?"

"She wasn't—"

Otto grabbed the boy's arm, and spun him toward the bridge. "Get gone!" Garfield whimpered. "She's got you partway in her thrall."

I had never switched to another language.

"Don't kill her," said Garfield.

"Garfield, stop," I said.

"Stop!" Otto stomped a lunge at Garfield. "Get!"

Garfield got.

Otto turned to me with a new pallor beneath his body hair. "If it were up to me, Witch, you'd be dead." Caspar wouldn't allow it. "But killing you for this would implicate the boy."

I said, "It was all my fault."

"You shut your mouth." He stood post at my door. "So you were casting spells at him, in a different language, because that's what the Church says you do." Sweat beaded in his neck stubble. "You confused him. And you will never speak to him again."

chapter 16

NIGHT

part ONE

When we left the priory, the abbey's white and shadow spread like a reversal of everything I knew to be true. Although I could see the ground, with its thick grass and gravel, I felt for a moment that my foot would fall through it, that this first tread after meeting Caspar would send us headlong into an abyss. All things considered, I wasn't wrong. Even up in my hanging cell, I fear the abyss more than I fear a sudden fall to any cavern floor. In his priory, with his feast, and his speeches, and even his book, Caspar, the servant of so-called light, had tried to draw me to a moral pit—a devilry. He gave it hooks. This temptation, perhaps, is why I find it so possible to love boys like Garfield, or even those who aren't like Garfield. In other circumstances, Caspar might have recruited me too. Thank God for Jillian. Thank God she was an intrepid, a trap-runner, a scout who could feel for all of corruption's pits and seams. In my life, I've become a nun and an advisor, a pilgrim and a strategist. But for the boys in Ordinal's yard below me, I try to be an intrepid too.

When we left the priory, sun had just set. We walked in silence, with guards on either side. Jillian had let go of my shoulder, but I still felt her grasp, as if she had left a scar of the moment when she had stumbled and I had caught her. I would have been proud of what I'd done, if Caspar hadn't also approved. As we walked, I wondered if Jillian was counting, if she had taken my advice. Of course, what I'd urged was her advice, reflected back at her. She kept her face tight and drawn. As she moved, she held her arms straight at her sides. The monastery offered no field for her to wander in, and her temper had nowhere to run.

"Caspar knew just what to do to you," I said. He had. He'd wielded the carriage ride, the interest in her niece, the robbing of her time with Eleanor, the inquest, the reform, the black powder, even the speeches.

We reached the guesthouse, and the guards waited. Jillian leaned against the lintel. "Jillian," I said.

She threw open the door, and the guards left. "He was testing us," she said.

I wanted to bury his look of approval.

She shut the door behind us, keeping a hand on it and a hand on me. "I'd say you passed," she said.

Part of me rose with all the anger I had tried to squelch from her when we were at dinner. "I didn't want to pass."

"I didn't mean you did." She made a hush sign with her hand. "But I didn't think he would test you. I didn't see what he'd do. Or maybe I did, and it just didn't matter."

"What does it mean that I passed?"

"It's all right." She lifted her head from her hands. "It's a good thing. You showed him you were strong, calm, not a speech-maker's fool." She sat on her bed, and a flea jumped. She leaned over her thighs, and dropped her hands to her feet. "I didn't."

Outside, the river frogs began to boom. Jillian was the one who didn't pass. She knew it and I knew it. I lit a lamp, and set it on the floor between us. "This couldn't be the first time you've yelled at him."

"No." She rose from her lap. Her face had blotched. "No, but not since Miriamne."

"Well, nobody here is Miriamne."

"I don't know. I don't know anything." She stood. She'd never admitted anything like this before. "We'll be fine," she said. She unfastened her armor, and peeled herself halfway out of it. Her tunic beneath had gone damp along her sides and her back. A mosquito drifted through the wall holes for which there were simply not enough plugs. She scratched her chest, and I thought of the tattoo lower down.

She said, "What angered me—"

"There was plenty to anger—"

"Is how there could be plenty of Miriamnes." The leather's greaves dangled from her knees. A mosquito landed on my thigh, but I didn't move. "That's what got me, you know. That was the biggest blow."

Miriamne seemed rather singular. "You think there are other Miriamnes?"

"Other people Caspar's started the precedent for with his inquest. Whole groups he'll scoop up with his black powder and his regimentation and his so-very-calculated reform. He'll fill his war-chest that way."

I shouldn't have eaten his food. "How's he going to regiment the communities?"

She held her arms akimbo, and the bottom of her ribs poked from beneath her tunic. "I think he's going to become principe." She'd read his plan as she would read a trap. "He'll command the whole Empire. And then I think he is going to start a war."

"A war?"

"I could be wrong." But she wasn't. Not in light of the mindless, the black powder, everything Eleanor tried to tell us. Now Jillian lowered the lamp. "We need to be quiet, tonight. We need to prepare." She looked somehow lost. "We need to try to sleep."

I sat on my bed. "How in the world can we sleep?"

"You have to try." She gave a watery smile. "The sun's gone down. You're more tired than you think."

"You think it's a war, Jillian?"

"And if you can't sleep, then just rest."

In the shadows, she sat straight. She was barely balanced; through the Opposite Silence game, this whole trip had shoved her off balance. Regardless of what Jillian said about quiet and sleep, I could not leave her that way. Tomorrow they'd direct her to a murderer's lair. We could die, if I left her unbalanced. She could die. In a way, we were back in the prison carriage. I waited for soldiers, and I listened for Mellion, and I couldn't lie down.

Jillian still wore her greaves. Where she sat in the dimness, she grasped the bed the way she'd grasped Caspar's table. Her posture—its readiness—showed she didn't want to be vulnerable.

Of course she didn't. But, of course, she was. Of course, she had been. Her shuddering meant that, both in the priory and at our cottage. "Jillian."

She dabbed a corner of her eye.

Her shuddering must have been her clutching at air.

"You were afraid," I said.

"I have taught you to control fear."

"But that doesn't mean you're immune to fear."

"And tonight, I let him see it."

"Well don't you think he's like Mellion? Don't you think he can plant fear?"

She hunched, and leaned onto her side. She lay on her bed, and either it squeaked or she did.

"Jillian."

"I'm so sorry."

I blew out the lamp. I couldn't see her like this. "Jillian—"

"I let him win."

"No."

"I showed him weakness. Fear is a weakness in how it fuels so much of this anger!" She'd kicked the bed, and her leather clinked.

My father could say something to help her. So would my mother, Miriamne, Eleanor, Teph. Tonight, I had to be old enough to say it. "Jillian, he has to be afraid of you too, or else he wouldn't drag you here."

"And now he's just a little less."

The night lowered and pressed. I felt I was still in the solarium, standing between her and that man.

"There are two of us now," I said. "For Caspar to fear."

"No. I don't want you to have this."

I crossed to her bed. "I think I can decide for myself."

"No. You do not want my life."

"No." No, I did want her life as a way of inhabiting her; no, I did accept it as something inevitable. No, I didn't want its loneliness but I did aspire to show all the world everything she'd taught. The light, dim through the wall-holes, reminded me of Wilm's stars. I put my hands on her shoulders—thin.

She pressed my hands. Then she pulled off her greaves, and smoothed out the breeches she wore underneath. "Caspar told you to take care of me."

I stood by her bed. I couldn't tell her I would take care of her, that we stood together as one big thing. But part of me tried to extend, like the almond branch, to reach for what I needed. "Maybe he had to find something I'd already do to make it look like I was obeying."

She grunted, and lay back. "Gaelle, go to sleep."

I took a deep breath. "I think you need me to help you carry this."

"I don't."

"This fear, Jillian, you can't leave it all in a box."

"Just—"

"Nobody can."

As she lay, she shivered. I could barely see her down on her bed, but I could feel her, the way she sometimes felt bigger out of sight.

I stilled my breath, and waited for her to say something. She was bigger, but only in how she was stretched.

"He's going to topple the world," she said.

"He's going to try."

"He's going to win, although he has no right to—although thousands, far more heroic, stand in his way."

"All right."

I knelt by the bed. She huffed. I sat on it, beside her, and I found her fingers, clasped as knots. I said, "You know Eleanor loves you."

"You need to get to Eleanor, if you ever lose me here. Gaelle, she is my friend."

"I know she's your friend."

"You have to go to her, and she will tell you what to do."

"All right." I looked into the dark. She spread out beneath me. "You know Lloyd loves you." I untwined her fingers the way she'd undo me from the ox cart. "You know Barbara loves you." I heard myself, and flushed. "Miriamne loves you." I breathed, deep and even. "Teph might love you." I could feel her shaking her head. "Wilm respects you."

"Wilm respects you."

She trembled. I said, "There are people I haven't even met who love you."

"You're supposed to count the people you love, not—"

"I love you." A tear welled in my eye's far corner. "You know I do." I found her head with my hand.

"You can't ever let them hear you say that."

"They already know I do." When Caspar saw me nearly touch him, he saw me ready to hug a fire.

Jillian had begun to weep, and I kept my hand on her crown. This night was like the one after my father died, except finally, nearly six years later, I had followed her upstairs.

chapter 17

List of Goods

The night when Otto caught me preaching to Garfield, he stood the rest of the boy's shift with such blank malice that I didn't even try to sleep. The next evening, Otto took Garfield's post again. When he arrived, I backed deeper into the cell, and he threw at me a handful of salt. For the next few nights, Otto stood at the far edge of the portico, almost to the bridge, and positioned himself, wide-stanced and wind-bent, as if he would personally keep all others from the influence of my witchcraft. I will admit Otto was touching in his guilt, even if it left no doubt he would happily see me killed.

This morning, I told Increase that likely from all its gold, Ordinal's treasury house is sinking. He met the news with his livid eye. Maybe the sinking meant something to him, as if it signified some reduction in the Church's demonism. Either that, or the bird just liked the hope in my voice. He clicks his beak whenever I weep. A sadist might say he's applauding, the way the Azmen clap their dagger blades. But I believe Increase is trying to cut through something, or to draw attention to himself. He sits closer to me when I sound hopeful, anyway. He still won't let me touch him, but he rests between the candle and me, and he'll splay one of his legs in my direction, if I pretend not to notice. Perhaps, with Garfield gone, Increase knows I need his company more than ever. Along his back, he's grown a blue chevron that's iridescent enough to present a sleekness at odds with his milk eye. But I like how his stay with me might have increased him, as it were. And I like how the growth is happening slower, and at a more sustainable rate, than what befell my beloved Garfield.

Later this morning, Increase scrambled out the window fast enough to waver the candle's flame. By instinct maybe, I watched the door. Otto, blocking the bridge, spoke with someone I couldn't see. The sergeant had the declarative tone he used with the boys, and at first I hoped he let Garfield return. But Otto's audience sounded older and out of breath. They told Otto to stand clear.

The door swung open, with nothing to show for it. Then two mailed men lugged in what resembled a small drawbridge winch, while a pug-nosed boy followed them. He looked maybe ten; he wore a leather apron; and he carried a coil of rope someone had looped around his shoulders. When he entered the Bell, he made a face as if he smelled something, and for an instant, I stiffened at the impertinence.

The men wore blue tabards with a gold elephant on the front. They were Church engineers. Thank God they weren't torturers; the winch had made me wonder. I said, "You brought the proverbial two men and a boy."

"Otto told us not to let you speak," said one of the men.

By the southern window, the engineers set down the winch. The Bell rocked, and the boy threw a wild glance at his companions. One of them—a blond—tugged at the boy's rope. "You aren't falling, Cole, long as you've got a line to her." The other end of the boy's coil spooled into the winch. Clearly the device was his anchor, but if the engineers had dropped that hoist while they crossed the bridge, Cole would have gone over the side. I almost said so, but it wouldn't have helped.

The men muttered to each other as they situated the winch. Cole carried probably half his weight in rope. The men beckoned the boy over to watch; he must have been the engineers' apprentice. Then the blond held the winch end of the rope, and had Cole twirl out of what he carried. The boy smiled, in spite of himself. The other engineer was short, bald, and full-lipped. He grunted as he picked up the uncoiled rope. The blond leaned, square, on the winch's frame, and the bald man tossed the rope out the window.

"What's with the lift?" I said.

"Otto said no talking," said the blond.

I stepped toward the other window, on the far side of the room. Maybe they'd use the winch to pull up a mindless, or an angry badger, or a piece of the altar's yellow brick. Cole sat by my pallet, and squashed an ant.

The bald man waved out the window, and the blond started to crank the winch. "Keep it dry," the blond said to me, "and it will crank better."

"Wait," I said. "I'm going to turn the winch?"

"If you want to eat, you will." He worked the winch with one hand, but his knuckles turned white from the work.

"They bring me my food," I said. "The guards do."

"Won't be easy without the bridge," said the boy.

"The bridge?" I said.

"Excommunication." The blond grunted, as he lifted a cask the winch had raised. "It means *cut off*, right?" He hoisted the cask from the window, and rested it on the floor.

"You're cutting away the bridge?"

"I think she might be hard of hearing," said Cole.

"No, she's just grasping the shape of things," said the blond. "We're maybe not literally cutting. But it ends at the same."

My heart fluttered. I glanced at the burlap gloves I'd knitted. "So this is my hermitage?"

Cole wiped his fingers on my stones.

The bald engineer spat out the winch's opposite window. "They'll fill the cask for you about every few weeks."

"Every few weeks?" I said.

He said, "Maybe more in the winter."

"But the rope is thin, see?" said the blond. "Wouldn't hold even half of you."

"Splat," said the bald one. "Not even long enough for the archers to shoot."

"And that's to say nothing of the wind," said the blond.

"And we should treat the rope with grease," said the other. "And a bell."

"Well," I said. "You're engineers down to the bone."

They peered at me. "We aren't supposed to talk to her," said the bald man.

"He's almost done it," said Cole. The boy had crossed to the door, and we followed.

Otto stood on the portico with a bucket and a brush. He'd painted what looked like red grease along the entirety of the bridge ropes.

"You're going to burn the bridge," I said.

"Now that's a little cliche," said Otto.

"Wouldn't need blood in the lard for burning," said the boy.

"Besides," said the blond, "the 'mancers say the fire would bother the bones in the scaffold."

"And," said Otto, "we don't want this thing bucking in the air."

"Please?" said Cole. "I want to see it when it gets here."

"No, you don't," said the blond.

"I'll watch from inside," said Cole.

"The watching would be bad enough," said the blond. "But what you don't want is the stink."

The bald man started across the bridge, and Cole reached for Mama.

"Can you guess, Witch," said Otto, "how we're going to cut you off?"

"No," I said. But perhaps I could.

"I want to see," said Cole.

"You'll see yourself across this bridge," said Otto.

"You said you'd help me across the bridge," said Cole.

"If you can't get your own self across the bridge, then you don't get to see what happens on the bridge." Otto pulled Cole off Mama. He shoved him to the edge of the portico, and the boy shrieked.

"Otto," I said.

"Ready to concede?" said Otto.

The boy's teeth chattered. "Aye."

Otto held Cole's biceps. "You didn't talk to the witch, did you?"

"No," said Col.

"Otto," I said. "He didn't."

Otto scorched me a look. "Climb on, then."

Otto hunched, and Cole mounted Otto's back.

"Bet I'm lighter without all the rope," said Cole.

"Would be lighter without all your yapping," said Otto. He hoisted the boy, and they took a step. "Don't worry, Witch." Over his shoulder, he fetched me a smirk. "They can't open doors."

The Church wouldn't use mindless on the bridge; they wouldn't let mindless inside the castle. But mindless aren't the only creatures in the Church menagerie that stink. Two steps onto the causeway, Otto told Cole not to touch the larded parts of the ropes. "Devorares eat anything what's got blood on it."

I slammed the cell door, and pulled it hard. I hollered for Increase, and I let Otto hear me. Anyone would scream a little, if her jailers had just marooned her midair. She'd certainly scream if she knew what a devorare is.

People also call a devorare a night hound, because it carries a stench strong enough to invade sleep. If the Church planned to bring one near Ordinal, they would send it off before sundown. And in the meantime, they would roust the monks who usually sleep through the day shift. The smell of a devorare can infect the slumber of those who live nearby, so the sleepers suffer visions that cross from the usual dreamlike into madness. The first time my battlefield Riven found a devorare, I had nightmares of a portly man, naked and hunched, with blood for eyes and an elephant's trunk. My comrades screamed in their sleep; the screams gave away our position. And the night hound simply stalked us, for a week, while the soldiers grew sleep-deprived and slow.

Now, from the Bell's north window, I called again for Increase. The blood-lard dripped. The Church could drive me mad with a devorare, assuming they didn't care about the sanity of everyone else nearby. The yard below me had emptied, as if instead of late morning, we'd moved into curfew. In fact, the guard might have imposed a curfew. The marksmen's towers had shuttered their arrow slits. Someone had taken hold of the drum the guard usually beats for executions, and now they started a slow tattoo that served either as a warning or as a means of keeping everybody awake. Honestly, though, I would bet my life nobody slept.

The stink arrived, and I pressed my crooked fingers to my mouth. The stench was a cross between the breath of a plague victim and something metallic—not blood, but harder, the way I imagine the scent of a lightning rod after it's struck. Now I called once more for Increase, and my voice was alone in the courtyard. Even the mindless had gone quiet. Perhaps they lay in a heap.

I scanned the plain, and pitied it the way I'd apologize to a battlefield before our armies started artillery. The devorare is drawn to blood, but it doesn't eat. Instead, it disappears whatever it puts in its maw, slowly, almost dissolving the mouthful. The creature gnashes its teeth, in the meantime, as if it's trying to keep purchase on whatever it annihilates.

I turned toward the south window, and nearly wept. Increase perched on the winch's provisions cask. "Where in the world do you go?" I said.

The stench thickened. I shoved the stool in one window and the chair in the other. God willing, the blood-lard would hold the creature's interest. And the furniture might hold for a moment, if the bait did not.

Increase's talons, twice-thick as my fingers, cracked the rim of the cask where he perched.

The devorare had climbed halfway up the face of the tower that anchored the bridge. The creatures are dogs, yes, as long as a wagon. But thumbless hands end both their fore and hind legs, so they can scale rough walls and ladders. This hound scrabbled the wall.

Somebody slammed tighter the tower's shutters. The devorare sniffed the ropes. On the ground, the creature resembles a coyote that someone has pulled higher and longer until the legs stretch tall as a pony's. This stretching is something that happens among other servants of the Church, and I've come to believe it's all part of a piece. But the devorare itself also has pointed ears, and a russet coat with blotches on those impossible legs. Now, splayed on the tower face with all its claws and muscles, the thing resembled a flattened gargoyle. It peered across the bridge with eyes gleaming and gray as fresh cartilage. The drum beat. The devorare reached from the tower, standing almost horizontally on its back feet, until it grasped the bloodied bridge ropes, and it landed on the planks without sound.

It clamped its mouth over the first portion of the rope, and slid its maw along the line, almost as if the creature was on a pulley. The hound took its time, as if it had been well fed. It lifted the lines, and it tugged, chewing faster and faster, as the exterior of the rope disappeared, and the interior showed white as sinew. My cartomancer friend with an eye for the cosmos: he wondered once if devorares simply displace what they eat, so that a pile of it accrues somewhere, like a midden. Now the bridge's devorare dismembered the far end of the ropes. Then it clung to the lines as the whole structure fell.

Increase fluttered. The devorare probably dangled with the rest of the bridge, from my Bell.

I couldn't see the creature, but the stench breathed wide beneath me. Increase hunkered; if anyone tells you birds can't smell, the person's mistaken. The Bell jostled while the devorare likely climbed. I pressed myself to the wall, and swallowed a retch. Then I lurched, as fast as these bones could clamber, to the winch.

It sat high enough that none of the rope hung lower than my floor. I almost collapsed from the relief. The devorare could still clamber right though my windows, if it traversed the underside of the Bell. But it had no easy access. And unless, God forbid, the guard stuffed my provision barrel with raw meat, the creature wouldn't have incentive.

Increase growled.

"Good Mother," I said.

He faced outside, and raised his back end, where maybe a plume would usually grow.

The sound that next washed over the yard was more of a force than a noise: deep enough that it felt to push through the fortress walls instead of over them. I'd heard the sound before, if not from the church choirs then from Caspar, their choirmaster. The signal—the note—is more of a hum than a rumble. Or perhaps a person could term it a call. Dangling from my cell, the devorare probably cocked its head the way Lucinda may have done, if she'd ever listened for an answer to her keening.

The Bell bounced, as if it had come free of ballast. I clutched the windowsill, and watched the devorare spring along the ground, out toward the plain. If Caspar was the caller, he could have been near Ordinal; that wasn't unheard of. Or he might have summoned the creature from leagues away. Whatever the case, the devorare's departure was stark as it was sudden, as if its master could also erase. Or at least he could insert and withdraw terror like a blade.

On all fours now, I closed my eyes to the cold that rose from the floor drain. The air felt good on my sweat; I'd nearly soaked my clothes. I Touched, for someone.

The cool slowed my pulse, as it pressed like an old memory of Jillian's hand. And I let my heart tap out the countable good: Caspar didn't want to kill me just yet; if he had, the devorare could have done so easily. Furthermore, Garfield was all right. Otto's vengeance toward me showed a particular protectiveness for the boy, and if Garfield had died, Otto would have bludgeoned me with the news. Finally, the jailers had gone through considerable trouble to engineer a way to bring me a reliable source of food. These were three blessings, and I drew my breaths for the count of three.

I smoothed my cassock, and used its hem to wipe the sweat from my lip. Increase had left again, which suggested the devorare had long gone. Still, its stench hung. The smell would probably linger for days. And you didn't need to be a poet to recognize the metaphor in the jailers using the creatures to dismember my Bell from everything else.

The suspension bridge likely hung from my cell, as a severed umbilicus. Certainly, none of the bloodied ropes remained. The drumming had stopped, and the boys probably removed their helmets to get away from the stink that clung there. Maybe they cracked wise about demon flatulence, as the jokes could be crude right now, as long as they kept coming. Maybe Otto clapped Garfield on the shoulder.

I sat, and tried to think of everyone but me. I couldn't think about me. If I started to do that, grief would send me crashing to the floor. I pulled the stool from the window, and dusted it with my burlap. I bent to my toes, and imagined mid-exercise, that I emulated Increase's own raised end. My laughter at the thought was a little too close to crying, so I sat again. I sat for a while.

I decided my marooning in the Bell wasn't the first time I'd been trapped up high. And if I fell, as the creak of the chains made me fear I might, it wouldn't be the first time I did that either. Better to think of my circumstance as the beginning of an ascent. I had already been born in fear. And if the whole of my life, both up and down, had taught me anything, it showed I didn't have to carry so much terror with me when I started to die.

I turned to the provisions barrel the winch had raised. Inside was a flour sack and an assortment of carrots and parsnips. Someone had packed about half a horse blanket, a scatter of candles, a mug of lard, a bottle of wine, a brown-bumped sausage, and a spoon.

"I've eaten worse," I said. Soldiers and farmers eat everything.

At the bottom of the barrel, a piece of rabbit hide lay in a roll. My hands went cold. My hair dongle—the one that a boy had smacked with a boot—it's what tied the pelt together. It might serve as a decent foot wrap. I unrolled the skin, and sat. On the other side, someone had written *List of Goods*. Then, perhaps to throw off suspicion, someone had itemized everything in the barrel, except the hair dongle.

I pressed the rabbit fur to my face. I clutched the dongle, and something jabbed my thumb. Poking from a split along the interior of the dongle, was an iron tab. It was a miniature scale pan. I pulled it from the dongle's slit, and brought out the perpendicular scale post to which the pan was still attached. "Oh, Garfield." He'd broken off the other pan from what was almost certainly his own holy symbol. Perhaps he'd thrown this second part away, but I suspected that in the place where he'd once hidden my hair dongle, he kept it now. I sat on the floor, and held the piece. So recently, it had been in Garfield's hands. Then I heard the sound of scraping. Without thinking, I'd begun to sharpen the symbol's tip against the stone.

chapter 18

CLOISTER

part ONE

I awoke to Jillian pulling me nearly from bed. She'd lit the lantern. Now she sweated in her armor, and threw a sack into my arms. In my half-sleep, I bumbled to keep from dropping it.

"We aren't in a panic," she said, "but we aren't going to rest."

A bouquet lay on the bed. "I don't—"

"We've had a gift of flowers." She pulled tight her belt. "Begonia, mock orange."

"From Casp—"

"No. Think."

I thought of the Treehanded. Then I thought of Eleanor stuffing the flowers in through the wall holes. Of course they were from her.

"Every flower's a message." Jillian passed me my boots. "It's quaint. Fussy. I didn't ever teach you." She pointed to the bouquet. "Beware. Deceit."

"Beware what?"

"I don't know. I don't know any more." She snatched a look out a wall hole. "But we will not wait for them to find us here."

Them was the deceiver, who was almost certainly the Church. A hope soared in me. "So we're going home?"

"No." She wore her traveling cloak. "No, we can't go home without leave."

"You mean from the people we distrust?"

She looked at me with a wan face, as if, from now on, I would always see how tired she was. "Gaelle, it could result in such wide retribution if we left—"

"I know." Such was the constant prison.

I stood half in and out of my boots, as if I reprised her stance from last night. "So they're just going to deal us some treachery we can't see coming."

"Now, deceit can mean anything."

"This isn't helping."

"Our messenger doesn't think they'll kill us, or else she'd have left us monkshood."

"How appropriate."

"It means mortal peril."

"Mortal—"

"Of course, monkshood is also poisonous. So it could have been too much of a liability."

I sat on the bed, and stood again. The flowers wafted a bright smell. "I don't know what to do with any of this."

Jillian met my eyes long enough for me to see her thinking. Maybe these sorts of things—these stakes—were what she was always thinking, what she'd arranged and balanced while she leaned on her dead sister's box.

"Gaelle. You're going to have to come with me."

"I am already with you."

I knew what she meant, but I didn't want to hear it.

"I mean the Lowers," she said. "The expedition."

"I don't want to do that."

"I know."

I hadn't meant to tell her no, but part of me, the stalling part, knew I would.

Now she told me it was better for us to be together, how down in the old killer's lair, we'd be alone with just a squad of church soldiers, instead of my staying up here with, she rummaged her sack, "an entire order."

"And Eleanor?" I glanced at the flower's vivid bunch. "What about her?"

Jillian looked up from her search, and shook her head. She seemed almost relieved. "I don't know." Somewhere a soft bell sounded. "He'd have to overcome a lot to kill her."

"You mean he has a thing for her."

"What he has is an appetite. And an attraction to the impossible." From her bag, she drew a dagger. It was the same one I'd used when Wilm had stopped the smoke. "We're going to find you an ax." I imagined pulling it from a monk. "I pray you won't use it." She pressed me the knife. "A fight up here could kill all of us." She closed my hand around the sheath. "You think this will do in the meantime?"

"Sure." I remembered the cold of this thing.

"Finding an ax is our excuse for us to get out of the guest house." For us to move. For us to put them off balance. "If the guards stop us out there, we'll just say we need to find you some equipment for the descent." I didn't like the word she'd used. "And honestly," she looked around, "equipment wouldn't hurt."

I imagined myself dressed as the guard, Rudyard. "Maybe we could also find something out along the way."

"That's never bad."

"No." I watched her not shudder. She put her hand on the door, and I expected her to place the other on me, the way she'd done just before she'd gone stiff with fear. "Gaelle, we cannot fight."

"Well, I'll fight to defend you."

"Then defend me by keeping calm." She touched my head. Then she handed me the wedge she'd shoved in the crack beneath the door. "As it is with your parents, my memorial will always be you."

What she said made me sniff. "Your memorial won't arrive for another fifty years."

"Forty." She opened the door. "I don't want to be infirm."

part TWO

Outside, the sky had rolled to a lightening pink. A gust blew from the barnyards, and I leaned into the smell of life, of home. Days like these had held Bocephus, the pig, and the Silence game. What we were doing now was a kind of Silence game.

Jillian drifted along the back side of the guest house. She walked, upright, at a regular speed, and she ran her hand along the abbey's eastern wall. This position put her in the shadows, beneath the battlements, and at the same time, her gait made her casual. She had me follow.

"Most of the guards are young," she said. "This time of morning, much of the upper order is at prime."

"Except for maybe someone who's coming to get us?"

She glanced back at me. We stood behind part of the winery, and fruit flies swarmed the open mouth of a spent barrel. "Let me talk, if they find us." Maybe Rudyard would. "Sometimes they listen." I thought of Laird, our escort, misplacing his dagger.

We stepped over a horse pile. I said, "What are we trying to find?"

"What we talked about." She stopped at an intersection. "Ax. Information. Position."

"Advantage."

"If they ask us, we'll tell them the first."

We could simply tell them the last, and watch them blink in their helmets. Down the road, a brindled dog drank from a puddle. He raised his head, and looked to the north of us, toward the cloister. We walked south, toward the village and the wide stink of the river. But if we wanted to get almost any of the things we needed, this route was only temporarily the right way, a simple detour of avoidance. And besides, it wouldn't be exactly safe to trust the circumspection of a vendor who'd, say, come to the market early to set up his pickles.

Maybe we'd find the bird merchant who dressed as a domino. He would know something we needed; I could feel it. But I also knew his information didn't involve the plans for this morning.

We skirted the backside of the merchant district. Jillian cased a barrel maker's stall for an ax, but all she could find was a wooden mallet.

Horses approached, and we crouched behind a stack of barrel staves. Along the main road, a single prison carriage rumbled slowly, with a single driver. Jillian muttered there was something off about the coach. The rising sun reflected off the dark of the carriage, in a kind of blurry smear. The walls were metal.

"Iron?" I said. "Have you ever been in iron?"

"No." She put her palm between my shoulders, and stalked back to retrieve the mallet. She held it out to me. "The balance is different, but it's the same throwing principal." Over my shoulder, she watched the carriage. "That, and you're likely to stun instead of cut."

"You think I'll need this?"

"It's better than a dagger."

I put the knife in my belt. The mallet felt cool with the morning. Mallets are more versatile than knives, and this one would do until we found an ax. The carriage turned a corner, and Jillian moved us after it, down a parallel street.

"What's in the carriage?" I said.

"Nothing, at the moment." We had to hurry, now, outside the shadows. "See how it bounces?"

The sky loomed, bare. The fact that Jillian chased the carriage meant something. "Then who's the carriage for?"

"I don't know." She likely didn't, but she had an instinct. She pushed us past a bakery, where I heard a young man laugh. The cart rattled east, toward a part of the abbey I hadn't yet seen. Jillian stopped, and turned to me. "It's for someone very strong, I reckon. Or someone with very strong friends."

"Then it's important."

She had my arm. "But I don't know how."

"Is it for us?"

"I don't know. I told him I'd go to the Lowers."

"Then is it," the thought barely made sense, "is it for me?"

She clutched her kukri. Treachery. Deceit. "Then why a metal one?" she said.

Because they knew she'd move heaven and earth to save me. Because they knew she could rouse her friends. Because even though she'd been telling us both not to commit violence, she would risk it all for—well, for her child. "We'll go see," she said.

I knew why she wanted to see. Learning about the carriage would give us advantage if it was for us. And it would give us information (and even room for blackmail) if it was not. "We can't do violence," I said. I wondered if this warning would be how we balanced each other from now on. "I mean it, Jillian. Not even for me." She watched me the way she'd watched me decide with Lucinda. "Jillian, promise me you won't make people die for me."

And then I realized that this very thing is what Miriamne must have said to her, how Miriamne made Jillian do what she did for her sister.

"Maybe it's a bad idea," Jillian said. The carriage rumbled farther. "Maybe you should go back."

"No." Her going alone had broken the question. "We go." What would I have done instead? Gone back to Eleanor, so she could get caught up in the deceit? Gone back to wait where they wanted us? "You think maybe we can watch from afar?"

She nodded, and we moved. Heaven help us if the carriage rounded back to scoop us up. "Gaelle, if I need to, I'll pretend I took you hostage—"

"What?"

"Made you go with me into the grounds."

"No!"

"It'll make you look innocent."

"And it will make you look like a monster."

Her reflection smeared in a puddle. "We all play to expectations when we play with sleight-of-hand."

She was the other half of my staying pliable.

We moved after the carriage, along the monastery wall, and we met the scent of a tannery. The battlements' surrounding stone grayed to a brown-mortared granite, and weeds grew from the foot of the wall.

"This isn't the cloister," I said.

"That's good." She glanced at a pen of geese. "It means we aren't committing the most capital trespass." She edged around the pen. "Don't upset them." Few things better announce a stranger than a gaggle of geese.

We passed beneath a crumbling archway, and I bowed in the stink. The yard here smelled of a charnel house: of blood, and mud, and something rotten within it. It all reminded me of the bottom of Lake Kelmer. "Is this where they keep the well bodies?"

She held the back of her hand to her nose and mouth. "I thought they burned most of those."

The carriage had put tracks in the mud, but beyond those, we couldn't see where it had gone. The wagon was easier to lose here, among the mud and dark stone. The road's cobble had started to space out, and then become as sparse as broken teeth, until it faded to the silence of sawdust. Jillian moved us along the eastern wall, past some abandoned pig hutches. Then we crept beside a grayed, close-slatted fence that seemed to reinforce tumbled gaps in the wall.

She pointed to a closed portcullis. The wagon tracks led there. The gate made us a dead end, but the bars would also let us peer at whatever was back there, from the relative cover of the metal and the wall.

I held the mallet while I peered at a half-rotted woodpile. The logs had bite marks.

Jillian fell on her side, clutching at a head-sized hook that had grappled her neck. The hook sat at the end of a long, metal pole. The pole sat in the grip of large, brown-robed man.

I threw the mallet, and it bounced, lengthwise, off the slope of his back. Without changing his grip on Jillian, the man turned to look me in the eye. His were the deepest blue. He had pockmarks and scarred lips.

Jillian yanked the pole, and the man grunted. She slid out the hook's open end, and rammed the man's portion of the pole toward his belly.

He stopped it before it reached him. The mallet lay between his feet.

"We got a thinker," he said.

He yanked. She let go, and he flung the hook-pole behind him, into the fence. He circled his arms.

"Nobody's hurt here." She stepped back. "We took a wrong turn. We surprised you. You surprised us."

He picked up the mallet.

"We serve as part of Caspar's expedition." She held up her palms. "And we're just trying to find my young niece an ax."

He sucked his lower lip. "Now that's a new one." He wiped his free hand on the leather apron he wore. "This one's got her brains all inside of her head."

Behind the fence, something snuffled.

"Gaelle, run."

The mallet hit me in the shoulder. Jillian gave a high kick to the side of the man's face. He stumbled to the left. She dashed to the fence, to the pole-hook. She stumbled back, without it. "Gaelle, go!"

I pressed my shoulder, still in its socket. I grabbed the mallet, and the man drew a knife. Jillian drew her kukri. A shape ran along the inside of the fence.

"Tssssk," the man said.

"Jillian." If she stabbed him, there'd be no returning. I threw a Touch, and she glanced at me.

"Spill Church blood, and they'll taste it," he said.

Something grated. The pole-hook slid along the cobble, where the creature behind the fence had grasped it through the weeds.

My head felt to float. We were in another forest, but this time, the water and the wood already held ruin.

Jilliam stepped, and the man matched her so that her back was to me and his back was to the fence.

"You keep mindless," she said.

"Oh, you keep mindless," he said.

"Esaosh, we don't keep mindless," I said.

He mule kicked the fence, and the pole clattered on the stone. "That's what all the casters say, Lovie. Before the Sword sends them to get et."

"You feed your so-called necromancers to the mindless?" said Jillian.

With his free hand, the man retrieved the pole-hook. I thought of the peasant man who gave away his dog. "Partly."

He swung the pole, and Jillian jumped. A rock I threw hit him in the thigh. He threw his knife, and it went wide of Jillian's. Jillian caught his arm, and he threw her into the fence. The creature scrabbled the planks. Jillian did a handspring off the wood, and landed by me. I snatched the knife he'd pitched, and I cocked it to throw at the man.

"No!" said Jillian.

I threw it over the mindless wall.

Behind it, rose a keening. The man edged toward the portcullis. "Sounds like a direct hit."

I drew our old dagger from my belt.

"Run," said Jillian. "Now."

I wheeled to flee, and Jillian cried. The man had thrown puddle water into her eyes. I reached for her. The hook slammed my neck. My face went into the mud, and the dagger fell from my hands. The man was on me, thick fingers inside my collar. He lifted me off my feet, and slammed my back against the fence. He gusted a smile. He had an extra canine tooth.

The mindless snuffled. They scrabbled the fence, splintering, the way they'd jumbled the trees. I pried at the hook around my neck. I Touched, and I remembered the first time I'd Touched.

"One word." He peered at Jillian over his shoulder. "I can command them to take her the fast way, which gives exercise to the lads." Tattered fingers clutched the top of the fence. "Or I can command them the slow way, which gives exercise to you."

The man's jugular pumped. Jillian crouched with her kukri, but she likely wouldn't be able to stab him in time to stop the mindless. Farther off, the geese honked. A mindless keened, and I felt its sound in the boards.

"Gaelleda," Wilm once said, "you are all grown up."

The man turned back to me, but not fast enough to get his chin down. This was something Jillian had taught me, one afternoon, when we were trying to keep my arms from becoming snakes. After a man leans in, a closed-handed strike will break his windpipe. An open-handed lift, under the jaw, will send him flying. The mindless cries were like the wind calling from the trees. Their keeper landed on his back.

Jillian landed on him, and I threw off the hook. He rolled to his side, and she pressed her kukri to his neck.

"I'll kill you," she said. "I'll throw you to the mindless, and everyone will think you just fell in."

He bulged his eyes. "You have enough salt then, Love?"

Men shouted. A dozen Rudyards jogged in from the geese, and they lowered their halberds. Rudyard—halberd. I gave a dizzy laugh. The squad approached the fence, and stepped back.

The mindless keeper got to his feet. Jillian sat. He kicked Jillian's back. I rushed, and she gave me a look to stop me cold.

"Stand down, Greegan." One of the older men, who stood nearest the fence, pointed the spear of his weapon. "We saw you had the young one pinned."

Greegan said, "All the peasants he sends here are mine."

"We're with Caspar," said Jillian.

"We know who you are, Yeoman." The older guard had to shout over the geese and the keening. He glanced at the cracked slats of the fence. "The abbot will sort it."

One of his men offered his hand to help Jillian out of the dirt. Greegan coughed. Nobody helped him. I stumbled over the pole-hook, and the captain—the older man—told me not to touch it.

"I tripped over it," I said.

He steeled me a look. He wasn't so old, maybe thirty. He was just thin.

"You have mindless," I said.

"Gaelle," said Jillian.

The captain's eyes went wide, and they gave him back some of his youth. He smacked me, hard, against the left ear. "You will not question the Church's right to study the enemy!" I'd fallen to my knees. "You will not question how we test their weapons," he spoke over my head, "and you will not question how we try those mages who wield them!" What he said sounded almost like a recitation. Jillian Touched, as if to fill me. "We trust the abbot to purge the heretics' filth. To feed them their own tail."

"And the abbot trusts the same filth's keeper," said Greegan.

The captain's mail clinked as he turned. "We must also trust that Abbot Caspar may use even the miscreants to the extent they're useful." His gaze landed back on me. "All brothers say amen."

"Amen!"

I knelt amid the force of the guards. Behind, a single mindless keened. Jillian stumbled to me, apparently from where the sentries had held her. She helped me up, and the squad closed ranks around us. They led us past the geese, who had calmed. So had the guards, as they'd fallen in with their captain. Perhaps the smack he'd given hadn't been just for me.

The soldiers pushed us along. Greegan hacked. The captain had separated him from the two of us. The keeper coughed again, and coughed louder. I whispered to Jillian. "I didn't hit him that hard."

"I know. I saw you." She peered at the men around us. "They saw you." I wanted to hold her hand, to let it keep me from running. "You did so very well."

I had. Part of me still felt the sweat and softness of Greegan's throat. It stayed with me as an answer to how I still carried the rip of the ferals' snake.

I remembered how the guards helped me up, and did not help the keeper. I remembered what Greegan had said to them about peasants, and how both the captain and my aunt had called us Caspar's. The abbot himself had greeted us with a feast. The realization, and its perversion, slowed me. Jillian and I were privileged. That's what the monks meant, at least in part, whenever they called us yeomen.

The Church had mindless. The Church fed them. The Observer told me not to consider them, at the moment, and Jillian would likely tell me the same. The mud squelched, and I tried to use the sound to bury all thoughts of the creatures. We stepped through a trample of chicken feathers, and I remembered the mother hen hunching over her brood. We passed the heat from the kiln yard, and I thought of Miriamne. A lump rose in my throat. The protection Caspar gave us was simply a kind of blackmail. And there was no telling what it would weigh now that we had seen the mindless. Maybe what the guard captain said was true: these were somehow captured mindless. And in the name of some retributive study, Greegan was supposed to feed these mindless the so-called mindless makers. Such an arrangement was the best of all possibilities, but it wasn't the most probable. To this day, I still don't know how long the Church kept their own mindless before they killed the peasants with the inquest.

part THREE

On our march, our company shouted a password—hawthorn—to a sudden guard tower. A gatekeeper raised a portcullis to an alabaster commons. This was not the way we'd come in. Stone pathways made a six-way intersection, in the manner of a cross with a diagonal passing through it. The pavers were white and they were pristine. In the center of the intersection, a gold slab sat maybe a handspan deeper, so it appeared as the pan of a scale. In one of the indention's corners, a blue robe lay in a heap. All of us walked a scalloped path around the gold.

Jillian had her head bowed. Maybe she collected herself in the way she'd done in the prison carriage, as if in some way, we had arrived at the abbey all over again.

"Do I have to blind you?" The captain was yelling. The company had stopped. He was yelling at me. "Head down, I say."

"She doesn't know the rules of the cloister," said Jillian.

"She doesn't know to listen," said the captain.

"I'm sorry." I stared at my feet. "It's all just so," I made myself sigh, "so majestic." There. Pliable.

"Except in extremis," said the captain, "no layperson is allowed in the cloister to begin with." I knew this. "I doubt you have the education to understand what you're seeing, and my guess is that you're trying to save your skin with an act." I knew I shouldn't have used that second so. "But an act, says the dean, has a way of coming true."

A guard ran to the place we'd stopped. "The abbot's in the stable, Sir."

The captain straightened his belt. "At least he isn't at prayer." He clutched his scabbard "Is he?"

"Not that I saw, Sir."

Greegan hacked.

"Everyone, stop the theater!" said the captain.

We were going to see Caspar. Caspar was going to see us. I started to sweat and my bowels felt hot. While looking down, I reached for Jillian's arm. The guards let me—maybe out of confidence that we'd been beaten, or maybe out of pity. I didn't want to see Caspar, to let him see me again, so I might stand between him and my aunt, and he could wonder if I would touch him.

My head reeled. I was going to be sick. Right on these majestic pavers, I was going to throw up what remained of our feast. Jillian Touched. I remembered Greegan's extra canine tooth, the mindless's fingers curling over the fence top. Perhaps the mindless had Caspar's spectacles. I bent over my knees. Greegan hacked, and I squeezed shut my eyes.

"Keep moving," said the captain.

"The mindless have her spooked," said Jillian. "They have your own men spooked." I hung my mouth open. "And this shows, incidentally, that we have nothing to do with them."

I opened my eyes. An ant, tiny, bustled across the pavement's white. My breath started to slow me. The ant trundled its unbowed path. It was an upstart, a rebel. It was all these things, just by being. My insides felt spacious. The creature was free. Black against the alabaster, it was like the bird man. I straightened. I almost looked for the bird man, as if he might be feeding the hummingbird that, so long ago, ascended into the rain.

"There's an ant," I said.

I walked next to Jillian, and she searched my face. "We're going to be all right," she said.

Maybe we were. I used the idea to move my feet. We weren't the only strangers here.

We followed the path deep into the cloister, far deeper than we likely had any right to go. Novices pinned the robes of the upper orders on drying lines. A red-haired dean addressed a ring of standing students, and when he saw us, his speech trailed.

Jillian sniffed. She tapped a Touch, and she sniffed again. The grounds smelled of the fens, but that wasn't new. They smelled of bread and laundry and mud and adolescent boy. I couldn't catch the slightest whiff of horses.

Maybe we were still far out from the stable. But if so, the grounds of the cloister were immense. Maybe Caspar kept something else in the stables, such as a halter for the mindless. The thought of it made me grip Jillian's sleeve, and she touched my fist with the fingers of her other hand. They were cool and clean as the walls of Teph's shed. They could untie almost any knot. She clutched my hand now, and pulled me to slow.

Caspar stood in the center of an open, double-wide stall. The walls comprised of vertically-slatted alabaster, so the whole of the structure resembled a kind of cage, or a tomb. The insides gleamed so much I thought he'd fitted them with mirrors. But then I realized they shone in the way of the iron carriage, likely a mindless carriage. Between the walls and Caspar stood not a horse, but a stand that held a saddle and barding.

Caspar had his hand on the captain's shoulder, as he spoke into the captain's ear, but I couldn't hear for the blood rushing in mine. The barding was a kind of black, boiled leather. Every few handspans, someone had mounted mirrors, true mirrors, in the shape of starbursts, within the leather. It would have been comical, all the sun-shaped dots, if the light didn't reflect every which way. Their dazzle would have confused people near the horse on a normal day, if not outright blind them in battle.

The armor further had ear portions, which themselves seemed unusual, but the covers were also large and padded, almost like mittens. And beyond everything else, the barding had reins, thin and black, that drooped stiffly instead of hung, and looked hard enough to clack in the manner of spines.

"Jillian—"

"No." She spoke and Touched at once. She gripped my hand so hard that she probably wished to hold my mouth. Caspar didn't know we'd kept Lucinda—and spared her. And for the sake of what felt like life itself, we could not divulge that we recognized what looked like some sort of Treehand-style barding for an absent warhorse. Now I first began to reckon how the creature I'd spared was like a hole toward which the whole world drained.

Where Jillian and I held hands, our pulses pounded in my palm.

Caspar, having left the captain, stood before us. He tapped his cheek with a finger that appeared slightly too long for his hand. "Did you find what you were looking for?"

Jillian let go of me. "You must have one spectacular horse."

He pivoted a look behind him. "Let's just say her procurement is an ongoing project." That likely meant he didn't know were Lucinda had gone. "Maybe one day you, or your niece, will help with it all."

"I see," said Jillian. "I'll have to bring some carrots."

"Oh," he said, "you'd have to bring everything you've got."

Looking back, I reckon Caspar knew of the war—of the Reordering War for world dominance, and of how Lucinda, the steed, would bring it about. But what I would love to know is if he'd yet discerned how the entity who first told him these things, also sought to control him.

Greegan hacked. Caspar brushed sawdust from Jillian's elbow. He said, "I hear you had a spectacular walk."

"Right until we ran into your mindless," she said.

"Would you like me to explain the mindless?" said Caspar. "It would be a gift from me, seeing how you and your niece have wandered where you weren't invited. Not to mention nearly costing one of my keepers his life—"

"We pulled our punch to save his life," said Jillian.

"That little one hit me in the throat," said Greegan.

"That little one tossed you by the throat," said Caspar, "and this is not the cost I mean." He gave Jillian what was nearly a commiserating look.

"Despite the fact that you don't deserve to know," he bounced his head in resigned consideration. "Despite so many things, I will remind you how every army does its best both to capture and study the enemy's weapons."

"By feeding them supposed necromancers," said Jillian. I Touched the way I'd put my finger to her forearm at dinner.

"You shouldn't take their side," said Caspar. "Gaelle, never make a bad alliance."

"You don't get to teach her," said Jillian.

"Then back to the mindless, of which I'll teach you," said Caspar.

He'd used the two of us in some chess-player's double-threat.

"Being practical, of course," he said, "you would realize that the one thing better than acquiring the enemy's weapon is observing the maker, as it's tasked with controlling said weapon."

Especially when that maker will die during the observation. I saw that retort in Jillian's eyes, and I also saw how she swallowed it down. She said, "Your captain has already fed us as much."

"He's a good man. But let's consider Greegan." Caspar beckoned, and the guards brought the keeper. "Greegan has made a mistake."

"They were peasants in my shambles," said Greegan.

"They aren't peasants," said Caspar.

"Yah," said Greegan, "I know that now."

"But what they have," furrowed Caspar, "is a way of attracting the churchmen who most reflect us at our worst."

Jillian puckered another retort.

"Gaelle," said Caspar, "you seem impressively taken with the barding."

"No," I said.

"You've been staring," he said.

I probably had been. The glass on the barding looked as if the stars had landed. "It's just the mirrors," I said.

"Well, yes," he said. "They are impressive." He stepped to the barding, and motioned for the guards to bring Greegan. "The mirrors are much like those in a sanctuary, as I'm sure you know." I mustered my catechism. "This means, in case you forgot, that the mirrors confront anyone who approaches, with a view of himself." He had the keeper stand before the suit. "In the rareness of the clearest glass, the viewer can get a rare gander at his own worth." One of the guards jangled his gauntlet against his thigh. Caspar looked up, and the guard stopped. "Now here," said Caspar, "the mirror shows how Greegan is in charge of beasts, because he is, in fact, mostly beast himself." Greegan wheezed a little laugh. "He never had the will or ability to gather much subtlety—which is why, I suppose, he failed to recognize you." Caspar rubbed his knuckles under his own eyes. "You made a mistake, Greegan." I began to fear for the brute. "You took more initiative than you were warranted."

"Sire, they were trespassing," said Greegan.

"Now, I've told you not to call me Sire," said Caspar. "But they were trespassing. And if I didn't have use for them, I couldn't afford their mistake."

"But," huffed Greegan, "I didn't know."

"But I have use for you too, Greegan. No matter if I also have to teach you." Caspar held out his own palm.

Greegan breathed in little gasps.

"This yard will remain your country," said Caspar.

Greegan rubbed where I'd thrown him.

"Please," said Caspar, "give me your hand."

Greegan stopped his breath. Jillian lay her Touch like a hand. Greegan set his face, and held out his left palm.

"Sometimes," Caspar fished in the front of his robes. "Sometimes, the smallest member is also one of the most indispensable." He patted his front. "And sometimes the larger one is much more expendable." He muttered while he patted some more. To the group he said, "You'll notice this if you ever try to climb a tree, say, with your pinkies raised."

"Gaelle," said Jillian. "Look away."

"I seem to have misplaced my knife," said Caspar. "May I?" From where I bowed my head, I heard the captain move. "Thank you, Oliver."

"I'll do better," said Greegan.

"All you need to do is remember," said Caspar, "that regardless of size, one's worth is in constant need of examination."

"I can remember," said Greegan.

"Oh, I'm sure you will," said Caspar. "We'll take the middle one. Somebody ready a belt to stanch the bleeding." Greegan started to gasp. "I promise you'll still have your post, Greegan."

"Abbot, please," he said.

Caspar mumbled to a guard about using a rope to hold fast Greegan's hand. "Now. All I ask is you leave the finger in the yard afterward, so it will remind everybody how much the Church actually owns."

Greegan whimpered. The stanch-belt reminded me of the strap I once had around my elbow. A fish I once saved hung as a proclamation in the water of Lake Kelmer. Greegan was screaming. Teph was smiling from beneath his rider's crouch, as Lucinda bore him away.

The soldiers moved us now, and my feet felt as if Greegan's yard clung to them. I held to Jillian, and if she was like me, we both took account of the other one's hands.

I thought again of how we should have killed Lucinda. Caspar—with his black powder and his reform and his inquest and his own pen of mindless—he sought Lucinda. Or at the very least, he sought a Treehanded warhorse. I took wooden steps, and remembered what Teph called compassion's complication, remembered hollering in the horse pen after the failure with Mellion. And then I remembered Jillian's voice as if she spoke now. As if, for this once, her Touch could communicate words, she told me that if Lucinda really was who Caspar wanted, we could not have killed her at all. We couldn't. I had reached this conclusion once before, so many years ago. We couldn't do anything of the sort, without so much help, without whatever we'd need in preparation. Not while the horse attracted the attention of so much power. Not while she herself wanted to be somewhere other than in anyone's barnyard. I kicked a rock, and I stumbled. Jillian hoisted my balance. Even without that armor, Lucinda had shown us ourselves.

Caspar, having returned the knife, led us to a guard barracks. The soldiers who escorted us stood to the side, while five other men, in packs and maces and swords, filed out. They bowed to Caspar, and seemed to size up Jillian and me.

"This is your party," Caspar said to Jillian. He rubbed his fingers against his palm. "I'm afraid that after Greegan, I need to leave you to change my robe." He flicked his fingers. "Do well, Intrepid." He turned to the crowd. "You descend to the ruins of the abbey's lower halls—to the Lowers, as they say—to bring yourselves higher than you've ever been. You will excavate the lair of a madman, of a murderer who, while now dead, still manages to plague us. You will put an end to such plague." Caspar raised his arm, and the men knelt. "You may find evidence of Visjaes's mortal influence, of a man who once stooped to magic. You will most certainly find more of this man's dead. And because of the epidemic of darkness we fight, even now as we hold fast against necromancy, you must deliver us those same dead. In doing so, you will both give peace to their families and deny access to anyone who seeks to blaspheme the corpses with re-animation." He stood before a man I hadn't seen approach. The man wore a full suit of plate armor, with gold scales on its front crest and red edging around its joints. Caspar raised his hand before the man's chest, and spoke a guttural language in a sing-song. The man swayed a bit in his armor. "We send with you an exorcist." Caspar stepped back, as if to give the man room. "This man has the authority to drive back whatever baseness he finds." He turned again to the kneeling group. "I doubt you will need him. You will likely find a criminal's remains, which is almost certainly the source of our current discomfort." Caspar stood by Jillian. "But the Church values its people enough that it will provide every asset as a means of setting things to right." He held out his palms as if he were mimicking the pans of a scale. "May Esaosh find us all worthy of the task." The crowd said amen. The soldiers rose. And upon leaving, Caspar winked to me. "Maybe I'll come and visit you at the herbalist's."

Then he was gone.

Jillian had laid her hand on my sleeve.

"Will he punish us," I whispered, "for my going with you?"

"Well, he'd have to think of a reason why he would, and a reason why you couldn't come." We walked with the group. "He's still playing nicely. He's trying to entice. But—"

"But," I said, "the treachery he wants to commit probably involves my staying up top."

She kept her hand on my arm. Seeing how nothing hostile had happened this morning, aside from our own sneaking around, we had either completely avoided the assault, or left it biding its time all along. My eyes watered. Nothing proved any of what we thought.

part FOUR

"Yeoman." One of the sword-wielding soldiers fell in beside us. "Are you all assembled?"

"My niece will come with us. That's a change to our party."

"Are you certain, Mum?"

"She's my amanuensis," said Jillian. "And at my age, Caspar's aware she's stronger than I."

He said, "That's understandable, mum."

She flattened her mouth. "She needs weapons. An ax. Some armor." The swordsman considered me. "We couldn't retrieve them after the fight with Greegan."

He looked behind him. The squad continued its march. "We can't be late."

"She can't be unprotected," said Jillian.

The soldiers slowed their gait.

The sword-wielder wrinkled his face, and looked around. He sprinted to a post guard, and brought me a helmet and a mace.

The helmet was too big. "I don't know how to use these," I said.

He gave a sort of frantic shrug. "We can redistribute when we reach bottom."

"Why can't we be late?" I said.

"Because the town has been mustered to watch us," said Jillian. "And any delay will show them we aren't as assured as we should be."

I wasn't assured, not in the slightest. If Caspar had Lucinda's barding, Caspar sought to ride her. If Caspar had the mindless, he at least tried to control them. If Caspar meant reform, what he also plotted was war. And this said nothing of the Treehanded, whom he acknowledged with the barding's spines. If Lucinda was the hole toward which all the world drained, and if Caspar meant to control her, he meant to control everything in the world. In the coming years, we would watch each province respond in kind. And we'd also learn how beneath us, right then, was the entity who may still control Caspar.

As our expedition assembled, the dawn grew orange. The light must have come while we hadn't noticed, as if everything moved faster today. The sun gilded the fray of the moss that poked between the timber of the work buildings. We turned a corner, and a dog barked. The man in the ornate armor—the exorcist—squeaked to the center of the squad. Two of the soldiers—young men—tittered behind him.

We passed the marketplace where the merchants paused while they uncovered their goods. I looked for the bird man, but all that remained of his spot was a scatter of down in the sun.

The town stood as we passed, and they bowed their heads. The breeze brought the scent of smoke and mud. We marched from the streets to the hedgerows. I pushed away the thought of snuffling behind a fence, of the soft bristle of Greegan's neck. Instead I smelled the last of the eddleblossoms in a nearby orchard. I thought of Wilm and my father, of my mother and Miriamne. I was afraid to look for Eleanor, and I was afraid to look to Jillian.

We wound into the fields. The exorcist stumbled, and adjusted his helmet. We'd marched far from all the other people. And among the dew and the soil, I wanted to sit, to feel a sudden rain.

The company stopped us at a barn, where inside, a cow huffed. A monk in white stood by a bare piece of floor. All the planks, in fact, had the color of new wood. The cow shuffled. In the center of the floor, two of the soldiers opened a hatch whose peg held a rope dangling down.

"Esaosh grant you power," said the monk. "Esaosh grant you light." The soldiers descended the rope. The lightbearer passed me a torch, unlit, and I thrust it in my belt. Outside, I glanced a rustle of brown leaves, and thought of the tree where I'd learned of my father. The breeze blew, and the leaves lifted, and then I realized they were actually sparrows. The morning warmed my face, and I counted my loved ones, up to seven. Jillian waited in torchlight, at the bottom of the shaft. I climbed again—this time, down.

List of Characters

(As many characters have only one name, this list alphabetizes them by first name. In Celd, Imperial naming convention holds that people don't receive a surname until they choose one after they come of age. Most monks of common rank simply go by their title—Brother—and their first name. Within their communities, Brother is dropped in usual parlance.)

Alder: A dog.

Ambrusso the Heretic Vivisector: A one-time monk who allegedly murdered and dissected his victims.

Babath: A demon who poses as dried meat to ambush travelers at waystations.

Barbara of Lloyd: Gaelle's mother. The sister to Jillian and Miriamne.

Bocephus: A pig.

Bone Wagons: Demons who infest necromancers' houses, until they carry their victims away.

Cole: An engineer's apprentice.

Eleanor: The Abbey-Holding herbalist.

Esaosh: The God of the Church, who embodies strength, clarity, and reason.

Father Felderan: The chief exorcist at Abbey Holding.

Gaelle: An orphan raised by heretics, and who's kept in prison when she's aged.

Garfield: A fourteen-year-old Church guard in Ordinal, who watches over aged Gaelle.

Godiva: An old mare that lives at Lloyd Orchard.

Greegan: A livestock keeper.

Increase: A near-naked bird who has taken up roost in Gaelle's hanging cell.

Jaes: The mother of Visjaes.

Jarek: A young and unfortunate monk.

Jillian of Ludington: Gaelle's aunt and surrogate mother. An outlaw and a heretic whom the Church has conscripted as an intrepid. The sister to Barbara and Miriamne.

Harwell and Lind: Outlaw trap-runners who mentored Jillian.

Helbore: An interesting history teacher at Ordinal.

Laird: A young, abbey monk.

Limdul the Marchman: A demon that turns its victims into a field of howling grass.

Lloyd of Clyde: Gaelle's father, an orchardist.

Lloyd Orchard: Gaelle's family orchard, near Ludington.

Lucinda: A carnivorous and bewildered horse.

Lumis Caspar: The present-day abbot-principe of the Imperial Church, who was the abbot of Abbey Holding, in Gaelle's youth.

Martin: A thirteen-year-old friend of Garfield.

Mellion: A longtime member of the Sword Potent.

Miriamne of the Book: A mystic and Church critic, burned for her writing. The sister to Jillian and Barbara.

Oliver: A leader of a squad of abbey guards.

Olvin Niels: The Abbey-Holding abbot whom Caspar succeeded.

Otto: A guard sergeant in Ordinal's prison.

Rudyard: A young, abbey guard.

Soot and Portence: Two cats.

Tasha: A horse.

Teph the Azman: A traveler from Azmon.

Visjaes: The so-called demon-god who opposes Esaosh, and is said to embody passion, magic, and trickery.

Wegman: An unpleasant history teacher at Ordinal.

Wilm Albertson: An astronomer and pasture man, who neighbors Lloyd Orchard.

Glossary

Abbey Holding: A Church monastery in Holding, famous for its spiritual teachings.

Abbot: The head of all spiritual matters in the Church. He is second only to the principe. Caspar later combines this position with the principe, to become the abbot-principe.

Abbot-Principe: A new position Caspar invents when, in present day, he serves as both abbot and principe.

Af: The second month of the Imperial calendar.

Alpion: The sixth month of the Imperial calendar.

Altarib: The eleventh month of the Imperial calendar.

Ariadne River: A river that flows through Treehand, and bisects Celd.

Azmon: The desert province in southwestern Celd. It's nominally an Imperial province, but it irks the Church by creating mindless.

Bakeet: A chain of islands off Cadmus and Holding, famous for peacefully winning independence from Holding.

The Bale: The cataclysm that occurred when Visjaes invaded Celd. Esaosh and the Princes drove Visjaes out, and they chase him still. But their absence has left Celd to govern itself, while it awaits Esaosh's return.

Bardion: The third month of the Imperial calendar.

The Bell: The colloquial name for Gaelle's hanging cell at Ordinal.

Black Sap: A Treehanded sap that paralyzes anyone who absorbs it.

Cadmul: Of, or from, Cadmus.

Cadmus: The northeastern province of Celd. It's mostly arid, with a frozen north, and it's home to Ordinal.

Cathedral Ordinal: An arch-cathedral of the Imperial Church. It's found in the capital city of Ordinal, which is in coastal Cadmus.

Celd: This world, found and established, but not created, by Esaosh.

Chancellor: The head of all secular matters in the Church. He is second only to the principe.

Choir: A type of Church artillery.

Clearing Wars: A historic conflict between Treehand and the Church, where the victorious Church pushed its boundaries farther west than ever before.

The Cleft: A resistance group, mostly run by women, that gives relief to the poor.

Core: The fourth month of the Imperial calendar.

Dean: A Church teacher, usually in charge of other instructors.

Devorare: A monstrous dog that climbs. It has a terrifying stench.

Eddlefruit: A purple, edible fruit about the size of a baby pumpkin and with an inside like an artichoke.

Exorcist: The unit of the Sword Potent that treats heretics.

Feaster: A carrion bird about the size of an eagle. They feed in packs, and in sufficient numbers, they will feed on the injured.

Ferals: The part of Lloyd orchard that has become neglected and overgrown.

Girash: A Cadmul term for an adult who hasn't come of age by killing an animal larger than they are.

Gomadong Plain: A steppe that spreads from northern Cadmus to the central coast. Ordinal sits on the rim of the Gomadong. Gaelle's hanging cell overlooks the Gomadong.

Great Man: The title for the leader of Azmon.

Grove: The name of the Treehanded church.

Groveman's Romp: A Holden term for a sap-drunken wander into the woods, that usually leads toward fatal results.

Haft River: A river extending from inner Holding to the coast.

Hal's Bride: A village that has sister settlements in Ludington and Northcraft. It's home to a decent blacksmith.

Harbinger: A Church missionary.

Head Wider Than the World: A Church idiom for an aristocrat who acts higher than his station.

Holden: Of, or from, Holding.

Holding: The southeastern province of Celd. It's comparatively temperate, and it's home to Ludington and Abbey Holding.

Imperial Church of Esaosh: The major governing body of Celd. It wields a bureaucracy, a military, and an array of laws and catechisms.

Inquest: The Church campaign against necromancy and mindless.

Inquisitor: The unit of the Sword Potent that judges heretics.

Intrepid: A trap-runner, especially in service of the Church. She usually clears the dangers from ruins. The Church has conscripted Jillian as an intrepid.

Jan's Rest: A village far to the west of Northcraft. It's home to a shoddy blacksmith.

Ketch: A battlefield in southern Cadmus, where the Church routed the Riven.

Knight: The unit of the Sword Potent that arrests heretics.

Lake Kelmer: A small lake near Ludington, where Lloyd Orchard draws most of its water.

Law of Hospitality: A Church law stipulating that a traveler seeking shelter must either pay or work for his lodging.

Law of Retribution: A Church law stipulating that when the Church garrison isn't available, a crime victim's closest kin must deliver punishment to the perpetrator.

Law of Trespass: A Church law stipulating that strangers arriving after dark must announce themselves, or lose protection against violence.

Lehashon: The seventh month of the Imperial calendar.

Light and Allegiance: The Church motto, popularized near the start of the Reordering War.

The Lowers: A warren of tunnels beneath Abbey Holding. They were once the abbey proper.

Ludington: A village in the central breadbasket of Holding. It's a sister settlement with Northcraft and Hal's Bride.

Mama: A rope that young guards hold, when they stand sentry at the Bell.

Merrial: The toxic and blasted province in northwest Celd. Nobody seems to live there. The Church claims this is where Esaosh first landed in Celd, and where he exited the world through Nabush.

Mindless: A brutal and catatonic flesh golem raised from the dead. The people of Azmon sometimes make mindless into slaves. The Imperial Church officially condemns mindless making.

Minting: A weekly Church service that refreshes a follower's dedication to the cause.

Moaske Shrub: A Treehanded plant that renders the black sap.

Nabush: A gargantuan, chitinous stalk that reaches from the wastes of Merrial, out of the world. Esaosh created Nabush.

Northcraft: The largest of the sister villages comprising of it, Hal's Bride, and Ludington. It keeps the largest market in the region.

Oading Rout: A major Church defeat in the Clearing Wars.

Pegrum: An infamous Church prison that also serves as a training ground for the Sword Potent.

Potch: The tenth month of the Imperial calendar.

Prince: One of Esaosh's great lieutenants, where Esaosh appointed each to oversee a province of Celd. When the Bale occurred, the Princes either fell to torpor, or joined with Esaosh in pursuing Visjaes from Celd.

Principe: The head of the Imperial Church. Caspar later combines this position with the abbot, to become the abbot-principe.

Profundus: The old Church language.

Reaching Man: An aspect of Visjaes that the Church calls an arch-demon. The Church declares the Reaching Man steals and kills children.

Recruitment: The Church practice of conscripting young boys as soldiers and monks.

Rector: A Church preacher, especially to the faithful.

Red Head: A mid-sized town in northern Holding.

Reordering War: The coming world war that will decide who will dominate Celd while Esaosh overtakes, and enters the final battle with, Visjaes.

The Resistance: A collective term for those who actively oppose the Church.

Retriever: Hunters from Azmon tasked to recapture lost goods or persons.

Rimstack: A gambling game played with dominoes.

The Riven: An army of those who fight for Visjaes, against the Church. Gaelle has served as an adviser for this army.

Roc: A raptor about twice the size of an eagle.

Rochon: The fifth month of the Imperial calendar.

Sanchal: A type of salt that can affect all mindless on contact.

Screel: The howling and persistent wind in Azmon, that, depending on intensity, can erode both stone and flesh.

Sets Down His Pail: The Holden and Azmonian idiom meaning "to set up house."

Shield Potent: The arm of the Church military that sees to secular crimes.

Simpleman: Someone who is unpretentious and dependable.

Sire Tree: The oldest tree in a grove. It's a Treehanded term that's entered everyday usage.

Sislau: The eighth month of the Imperial calendar.

Star Fall: A far-future event when the stars overtake Celd.

Stuttering Plague: A virulent respiratory disease whose signs involve stammering.

Sword Potent: The arm of the Church military that sees to ecclesiastical crimes.

The Syndicate: A network of heralds and criers who spread the news according to their own profit and bias. They're useful to both the resistance and the Church, but are more sympathetic to the resistance, whom they occasionally serve as spies.

Talent: The basic unit of Imperial currency.

Tonn Man: Nomadic horsemen in northern Cadmus.

Touch: A mental call and response between two people.

Tree Ghosts: A derogatory word for someone from Treehand.

Treehand: The province that runs down the center of Celd. It's home to the insular Treehanded and their heretical arbor cults. Treehand engaged with the Imperial Church in the Clearing Wars.

Treeman: A colloquial name for someone from Treehand.

Wax: The twelfth month of the Imperial calendar.

Worg: A ferocious breed of wolf the size of a boar.

Zaffion: The ninth month of the Imperial calendar.

Zeffar: The first month of the Imperial calendar.

Selected References

Applebaum, Anne. *Gulag*.

Brenden, Piers. *The Dark Valley: A panorama of the 1930s*.

The Code of Hammurabi.

Cole, David & Watchtell Stinnett, Melanie. *Rules for Resistance: Advice from around the globe in the age of Trump*.

Coleman, Loren & Clark, Jerome. *Cryptozoology A to Z: The encyclopedia of loch monsters, sasquatch, chupacabras, and other authentic mysteries of nature*.

Davis, Graeme. *GURPS Middle Ages*.

Davis, Wade. *The Serpent and the Rainbow*.

Department of the Army & Underwood, Peter. *The Official US Army Survival Manual Updated*.

Ehrenreich, Barbara. *Witches, Midwives, and Nurses: A history of women healers*.

Foucault, Michel. *Discipline and Punish: The birth of the prison*.

Garthwaite, Rosie. *How to Avoid Being Killed in a Warzone*.

The Geneva Bible.

Grice, Gordon. *Deadly Kingdom: The book of dangerous animals*.

Keegan, John. *The Face of Battle: A study of Agincourt, Waterloo, and the Somme*.

Morris, Norvil & Rothman, David J. (Eds.). *The Oxford History of the Prison: The practice of punishment in western society*.

Mortimer, Ian. *A Time Traveler's Guide to Medieval England: A handbook for visitors to the fourteenth century*.

Ross, John S. *GURPS Russia*.

Scott, Samuel P. & Sites Roy A. *Roman Civil Law: Including the Twelve Tables, The Institutes of Gaius, The Rules of Ulpian & The Opinions of Paulus*.

Stewart, Amy. *Wicked Plants: The weed that killed Lincoln's mother and other botanical atrocities*.

White, Matthew. *The Great Big Book of Horrible Things: The definitive chronicle of history's worst atrocities*.

photo credit James Robinson

ABOUT THE AUTHOR

MEGAN CARNES is a graduate of Oberlin College and the University of Iowa Writers' Workshop. She has taught writing, life skills, and humanities at Davenport University. With her husband and three cats, she lives in Iowa City, Iowa.

Thank you for supporting the creative works of veterans and military family members by purchasing this book. If you enjoyed your reading experience, we're certain you'll enjoy these other great reads.

AMERICAN DELPHI
by M.C. Armstrong

During America's summer of plague and protest, fifteen-year-old Zora Box worries her pesky younger brother is a psychopath for sneaking out at night to hang with their suspicious new neighbor, Buck London, who's old enough to be their father. Their father, a combat veteran, is dead—suicide. Or so everyone thinks, until Buck sets Zora and her brother Zach straight, revealing their father as the genius inventor of a truth-telling, future-altering device called American Delphi.

SALMON IN THE SEINE
by Norris Comer

One moment eighteen-year-old Norris Comer is throwing his high school graduation cap in the air and setting off for Alaska to earn money, and the next he's comforting a wounded commercial fisherman who's desperate for the mercy of a rescue helicopter. From landlubber to deckhand, Comer's harrowing adventures at sea and during a solo search in the Denali backcountry for wolves provide a transformative bridge from adolescence to adulthood.

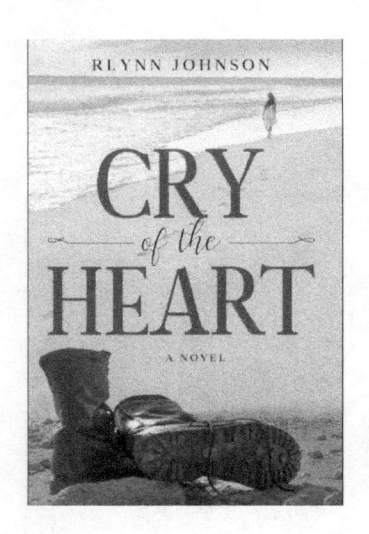

CRY OF THE HEART
by Rlynn Johnson

After law school, a group of women calling themselves the Alphas embark on diverse legal careers—Pauline joins the Army as a Judge Advocate. For twenty years, the Alphas gather for annual weekend retreats where the shenanigans and truth-telling will test and transform the bonds of sisterhood.

COLLATERAL DAMAGE
2ND EDITION
by Kevin C. Jones

These stories live in the realworld psychedelics of warfare, poverty, love, hate, and just trying to get by. Jones's evocative language, the high stakes, and heartfelt characters create worlds of wonder and grace. The explosions, real and psychological, have a burning effect on the reader. Nothing here is easy, but so much is gained.

—ANTHONY SWOFFORD, author of *Jarhead: A Marine's Chronicle of the Gulf War and Other Battles*

SUB WIFE
by Samantha Otto Brown

A Navy wife's account of life within the super-secret sector of the submarine community, and of the support among spouses who often wait and worry through long stretches of silence from loved ones who are deeply submerged.

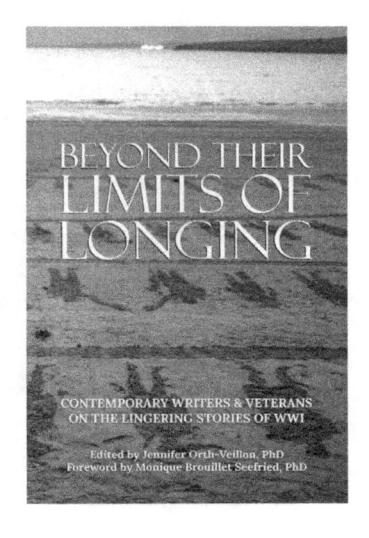

BEYOND THEIR LIMITS OF LONGING
edited by
Jennifer Orth-Veillon, PhD

In America, WWI became overshadowed by WWII and Vietnam, further diluting the voices of poets, novelists, essayists, and scholars who unknowingly set a precedent for the sixty-two successive, and notable, war writers who appear in this collection to explore the complexity both of war's physical and mental horrors and of its historical significance in today's world in crises.

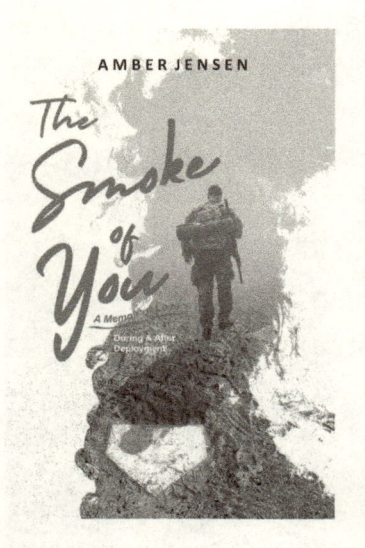

THE SMOKE OF YOU
by Amber Jensen

A young couple's love and marriage are tested during and after a military deployment with the National Guard to Iraq that results in a battle with chronic pain and the slow-burning challenges of married life. A story of selfless love and self-discovery, of hardship and hope, *The Smoke of You* will resonate with anyone who has ever suffered, and still bravely loved.

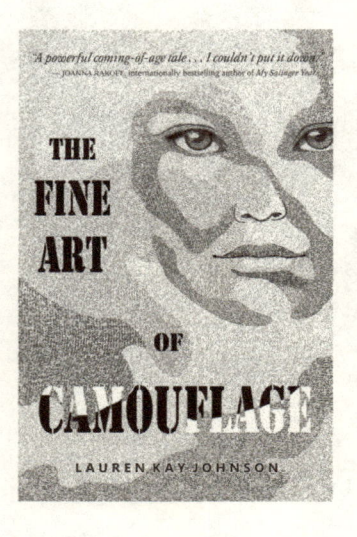

THE FINE ART OF CAMOUFLAGE
by Lauren Kay Johnson

A young woman's coming-of-age in the military against a backdrop of war, viewed through her lens as an information operations officer who wrestles with the nature of truth in the stories we hear from the media and official sources, and in the stories we tell about ourselves and our families.

KURTZ
by John Lawson III

Nick Willard may be three years her junior but he has pined for Annie Kurtz since they were both prep school students. However, after 9/11, Annie joins the Marines, eventually making a split-second decision her superiors never wanted her to make, and wrestles with whether she should have followed orders or her conscience. Nick—now a successful journalist—and Annie explore the tensions between love and friendship, even those between morality and law, as they come of age amid the psychological traumas that result when war makers sweep reality under a rug of ridiculous details.

FALLING OFF HORSES
by Karen Donley-Hayes

A mutual love for horses unites two young women as teenagers who forge an undying friendship that will steady them after countless falls from horses, a roller coaster of love losses and triumphs, the emotional pitfalls of equestrian breeding and competing—and finally, through the heartbreaking diagnosis of a fatal illness.

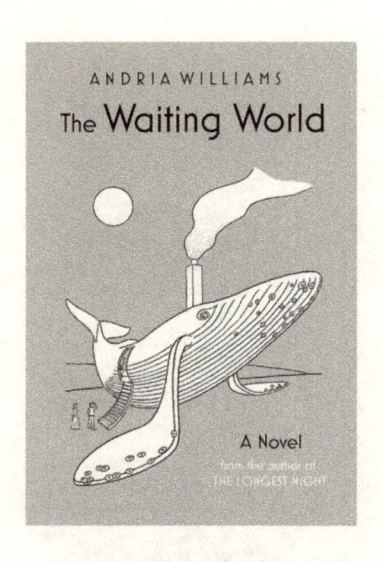

THE WAITING WORLD
by Andria Williams

In 1929, two Irish housemaids, Nessa and Aoife, bonded through their journey to America, stumble upon and pocket a strange find on the shoreline of the home belonging to larger-than-life business magnate Titus McAvoy. When their path crosses a young white-passing British World War I veteran, John, who suspects the enormous worth of their find, the three friends forge a different life together—one free from the dark underbelly of how the rich treat the poor, and free from the pervasive rot of nationalist and racist behaviour, not to mention the injustices and dangers that too often befall women. But...nobody walks away from Titus McAvoy.

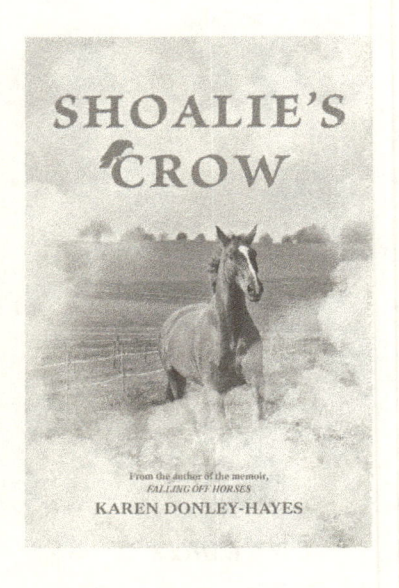

SHOALIE'S CROW
by Karen Donley-Hayes

A horrific fatal accident during an equestrian jumping event leads to the reincarnation of a newborn foal who discovers the only being who speaks her non-horsemanlike language is, of all things, a crow. Together, Shoalie and her crow-friend struggle to unravel a mystery that's leading toward another horrific fatal accident. (Published under our imprint Family of Light Books)

HILLS HIDE MOUNTAINS
by Travis Klempan

By all accounts, Mo's new life in Chicago appears picture-perfect—poised, static, and artificial. But when her boyfriend, Kirk, breaks the frame and kicks her out of his condo on their anniversary, Mo is too embarrassed to head East to face her parents' disappointment. Instead, she
reaches out to the only lifeline she has left—her deceased best friend's lover, John, a former soldier now living on the edge of Montana's wilderness and facing a battle that will require supernatural powers from them both if they're to win this one.

Printed in the USA
CPSIA information can be obtained
at www.ICGtesting.com
LVHW040504060324
773595LV00001B/74